Praise for Craig Robertson

'A tale that takes the reader on a wickedly entertaining ride through a **fascinatingly SINISTER world**'
Sunday Mirror

'Robertson's work is marked by crisp prose, smart storylines and an **INVENTIVENESS most authors would envy**'
Eva Dolan

'In ***Murderabilia***, Craig Robertson has created a **crime novel like no other** I've read . . . I really didn't want to put it down!'
Crime Fiction Lover

'**BLIMEY this book was BANGING . . .** Top notch crime fiction of the type all us avid crime fans devour with the fervour of true fanatics'
Liz Loves Books

'**MASTERFUL!** Craig Robertson certainly knows how to hook a reader'
Kati Hiekkapelto

'**A revenge thriller** with a twist'
Sun

'Doing for **Glasgow**, what Rankin did for **Edinburgh**'
Mirror

'**A TENSE torch-lit trek** through a hidden city you never knew existed'
Christopher Brookmyre

During his 20-year career in Glasgow with a Scottish Sunday newspaper, Craig Robertson interviewed three recent Prime Ministers and attended major stories including 9/11, Dunblane, the Omagh bombing and the disappearance of Madeleine McCann. He was pilloried on breakfast television, beat Oprah Winfrey to a major scoop, spent time on Death Row in the USA and dispensed polio drops in the backstreets of India. His debut novel, *Random*, was shortlisted for the CWA New Blood Dagger and was a *Sunday Times* bestseller.

Also by Craig Robertson

In Place of Death
The Last Refuge
Witness the Dead
Cold Grave
Snapshot
Random

CRAIG ROBERTSON

MURDERABILIA

SIMON &
SCHUSTER

London · New York · Sydney · Toronto · New Delhi

A CBS COMPANY

First published in Great Britain by Simon & Schuster UK Ltd, 2016
This paperback edition first published in 2017
A CBS COMPANY

1 3 5 7 9 10 8 6 4 2

Simon & Schuster UK Ltd
1st Floor
222 Gray's Inn Road
London WC1X 8HB

www.simonandschuster.co.uk

Simon & Schuster Australia, Sydney
Simon & Schuster India, New Delhi

A CIP catalogue record for this book
is available from the British Library

Paperback ISBN: 978-1-4711-5659-5
eBook ISBN: 978-1-4711-5660-1

Typeset by M Rules
Printed and bound by CPI Group (UK) Ltd, Croydon, CR0 4YY

'Every man has to have a hobby'

– Ed Gein, American murderer and grave robber who made household objects from human body parts. He gave the reply when asked why he'd done what he did.

Prologue

We saw her the minute she stepped inside, thinking herself so clever just for being there. It must have taken all of two seconds for her to switch from smug to scared. The unwarranted confidence spilling from her like blood from a slashed wrist.

Coming in here is like entering a maze with all the lights turned off. We're here, waiting for her, watching her stumble around in search of us. She's sure we're inside but now she's afraid because she realises she doesn't know where she's going. Us? We can see in the dark.

This is our place. Us and people like us. She, on the other hand, is an intruder.

She's just blundering around, pushing buttons, hoping for the best. She's treading on mines and traps every step she takes but she's too stupid to even notice.

She is inside the most dangerous place on the planet and she doesn't know it.

This is the darkest place you can imagine. She'll find that out soon enough.

We don't mind her coming looking because it was

inevitable that someone would eventually do so. We do resent her misplaced confidence, though. We object to her cheek.

Someone must have given her a key, because there's no other way in. This place is impenetrable without an invitation. Governments have tried and failed to get in – and stay in – here. Experts in terrorism, fraud, money laundering and people trafficking have spent millions trying to be inside. Representatives of every significant branch of law enforcement have done the same. It remains beyond their reach.

This is a place where people are actively working to have a world leader assassinated. Where you can buy or sell children. Or guns or drugs. Where you can have someone killed or abducted, provide a new identity or the opportunity to disappear. And us? We deal in murder.

In this place you will find anything you want and everything you fear.

Welcome to the dark web. Good luck trying to get out again. Good luck trying to stay alive.

CHAPTER 1

Thursday, 21 April 2016

A Glasgow railway station on a cold April morning is a lonely place to die. It's a pretty soulless place to wait for a train, too.

Not even the promise of sunrise offers much hope of chasing away the chill and putting heat into their bones. They're all sleepwalkers, lumbering from foot to foot and shivering as they await their train north.

Nathan watches them with amusement and contempt, seeing the same old dance ready to repeat itself. Unsociable bastards, the lot of them. They barely look at each other, instead staring at the electronic noticeboard high above Queen Street's concourse, willing the platform number to appear. They all know it will soon say platform seven but, no, they need the proof before their eyes.

They need to actually see it change before they'll allow themselves to shamble through the barriers and get on board in search of a seat to themselves. It's always the same.

He looks around and doesn't see any familiar faces, but they're all recognisable in their own ways. There's the guys in the suits stuffed with self-importance and trying to hide whisky breath with packets of mints. There's women in sharp two-piece numbers, clutching laptops, newspapers and handbags, their collars turned up against the morning air. Then there's the rucksack crew in walking shoes and fleeces and three days of stubble, all ready to sleep until somewhere north of Perth. There are teenagers in hoodies, night-shift workers heading for their beds and a few who look like they missed the last train and are being poured onto the first one instead.

There are holdalls and suitcases, sports bags and shoulder bags and there are plastic bags that clink with fuel for the journey. They're all here, cold and weary and ready to go. All waiting for the platform number to become the magic seven.

Nathan isn't any different. He's keen to get going, too, and frustrated at seeing the four-carriage train just sitting there but not being allowed on board. Come on. It's bloody freezing out here, just finish whatever it is you have to do and let us inside.

It isn't six o'clock yet but there are maybe fifty or sixty people waiting and doing the cold-feet shuffle. Some of them are hugging plastic cups of coffee, others are rubbing their hands and blowing out air that fogs in front of their faces. All just looking at the board and waiting and . . .

There. The digital numbers flash and change and, sure enough, it's platform seven. About time. You can almost hear them all think it. Everyone moves.

Here we go, the same old nonsense as they get on. Look at them pretending not to hurry but desperate to get there before anyone else, quickening their step in the hope of a seat with a table and no neighbours, ready to put down bags or newspapers to mark their territory and, above all, eager to be facing forward. Oh, and his personal favourite, the selfish sods that sit on the outside of two seats to stop anyone else sitting beside them. People are pathetic.

There they go, moving to the far carriages in the hope that they will be empty and they won't have to look at anyone else or have their space invaded. And God forbid they might actually have to talk to another human being. Train passengers may be the most unsociable bunch on the planet. Nathan despises them and maybe that just makes him as bad as they are.

He shakes his head as he watches them go to the far end and smiles, knowing they won't be able to get the peaceful commute they seek. It's like a plane load of tourists all flying to the same deserted island in search of paradise. It just doesn't work out the way you want.

He gets into the first carriage. It will do him just fine.

There's still four minutes to go and the seats are filling up around him. A young Chinese couple get in the seats in front and he can hear their low chatter, doubtless complaining about the cold. A large guy sits down across the aisle and spends a couple of minutes noisily stuffing a jacket, a coat, a scarf and hat and a duffel bag into the overhead space.

It's 05.55 and the doors are closed. One minute to go until the first train stretches and yawns and lurches out of

Glasgow towards Aberdeen. The guard on the platform looks like he's just fallen out of his bed, hair dishevelled and eyes bleary. He takes a final scratch at his beard and a last look at the clock before raising his flag and blowing his whistle. 05.56. Time to go.

The train rocks and moves and the carriages are reluctantly forced to follow. The Chinese teenagers move their heads together and kiss. All the antisocial bastards in their individual little neighbourless seats breathe a sad wee sigh of relief that they've secured some room for themselves.

They slide down the right-hand side of Queen Street's walls, a low rumble as they take their leave. The nose of the train enters the tunnel under the city's streets and leads them slowly into blackness before remerging just moments later back into the mist-shrouded break of day.

He hears the first scream, or maybe it's the second. It's distant but unmistakable and ripples back through the carriages in waves. The people round him hear it, too, and there's instant confusion and panic. The young couple in front are straining forward to hear and the large guy opposite is standing as he tries to see what the hell is going on.

The screams are closer and louder and multiplied. They're not rippling back now, they're flowing. It's a tsunami. Shouting and obvious panic from up ahead.

Then a screech and a sudden stall that sends everyone back in their seat as the train slows dramatically. He knows someone has pulled the emergency cord and stopped the beast in its tracks. The brakes are on and they are only inching forward now.

The screams become deafening. The screams are from the carriage in front and from his.

Everyone is looking at it. The blue latticed bridge up to their right. The bridge and the naked body that's hanging from it.

He pushes his face to the window, frosting the glass with the sudden explosion of his breath. The man's head is slumped forward, choked at the neck, but they can all still see his eyes bulging, wide and terrified but lifeless. His arms are by his sides and two dark streaks of red run from his chest down across the white of his bare flesh. It's blood, streaming down his torso and thighs.

From around him, Nathan hears familiar metallic clicks and looks up and down the carriage to see people on their mobile phones. They are photographing the body that is swinging from the rope.

The Chinese girl has her head buried in her boyfriend's chest but, even as she does that, he is snapping away. Click. Click. Click.

They don't know what else to do. They scream and they photograph. They are horrified and bewildered and disgusted but they click and click and click.

Nathan takes a photograph too. He takes several. However, he isn't as shocked as everyone else is to see the hanging body. Nathan put him there.

CHAPTER 2

Standing still in a crime scene is like catching your breath in a whirlpool. Controlled chaos reigns around you and for a moment you can be fooled into thinking it's you who are moving and that everything and everyone else is a frozen blur.

Tony Winter stood just long enough to fall into the trap. He drank in the familiarity of his surroundings, the barked orders and the frenzied flit of bodies, the unhurried haste and the guilty vibe of people high on the rush of something awful. It had been his world for so long and, even now, when it had turned upside down, it seemed as right as it was wrong.

A few yards away, and maybe forty feet above his head, hung the body that was at the centre of the vortex. Everything worked round that. It was their reason for being.

He took the camera that was slung around his neck and used the zoom to focus in on the man. Fair hair, pale skin turned paler still. Already there was vivid purple discoloration in his legs and feet, gravity causing the blood to settle.

The twin streaks of blood down his pallid torso were – Winter closed in further – coming directly from the man's nipples. Or rather where the nipples should have been.

Winter's camera picked out the rough fibres of the thick rope that clung to the victim's neck and suspended him from the bridge. He traced back down to the man's slumped head and those straining eyes, down, down, all the way to the rough ground spattered in blood and the strange stack of clothing that sat way below the body.

He backed up a few yards, taking in more of the scene between him and the hanging figure. Lifting his camera again, he made a few quick adjustments to change the exposure, then framed the man and let the busy army of uniformed cops, detectives and forensics walk across his shot. The effect was to leave the body perfectly in focus but the white-suited figures became shadows of themselves, a welcome party of ghosts for the recently departed.

Slowly, however, one of the ghosts turned and looked straight back at him through the lens. This one was fully focused.

'Tony, what the hell are you doing behind the tape? You forget you don't work for us any more?'

It was less than a year since Winter had made the leap from police photographer to photo-journalist. From Forensic Services to the *Scottish Standard*. He still wasn't sure if it made him poacher turned gamekeeper or the other way round. Maybe it just meant he was now outside the tent, peering in. Except he had just been caught sneaking inside.

He shrugged unapologetically at DS Rico Giannandrea, a hint of a smile playing on his lips. 'No, but I think a couple of the uniforms forgot again. They recognised me but no one wanted to stop me.'

Giannandrea scowled at him. 'Well I'm stopping you now. Do I need to rip the memory card from that camera or are you going to remember the rules? And the law?'

'No need. I'm just trying to do my job, Rico.'

Giannandrea shook his head and lowered his voice. 'Just don't make mine any harder. You know if it was anyone else I'd kick their arse. And don't call me Rico. Not here. Go on, beat it, Tony. You'll be in even more trouble if *she* catches you in here.'

Winter didn't doubt the truth of that but in itself it wouldn't make him stop. He had a job to do and so did she. The trouble was that his job and hers weren't always exactly compatible.

Giannandrea's phone buzzed and he listened briefly before ending the call. 'That's her coming now, Tony. Do us both a favour and get fifty yards back that way as fast as you can.'

With a sharp nod, Winter hustled back towards the station, managing to duck under the tape next to a startled constable just before she got there. Job to do or not, he didn't see the point in making life any more difficult for himself than he needed to. In any case, he already had what he came for.

When DI Rachel Narey reached the tape and saw him standing there, a fleeting look of exasperation crossed her face. Her eyebrows lifted in a familiar expression. It said,

'Here we go again.' It said, 'Speak later' and it said, 'Stay the hell out of my crime scene.'

Narey and Giannandrea were standing on the rubble-strewn path next to the track out of Queen Street. Directly above their heads the naked figure swung slowly in the morning breeze, making them dizzy.

They stretched their necks back, looking up into the light mist, seeing the soles of the young man's feet, seeing the streaks of red down his torso and legs, and the purple settling of lividity. His eyes popped and his neck was scored raw by the rope that hung him. It was a horrific sight and they couldn't help but stare.

Beyond the body, all they could see was bridge and brick, then a misty, miserable canvas of grey. Against that, he swayed, ashen white as if crucified on an invisible cross. A scrub of fair chest hair was daubed in blood and his mouth hung open, frozen in a twist of terror.

'Fuck.'

The word slipped so casually from Giannandrea that she wasn't sure he even knew he'd said it. They'd both seen plenty in their time and this was more of the same but different. Another shade of the familiar still had the power to shock.

The site smelled of death and daybreak. Something dead and something reborn. She imagined she could smell his flesh decaying over the freshness of morning dew and clean air.

The ground at their feet was a minefield of blood spots and they had to pick where they stood with care. Looking straight up, necks craned, it was all too easy to imagine fresh drops falling like rain onto their faces. Narey blinked but, when she reopened her eyes, the body was still there, still swinging, still dead.

Behind them, the noise from the station was chaotic. Restless engines rumbled, eager to move but confined to base. Sirens blared as emergency reinforcements arrived, struggling to be heard over the incessant excited chatter that rose to the roof and back again. Closer, the scene buzzed with people and questions, everyone with a job to do but everyone taking time to sneak another look at the young man on the rope.

'Fuck,' Giannandrea muttered again.

The area within the arc of the body was already salted with yellow numbered markers indicating blood drops and a couple of partial footprints. Marker number six was next to a neat pile of clothing positioned on the stones way below the body. Jeans, shirt, jacket, sweater. All perfectly folded and stacked on top of a pair of white trainers. It looked like they'd been tidied and placed there by an over-attentive mother.

The corners of each piece of clothing matched the others perfectly. It was obsessively neat. Like a return from the best laundry in town, except they were spattered with blood drops from the swinging figure above.

Narey crouched down and saw that the clothes were worn but fresh, good-quality and fashionable. She poked a gloved finger into the pile and revealed a designer label sticking out of the collar of the shirt and saw another expensive logo on the breast of the sweater.

She knew the initial search of the clothes had produced a photo driving licence in a pocket of the jeans. It declared him to be Aiden McAlpine, a twenty-three-year-old from Knightswood in the city's West End. As she looked up again, he looked even younger. Pale and scared. Lost and needing to be rescued. He needed to be taken home to his mother.

Narey stood again, turning to walk across to the track, positioning herself where the train would have been, trying to see what the passengers would have seen. They couldn't have missed him.

Giannandrea had said it had been the first train out of the station. The driver saw him initially but then the whole train did. Someone hit the emergency alarm and the driver slammed on the brakes. It hadn't picked up any speed so was able to stop quickly. That turned out not to be the best idea, as it left two carriages with a front row-seat.

In seconds, the bloody photos were all over Twitter. Ghoulish? Of course it was, but that's how people are. It went viral in no time. In the twenty minutes it had taken her to get to the track, the body had been seen all over the world.

They hadn't been able to back the train into Queen Street because there were other trains waiting to get out, so they went on to Bishopbriggs and got people off there. Some of them were treated for shock, but only once they got off their phones and social media.

Was the body still swaying? She'd swear that it was. Either *it* was moving or *she* was. She wanted the poor sod cut down and covered as soon as possible. There was also no way trains could move down that track until it was done, and there was mounting chaos behind them.

The first alert labelled it as a possible suicide but that just didn't fly at all. One look and she knew that wasn't the case. This was murder. Neither pure nor simple, but certainly murder.

There was no obvious way back up to the bridge from the ground and it beggared belief that this young man had stripped there by the track, arranged his clothes into that weirdly neat pile, then somehow made his way, naked, up to the bridge and tied a rope round his neck.

No, someone had done all that for him. They'd killed him in the dark of night and tied the body to the bridge before throwing him over the edge to hang there for the train to pass.

There were probably hundreds of bridges in Glasgow but few of them would have left such a public viewing area. This was *meant* to be seen. That was the whole point. Jeez, those bloody mobile phones. It had been seen everywhere.

Someone had put on quite a show.

Giannandrea joined her again, shoving his phone back in his pocket and his face suggesting even more good news.

'What's up, now?'

He breathed out hard, as if it would somehow help. 'We've got an ID on the victim. Aiden McAlpine is the only son of Mark McAlpine.'

'The MSP?'

'Yep.'

'Fuck.'

*

They stood in silence for an age, both looking up, seeing the man and the rope and the bridge. Both joining dots and asking and answering questions in their heads. Both looking back down at the pile of clothing.

'Why have his clothes been left like that, Rico?'

'To freak us out. To add to the whole staging of it. And to make sure we know it's not a suicide. Whoever did this was making sure he didn't miss out on the credit.'

She nodded without taking her eyes off the body.

'Yes. It's exactly that. It's showing off. It *is* all staged. A bridge in front of a train-load of passengers. Daylight breaking. The clothing. Is there CCTV covering the bridge?'

Giannandrea shook his head. 'No. Nothing. There's no shop or businesses up there that would have their own, either.'

'Great. And something else about these clothes, Rico. What's missing?'

He looked again, trying to work it out. 'There's no underwear. No boxer shorts or socks. But he could just have gone commando and some kids still go sockless for fashion.'

'Yeah, maybe. But the way these clothes are stacked? Someone's taking the piss and I don't like it one bit. Rico, Google something for me, will you? What time was sunrise this morning? Exactly.'

Giannandrea worked his mobile phone and had the answer in seconds. 'Glasgow sunrise, 05.56.' He lifted his head and looked at her. 'The same time as the train left.'

'Fuck.'

CHAPTER 3

He had maybe twenty photographs he could have chosen from. Scene shots, body shots. Close-ups of the rope or the hands. A shot of the blood that had trickled down the torso. Maybe the horrified look on the faces of passengers or the studied shock of attending cops.

Twenty photographs, but in the end the choice was easy. There is always one. *The* picture. This one was almost identical to six others but different enough that it stood head and shoulders above them.

The words were the hard bit but, luckily for him, one good photograph was said to be worth a thousand of those. He wasn't quite sure about the arithmetic but he was happy to go with the principle. One good photograph. Used big and bold and keeping the words to a minimum. Said it all.

It was the clothes. The neat, folded clothing that Aiden McAlpine had been wearing before someone stripped him and murdered him.

Winter had framed it carefully, probably just as obsessively as the killer who'd stacked it with hospital corners and military precision. He'd offered it to the picture desk who initially threw up their hands at the uselessness of it, hadn't he got the body, then got more interested when they actually looked at it.

They took it to the editor, Jack Hendrie, who was all over it in an instant. He decided to splash with it. Front page. Large.

There it was, big as a house on the front page of the *Standard*. Almost life-size. Almost death-size. Winter guessed not everyone would have seen the shadow at first. The clothing itself grabbed your eye. The crisp pale blue of the shirt. The dark and faded blue of the denims. The white trainers with the flash of navy. The so-recently worn, the perfect folds and immaculate corners. All that took the eye away from the shadow. At first.

Then when you saw it, your eyes grew wide with the dawning realisation of it. The unmistakeable silhouette of the hanging man, the macabre shadow posed perfectly across the clothes he'd been ripped from. His death painted theatrically across the remnants of his life.

It showed the body in a way no direct photograph of it could. Not in a national newspaper at least. Nor on any news programme. It conveyed the horror of it without actually showing any. The world leapt on it, helped by the fact that Hendrie decided to put in on the paper's online edition first.

In the digital age, to wait was to lose. He couldn't take the chance of being beaten to the punch with something similar, so got it out there fast. The picture went live before the first pint had hit the back of the first throat in the Horseshoe. All copyright *The Scottish Standard*.

The other papers led with variations on the same headlines and the best pic they had available, which wasn't much. 'Sunrise Killer', said the *Sun*. 'MSP's son murdered', said the *Herald*. None of them could match the power of the *Standard*'s front page led by Winter's photograph.

The first request came from the *Telegraph* in London, quickly followed by its rival, *The Times*. CNN International wanted it and then so too did its senior partner in the US. The *Standard*'s newsdesk was swamped with requests. The BBC, ITV, *Bild*, the *New York Daily News*, ABC, Fox News, *Le Monde*. All willing to pay top dollar.

Winter's photograph had the unique stamp of being palatable yet shocking. Editors could pretend they were defending the sensibilities of their readers and viewers while simultaneously feeding their hunger for gore. It went global and it carried the murder of Aiden McAlpine with it.

The Internet, quickly sated on the revulsion of the mobile phone pictures from the morning, fastened on to the clothing photograph as if it was some sanitised version that pardoned their own bloodlust. Facebook and Twitter gorged on it. It was shared and liked, tweeted and retweeted. Thousands of times every minute.

The speed of it scared him a bit. Every use of the photo bred a hundred more, each of those hundred spawned a thousand. He'd never properly understood the word viral till then. If his picture had been a disease, the world would have been dead.

The feedback came via the *Standard*'s Facebook page. Messages poured in. To the photographer, to the journalist, and to variations on 'the scumbag who took that picture':

'Amazing pic.'

'You should be ashamed of yourself.'

'That creeped me out. But I liked it.'

'Good job. Thank you.'

'Gross. Cool but gross.'

'Disgusting. Get a life.'

'Spooky.'

The worst if it was that he became part of the story and that had never been in the deal. The more impressions the photo made, the more people wanted to know who had taken it. His news editor, Archie Cameron, a twenty-year reporter who'd survived the culls and was now running the desk because no else remained who could do it, told him he'd had eight requests for an interview before two o'clock.

Winter flat out refused. He wasn't the story. Aiden McAlpine was the story.

Archie had sighed and told him he agreed, but that wasn't the way the world worked any more. The *Standard*'s owners liked the fact they were the subject of global attention and they were very keen that Winter did the interviews. In the end, he didn't have much choice but to agree.

Everything about it left him feeling a bit dirty. It was his photograph but it was like he didn't own it any more. It was out there, seen and devoured by the world. Sure, that was his job but he couldn't escape a feeling of dread. He felt that somehow he was being used and that maybe he'd done the one thing that Aiden McAlpine's killer wanted. More headlines, more exposure.

'Good job. Thank you.'

CHAPTER 4

The message that a press conference had been called for three that afternoon had immediately made Narey uncomfortable. The presser was no great surprise given who Aiden McAlpine's father was, and the timing was perfect for the TV companies, who'd be desperate for a teatime news slot. Detective Chief Superintendent Tom Crosbie, the lead for the Major Investigation Team, was fronting it up, but she wouldn't have expected anything else. A high-profile case always suits the suits.

Be there, was what she was told. Get your lippy on for the cameras. Press room. Three o'clock. That was it. She was bothered not by what had been said to her but what hadn't. Sure, it had all been a rush job, so maybe she was worrying unnecessarily, but she didn't think so.

The press was there before she was and a couple of reporters who knew her by sight approached to try to ask her questions. She brushed them aside, telling them they'd just have to wait. She needed to talk to DCI Addison, to find out what the hell was going on, but there was no sign of him, and it was just a couple of minutes before the thing was due to start.

She felt another hand at her elbow from the press pack and turned with half a mind to twist it up the perpetrator's back. It was Winter.

'Fancy seeing you here!' He kept his voice low enough that his fellow journalists couldn't hear. 'Can you tell the *Standard* who the killer is?'

'No comment. You know, I still can't get used to you being here. Being one of *them*.'

He laughed. 'Well get used to it. It's what's going to have to pay our mortgage.'

'The wages of sin.' She spat it out but a hint of a smile played on her lips. 'I don't like the way this conference is going. I've a feeling you might have one pissed-off police officer to placate later.'

'Why? What's up?'

'Maybe nothing. I'm not . . . Hang on, there's Addison. I need to speak to him. Look, I have to go.'

DCI Derek Addison was her longtime boss and a good friend of Winter's. Thick as thieves, the two men were drinking buddies and football fans together. You'd think that might have cut her some slack as far as knowing what was happening in the station was concerned, but it didn't seem to today. Addison's lanky six-foot-four frame rose above most of the other cops in the media room and she'd spotted him the moment he entered.

She managed to catch his gaze and made an exaggerated shrug of her shoulders to throw him the question. He immediately looked awkward and she could see him swear under his breath, fuelling her fears further. He started to make his way across the room towards her but, just behind him, Crosbie entered the room signalling the press conference was about to start and he had to abandon the move with an apologetic shrug of his own.

Fuck it. Fuck it. She could feel the anger rise from her toes.

There was a seat behind the desk with a piece of folded card in front of it with her name printed in bold letters. She manoeuvred her way behind the other seats and took her place. She had no sooner sat down than she wanted out, wanted to be anywhere else. She was trapped, though, stuck where she was in full view of the media and the cameras.

All she could do was pick a spot on the far wall, somewhere just above the heads of the assembled reporters and other cops, and stare at it with as impassive an expression on her face as she could maintain. She fixed on that to the extent that, although she was aware of other people taking their seats beside her, she couldn't see who they were.

When Crosbie began to speak, she could register only every other word and phrase. All were delivered in that deadly sombre tone that comes only with media coaching. Crosbie could have been reading Billy Connolly's greatest routine and it would still come out as if a little girl's dog had been run over by a bus. No drama, no sensitivity, just a big dollop of gravitas.

She knew where it was going and didn't need to listen to it all. She kept her focus on the far wall and on looking nothing other than professional.

'Officers were called ... attended immediately ... parents notified ... greatest sympathy ... understanding at this time ...'

Get to it. Ah, here we go.

'Because of the high-profile nature of this investigation and of the extensive media exposure that it has already created and will continue to receive ...' Coming right around the bend. It needed just three words to put the tin lid on it: 'Detective Chief Inspector.' There we go, bingo, full house. '... Denny Kelbie will lead for Police Scotland on this case. He has already familiarised himself with the work done until this point and will waste no ...'

Kelbie. Of all people. The malevolent, incompetent little shite. Denny Kelbie. Oh just perfect.

She didn't need to look, didn't dare to look, but she was sure he was there a few feet away, all five-foot midget of him, sitting next to Crosbie with his chest puffed out and the word 'smug' painted on his forehead. Anyone, anyone but him.

She kept staring at the wall ahead, her face blank. Try as she might, though, she couldn't escape the image of some ugly goblin standing at her side, ratcheting up the blood pressure on her wrist, tightening some spiked medieval instrument of torture that twisted her arteries to bursting point. An ugly goblin named Kelbie.

She let her eyes drop just enough to look for Winter among the seated reporters. Sure enough, he was looking right back at her, one person at least who could feel her pain. He grimaced in sympathy but then he was signalling something else, motioning her back to the table. Focusing again, she could hear her name being mentioned but it came as if from an echo chamber and it took her a second or two to process that she'd been called on to speak. She saw that the rest of the assembled press corps was looking at her expectantly.

'DI Narey,' Crosbie was repeating. 'Can you tell us what you found at the scene at Queen Street Station this morning, please.'

Demoted to second chair but still called on to sing for her supper. Sure thing. She took just a breath to calm herself down enough to present a professional face then launched into it. She gave chapter and verse on the morning's events, appealed for anyone in the area at that time to come forward with information, then sat back to take questions.

'DI Narey, can you comment on the public nature of where the body was found, seemingly deliberately in front of the commuter train?'

She'd formed the reply on her lips but didn't get a chance to utter it. Kelbie leaned into the microphone in front of him and spoke across her.

'That would require speculation rather than comment and DI Narey isn't going to indulge in speculation at this stage. What we can say is that we are keeping an open mind on every aspect of the investigation.'

Her ears burned at that. She would never indulge in fucking speculation and didn't need to be protected from the question or told not to do so. She swallowed it and answered the reporter directly.

'As DCI Kelbie has suggested, we will explore all aspects of both the timing and location of the victim's body.'

'Do you think that Mr McAlpine's prominent position as an MSP is connected to his son's death?'

'Okay, let me take that,' Kelbie said, stepping in again. 'Ladies and gentlemen, let me be clear on one thing. Aiden McAlpine's death is a terrible tragedy and our sympathies are with his parents. However, we will investigate as we would any other victim of any other grieving family. Mr McAlpine's public role will not change our efforts to bring justice in this case. We will be working diligently to find exactly what happened to Aiden McAlpine and will of course speak to his father as part of our enquiries.'

Lots of words, little substance, little man. He knew nothing about the case but he liked the cameras, loved the spotlight. Kelbie was going to milk this for all it was worth.

When the press conference was over and the reporters and film crews began to filter from the room, Narey let her blank expression drop and one of clear displeasure took its place. She stood and began to push her way out from behind the table. Addison saw the move and made his own way round from the opposite end of the table. Unfortunately for him, DCI Crosbie had the same idea and he was nearer to Narey. Addison was always a couple of strides behind and struggled to cut Crosbie off before he got to her. Or she to him.

She saw them both approach and was content to have both in the firing line. Crosbie began to speak with his practised diplomacy.

'DI Narey. I expect you will be—'

'No one thought that maybe I should have been told this face to face rather than hearing it during a broadcast press conference? No one thought that would be courtesy to say the least, not to mention issues of professional standards and common decency? No?'

'DI Narey,' Crosbie persisted, becoming irritated, 'I understand your frustration but—'

'With all respect, sir, I'm not sure you do.'

'Rachel!'

'As I was saying, I *do* appreciate and understand your frustration, but time was very much against us here. Mr McAlpine's status has drastically altered the clock on this. In an ideal world, we would have sat down and had a one-to-one before the press conference, but time simply didn't allow for that. A decision's been made and, while it may have been communicated better, it is no longer up for discussion. DCI Kelbie will be leading this investigation and you will be reporting to him.'

'The clock altered because the victim's father is an MSP? Sir, I've always operated on the basis that all murder victims should be afforded that sort of urgency. Even DCI Kelbie pretended he thought that too. On top of that, urgency should always come second to accuracy, and I'm much more likely to give you that than Kelbie.'

The DCI heard her spit out his name and came running like a dog eager for a fight. She could see the snarl form on his face and began to arrange one of her own.

'*Rachel!*' Addison's voice was thick with warning but she ignored it and plunged headlong down the path of righteous self-destruction.

'This is not only unfair and most probably sexist, it is entirely detrimental to the investigation. DCI Kelbie's credentials for solving a case of this kind are dubious to say the least. His career—'

'Rachel!'

'His career has been mediocre at best and his history of failure is—'

'Rachel!'

Her head was swimming with it now, indignation and resentment and anger and frustration. It was hot in the squad room and getting hotter. She couldn't stop herself even if she'd wanted to. She was on some sort of spiral that was irresistible. Kelbie wasn't exactly helping by being in her face now, shouting back at her even though she couldn't make out a word through the fog of adrenalin and the oxygen that seemed to be making her head lighter with each passing second.

She couldn't even hear her own words and had no idea what she'd just said. All she knew was that everyone remaining in the room was looking at her. Kelbie, Addison, Giannandrea, Crosbie. She could see Winter staring in through the window, too. All with their mouths open and concern or shock written on their faces. They were all spinning, moving, distorting. Suddenly, they were above her and she'd no idea how they'd got there.

'Rachel!'

Something bumped against her head and she'd vaguely wondered what it was. Turning to look, she realised her cheek was cold against the floor and it felt comforting, like ice against a cut. She was on the floor yet still falling and had no idea if there would ever be a bottom to it. She was just about to ask what the hell was going on when she realised she had no voice and someone had turned out all the lights.

CHAPTER 5

'Rachel. Rachel!'

The voice came to her through a curtain of pain and confusion. Something deep in the middle of her pierced and stung and bent her double. It made her teeth grind and her eyes water. Crying. She was crying in pain.

Lots of voices. All urgent. All somewhere above and distant. They were drifting in and out – or else she was. The floor so cold. Her face so hot.

'Rachel!'

Tony. He was loud and angry and worried. She couldn't lift her head, but looked up to see him pushing Denny Kelbie forcefully aside. His face loomed large over hers and she saw him mouth something close to a scream.

No! Don't tell them. She didn't have words. *Don't tell them. Not yet. Too soon. Please.*

Shit, how could it hurt so much? Had someone stabbed her in the stomach and then sliced her veins?

All those voices. Everyone shouting at her. But there was darkness calling at her, too, and it seemed much more inviting. Just slide into the dark and the pain might stop. Seemed so obvious and easy.

'Rachel!'

She looked up into his eyes to say goodbye. Bye-bye before she went to the dark. It hurt so much.

'She's pregnant,' she heard him tell them. 'Get an ambulance, now. She's pregnant!'

CHAPTER 6

She couldn't actually be sure she remembered being on the floor with the men above her. She may have dreamed it or overheard it second-hand from the doctors and nurses who fussed round her bed thinking she was asleep. She was in the Southern General, she knew that much, but whether she'd been there five minutes or five days she couldn't say. The pain had largely gone, drowned in something that had been shot through her veins for that very purpose, something that killed the discomfort and her ability to be awake.

When the effect of that eased enough that she could hear and see at the same time, the room settled into a soft focus and she rediscovered the ability to speak. The two words croaked out of her, scratching their way free of a throat denied water for too long.

'My baby.'

Even as the nurse turned to look at her, Narey realised she was questioning her own words. *Baby.* If anyone else had used the term just a little over four months into pregnancy, she might have doubted that it was even that. Can it be a baby yet? But it was suddenly very, very different when it was growing inside her and at clear risk. It – he or she – hadn't been planned and had come as a rude shock. She'd spent four unhappy, uncertain days before she'd told Tony. Even then the pair of them had been more overwhelmed than overjoyed. His job, her job, her dad. They had so much to deal with already and, while of course they wanted this, or at least they were pretty sure they did, someday – but today? The nine-month tomorrow today? Now?

It changed with the growing acceptance and the end of shock. It changed completely with the sixteen-week scan and the sight of the little someone with definable ears and a nose. It changed beyond all recognition when she hit the media room floor and the unborn life was in severe danger of being snatched away.

'My baby.'

The nurse's plump face assumed business and she gave an insistent nod of the head, holding out a hand to plead with her to wait as she turned on her heels and went in search of someone else.

It took an age. Long enough for her to launch a search within herself. Some bizarre, inexplicable, mind exploration for the something that she needed to be there. Could she not feel it? Surely she would know? The panic grew with every passing second and didn't ease as she heard the urgent clatter of shoes on the polished corridor floor getting closer and closer to her bed.

She looked up to see the irritatingly calm features of a man in his fifties, his dark-brown eyes peering at her with concern.

'Do you know where you are, Rachel? And how you got here?'

'Yes and no. And it doesn't matter. My baby, Doctor. How is my baby?'

He took a deep breath and leaned back, straightening up away from her in a way she didn't like. He was preparing himself. She'd seen it, done it, often enough to know the signs. It scared her.

'Don't feel the need to sugar-coat it for me, Doctor. I'm as used to breaking bad news as you are. I'd appreciate if you just told me straight.'

'Your partner, Mr Winter, is on his way. We—'

'Tell me now, please. I don't need my hand held.'

The doctor was Asian and a mister according to his name badge. Mr Tillikaratne. She wasn't quite sure of the significance of the mister, maybe just a specialist rather than a surgeon, but she didn't take it as a good sign. He had a good face, though. Kind with nice brown eyes under grey hair.

'I'm sorry to tell you that you may be suffering from pre-eclampsia.'

The colour drained from her face and her eyes reddened. 'But I can't be. Not yet. The baby . . .'

'Is at risk but with the right care and rest I'd be hopeful that he or she will go full term and suffer no ill effects.'

Risk. Hopeful. Suffer.

She did need her hand held. She needed all of her held.

'It is incredibly rare for pre-eclampsia to occur before twenty weeks. There have been instances of it, however, and my opinion is you are not yet suffering from the condition. But we cannot take any chances or it could develop. We must take steps to protect both of you.'

'Both?'

'Pre-eclampsia can be fatal for the mother too. We cannot allow you to endanger yourself. I have to be quite clear and honest with you, Ms Narey. If necessary, we will terminate your pregnancy to save your life.'

The air was sucked out of the room and she couldn't hear a word. The doctor was still talking but she could only see his mouth opening and closing. Trying to process what he'd said was all she could cope with. If she could cope with anything at all. Her hands went to her stomach, cradling herself and her own.

'... only with complete bed rest,' he was saying. 'You do understand that?'

What? She didn't understand anything. Where was Tony? She needed him. Needed him to explain and reassure and just to be there.

'I feel fine,' she heard herself saying. 'Whatever it was, I'm fine now.'

The doctor's headshake was kind but firm. 'You're really not.'

'You don't understand. I'm in the middle of a case and my maternity leave doesn't start until—'

The doctor put out a hand to cut her off in midstream. 'DI Narey, I'm sorry but it's *you* that doesn't understand. You won't be working any case for a considerable time. Your maternity leave started the minute you hit the floor. You will be confined not only to home but to bed for at least five weeks. There is no alternative.'

'But—'

'No alternative. None.'

'You can't do that. Please.'

Another voice came from near the door. 'He can and it's already done. She looked up to see Addison walking in.

'Boss, you need to have a word with this doctor because he—'

Even in the middle of denial, she knew how ridiculous everything she was saying was. She was reaching, looking for some reversal of a reality she couldn't cope with.

Addison grimaced. 'I see you've been told the news. Don't take it out on him and don't even think of starting on me. This isn't up for discussion. You're off the Queen Street case completely and your enforced leave of absence has already begun. You've been stood down, Rachel. Accept it.'

'This is ridiculous. I'm fine. I just had a dizzy spell and once I've—'

'No!'

'Can no one let me finish a sentence round here? It's my body. Surely I'm best placed to judge what I can and can't do?'

Addison shook his head and loosened his tie. 'Rachel, if you don't do exactly what you're told and stay in bed, then I'll arrest you myself. I'll charge you with . . .' He struggled for an option. 'Doc, give me something here.'

'Endangering the life of an unborn child.'

'Yes, that. Exactly that. Be sensible, Rachel. Please. I'm counting on being a godfather in five months' time.'

'*You?* No chance.'

'What? I'm offended. Who means more to you two than me?'

'Piss off. Sir. Seriously, this is how it's got to be?'

His voice softened. 'Yes. Anything else is way too risky.'

The air and the anger escaped from her, drifting away on a heavy sigh as her eyes closed over.

'In that case, leave me alone now. Please. I'm pretty sure I'm going to cry and the last thing I want is to do that in front of you.'

CHAPTER 7

He was there about ten minutes later, bursting through the door as slowly and as quickly as he could. She knew it was him without lifting her face from where it was buried in the pillow. Smell or sense or need or something. Something she didn't need to begin to explain. All she knew was that, when his hand went through her hair, she knew. When his mouth pressed itself against her forehead, she knew.

She knew and she felt better for it. He couldn't take away all of the pain and the fear and the risk but he could take some of it. His share.

The dread wasn't all hers, she knew that. She could hear his in the shallowness of his breathing and feel it in the tremor in his hands. He was striving to be strong for her but he needed to be held as much as he needed to hold. This was two-way hugging.

He was remembering the look he felt must have been on his face when she'd first told him she was pregnant. His mouth must have been stuck open. As if her being pregnant were the most unlikely thing in the world. As if it were a bad thing. As if he were the most selfish bastard in the world. He was ashamed and embarrassed now just thinking about it.

He couldn't get his head round it at first. A baby. Their baby. Out of the loins of a tumultuous relationship, another being. It had scared him right from the off. Nothing compared to how it scared him now, though.

And her, her. He loved her so much that it frightened him to death.

She could feel he was nervous to hold her too tight, as though there were a risk of breaking her. She wanted to tell him she was unbreakable, that she'd survive this, survive anything. She'd always told herself that was true. Any situation, any problem, she'd cope. But how did she cope when her body was betraying her?

She felt his hand slip its way into one of hers, fingers entwining like the roots of a tree. He was bonding his body with hers for mutual support, scaffolding for each other. Whatever his faults, he'd be there every step, do whatever he could. He held on for dear life and she did the same.

It had easily been ten minutes without either of them saying a word. She finally spoke but the words could have come from either.

'It will be all right.'

Neither of them knew that would be the case but they were desperate to believe it, so they did. Fingers brushed at wet eyes and they both managed a laugh at their shared thinking.

She half sat up, half propped herself on his shoulder. 'Great work with that photograph. It's been everywhere.'

'Forget that. It doesn't matter.'

'Oh, but it does. Our baby is going to need shoes. So you need to go to work.'

'You're something else, you know that?'

'I do. The clothing that you photographed. That's your story. They weren't all there.'

'What? Rachel, stop—'

'No, listen to me. Kelbie will never see it because he's an idiot but the way those clothes were left was a message being sent. It was all very deliberate. And there were items missing. That's your story. That's the key.'

CHAPTER 8

Being a journalist was not something that had come easily to Winter. If it was a natural skill of some sort, then he was missing the gene.

It had been nearly a year since he'd picked up pen, notebook and laptop and added them to his cameras when he went to work. He was still much more comfortable with a lens than interviewing someone, but he was getting there. He knew what questions to ask and which ones not to. He knew when to walk away and when to run. Maybe most importantly, he now knew a story when he smelled one.

That final piece of knowledge had been earned the hard way. He'd had plenty of those that turned out not to be stories at all – in the eyes of those that mattered – to finally recognise the difference.

He was never going to win a Pulitzer prize but at least he could now get through the day without completely embarrassing himself. Usually.

Much of that was thanks to the man he was going to speak to now, Archie Cameron, the news editor. He was a good guy, solid and smart, and had been round the houses often enough to know which doors to knock and which to avoid. Archie had been around for two decades and that qualified him as old-school even though he'd just turned forty. He was last man standing as far as the newsroom was concerned, the only competent one not earning enough to get bulleted by the accountants. By the measure of that double-edged compliment, he was now in charge.

He could, despite his undoubted good points, be a grumpy and short-tempered bastard but that was par for the course for journalists, and if you ignored that then you'd see he was more than okay. He'd talked Winter through the tough early days, shown him the ropes that were left and kept him from getting sacked. Archie had either seen enough in him to make it worthwhile to coach him or was just a decent enough guy that he'd have done it anyway. Either way, Winter was grateful.

He didn't look up from his computer screen as Winter approached the desk, his gaze fixed on whatever was scrolling before his eyes. He looked frazzled, with worried waves printed on his forehead, but Winter had never known him to look any other way. He'd seen photographs of Archie as a young reporter and the man now looked like his own grandfather.

'I hope you're coming to my desk with a good story or a great photograph, Tony. If not, do us both a favour and fuck off again. I don't have time for anything other than good news right now.'

He hadn't looked up but Winter wasn't surprised he'd known it was him. Archie had some superhero form of peripheral vision that negated the need to lift his head.

'It's possibly good news.'

Archie did glance up this time but only to give a look that made it clear that 'possibly' wasn't good enough. His eyebrows mocked the credibility of Winter's words; indeed he was incredulous they'd even been uttered.

'*Possibly*? Partick Thistle are *possibly* going to win the Champions League next season and I'm *possibly* going to find cream that will sort my piles, but I wouldn't bet two bob on either of them.'

It's what he did, or tried to do. Full-on irascible journo in the way he'd been brought up, witnessing *real* news editors do their stuff. Whisky-soaked arseholes with nicotine on their fingers and ink in their blood, prime ministers' home numbers in their contact books and a complete inability to be nice about anyone other than their mother as long as anyone was watching. Archie tried the best he could but few of the staff really thought he meant it. It was a half-hearted nod to the past; it was what he thought he should do.

'So what the fuck is it?' Archie was playing the hard man but he wasn't winning.

'I've got a lead on the McAlpine killing and I want to pursue it. I think it's worth a go.'

That won him a heavy sigh and a long stare. 'What kind of lead? The kind that means you're going to disappear for a few days and come back with nothing but a handful of expense receipts? Or the kind that's going to make my life easier and fill the front page?'

Winter played the best card he currently had. 'The kind that has already filled the front page. The kind that has been picked up by the London papers and all those TV stations. That kind, Archie.'

The coverage of Winter's murder-scene pic had made Archie as happy as Archie was likely to get, but it had left the paper's owners ecstatic. Their happiness was pound-shaped.

Archie drummed his fingers on the desk as he thought. 'What's the lead?'

'Can't say.'

'Can say.'

'Can't.'

'*You're* the can't, Tony. You know how strapped I am for staff. If you're buggering off leaving everyone else to fill the paper, then this better be good.'

The *Standard* office used to be a big building in the Merchant City, home to forty-odd journalists plus another dozen office staff. Now all Archie had were five reporters and a secretary in a modern block in Anderston plus four freelance subeditors on the other end of a fibre-optic connection in Wales. The days of the Raj were long gone.

'It will be good, Archie. Promise.'

'Promise? I can't print fucking promises. Fine, go follow this lead. But you come back to me with a good story or start looking for a new job. Okay?'

'Okay.' Winter knew Archie didn't mean it but the game was they'd both pretend that he did.

'I haven't finished. There's an antiwar march in George Square tomorrow. With a bit of luck someone will start a fight or attack the polis. Get me pics and words on that.'

'Will do.'

'And there's some exhibition opening about shipbuilding on the Clyde. It sounds dull as fuck but it will fill a space. Cover that too.'

'Cheers, Archie.'

'Piss off.'

Winter had the time he needed to look into the stack of Aiden McAlpine's clothing, but he had one slight problem. He didn't have a clue where to start. His promises to Archie were as hollow as a banker's conscience.

His gut told him Rachel was right about its being the key to understanding the boy's murder, but that didn't mean he knew how to do it. He was going to need help.

His mum had always told him, if you're in trouble, call the police. He pulled out his mobile, found the number and punched it. Addison answered right away.

'Hey, wee man. How's Rachel?'

It was a good question.

'She's doing okay, Addy. Bored out of her skull and getting more bad-tempered by the day. But she's all right and the baby's all right. I'll settle for that.'

'Glad to hear it. Tell her I was asking for her. What about you? I saw your photograph everywhere. Nice work. Must have bought you a million brownie points in the gutter press.'

'I wish. Yesterday's news, tomorrow's chip wrapping. I've promised them a follow up on the McAlpine kid but truth is I've got nothing.'

There was silence on the other end of the line as Addison digested that.

'And you're telling me this, why?'

'I was wondering if you . . .'

'It's not my case. Not that I'd be telling you anything if it was. It's Kelbie's. That little shite will be desperate to get himself in front of the cameras somewhere. If only he was as keen to get himself in front of a speeding train. Sorry Tony, I can't help you.'

'Come on. It's not your case but that doesn't mean you don't know things. There's nothing going on that you don't know about. Give me a break here, will you? I can just ask you a couple of questions and you can just say yes or no. How does that sound?'

Addison grunted. 'Listen, wee man. Are you trying to trick information out of me to make DCI Kelbie's case look bad? To con me into telling you things he wouldn't want revealed to the press?'

'Yes.'

'Okay, good. What do you want to know?'

CHAPTER 9

She was trapped.

Trapped in a four-bedroom Victorian conversion that had appeared huge when there was just the two of them rattling around in it, but now seemed tiny. It had shrunk to one bedroom and the occasional, although ever-increasing, use of the bathroom.

She used to love this room. They'd redecorated when they'd moved in just under a year ago and she'd been so happy with what they'd done to it. Now? Now she was wondering why they'd ever bothered.

She was trapped.

Trapped with a creature growing inside her. A little human being who'd moved in without asking and had turned her life upside down. An invader. An asylum seeker. Not a refugee. Not yet. It was still awaiting her approval for that status.

She hadn't planned to be pregnant. She hadn't asked for any of this. She had a career that she'd worked bloody hard to advance in and be respected in, and all that was in danger of going down the pan because of a design fault in her body. She could just imagine all the male cops, all the amateur glaziers who had helped fit that glass ceiling, pissing themselves laughing. Told you, they'd be saying, nudging their Neanderthal mates; told you she couldn't hack it without having a sprog. That's her finished. That's that stuck-up bitch done.

It wasn't being pregnant that was bothering her. Not really. She'd been happy, they both had after the shock. They'd been open-mouthed and scared and really happy. But then there was the whole falling-on-her-arse-and-passing-out thing. That had scared the shit out of her and it had been embarrassing and given those wankers all the ammunition they needed to say they'd been right about why she shouldn't have been promoted. She passed out for chrissakes. In front of them.

So she resented the growth inside her. She hated herself a bit for doing so but couldn't deny it. Application for refugee status denied. For now.

Trapped. Trapped in a king-size bed with four walls to look at and just the sounds of the street for music. Sure, he'd brought in speakers so she could play tunes from her phone but she couldn't be arsed. She'd rather be an angry frustrated martyr with the noise of Great Western Road as a backing track. The more she had to complain about the better.

There was just ten yards or so from the front of their house on Bellhaven Terrace to the crazy traffic on GWR. She'd made him crack the bedroom window so she could hear the world, shooing away his motherly worries about the cold or someone breaking in. She wanted to hear. If she couldn't see anything or speak to anyone, then at least let her ears do some work.

There were buses all day long, the squeal of air brakes driving her a bit demented, but at least lassoing her to some reality. At rush hour, there was regular blasting of horns as cars snuck into the bus lanes and the drivers played horn tag to see who had the biggest.

At mornings, lunch and tea she'd hear high-pitched teenage chatter as the schoolkids made their way to and from Notre Dame or the primary school. At lunch she knew they'd be queuing up in Churchill's Convenience store and munching on rolls and crisps and whatever fizzy drink floated their arteries.

They were the sounds of her unseen West End. She hated it and loved it and hated it.

They'd bought this house with the idea that her dad would live there with them, at least part of the week. Him and a room for his carer, Jess, for when she and Tony were both working.

Dad had been in his nursing home for too long. Him trapped there the way she felt now. Him trapped in his own head most of the time. Alzheimer's. Such a horrendous thing for a man like her dad to have.

So Tony had suggested they buy this monstrosity of a place so that her dad could stay. She'd loved him for it and for a while it worked. Tough, very tough, but easier on her conscience than having him in that home.

Then came the invader and they just couldn't do it any more. Another reason to resent her own baby and to wallow in double guilt.

The extra three bedrooms laughed at her now that they'd both gone. Hollow, empty rooms that rang with malicious amusement above the buses and the schoolkids. Still, one would hopefully be for the asylum seeker. God, she so hoped it would be. She couldn't bear the thought of losing him or her. She couldn't imagine anything worse than losing her little refugee.

All she could do was lie there. Lie there and plot.

CHAPTER 10

Winter didn't have much. Even with the little he'd persuaded Addison to give up, he barely had enough to fill a second lead. It was far from what he'd promised Archie Cameron but he'd decided to file it along with disclaimers about its being a holding story until the real thing came along.

Any story about Aiden McAlpine was a story, though. In many ways, he was the only story in town. Being a prominent MSP's son would have been enough. Being hanged in front of the dawn train would have been enough. The double whammy made it huge.

Still, Winter was ready for Archie to jump all over his story with boots on. He'd see it for the threadbare half-story it was. But, this week being Aiden McAlpine week, it might just be good enough.

Archie had his head pressed against the screen of his computer. For a second, Winter thought he was sleeping against it but then realised it was the more common occurrence of Archie trying to put his head through the monitor so it would magically cure whatever the problem was.

There were slight bumping motions against the screen that were getting progressively louder and Archie had to be saved from himself.

'Boss. Archie.'

Cameron looked up and didn't seem to be made any happier at seeing him standing there.

'Make it good and make it fast.'

He took a deep breath and began the pitch. 'The clothes that were left at the scene of Aiden McAlpine's murder? The ones I photographed.'

Archie shook his head slowly. 'The pic that went worldwide? I vaguely remember, yes. Get the fuck on with it.'

'Right, sorry. Those clothes. Some of them were missing.'

Archie was almost interested. He sat back and ran his hand through his thinning locks. 'Missing? What kind of missing? How?'

'Missing in a way the cops haven't admitted. Missing in a way they haven't told Mark McAlpine.'

Archie smiled, an increasingly rare occurrence these days. 'Tell me more. And please tell me you have this locked down.'

'I've got it from cop sources. Impeccable sources.'

'Nice. Sources that will be quoted?'

'No.'

'Of course not. So, these clothes went missing after you photographed them?'

'Um, no. Before. They weren't put there with the others. That's the point. They've been taken by the killer, and the cops have refused to tell anyone this.'

'Taken by ... You're pishing on your own chips here. Why don't you just tell what you think has happened here?'

'Okay, so there was no underwear among the clothes. No shorts, no socks. Possibly Aiden McAlpine wasn't wearing any but more likely he was. So either the killer had dumped them or he's kept them. It's a story either way.'

'So you don't actually know what happened? Fuck's sake, listen to me. It's not a story. Aiden McAlpine might not have been wearing socks. That's your story? Geez peace!'

'No, he was wearing them *and* underwear, but they've gone missing. I think they've been taken as a trophy by the killer. And the cops are keeping it quiet. Surely that's a story. And we have the pic to prove it.'

The trophy bit came out of his mouth before he knew it had been in his head. It might have been better if he'd thought this through. Archie made a face as if he were chewing bleach.

'I don't know. What do you mean the cops are keeping it quiet? They're whispering it?'

'They're refusing to confirm what was or wasn't among the clothing. They're claiming the information could be evidential and won't be released. Come on, Archie. It's a story, you know it is.'

'Don't tell me what I know! You've been doing this for less time than it takes me to process a chicken Balti so don't tell me what I know. Go write it up and let me see it. Then I'll decide.'

'It's a story, Archie. A front-page story.'

'Yeah, maybe. If it runs at all it's going to need Betteridge.'

'Who?'

'See what I mean? Less time than it takes me to get a good curry through my system. Go fuck off and write it.'

*

Archie had had the piece for half an hour, all of which he'd spent with his door closed and resisting any attempt by Winter to find out what he was thinking. Finally, he emerged far enough to look over to Winter's desk and motion him inside with a brusque nod of his head.

By the time he got there, Archie was already back behind his desk, staring at his screen.

'This is all you've got?'

'Yes but—'

'And you haven't got a quote from the cops or McAlpine?'

'Not yet, I wanted—'

'And you can't actually prove these clothes have gone missing?'

'No but—'

'And yet you expect me to run this as it is? And you think management aren't going to crap themselves when they hear about it? And you think the lawyer will okay it?'

Winter digested all of that. 'Yes. No. Yes.'

'Aye, that's what you hope the answer is, not what you think it is. There's no way I'm running this without comment from Police Scotland or McAlpine.'

'So you'll run it if I get those?'

'I might.'

'Fantastic. I—'

'Haud your horses, I haven't said yes. Best I might do is some kind of "Have MSP's son's murder clothes gone missing?" With a question mark.'

'Okay. Well—'

'No, it's *not* okay. That bring us back to Betteridge. Have you had a chance to Google it yet?'

'I've been a bit busy writing a page lead. Who's Betteridge?'

'Betteridge's law of headlines.' Archie muttered. 'It says that any newspaper headline that ends in a question mark can be answered with no. Basically it means the story is bullshit. The reporter knows it's bullshit and the sub knows it's bullshit. Bang a question mark on the end and you might just get away with it.'

'And you think that's what this is?'

Archie shrugged. 'If it can't walk like a duck and can't swim like a duck and can't quack like a duck, then it's probably a pile of duck shit. But today it happens to be the best bit of duck shit we've got. So you're getting the Betteridge question mark. And that's the best I can do for you.'

'I'll take it.'

'Like you've got a choice.'

CHAPTER 11

Nathan had read quite a bit about other people like him. Or people who were *possibly* like him – he had no real idea of what they were like. Probably what he really meant was people who did the same thing he did. Kill.

For a long time, it didn't make any difference to him. He did it. He had the taste for it and he wanted more. That was all he knew or cared about. Why anyone else did it? He couldn't care less.

Then, after a while, and on one of his periods of down-time, he started to wonder. He wasn't even sure if he was wondering about them or about him. Maybe if he could work out why they did, he'd know why he did.

He read psychology books, watched documentaries and looked up all he could find online. It gave him a bit of a hard-on, if he was honest. There were theories on prefrontal cortices, something called the amygdala, and how that meant killers didn't give a fuck about anything and that's why they just did what they wanted. Others argued about upbringing, nurture rather than nature and all that, how most killers had been sexually abused.

Then there was shite about evil. How you were just born bad.

He read about people whose names he'd known but little else. Macy. Dahmer. Nilsen. Bundy. Charles Ng. Otis Toole. David Berkowitz. Peter Manuel. Tommy Lyn Sells.

He read about kidnappings, serial killings and spree killings. Bodies dumped, mutilated and buried. Decapitations, heads as trophies, body parts stuffed in drains. Mutilation. Torture.

There was a thrill he hadn't expected. A second-hand excitement that heated his blood and gave him ideas.

All that from reading about people like him. Except they were known and he wasn't. Everyone knew their names. No one knew his. Not yet.

What he really wanted to know from those like him was how they felt. *After.* Not before. He knew how they felt before. How did they feel *after* they'd done it? Come to that, how did *he* feel?

It varied. Elated. Jumping. Buzzing. Or else down, dirty, as if he'd given in to it again. Worst was if he felt indifferent. As if it hadn't done anything for him. That made it seem like a waste of time.

Mostly, he felt like he imagined an animal did after it had caught and killed its prey, like a lion bringing down an antelope or a wolf a deer. Sated. Fulfilled. Excited in its skin. Belly full and nerve ends jangling. Alive.

There were other kinds of killer, too, ones that he knew were nothing like him. Guys who got drunk and beat their wives to death. Nothing like him. Robbers who clubbed security guards over the head. Nothing like him. People who lashed out or killed for revenge or in self-defence or in anger. Thieves who killed for money. Nothing like him.

Those people did it once. Maybe twice if something strange happened. They didn't set out to do it and probably wished they hadn't. Nothing like him.

Because, if there was one thing he'd learned from reading about Dahmer, Bundy and the rest, it was that he was like them in one way more than any other. The *why*. He did it because he wanted to, because he had to. Above all, he did it because he liked it.

CHAPTER 12

A week. She'd been at home for a week. A long week of seven long days.

Don't think a day consists of only twenty-four hours. Most of the preceding seven had run to thirty or forty hours each. Each of those hours easily ran to eighty or one hundred minutes. Each and every day of drudging tedium had lasted an eternity and yet the week itself had gone in an instant and she'd done nothing, achieved nothing and been worth nothing. She'd got a week fatter and a week duller, but that was it.

She'd tried crosswords, online quizzes, memory tests, anything she could think of to keep her brain in some kind of shape, but little of it could hold her attention for long. Books had been half-read and discarded, TV channels had been switched with a regularity that threatened to break the remote control. Did people really stay at home and watch this stuff?

She'd made promises to herself and to Tony, and to the little person that was forming inside her. She said she would relax, that she'd stay in bed and keep movement to a minimum. Of course she wouldn't stress about the job or the case she'd been ripped from. She wouldn't think about Denny Kelbie or the Queen Street body or the stack of clothing that was placed under the body or the fact that not all the clothes were there and that bugged the hell out of her. She wouldn't think about any of that. Not for another ten minutes. Promise. Five at least.

The room, their bedroom, had begun to shrink, she was sure of it. It used to seem a big, generous room, the kind of high-ceilinged Victorian expanse that their part of the West End specialised in. Now, it was closing in on her, edging closer to the bed day by day, till she could almost reach out and touch the walls. She was beginning to dislike it, too, wearying of the pale blue of three of them and the patterned wallpaper of the other. Why had she ever liked the painting of the old man, the one they'd got at the university art show? He just looked gloomy and was beginning to seriously piss her off. She wondered, if she picked up the glass next to the bed, whether she'd be able to knock the painting off the wall with a decent throw.

What shade of blue were these bloody walls anyway? She remembered the tin had said it was something stupid like Mineral Mist, but that sounded more like a non-alcoholic cocktail than a colour. She'd spent seven days trying to determine what they really were. For a while, she'd thought it might be cornflower blue but she realised she had no idea what cornflower was, never mind what colour it was. Maybe the walls were baby blue like Frank Sinatra's eyes. Or powder blue. Except that was one of those things you just said without really knowing was it was. What kind of bloody shade was powder? Maybe it was azure. Like the sky on a summer's day. Like sky blue. If she could remember what that looked like.

There was too much time, too, to contemplate her bump. In fact, it wasn't even a bump yet. It was an internal bump. Hers. The weirdness of it freaked her. It – he or she – was actually growing inside her. She had so much time to lie still and think about this that she sometimes tried to feel it growing, feel it forming. She also had time to resent it. It wasn't the baby bump's fault that she was where she was, forced to play invalid while feeling perfectly healthy, she knew that, but it was the reason. *Your fault*, she heard herself saying.

She felt other things, too, though. Like fear and hope and a fierce protection she'd never quite known. Her emotions were being held hostage and she couldn't afford the ransom.

It was also irresistibly physical. She'd always been firm in her belief that it was her body and she'd decide anything and everything connected to it. Suddenly, annoyingly, infuriatingly, it wasn't just hers any more. She was sharing it with another being who was taking and giving without bothering to ask for consent, flooding her brain with all sorts of stuff while simultaneously sabotaging her bladder.

The walls weren't royal blue or steel blue or navy blue. They weren't turquoise or cyan or sapphire or cobalt. Maybe they were Oxford blue, whatever that was, or true blue. How could her bosses possibly think Denny Kelbie could run an investigation like that? He was too one-dimensional, too old-school dinosaur, too bloody thick.

The man in the painting on the wall was old-school too. Old-school Glasgow. He had a face battered by life, booze and cigarettes, with eyes that were even older than he was. He was sat in the corner of a pub, her guess was Tennent's on Byres Road, judging by the wood panelling behind him, and half-glaring, half-smiling at the girl who sketched him. Mona Lisa, Glesga-stylee with a half and a half-pint. The old bugger had been staring at her from that wall for a week now and she was getting fed up with it.

A week. Seven long, long days.

Tony was out there, working, not saying much when he was at home. Not about the Queen Street case, anyway. He said plenty about how she should take it easy. A lot about how she needed to try to relax. Every word making her relax less. He was fussing and fretting and conscientiously driving her crazy. He'd continually try to feed her, as if she weren't going to get fat enough. He wanted to check her temperature and her blood pressure every five minutes. He'd plump her pillows for Christ's sake!

It was actually all his fault. He'd done this to her. He'd got her pregnant. He'd made her an invalid. Left her debilitated, incapacitated. He'd made her bloody useless.

There was no way the neatly arranged pile of Aiden McAlpine's clothes weren't linked to the murder. No chance. The mind of the person who'd laid them out like that, so obsessively, so neurotically, that was the key. Work out the issue with the clothes and you will be halfway to finding the killer.

The old man sneered down at her from the corner of Tennent's, laughing at her for being so inadequate. Find out about the clothes? She could barely find her way to the toilet in time. She half sat up, reaching for the pillow and wrenched it out from beneath her, throwing it at the painting on the cornflower wall in the same movement. It missed by a couple of feet and landed on the floor with a pathetic, deflating thud.

She looked down at her fists, clenched like an angry child's. It was just as well Tony wasn't there to take her blood pressure. She forced herself to breathe out and take a lungful of something more relaxing. Except she knew there was only one thing that would let her relax at all. She was going to do it. For her sake, for the baby's sake, for Tony's sake, for everyone's sake. For Aiden McAlpine's.

She reached for her laptop, opened it up and mouthed a silent apology for the promises she was about to break.

She was physically imprisoned but the Internet was her way over the walls. It would be her way of staying sane or going completely crazy.

The latest newspaper reports on the case showed, inevitably, that Kelbie's investigation had stalled, plenty of bluster and bravado but no progress. No one out there seemed to know any more than she did and she'd been locked up like an invalid. There was information to be had, she was sure of it, and all her instincts told her the clothing was key.

If Aiden had been wearing boxers and socks before he was killed, which seemed likely, where were they now? As far as she could see, the choices were that the killer had discarded them after he'd stripped the body, that someone else had pinched them, or that the killer had deliberately removed them from the pile he left on show. Given how deliberate everything else had been, that was where her money was going.

What it meant, she didn't know. They could have been kept as trophies, as Tony had suggested in his article. That had already occurred to her and she'd seen and known about cases of that in the past. It was never a good sign and hinted at a repeat offender.

Trophies were something she could understand, though. The psychology of it was pretty straightforward. Often they would dine out on it sexually, reliving the killing in their heads so as to get off on it. Sometimes they would give the trophies to a wife or girlfriend and get their kicks from seeing them unwittingly wandering around wearing objects from the victim. That didn't seem very likely with a pair of worn socks and pants, though.

Trophies were usually jewellery or locks of hair. Clothes, yes, but underwear was more likely if it was a female victim. She supposed the killer could have been gay and that might explain it, but it still didn't ring true. Or not true enough.

Maybe the whole thing had been set up to be photographed. Did the other items just mess with the neatness, with the whole weird choreography? Maybe she'd just been in this room too long.

The whole viral nature of what had happened didn't sit easily with her. The passengers on the train, then Tony's damn photograph. It was what the killer had wanted, that much was obvious. Just showing off, or something else?

A sudden stabbing in her stomach jolted her back into the room. The pain made her double over and her eyes water. Her refugee was not happy she was working when she wasn't supposed to be. Don't tell Daddy. The thought came to her through clenched teeth. Don't tell Daddy.

She did her relaxation exercises and suffered while praying for it to pass. The spasms made her curl on the bed and hold both arms around herself. When it had gone, it left her breathless.

She searched about killers and their trophies, not finding much she didn't already know or had been taught. It was about a reward for their accomplishments, about the thrill and their sense of invincibility. It was all about fantasy, one that never ends.

She searched, too, for information about staging and photographs, seeking clues to what it might be. She wasn't working a case: she was working her mind, for good or for ill. She couldn't stop herself and wasn't sure she wanted to.

The reading on staging all came back to fantasy. It was all about sex and power, but, then, what wasn't? Most often, it was a message to the police. A message of the 'you can't catch me' variety. Which only served to prove most repeat killers were also idiots, but it was that sort of brainlessness that led them to being caught.

She typed 'crime scene photographs' into her search engine but found it pointing to sites overloaded with explicit real-life crime-scene photos. A flick through a couple of them was enough to turn even her stomach.

She'd seen horrific sights in her time, but these were way beyond. Butchered bodies, rotting corpses and decapitated skulls. Some of the killers were well known; most of the pictured victims were not.

'Crime-scene photographs psychology' just got more of the same. Tony's old day job, which she didn't need to see. She was about to try another search term when she saw another listing a few hits down the page. 'Murder memorabilia site selling killer's crime scene photos'.

A specialist website was selling photographs taken by forensics and used in court to convict an American serial killer named John E. Robinson Snr from Kansas. The photos, described as 'horrible', 'gruesome' and 'very grisly', showed the bodies of women stuffed into barrels on Robinson's farm.

The website sold memorabilia. Serial-killer memorabilia. It opened her eyes wide. And it gave her a new word. In the trade, it was known as 'murderabilia'.

True-crime collectibles. Murder memorabilia. *Murderabilia*. People were buying and selling things related to killings and killers. Letters, weapons, artwork, clothing, anything connected to serial killers in particular seemed to have a value. There were websites dedicated to it, people who made a living from murder. And there was just so much of it.

She jumped into the first one she saw. The names, so many of them familiar, screamed out at her, mostly American. Ted Bundy, John Wayne Gacy, Jeffrey Dahmer, Richard Ramirez, Ed Gein. A further look found some nearer to home on two sites called KillingTime and Murder Mart. Ian Brady and Myra Hindley, Dennis Nilsen, Fred and Rose West, Archibald Atto, the Krays.

You could buy missing posters for victims, Christmas cards from killers, arrest warrants, death certificates, photographs, autographs and driving licences. If she had a mind to, she could buy a death mask of the gangster John Dillinger right there and then, delivered to her door in five working days. She could buy a lock of Charles Manson's hair for eight hundred dollars.

It was a world of its own. A weird, shocking, strange, grisly, thriving world where murder was the order of business. How could she have not known this existed?

She bookmarked page after page, trying to remain calm yet racing on ahead of herself. There was a handwritten letter from Brady, a bucket of tools that belonged to West, a corset worn by Rose, a razor used to slash Tobin in prison, a uniform worn by John Christie. There was soil taken from under an American serial killer's house, fingernail clippings from another. Napkins, towels, shirts, hats, gloves. Anything. Everything.

She was sickened and fascinated. Unable and unwilling to stop tearing through page after page of it but disturbed by what she saw. Was it anything to do with what she'd been looking for? Maybe, maybe not. But, either way, she couldn't stop.

How did you price things like these? She saw an autograph from the 1930s American child killer Albert Fish had sold for $30,000. The gun used to shoot Lee Harvey Oswald had gone for over $2 million. A Christmas card from Ted Bundy could be bought for $4,000. A pair of gloves made by a fellow inmate for Manson were selling for $775.

She knew it wasn't likely but she did it anyway. Couldn't stop herself. She went to the search function of KillingTime and put the name in, much more in hope than expectation. She got nothing and felt immediately deflated but also a bit stupid. It was an active, unsolved investigation; there was no way they could be seen to be selling such a thing.

It didn't stop her fingers typing their way to Murder Mart, though. She repeated the search and, when the screen shifted, she had to look again to be sure of what she was seeing.

Aiden McAlpine.

One result.

Boxer shorts and socks worn by Sunrise Killer victim Aiden McAlpine. MSP's son. 100% genuine. Unique item. Starting bid £3,000.

CHAPTER 13

She'd stared at the screen for an age. Minutes. Just reading and rereading, blinded by the cheek of it, the sheer immoral nerve of it.

Someone – going only by the name of Shadow123 – was actually selling Aiden McAlpine's underwear. *Selling it*.

There was a photograph to accompany the item. A pair of light blue cotton socks neatly piled over a pair of navy blue boxers, the Armani logo visible on the waistband.

It took a while for her to get her head around what she was most surprised and angry at. She really thought her days of being shocked by anything were long gone. When you'd seen a drunk man sleeping naked with his dead dog then you'd pretty much lost the thrill of being astonished. This was giving it a run for its money though.

Her first reaction was to pick up the phone and call Addison or Giannandrea but a bunch of voices in her head were shouting at her not to do it. For a start, it wasn't their case. Addy had nothing to do with it and Rico was having to doff his cap to Kelbie.

Kelbie. She'd be damned if he was getting a lead she came up with. The whole burning embarrassment and resentment of the row in the press conference that made her pass out; she'd never let that go.

Damn. Her stomach creased as the pains sneaked back. The little buggers had their knives out and were jabbing at her. She was doing her best to ignore them but they stabbed and stabbed.

She'd always played the good cop and didn't know any other way to do it. It came from her dad, she knew that. Straight arrow, straight shooter, do it by the book and do the right thing. Jesus, what he'd think if she didn't turn this in.

Whoever was selling this stuff wasn't necessarily the person who killed Aiden McAlpine. She told herself that again and it didn't sound too convincing. Whoever was selling it, needed to be found. That much she was sure of.

She really didn't want to give this to them but knew she couldn't keep it to herself. This was serious, way beyond her pride and her problems with Kelbie. Damn it.

In the end, she came up with a plan that relied on her doing something she'd rather have avoided but simply couldn't. Letting Tony know she'd been nosing around online. He was not going to be happy.

Unhappy was an understatement. How did you find this? What were you doing online? Have you forgotten what the doctor said? What were you thinking?

At every question, she tried to shift his focus away from the how and the why of what she'd done and to the opportunity she was giving him. Here's a story. Here's *your* story. Here's your *chance*.

He kept fretting at it, worrying about her stress levels, about the amount of rest she was getting, about what else she was doing when he wasn't there.

There's a story in this for you and a lead for the investigation team. This way, everyone wins. Except Kelbie. Embarrass him. Show everyone what he doesn't know.

But what were you even thinking about? You are supposed to be *away* from all this.

Yes, yes, but that doesn't matter. She kept telling him it. Your story. Your chance. Their lead. Everyone wins.

She was wearing him down when the first of the spasms kicked in. Just mild ones, but enough that she had to clamp her teeth together to avoid showing the pain. She had to twist it into a sarcastic grimace, covering the fact she wanted to scream.

He picked up on it, she was sure of that, but didn't say anything. Instead, he just nodded slowly and said okay. He'd do it her way.

He'd go to Mark McAlpine's news conference and he'd get his story while making sure the cops got the lead about the missing clothes being for sale. Everyone would win. But he'd only do it if she promised to get off the laptop and stay off. No more getting involved where she shouldn't.

No, of course not. Of course. Not.

CHAPTER 14

Inevitably, it took Winter half an hour longer than it should have done to negotiate Edinburgh's traffic. If the introduction of the trams had eased congestion it was in the same way that taking a cup of water out of the ocean improved your chances of not drowning in it.

It was a further half-hour to worry about being out of Glasgow and away from Rachel. He'd called before he'd left and he knew he'd call again as soon as he stopped, no matter how much it would annoy her. She felt fine and he felt helpless. It was a certain recipe for argument, but he'd take that.

Mark McAlpine was holding his press conference in a room in the Parliament building at the foot of the Royal Mile, increasing Winter's difficulty in getting there. It was pretty unusual for a victim's family to host a media session rather than the cops, but McAlpine was far from your usual grieving parent. He was one of the most recognisable and outspoken Members of Parliament and rarely shied away from the spotlight. Winter cringed at the thought of him using his son's murder to gain more screen time.

He was a Scottish National Party member but not part of the cabinet, having resigned his junior post in protest at cuts in local government budgets, the kind of grandstanding gesture that he specialised in. McAlpine was a very ambitious man and no one doubted he'd return in a higher post, most likely with a run at the leadership and to be First Minister down the line.

He was bombastic and loud, with a talent for practised one-liners and cruel putdowns of his opponents. He'd say anything that would get him an edge and dismiss it later as political banter and accuse his rivals of being bad losers or having no sense of humour. He had many principles, any of which could be swapped for a more convenient alternative. In short, he was the worst kind of politician, and so likely to do very well.

Winter's press pass got him past security and he entered the Parliament building for the first time. Up until that point he'd only been paying for it. He was immediately impressed by the intricate design of the place and had to fight to maintain his journalistic mask of disdain. He was pointed to a door at the rear of the entrance hall and he tagged onto the end of a group of other journalists, a couple of whom he recognised.

They made their way into a spacious room already half filled with reporters, photographers and a couple of TV crews. He was there to photograph as well as take notes and couldn't do both at once. He'd normally use his phone to record what was said but that meant not having it if

Rachel called. With a head full of worry, he reluctantly switched on the record function and left his mobile alongside the cluster of others by the lectern.

A few minutes later, the rear doors were pulled back and Mark McAlpine swept in, flanked by DCS Tom Crosbie, the head of MIT, and Denny Kelbie. Winter's jaw clenched at the sight of the short-arsed DCI as he strutted towards the stage. He'd never liked him but there was no way he'd ever forgive him for the way he'd treated Rachel.

Kelbie sat to McAlpine's right as Crosbie stood at the lectern. The DCS raised a hand and the room fell into silence apart from the clicking of camera triggers. Winter was standing at the side of the room, his own camera focused on Crosbie and McAlpine, Kelbie being kept quite deliberately out of the shot.

Crosbie kept it short and to the point. He'd been left in no doubt as to whose event this was and he was to delay McAlpine's moment no longer than he needed to. He thanked the press for coming, reminded them of the tragic details of the case and said he would take questions later. He sat down and the room waited for McAlpine to rise. The MSP milked it for all it was worth, staring at the floor and leaving a reflective silence before pushing back his chair and standing to face his audience.

He was a tall, slim man with a full head of fair hair and an infinite sense of his own importance. Winter tried to rein in his prejudice against him, given the circumstances, but it was a struggle. He couldn't escape the feeling that McAlpine was working this.

'Ladies and gentlemen, on behalf of my family . . .' – his

voice caught and he very visibly swallowed – 'I want to thank you for coming along this afternoon. The days since Aiden's murder have been extremely trying, unlike anything I've experienced in my personal or business life or in my political career. My wife Catriona and I have suffered a loss that only other parents could possibly imagine. And I would not wish that understanding on a single one of them. Our son, our beautiful boy, has been ripped from us. Our lives have been shattered.'

He paused to sip at the glass of water in front of him and to let his words percolate. When he raised the glass to his lips, Winter's lens saw that his hand was shaking. Real or for effect? He hated himself for even wondering.

'Our son was murdered and left to rot. He was killed, then publicly degraded in the most abhorrent way. The image that was seen by the world after being shamefully shared far and wide is not how I will remember him. It is not how my wife or our family will remember him. We will remember Aiden as sweet and smart, as being always laughing and helpful. We will remember how he slept with a smile on his face as a child, how he delighted his teachers and neighbours, how kind he was to his sister Chloe. We will remember him as the best son any parents could wish for.

'And . . .' – McAlpine's voice hardened and rose – 'we will *never* forget what was done to him. The person that committed this vile act, this barbarous atrocity against my son, has no place walking free amongst decent people. He has no place in society. I trust that the police' – he shot stern glances at Crosbie and Kelbie, who both made sure they stared straight ahead – 'will ensure that this monster is swiftly captured and given the strongest punishment that the law allows. I expect, as I would for any other parent, that every available officer will work tirelessly to identify and arrest this wicked individual and remove evil from our streets.'

Winter's camera closed right in on McAlpine as he worked his way towards a crescendo, seeing the blood rise in his cheeks and the hatred in his eyes. His lips were curled back as he spat out the words like an old-time preacher, full of fire and brimstone. His eyes were reddening, too, and fat tears began to roll down his cheeks.

'It has been suggested that Aiden was murdered as a means of getting at me. That he was killed because of my role in public life. I do not yet know if that is true, but I am assured it is a scenario that Police Scotland are examining and taking extremely seriously. I trust that they will ascertain the truth. In the meantime . . .' He paused for a gulp of water and steeled himself for the finish. 'In the meantime, my constituents, my party and the people of this country can rest assured that I will not be driven from my duty to them. I will not back off from things I believe in and will not be silenced. If it was the intention of the monster who murdered Aiden to derail the democratic process, then he will fail. I owe that to Aiden and to those who voted for me. I have a job to do and I will finish it.'

The last sentence was delivered in a breaking voice that only just managed to squeeze out the final few words. He stood, mouth hanging slightly open, looking out across the press pack towards the back of the hall where the TV cameras were. Staring out at the killer and his electorate.

Winter's camera caught the pain and the precision of the pose that McAlpine was striking, the one that would surely feature in the next day's newspapers. Denny Kelbie pushed back his chair and stood beside the MSP, a tacit offer of an arm if it were needed. McAlpine looked at him, shaking his head before lowering himself unsteadily back into his seat. It had been quite a performance and Winter couldn't tell what had been genuine and what had not.

Kelbie remained standing and announced that he and DCS Crosbie would take questions on operational matters relating to the case. The first few were entirely routine, a gentle warm-up for both sides.

'DCI Kelbie, can you tell us the latest in the investigation?'

'We are continuing to focus on a number of areas of enquiry, but it is fair to assume we are paying particular attention to Mr McAlpine's political position and looking at correspondence he has received in the course of his work.'

A voice called out from near the front, 'Has Mr McAlpine received specific threats?'

'I'm not able to answer that at this time.'

'Not able or not prepared to?'

Kelbie paused, then sighed. 'Next question.'

So there it was. The suggestion laid heavily that there had been a threat against Mark McAlpine, without anyone actually saying so, therefore easily deniable later.

'Do you have a suspect?'

'Not one that can be named publicly at this time.'

'But you do have an individual who you believe may've been responsible.'

'Neither naming nor confirming a specific suspect would be helpful at this time.'

'Can you tell us about Aiden's movements on the night before his murder?'

Kelbie hesitated and Winter was sure he saw a look flash between the DCI and McAlpine. 'We are continuing to retrace Aiden's steps that evening and, while we know most of where he was, we don't believe they have a bearing on what happened and we don't want to confirm them publicly while they and the remainder of his actions might be of use to us.'

So the fencing continued, with Kelbie saying little and hinting plenty. Winter had seen it before and was sure it said nothing more than that Kelbie was coming up empty-handed. He talked about witnesses being interviewed, about urgency and stones not being left unturned. He spoke of offering every care to the McAlpine family, about his own determination and how people could sleep safely in their beds knowing he was on the case.

Before Winter knew it, his own hand was in the air. Kelbie saw it out of the corner of his eye and nodded his acceptance of it before fully realising who it was. Winter saw his expression change but it was too late.

'I'd like to ask about the pile of clothing left at the scene.'

Kelbie tensed. 'What about it?'

He eased his way in. 'Can you confirm that it belonged to Mr McAlpine's son.'

He couldn't do anything else. 'Yes, it did; now next . . .'

'And you believe it was left there by the killer?'

Kelbie's face was tightening. 'We believe so yes but—'

'And can you tell us where the rest of his clothing is?'

Kelbie flushed and stared at Winter. He couldn't seem to find an answer beyond one that would have embarrassed him. He didn't know and probably hadn't considered it. The pause rippled round the room like a rumour. McAlpine was looking confused, wondering why Kelbie wasn't just answering and moving the questioning on elsewhere.

Kelbie did what he did best when cornered: he attacked. 'Sorry, but I was simply stunned that a member of the press would use this occasion as a chance for self-promotion. Mr Winter is trying to cash in further on personal grief by bringing attention to his rather disreputable photograph of Aiden McAlpine's clothing. Not only is it a complete red herring and irrelevant to the investigation at hand, it is completely disrespectful and hurtful to the McAlpine family. I will not dignify it by answering. Next question.'

Winter persevered. 'Are you looking for other items of Aiden's clothing?'

Kelbie bit his lip and for a moment Winter thought he'd have to admit the truth, but groans and murmurs rose from the press pack. 'Get on with it.' 'Get over yourself. 'Who cares?'

Winter had one last go, even though the will was seeping from him. 'Would it not interest the police to know—'

Mark McAlpine rose to his feet, blood curdling in his cheeks, glaring furiously at Winter. 'We are here to discuss the investigation into the murder of my son. Not to discuss his clothes. Not to discuss the frankly shameful way those clothes and the reflection of his body were plastered across newspapers all over the world.'

Kelbie raised a hand and demanded quiet. 'That line of questioning is over. I'll take something from someone else or the press conference is over too.'

Great, all he'd succeeded in doing was turning the ire of McAlpine and much of the room against him. He didn't imagine Archie Cameron or the *Standard*'s owners would be best pleased, either.

He'd been all set to work his way towards the revelations of the underwear for sale so that he could both get the story and do what Rachel needed him to do. Kelbie's mongrel attack had turned his good intentions into stubborn resistance, and now they could all whistle for it.

His bolshie self-congratulations lasted until he got home and opened the front door. She was in bed, waiting, expecting. He'd had one job to do and he'd let her down.

She was sitting up as he walked into the bedroom, arms crossed across her chest. He felt like he was slinking home after closing time with a burst pay packet in his pocket. He decided he'd get his retaliation in first.

'Look, Rach, don't start. Kelbie shut me down as soon as I started to speak and there was—'

She held up a hand to say stop. He did so.

'If you're starting to apologise then, first of all, it's a crap apology and, secondly, don't bother. I saw the press conference on TV and you gave them every chance. You gave Kelbie a chance he didn't deserve. They wouldn't listen, so I say you go and find who was selling these clothes, you get your exclusive and they get to look embarrassed.'

'Are you sure? Your conscience can live with not handing the information over to them?'

'I'm sure. Kelbie had his opportunity and he blew it. I'm not part of this and I don't owe them anything. Just do what you need to do.'

CHAPTER 15

KillingTime had 117 items of Charles Manson murderabilia listed for sale. Murder Mart had 96. Between them that was 213 things related to the murdering mad sod that was Manson. What were people thinking?

What was *she* thinking? She hadn't really meant to go back in but it had called to her. Just one more look.

The Manson items available started at a couple of bucks and went up to a staggering ten thousand dollars. For that you could purchase two booking cards, filled out when Manson was booked in for possession of marijuana just weeks before Sharon Tate and the others were murdered. Ten grand for Manson's inky prints? The seller's description listed Manson as 'an icon'.

For a buck under five thousand, you could buy a piece of red, blue and yellow string artwork that Manson made in his prison cell. According to the site it was a nine-inch rainbow scorpion and it did look a bit like one, she supposed.

Three and a half grand would get you a piston door from the Spahn Ranch, the old film studio set where the Manson Family lived for much of 1968 and 1969. For three thousand you could have a piece of doodled art that looked like it was done by a two-year-old.

There were letters and self-portraits, paintings and signed photographs. You could buy a pair of gloves, fashioned for Manson by another inmate. Or a broken guitar string or a signed legal document. There were signed book jackets and Christmas cards. There was even a copy of his parents' marriage certificate, signed of course by Manson himself.

There was hair. Lots and lots of hair. Manson's flowing locks, his trademark Jesus-lookalike look, had been cut away at many, many times over the years to make sellable slices of DNA for anyone wanting to build their own little Charlie from scratch.

Photographs and hair. Books and hair. Greetings cards and hair. Music and hair.

There was even more music than hair. Manson's music was everywhere. There were audio cassettes, vinyl and CDs. Charlie had transcended the formats and was now even available for download.

Charlie the singer-songwriter. He was so sure he was going to be bigger than the Beatles.

She was in iTunes before she could stop her fingers. Curiosity. Just the same as with the collectibles, she wanted a feel for it. She wanted to understand it.

With a silent apology to the refugee, she bought an album. A penny under eight pounds for twenty-six songs by a murderer. Even as she did it, she wondered what the hell she was doing.

She played his music as she read about Sharon Tate. She'd

known the name, of course, and probably the basics, but it was only when she began reading that Narey realised how little she actually knew about her or her murder. She scoured the Internet and read everything she could find. And wished she hadn't.

Blonde, glamorous and stunningly beautiful, Tate was an actress and model. She was talented and connected. She seemed to have had everything going for her.

She'd been nominated for a Golden Globe and for several newcomer awards. She'd starred in *Valley of the Dolls* and alongside Orson Welles, Dean Martin and Tony Curtis. She was married to Roman Polanski and lived in the Hollywood hills, where she hung out with friends such as Steve McQueen, Warren Beatty, Jacqueline Bisset, Peter Sellers and Mia Farrow. It was a golden life.

But, for all that, Sharon Tate is remembered for one thing above all else. For being murdered.

That just isn't right or fair. Her killers shouldn't be remembered with her. She shouldn't be remembered because of them. But it seems that's the way it is. All of us gorging on her death like vampires, like hyenas.

People selling stuff. People, *people like her*, buying stuff. Books, magazine articles, blogs, photographs. It was everywhere, kept alive by the bloodsuckers, by the morbid fascination. But it was real. Not some lurid fiction. It was real. Real people died.

On August 8 1969, Sharon Tate went out for dinner with friends at her favourite restaurant, El Coyote, on Beverly Boulevard. She was heavily pregnant.

It was the thing Narey either hadn't known or had

forgotten. Now that she read it, it shocked her. Sharon Tate was *eight and a half months* pregnant.

Around 10.30 that night, she returned to her home in Benedict Canyon along with the friends – hairdresser Jay Sebring, playboy Wojciech Frykowski and heiress Abigail Folger. Just after midnight, the house was broken into by four followers of Charles Manson.

Tex Watson, Susan Atkins and Patricia Krenwinkel went into the house in Cielo Drive while Linda Kasabian kept watch outside. What followed was inhuman savagery.

Sharon was stabbed and slashed sixteen times. Sixteen. In the back and the chest. Eight and a half months pregnant and stabbed to death. She pleaded for the life of her unborn child but they didn't care.

Atkins told her, 'Look, bitch, I don't have any mercy for you. You're going to die.'

They tied her by the neck to Sebring. That was how they were when they were found by the police the next morning, the rope looped over a ceiling beam. The ceiling was riddled with bullets and the floor covered in blood. Her nightdress was soaked crimson.

Manson wasn't there but he might as well have been. He planned it, he ordered it. He told them to go to the Cielo Drive address and kill everyone there. They did nothing unless he said so. Manson did it every bit as if he'd wielded the knife.

The word 'pig' was scrawled in Sharon's blood on the front door.

One of her breasts was cut off.

An X was carved into her stomach.

The killers threatened to cut out her baby and take it.

Narey felt her hands forming claws with every further word she read. Rage grew large and she was hammering at the keyboard as she scrolled through pages. She gnawed at her lip until it nearly bled.

She knew murder. She knew what it looked like, what it smelled like. She'd *dealt* with it. But reading this? It was beyond murder. It was savage.

Manson. Charlie fucking Manson. Murderer. And she had his music playing in her home. She'd bought a piece of him. And he'd done that to Sharon. To Sharon and her baby. She had to get rid of his music. Delete it. Scrub it. She couldn't have it in the house.

The pains inside her were probably inevitable.

They began as a single stab, then rained on her as if they came from a dozen hands. Piercing stings that flashed through her. Sympathy pains for Sharon. Agony for her. Shit, shit, shit! She thought she might have to phone Tony or even the doctor. Shit, shit! She breathed and breathed, breathed for two, until it finally subsided.

With her eyes closed, she slammed the laptop lid shut. It wouldn't do Sharon Tate any good for her to read more, and it wasn't doing *her* any good, either.

CHAPTER 16

Winter had a story, that much was obvious. Just the very idea that someone was selling Aiden McAlpine's clothes was enough to fill the front page of the *Standard*. He'd easily get the boy's father to be morally outraged, and that would be the quotes dealt with.

It would all be backed up by his own photograph, again, and it would be easy pickings. But it wasn't enough. There was a bigger story just out of reach, and he owed it to himself to find it.

Someone selling, or maybe just claiming to sell, the clothes would buy him a cheap splash but finding who it was . . . that went much further. That was stop-the-presses stuff. If they did that any more.

He'd done his own research online and found the names of a few collectors in Scotland who might be able to give him a lead on it. He'd phoned the nearest of them, and had said he wanted to do a feature on murderabilia. The man's ego said sure, he'd love to.

Barry Fyvie lived in a top-floor flat on Dumbarton Road in Partick, above the Rosevale pub and an Indian takeaway.

It maybe wasn't the most obvious place for a collection on murderers and their victims but it was where it was.

Winter buzzed the entry pad and a gruff voice from above checked he was the person who had been expected. 'Come on up.'

Fyvie was a big guy in his early fifties, tall and heavy-set with a black Stone Roses T-shirt barely containing a heaving beer gut. He had thick sideburns, a grey-flecked goatee and long, greying hair that was tied back in a ponytail. He certainly looked like he collected something.

'Thanks for seeing me.'

The big man shrugged. 'Why not? No such thing as bad publicity, right? Sit anywhere you want.'

That was easier said than done. Half of the black leather sofa and one of the room's two chairs were covered in plastic bags and cardboard boxes. The other was occupied by a large sleeping cat. Fyvie saw Winter's dilemma and weighed up which to clear to allow his guest to get a seat. After a moment's deliberation, he took a couple of steps and scooped the cat up and dropped it gently onto the floor. 'Sorry, Ted,' he told it 'but we've got a visitor.'

'Ted?' Winter asked.

'After Ted Bundy.'

'You named your cat after a serial killer?'

Fyvie pushed a bag to the side so he could grab a corner of the couch. 'Doesn't everybody? You want a tea or a coffee? I've got a couple of beers in the fridge.'

'No, I'm fine, thanks. So how long have you been into it, the serial-killer thing?'

'Since 1969. I watched *The Boston Strangler* at the

Odeon on Renfield Street and that was me hooked. I was too young to have watched it but that didn't seem to bother my mum or dad. What a film! Scared the shit out of me, but it was electric. Tony Curtis as Albert DeSalvo. He was only in the second half, but that was probably just as well, for DeSalvo wasn't actually the Strangler.'

'He wasn't?'

'Nah. No way. Chances are it was more than one person, and I reckon DeSalvo did one killing at most. Wouldn't stop me from buying stuff of his, though. Not if there's money in it.'

'And there *is* money in it?'

Fyvie spread his arms wide. 'Flat's bought and paid for. Collecting is my only job and it keeps me in beer and vinyl, so I'm as happy as a pig in shit. Yeah, there's money in it.'

'You mind if I take notes?'

'Nah, go for it. I've got nothing to hide. All legal and above board. Ask what you want, just make sure you spell my website address right.'

There wasn't a hint of embarrassment to the man. Absolutely shameless.

'So who or what do you collect?'

'Anything I can get my hands on. The more famous the killer, the better. The more kills, the more money. It's not rocket science.'

'So what's the most valuable or most famous thing you've got?'

'Right now it's probably a Thanksgiving card sent by Jeffrey Dahmer just a few days before he was murdered. It's a really nice piece. Want to see it?'

Winter's gut response was no but he heard the word 'yes' come out of his mouth. Maybe something deeper than his gut answered before he could.

Fyvie grinned wide and bounced out of his seat. As he disappeared into another room, Winter looked around. He eased open a plastic carrier bag at his feet and saw a bundle of opened envelopes, all addressed to Fyvie. The couple that he had time to sneak a look at were stamped with variations on a theme saying they'd been opened by a prison before being sent.

Fyvie lurched back into the room, carefully peeling back layers of bubble wrap as he did so. He didn't touch the card directly but held it open using the wrap for Winter to see.

Thanks for everything mom. Have a great day.
Sorry I'm not there to share it with you. Jeff.

Fyvie was smiling. 'Sweet, huh? Four days after Thanksgiving, Dahmer went on his assigned work detail in the Columbia Correctional Institution in Portage, Wisconsin. When he was in the showers of the prison gym, Christopher Scarver beat him about the head and face with a twenty-inch metal bar. Dahmer was dead within the hour. Now I'd rather have the metal bar but this'll do me fine. I'll make good money on this.'

'What else do you have?'

Fyvie scratched at his beard. 'Headline-grabbing stuff? I've got a piece of John Wayne Gacy art that I've been sitting on for a while till I get the right price. I won't let that go for less than a few thousand. And I had a long handwritten letter from David Berkowitz, Son of Sam, that would creep you right out, but I sold that a month back. Best thing I ever had was a gold necklace handmade by DeSalvo. Beautiful it was. Bought it for a grand, sold it for two.'

'And what about something more local?'

'Scottish? Well, I've got a long letter written by Dennis Nilsen to his lawyer. It's a nice piece. And I've got a few letters and signed photographs of Archibald Atto. An original missing poster for Martin Welsh. Some Peter Tobin things, too, but nothing special. It all sells, though.'

'What else of Atto's is on the market?'

A cautious shrug. 'The real money with him is in the trophies that he took off his victims. The jewellery. I know there's some of that doing the rounds but chances are I'll never get near it.'

'Why won't you get near it?'

'I'm legit. It isn't. Simple as that. Same reason why I only have that one Martin Welsh item. Someone else has got all that stuff. You see, the Welsh case is different. It's one of the few where the victim is more famous than the killer.'

'Because the killer was never caught.'

'Right. If he was then *his* stuff would be going for big bucks. But he wasn't, so the money is in the boy instead. I'd like more of it but there's nothing going around.'

'Don't you worry that it glorifies murder and murderers?'

Fyvie laughed loudly. 'Do I look like a worried man? Does it fuck. Listen, people have always been fascinated by killers. We're still talking about Cain and Abel and that was years ago. Sex sells. Murder sells. Sex and murder sell like naebody's business. I'm no killing anyone, I'm just collecting the stuff. If I don't do it some other fucker will. It's just business.'

'And what about the victims?'

'They're deid. That's what makes them victims.'

'What about their families?'

'Not my problem. I'm sorry and all that but me not buying or not selling isn't going to change anything. Like I say, somebody's going to make money out of it, so it may as well be me.'

The man was a real charmer. Winter didn't think he had to worry too much about offending his sensibilities.

'What about stuff that might still be part of an ongoing investigation?'

Fyvie's eyes narrowed warily. For the first time since Winter entered the flat, he felt the collector was on his guard.

'Like I said, I'm all legal and above board.'

'But you've maybe heard of things like that?'

'I'm completely legit.'

'But other people aren't?'

'I wouldn't know. Ask me something else.'

He may as well push it, he thought. The door was getting closed in his face anyway.

'If something like that was doing the rounds. Where would you go to buy it?'

'I wouldn't.'

'Okay, where would someone else go?'

Fyvie scowled. 'Listen. This isn't what I want to talk about. There's collecting and there's collecting. If you want to talk about the other side of it, then you've come to the wrong guy. Maybe you better go.'

'At least tell me what you mean. What's the other side?'

He huffed. 'No, forget it. I don't want to talk about it.'

'Okay. Do you know a collector, maybe just a seller, known as Shadow?'

'No.'

'Shadow123?

'I said no. Get back to interviewing about my site or get out the door. Or the window. And I'll help you out if you need it.'

As Winter crossed Dumbarton Road towards his car, he turned and looked back up at the top-floor flat. Barry Fyvie was standing at the window, half hidden behind a curtain but staring down at him. He had a phone in his hands and he was gesticulating wildly. When he saw Winter watching him, he quickly slipped out of sight.

CHAPTER 17

Winter came away from the meeting with Fyvie little wiser than he'd gone in. He'd learned a bit more about murderabilia but without much idea of what to do with it.

He was pretty damn sure the collector knew more than he was letting on though. The man had spooked at the very mention of the clothes being sold and shut up shop very quickly after that. Had the mention of Shadow123 been what had thrown him? Did Fyvie *know* the seller?

Winter had been back on the Murder Mart site but there was no sign of the clothes or the person that had tried to sell them. Whoever it was had named themselves well. *Shadow.* Who and where the hell were they?

The only thing he could think of was to contact them. Sign up and say hello.

Murder Mart let you message other users and as soon as Winter set up an account of his own he was able to do exactly that. He signed in, typed Shadow123 into the message field and prepared himself to talk to a possible, maybe probable, killer. He really didn't know where to start.

Re Aiden McAlpine clothing. I'd like to talk

It took over two hours before he had a reply.

Okay, so talk

I want to buy the clothes you were offering

Have you got the cash??

Yes.

The price has gone up.

Forget it, then.

What can you pay??

£3000

Okay. They're yours.

Where do I get them?

We'll meet. I'll tell you where.

Winter pushed back in his chair and edged the laptop away from him, pulse racing. This was way out of his comfort zone, this was *her* job, not his. Not any more though, he reminded himself. It was his now. She needed to be protected, not least from herself, and he had to step up and deal with this. Whatever the hell it was.

CHAPTER 18

It bothered Narey that the sites were almost all about the killers. Not enough that she closed her laptop and got the hell out of there as she knew she should, but it still grated. She'd known some of these people, she'd certainly known their type, and no way did they merit the headline treatment. They were pathetic creatures, completely unglamorous and a world away from the celebrity status these sites seemed to give them.

It was wrong that anyone should give the smallest of fucks about things belonging to rapists, torturers and murderers. These men, almost always men, weren't worthy of such interest. They were wired wrong, they were evil if you believed in such a thing, and certainly did evil things. They should be caught, sentenced and ignored. Not kept in people's minds by Internet auctions and what amounted to fandom.

The only real exception to its being about the killers was when the victim was known and the killer wasn't. Only then did it focus on the people who actually deserved it. So easily overlooked, so quickly forgotten when they weren't as famous as the serial killers who took their lives. Victims could rarely make headlines the way murderers did.

They either had to be famous to begin with, like Sharon Tate or JFK, like John Lennon or Gianni Versace, or else they had to be killed by someone who was never caught. The great unsolved mysteries made names for the dead. The killers went unpunished but the sick twist was that at least their prey were remembered by more than just friends and family.

People remember Elizabeth Stride, Catherine Eddowes, Annie Chapman, Mary Jane Kelly and Mary Ann Nichols, because they can't remember Jack. In Scotland, they know Patricia Docker, Jemima McDonald and Helen Puttock because they don't know who Bible John was.

Narey remembered more victims than she'd like to, people who'd been forgotten by all except those who buried them. Poor sods who were in the wrong place at the wrong time and whose deaths barely caused a ripple in the national consciousness. The ones the rest of the world remembered were those who never got any kind of justice. The likes of Renee MacRae, Genette Tate, Carl Bridgewater, Martin Welsh and Suzy Lamplugh. Famous for being murdered even if in some cases their bodies, like their killers, were never found.

There were items available online for that kind of victim, the prominent kind. The business was just as grubby, though, just as unpleasant, just as compelling. There was a trade in old school photos, clothing, signed documents, missing-person posters, even copies of death certificates.

She didn't want to look through this stuff any more than

she did for the killers, but there was that big empty room and the long days stretching beyond dark, and both needed to be filled. There was just her and the Internet, her and the auction sites. There was murderabilia and a tankful of time.

She was flicking through it now, loathing herself for it with every touch of the keyboard, making new excuses and disregarding them as she went, all the while burrowing deeper and deeper into the black soul of it.

There was another Martin Welsh collectible. An original missing-person poster from 1973, creasing to one corner and slightly weather-damaged but otherwise in perfect condition, according to the seller. Yours for bids starting at £300.

Martin Welsh. The boy who went to school and never came home. One of the most famous unsolved crimes in the country.

His name had caught her eye any time she'd seen it on KillingTime or the other sites. Her dad had worked the case at one point and, like any unsolved it had tugged at him, dragging him back to talk about it and pore over the details for something he'd missed. So, when she saw items for sale, they jumped out of the screen at her, as they did now.

It seemed a lot for a printed bit of paper that had been tied to a lamppost or stuck in a newsagent's window. There must have been thousands of them distributed, but she guessed that few survived. It would sell, and probably for a good bit over the starting price.

Wait. It disappeared, almost in front of her eyes. Auction closed, item purchased. It must have been up for less than an hour and was gone.

The usual protocol was that an item went to auction and the highest bid after the closing date won whatever it was. However, there was often the option to buy something outright at any time for a higher price, rather than wait or take the risk of being outbid. That had to be what had happened here.

But something else nagged at her. She'd thought she'd seen this before with Martin Welsh stuff. An item that had appeared but was almost immediately bought. It could have been her mind playing tricks on her, though. God knows, it had been doing that often enough of late.

She wanted to check if she was right, but there was no archive of previously sold items unless you were the person who'd bought them. It bugged her and she wanted to know more.

She'd always been stubborn and contrary. She remembered people commenting on it since before she went to school. A wilful little madam, her dad's aunt had said. And the old cow had been right. It turned out not to be a bad thing when she became a cop but probably made her a pain at other times.

Right now, she felt the urge to be a pain for whoever was snapping up the Martin Welsh collectibles. She was annoyed at not being able to remember for sure if she'd seen this happen before, irritated at someone buying this if they were, and generally just pissed off at being stuck in this room with only murderers and victims for company. She had an idea.

There was an alert system that you could use to be notified when a collectible about a particular murder went on the site. Use that and you got an email as soon as something went live. If someone had nothing to do but sit all day staring at their laptop, then they'd see that alert email immediately. And that was exactly what she was going to do.

She ticked the box, put in 'Martin Welsh' as the search term and it was done. Now she'd see how much of a pain she could be.

She sank back onto her pillow, the air escaping from her and the short-term fun of the alert disappearing with it. She stared at the walls in front of her and hated them.

Cornflower blue. It could definitely be cornflower blue.

CHAPTER 19

Winter had walked down Letherby Drive dozens of times. Each time he'd walked alongside thousands of others, usually tens of thousands, all crowded shoulder to shoulder, just one trip away from being trampled.

The street sloped steeply from top to bottom, from where it swung off Carmunnock Road and down towards Hampden Park, the national football stadium. In his head, it was always noisy and boisterous, the air thick with hope and booze, flags flying and songs raucously sung.

This time was very different, though.

He was walking down the hill in the dead of night, no one beside him except the ghosts of fellow supporters singing songs no one would hear. There was only the sound of his own footsteps, and they seemed to boom out like explosions in the silence. The quiet was all the stranger for the absence of the thousands.

The seller of Aiden McAlpine's clothes, the man who had maybe killed Aiden, was down there somewhere. The location had been his choice and he'd insisted Winter come on foot. He didn't want to see a single car in the car park or anyone else arrive but Winter.

He felt so exposed walking down there, no crowd to hide in, no one to help. The plan was to meet behind the north stand, opposite the main entrance and the car park. The most hidden and secluded part of the stadium.

He could hear cars in the distance, somewhere back over the tenements but a world away. Apart from that there was the wind and just a few discarded cans scooting along the tarmac. Just enough to jangle his nerves.

He got to the foot of Letherby Drive, the car park empty to his right and the stadium looming like a giant before him, bigger and more intimidating in the dark than it ever was under floodlights. He curved left round its perimeter, trying to muffle his footsteps by treading softly but failing miserably.

The Scotland supporters' song that came to mind was *We'll Be Coming Down the Road*. When you hear the noise of the Tartan Army boys, we'll be coming down the road. The thought made him keep to the shadow of the stand, clinging to it and the dark for security. Maybe he'd be heard, but he'd do his best not to be seen.

He was round the expanse of the west stand, the Rangers end as it was known, and knew he'd soon be there. Someone standing, as much in the dark as he was, waiting for him. Maybe armed, certainly ready. It suddenly seemed like a bad idea.

He drifted past closed turnstiles, on and on towards the halfway line, fully expecting someone to step from the shadows at any moment.

But they didn't. They turned him into a shadow instead.

A light flicked and blinded him, causing him to throw his hands up in front of his face to shield his eyes against a powerful torchlight.

'That's far enough.'

There was no more than a dark shape behind the light, the beam directed into his eyes. He squinted and could only listen rather than look.

'Turn the torch off.'

'No chance.'

The voice was low and brusque. Winter was sure it was being faked, deliberately deeper than it was to disguise it.

'Have you brought the money?'

'I need to know you're genuine first. That what you're selling is genuine.'

'It is.'

'How do I know that? You could be flogging any old shit. I need proof.'

There was a long silence. Winter tried to see behind the light and could make out only a six-foot frame and what seemed to be a balaclava or a woollen hat pulled low across the face.

'They're Aiden McAlpine's clothes. That's all you need to know. If you don't want them then fuck off and don't waste my time.'

'How did you get them?'

'I killed him.'

The words fell on the tarmac like nails on a coffin.

Winter considered rushing him, shutting his eyes to the light and trying to knock the guy to the ground. He'd no real idea of how big he was or if he was armed. Aiden had been—

Something metallic clanged against the wall of the stadium. Winter froze and, in the silence, it clanged again twice in quick succession. The seller had read his mind and was warning him against being brave or stupid.

He took the hint and stayed where he was.

'Why did you kill him?'

'Never mind. Have you got the money?'

'Why did you leave him at the station like that?'

The metal banged the wall again, harder. '*Have* you *got* the *money*?'

'Let me see the clothes!'

'Not without the money. If you're wasting my time, I'll kill you the way I did Aiden.'

'I've got the money. Come and get it.'

Winter barely believed the words had come out of his mouth. If there were any more, they were stuck in his throat.

The light flashed at his eyes and he saw the shape begin to slowly advance. He wasn't armed but the seller didn't know that. Maybe he'd back off. Maybe he'd kill him.

The torchlight snapped off and everything was darkness. He heard the footsteps quicken and he braced himself, his arms coming up to protect or to fight, he didn't know which. The steps clattered on the tarmac and reverberated off the wall but the attack didn't come.

As Winter's senses sorted out the jumble of sounds and lack of sight, he realised the footsteps were going away from him, not towards. Now they were softening, distance weakening them. The seller, whoever he was, had gone.

Maybe he'd heard the lie in his voice, realising there was no money; maybe he'd just sensed timewaster. Maybe it wasn't his time to kill.

Winter took a half-step back and planted himself against the wall, breath exploding from him. He wasn't cut out for this.

He stood and listened until long after even the faint tread of the man had gone. Chasing him wasn't an option he considered for even a moment.

He turned and made his way back round the stadium, hearing ghosts of boos slipping over the wall from the Rangers end. He'd had an open goal and he'd missed it. The catcalls and complaints followed him all the way round the west stand, and he expected more once he got home to tell Rachel the news.

As he turned the last bend of the curve and Letherby Drive was in front of him once more, he wondered if he'd blown the best chance he had. Maybe he really should have taken the money and bought the things. Maybe . . .

A hand gripped his shoulder and tugged at him, nearly pulling him off his feet as he was spun round. He threw an arm out but was off balance and it lashed hopelessly through fresh air.

'Easy, son. If that's the best punch you've got, you'd be better not throwing it.'

Danny Neilson stood there with a big grin on his face and Winter nearly moved to wipe it off in his embarrassment.

'You scared the shit out of me, Uncle Danny. And where were you when that crazy bastard had a knife on me?'

'I can't be in two places at once, Anthony. And it would have tipped him right off if I'd been on the north side too. Are you okay?'

Winter breathed hard. 'Yeah. I'm fine. Just shaken up a bit. Did you get a look at him?'

Danny nodded. 'Six foot one, I'd say. He pulled a balaclava off just as he was leaving the grounds. Long dark hair and a beard. On the skinny side of athletic. He was walking far too quick for me to catch up without running and with my weight he'd have heard me a mile off.'

'He sounds like Jesus.'

Danny grinned. 'Nah, son. Jesus never wore a balaclava. Far too hot in the Holy Land for that. And Jesus didn't drive a Vauxhall.'

'You saw the car?'

'Yes. It was a black Astra and I got a partial plate. Ending in KGV. We'll find him.'

'Dan, you're a genius.'

CHAPTER 20

She kept having the same dream. There was a woman with long, blonde hair standing on the other side of the room. She always had her back to her, so Narey could never see her face, but she still knew who she was. The woman was walking away and just beginning to turn round as she slipped from view, morphing into the blue wall. Every time, just as the she disappeared, Narey would notice that the woman's dress had turned from white to red. Then she'd see that it was dripping with blood. Soon after that she'd notice that *she* was bleeding, too, her thighs wet and sticky with it.

That was what would wake her up. Without fail, at the realisation of her own haemorrhage, she'd fight her way out of sleep and lie there terrified until she realised it had been the dream again. The Sharon Tate nightmare.

It would end with her cradling her belly like guards round a castle. Keeping her own safe from harm.

She was back at the laptop as if she'd never been away. Finding new layers of the selling sites, new depths of depravity that had been turned into cash.

She knew this dark world trapped people, grabbing them by the ankles, then wrapping tendrils round their entire bodies until their minds were lost. It was a dangerous place to visit and a deadly place to live.

All her career she'd been used to having to deal with human nature and the terrible things it brought about. She'd traded in murder and violence for far too long and, like everyone in law enforcement, she'd had to find her own way of living with that.

Some just cut off their feelings, becoming all but dead inside to insulate them against the worst the job had to offer. Others, mainly men, offered a big bluff to the world, pretending it was all fine and nothing bothered them. Most of them made out it was all a big joke, cracking gags as they stood over kids with knives stuck in them. Many just turned to booze, soaking up the horrors and the inhumanity the best they could.

The more balanced ones, and she used to be among them, learned to compartmentalise. She thought of it as having a series of drawers in her head. When she was on the job, they'd be open, dealing with whatever it was, taking it head on. When she was done they'd be closed.

Sure, that was sometimes easier said than done, and drawers had been known to slide open in the dark of night and let loose chaos. But she'd had to try to lock them because she knew one thing above all: you couldn't take it home with you. Not if you wanted to keep your relationships and mind in one piece.

The box at the bottom right of her screen popped up, telling her she had mail. It was from KillingTime, a response to the alert she'd created. There was a Martin Welsh item for sale.

She hated the rush of excitement she was feeling but let it sweep her along just the same. She clicked on the link and the listed item was in front of her. A front-page cover from the *Daily Record* from May 1973. The headline was big and bold: BOY (14) DISAPPEARS ON WAY HOME FROM SCHOOL. There was his photograph, instantly familiar, even though she hadn't even been born at the time. Bids starting at £75, the closing date two weeks away.

She didn't give herself time to think about it. Her fingers moved over the keyboard and she purchased it outright for £120. Successful bid. For better or for worse, it was hers.

What had she done? More to the point, why had she done it? She didn't know whether it was to annoy some collecting freak or because she was in this as deep as any of them. She knew it had felt good, she just wasn't sure why, and that worried her.

Worried her but didn't stop her. Instead, it opened a door she'd been trying to wedge shut.

Once you'd done it, it became easier to do it again.

She ordered a further six different items from KillingTime. Six. She spent nearly seven hundred pounds on murderabilia. She'd meant to buy maybe one, spend maybe fifty quid. Just to get the feel for it, just to see how the system worked. The problem was that once she started her spree she couldn't stop.

She bought a letter by Tex Watson, the Manson Family member who'd led the attack on Sharon Tate's house

A handwritten single sheet of lined paper had cost her

£225 and, when she woke after a sleep, she had to check that she'd actually purchased the thing. She couldn't honestly say *why* she'd bought it, though. Part professional curiosity, part compulsion, part revulsion, maybe something else entirely. All she knew was she clicked and paid and bought. Watson's letter was on its way.

It was the same with the two autographs she bought – or slaughtergraphs as she now knew they were called in the trade. There were all sorts available, from signed photographs, which seemed to be the killers' main way of manufacturing a bit of spending money, to any piece of paper or form they'd signed before ending up behind bars. She bought a note signed by another Manson Family member, Patricia Krenwinkel and a visitors' questionnaire signed by Linda Kasabian.

When she saw a subsection offering crime relics, she heaved a sigh of disgust and clicked immediately. The leading item was a piece of stone from the fireplace at 10050 Cielo Drive. The address was now instantly familiar.

The house where Sharon and the others were murdered had been demolished in the mid-1990s and, inevitably, some of the rubble had found its way into the hands of people who could make a fast buck from it. Private collectors, rich ghouls, snapped up most it, but some smaller pieces found their way into other hands and from there onto the market.

This fragment was one and three-quarter inches long, an inch thick and an inch deep. It was still sealed in the original packaging from a store named Hellhouse of Hollywood. A piece of Sharon's fireplace. The fireplace she was murdered in front of. Who in their right mind would buy something like that? With a handful of clicks, *she* did.

Maybe it was a short step from there to the piece of 'art', slaughtergraph and all, from Susan Atkins. Two bloody footprints were framed along with a handwritten note and signature from Atkins, the piece mimicking the bloody print she'd left on the floor of the Tate house.

It was a vile piece of exploitation. And Narey bought it.

Maybe it was to stop someone else from having it. Maybe it was an attempt to make sense of it. Maybe there was a space she had to fill with something, anything, to stop her staring at that blue wall. Maybe she didn't know what she was doing any more. That would certainly help explain why she also bought a lock of Charles Manson's hair.

She felt the way she might if she'd eaten a whole packet of chocolate biscuits in one sitting. Or if she'd drunk a bottle of prosecco when she'd planned to have only one glass. She felt sick and disgusted with herself. And glad she'd done it.

The corner of her screen flashed again. Another email from KillingTime. Surely no one could be selling another Martin Welsh item so soon after the last.

She had a direct message, not from the site itself but one of the users. Someone calling themselves RD. It was headed 'Re Martin Welsh purchase'.

> I see you purchased the newspaper front page that was offered earlier. I'd like to buy it from you. I'll give you twice what you paid for it. So, £250.

Two hundred and fifty pounds? For an old newspaper?

Her copper's nose twitched and didn't like what she smelled. Who the hell would be so desperate as to want to pay that? She'd set out to annoy whoever was buying this stuff and she'd succeeded. She'd make a profit, too, if she wanted it, without even getting out of bed. It wasn't enough, though.

'No thanks,' she typed. 'I'm happy with my purchase and I'll just keep it.'

She sent the reply, sure that it would piss him off even more and happy with that thought but still wondering what was going on. Feeling the slide from collector to cop, she knew she had to read up about the Welsh case, and it couldn't wait.

CHAPTER 21

Winter had tried mailing the Shadow on Murder Mart again but got no reply. Not even a fuck off. Not even a threat.

There was no other mention of Shadow123 on KillingTime or Murder Mart. No mention of him anywhere. The Shadow had slipped into the dark.

It felt odd that someone would make just one post. He'd learned enough to know that, in the world of murderabilia sites, your name is your bond. It's all about trust and feedback. You pay on time, you send on time. You always do what you say you'll do or no one deals with you again. You're dealing in death, so you have to be able to trust the other guy. It's all about being trusted by the other nuts.

Shadow123 had no rating that Winter could find. No record of sales or purchases, no queries, no other items on offer. He'd had the McAlpine underwear – or said he did – then disappeared off the face of the Internet.

Danny had run the partial number plate with his pals on the force but as yet they'd got nowhere. They were hopeful they could narrow it down but it would take time.

The only place Winter could think of to look was the family. The McAlpines.

There was no way Mark McAlpine was going to talk to him, but his wife might. It was pretty well known, if unsaid, among the media that they were barely together as a couple. He stayed in a flat in Edinburgh's New Town most of the time while she still lived in the family home on the south side of Glasgow.

He might well get the door slammed in his face followed quickly by a call to his bosses or the cops, but he had to try.

The McAlpines, at least one of them, lived in St Andrew's Drive in Pollokshields, in a large, four-bedroom, white-sandstone house sitting back off the road. Not quite a mansion, bad for the image, but little change from a million pounds. A broad, paved drive curved between a lush lawn and the front door.

He pressed the bell, crossed his fingers and waited. A clack of heels announced someone's arrival and seconds later the door opened just enough to reveal a woman in her fifties peeking round it. He'd seen the photographs and knew it was Barbara McAlpine, former cabin crew turned politician's wife. She was a fine-looking woman with barely a streak of grey in the dark hair that flowed back over her head. Her eyes told a different story from the well-manicured rest of her. Tears had been a regular visitor.

'Can I help you?'

'Mrs McAlpine. My name is Tony Winter and I—'

'I know you. You took the photograph. The one that went everywhere. The one of my Aiden.'

Her Aiden. Not theirs.

'Mrs McAlpine, I'm sorry that—'

'No, no. I'm glad you took it. I'm glad the whole world saw it. They all know what happened to him. My husband doesn't feel the same way, but there's no change there.'

That he didn't expect.

'I hope it helped in some way, Mrs McAlpine. Actually, it was that photograph I wanted to talk to you about. Would it be possible for me to come in so we can discuss it?'

She looked highly sceptical and her hand weighed up the door, ready to close it.

'Please. It's important. I think it can help.'

She blinked, maybe fighting back fresh tears, and nodded, turning away to let him follow her. They walked through a wide hallway and past a couple of closed doors before she led him into a large, white-walled room populated by two huge sofas and an armchair. She took the chair and left him to his choice of the couches.

'What is it you think we need to talk about, Mr Winter?'

'About the photograph and the clothes that were in it.'

'Aiden's clothes.'

'Yes. His clothes that were photographed and the ones that, seemingly, weren't there.'

She stared back at him for a while and he wondered if she'd taken it all in. She had.

'Let me stop you there. I won't have you quote me. On anything. Is that clear? If you agree to that then I'll talk to you. But I need your word on it.'

'You have it. I won't quote you. I'm looking for information rather than quotes.'

'Okay. Go ahead.'

'As the police may have said to you, not all of Aiden's clothes were in the pile left at the scene. There was no underwear. That may or may not be significant but I believe it is. If I were to show you a photograph of items said to be Aiden's do you think you might recognise them?'

Her face crumpled slightly. 'I might. I did wash them after all but . . . I don't know. I'll try.'

Winter produced an enhanced copy of the image that Rachel had screen-grabbed from KillingTime and handed it to her. His own photo skills had produced something he hoped the mother could recognise.

She stared at it intently, her eyes widening slightly. Recognition? He hoped so.

'Maybe. I mean I can't say they're his but boxer shorts like those . . . Yes, I'm sure he had those. The socks, too.'

'Could you check a drawer to see if the ones you remember are still there?'

The moment the words were out he regretted them. He had no idea if this woman had even been able to bring herself to go through her son's clothes. However she was tougher than he'd given her credit for.

'I'll look. Please stay here.'

She was back minutes later, her eyes red. 'The ones I remember aren't there. They're not in the wash, either.'

'Was there someone in Aiden's life. A girlfriend? Someone who might be able to give us a clue to what happened.'

Barbara McAlpine smiled. Winter initially thought it was tinged with sadness but there was something else. He let it go.

'There was no girlfriend, no.'

'Did he have any close friends. Anyone at all that it might be worth me speaking to?'

She considered it and decided to give up whatever she was mulling over. 'He didn't have many close friends. Not that he would confide in or turn to. There was a boy he was close to for a long time, a best friend if you like, but they fell out. Aiden took it quite badly and I wanted to tell him it was all part of the growing-up process and he'd get over it. No one wants to hear that, though, do they? He was as close a friend as Aiden had since he was little.'

'Who was this boy, Mrs McAlpine?'

She hesitated, reluctant to break a trust. But she wanted answers more than she did forgiveness.

'His name is Calvin Brownlie. He lived in Battlefield somewhere. I dropped Aiden off there a couple of times. Cartvale Road.'

CHAPTER 22

Cartvale Road was long, straight and narrow, like a sniper's alley. Red sandstones grew four storeys high from the pavement, making the street appear even tighter. Winter stood in its middle and saw it stretch a few hundred yards in each direction.

Brownlie was listed in the phone book and Winter could have phoned ahead but he didn't want the man to know he was coming. Instead, he pushed the door buzzers on all except flat six and waited for one to respond. The door popped and he pushed his way through and up the stairs.

It was just after nine and he'd seen the curtains on Brownlie's flat were still closed. Time for him to wake up. He rapped sharply on the door, trying not to sound like the cops he'd seen do the same thing so many times before.

The door was opened a minute later by a tall, bleary-eyed and bearded young man scratching at long, dishevelled hair. 'Yeah?'

'Calvin Brownlie?'

His name woke the hipster more quickly than the door

had and his eyes widened as if something sharp had been thrust into him. It was recognition.

His mouth dropped and he desperately tried to shove the door closed but ran into the boot Winter had thrust a few inches across the threshold. Brownlie put both hands on the door and feverishly pushed at it as if a horde of zombies were on the other side. The guy was terrified.

'Get out! Leave me alone. I didn't mean it. I swear I didn't.'

Winter got his shoulder into the door and shoved all his weight against it. He sent the guy falling back into the flat's hallway and walked through behind him. He wasn't and had never been a fighter but Brownlie didn't know it. He stood above him and glared.

He scrambled back further into the hall, trying to get away from Winter.

'Talk to me, Calvin. Tell me why you did it.'

'I didn't mean ... Please, don't hurt me. Please!'

The voice. Higher but it was the same voice. He was sure of it.

'Come on, Calvin, you know I know what you've done. So just tell me.'

'I just ... I didn't mean to hurt anyone.'

Winter got closer, bending over him, his eyes blazing. 'Are you going to tell me?'

'Yes! I will. Just don't hit me.'

'Get up. Get into the other room. Move.'

Brownlie got nervously to his feet, his eyes never leaving Winter's fists, and led them into a living room that didn't quite match up to the McAlpine's villa in St Andrew's Drive.

It was a mess. Ashtrays laden with roll-ups, cushions and empty beer cans on the floor. Shoes, magazines and glasses everywhere. 'Take a seat, I suppose.'

'Yeah? Where?'

Brownlie waved a hand through a clutter of papers and clothes and produced a torn leather armchair from beneath them. 'Sorry. There you go.'

He was in his early twenties, wearing just shorts and a T-shirt, and his tousled sleepiness had been replaced with fear. He wrung his wrists and shook noticeably as she stared at the floor to avoid Winter's eyes.

'You are Shadow123, aren't you?'

He didn't lift his head but he nodded.

'Look at me. I want to hear you say it. Are you Shadow123?'

Brownlie did as he was told and looked up. 'Yes.'

The voice was trembling and quiet, a range away from the one he affected at Hampden, but it was him. He was the seller of Aiden's clothes. By his own words, the person who'd killed him.

Winter was suddenly unsure where to go next. What to say to him. He could only manage one word.

'Why?'

There were tears. Brownlie's eyes reddened and they ran slowly down his cheeks.

'I needed the money. That was all.'

'You killed your friend for money?'

Brownlie's eyes grew large. 'I didn't kill him. I didn't kill Aiden!'

'No, of course you didn't.'

He tried to jump to his feet but Winter stepped forward and firmly pushed him back into the chair.

'I swear. I didn't kill anyone. You've got to believe me!'

'You told me that you did. At Hampden you said you'd killed him.'

'I lied.' It sounded pathetic. Pathetic enough that Winter believed him.

'Why would you say that?'

'To make you believe I had his clothes. His real ones. The ones he was wearing when he was killed. I wanted the money.'

'So what were you going to sell me?'

'His underwear. Aiden's. Just not the ones he'd worn when . . .'

'When he was murdered. How did you get the ones you were going to sell?'

'He left them here.'

It took Winter moments longer than it ought to have done to join the dots. The amused smile on Barbara McAlpine's face was the clincher.

'You and Aiden were lovers.'

'He was my boyfriend.' Some defiance had returned to the voice.

'That explains why he left them here but not why you'd try to sell them for cash. How could you do that?'

The tears started again, uncontrolled now.

'We fell out and broke up. I was mad at him because I hadn't wanted to finish it. It was just a stupid argument but I was angry. And when he died I was even angrier. I saw the story in the paper about the clothes being taken and how the killer had them. I thought . . .'

He broke down and Winter gave him the space to recover.

'I thought I could get back at him. I wasn't angry at him for the argument. I was angry at him for dying and leaving me. I knew I could get money for them and found a website to sell them on.'

Jesus Christ! Winter didn't know whether to hit him or hug him.

'I got scared, though, and took the sale down again. And then you contacted me and said you'd pay three grand. It's a lot of money. I'm pretty much skint. The only thing I've got of any value is this watch' – he held his wrist up showing an expensive-looking piece – 'but I got that from my parents and I never take it off. It was sell that or sell Aiden's clothes.'

'You could have got yourself killed.'

Brownlie wiped away tears and nodded. 'I thought you'd think I was the killer and be scared of me as long as I acted tough. But, when you told me to come and get the money, I panicked and had to run.'

'Did you have a knife?'

'No, just a metal ruler to hit against the wall and make it sound like one.'

'You idiot! I'm a journalist.' Brownlie's head snapped up in fresh fear. 'You know I could plaster your name all over the papers. Selling your murdered boyfriend's clothes. It would be everywhere.'

'No, no please! Please don't.'

'You'll just have to wait and see. In the meantime you *do not* tell this to anyone else. You keep your mouth shut about it. Now get me the clothes, and any others of Aiden's you have.'

'I will. Please don't . . .'

Winter climbed back down the stairs of the close onto Cartvale Road and got into his car. He knew he wouldn't run the story and wouldn't tell Archie Cameron. Calvin was only guilty of being stupid and heartbroken. There was no point in breaking his heart any more.

He'd never make a journalist. He had too much humanity in him.

First, though, he'd check Calvin's story. Shaking his head at himself, he called the mobile number she'd given him.

'Mrs McAlpine. It's Tony Winter.'

'Yes? Do you have news?'

'I do but I need to ask you a question first. Was Aiden gay, Mrs McAlpine?'

'Yes. Of course he was. And I couldn't have been prouder of him. I loved that boy from the day he was born till . . .' She struggled to say it. 'Till the day I die.'

'Did your husband know Aiden was gay?'

'He chose not to know.'

The condemnation in those few words was fierce. Barbara McAlpine was nurturing an anger against her husband that Winter had to use.

'I have found something but I'd rather it didn't go to the police just yet. It won't help find who killed Aiden but it might just hurt his friend Calvin. Mr McAlpine might like it go to the police, though, so it's your choice.'

The line went quiet for just a few moments. 'My husband

doesn't always know best, whatever he tells the voters. Do what you think is right, Mr Winter.'

'I will. And, it may be small consolation but I can bring some of Aiden's clothes home.'

'You're right. It's only small consolation, but it is some. Thank you.'

CHAPTER 23

There was a time when Martin Welsh was a household name, particularly in Scotland. Every newspaper, every news programme, every radio bulletin, every conversation in every pub or corner shop. Everyone had an opinion on what had happened to him.

There were emotional appeals and police reconstructions. Rivers were trawled, woods searched and quarries dug up. Psychics were called in. Rewards were offered. Known paedophiles were taken in for questioning. Questions were even asked in Parliament.

His face was instantly recognisable. The quiet smile, the summer-freckled face and the curly fair hair. He looked out of newspapers and shop windows and down from lampposts for the entire summer and autumn of 1973. Find me. Save me.

His mother, and to a lesser extent his father, became familiar faces, too. Jean Welsh was the one whom the television cameras sought out. Attractive and distraught, wet eyes pleading, voice breaking. She tore at heartstrings across the nation. Martin's dad, Alec, left her to do most of the appeals and interviews, although often he'd be standing at her shoulder, gruff and silent, not knowing how else to be.

Martin and his family were just as visible on the first anniversary of his disappearance, and the second. Maybe slightly less so after five years and much less so after ten. Most people stopped talking about him, most stopped looking. The case remained open and unsolved. No one doubted that he'd been murdered, but he wasn't news any more. He'd become, 'Remember that boy, what was his name, the one from Calderrigg in Lanarkshire, the one that went for the bus and never came home?'

Of course to Jean and Alec, to his young sister Alice, to his grandparents and aunt and uncle, it would forever be Wednesday the 2nd of May, 1973. The day Martin last went to school.

The entire country knew the story. Or the first part of it at least.

Martin got up at 7.30, wakened by his mother, his father already having left for his job at the dairy. The children had breakfast round the kitchen table, cereal and toast and standard sibling arguments. Jean Welsh walked Alice, then ten, to the local primary school, leaving fourteen-year-old Martin to get the bus from Calderrigg to his secondary school three miles away in Airdrie.

Martin was dressed in school uniform with a blue Adidas backpack over his shoulder containing homework and lunch. He was five foot six and weighed nine stone. He'd had a bad cold a week earlier but was otherwise completely healthy.

He arrived at school on time and began his day with an English class, followed by Geography. He ate his packed lunch – ham-and-coleslaw sandwiches, an apple, a Mars bar and a can of cola – with two of his pals, Gordon Tierney and Dylan Brown. They talked about football and having watched *The Goodies* on television the night before.

The only hassle they faced was from an older boy, a fifth-year named Johnny Wallace. He claimed Martin owed him money, although all three other boys denied this, and was threatening to break his arm or kill him if it wasn't paid quickly. Wallace was interviewed by the police and said he was just frightening Martin, he didn't mean it. His parents said Johnny came straight home after school and didn't go out again.

After the bell for home, Martin said goodbye to Tierney and Brown as they went for their bus and he for his. It was the last time they ever saw him.

From the moment she'd started searching, Narey had realised she knew much less about the details of the case than she thought she did. She knew he'd been taken, on his way from school, and knew the common consensus was he'd been murdered and . . . well, that was it. That and his face. Everyone had seen the photograph. It was part of the national consciousness.

Shyly smiling. Freckles. That tousle of fair hair. Instantly likable. Instantly recognisable. The boy.

She had to trawl the Internet for the detail. Martin had gone missing six years before she was born and the story had dropped off everyone's desk. He was still referenced, his case still open, his family still grieving, but so much of it now went unsaid.

Her search was hindered by the fact that there was no Internet when Martin disappeared, so there was little in the way of news stories from the time. She had to piece together what there was but it was superficial and sketchy. She wanted case files, investigating officers' reports, witness statements, the stuff that newspapers might have known but couldn't print, the things that cops knew but couldn't prove.

Her instincts had kicked in and she wanted to know everything. She grabbed a pad and pen from the living room and began to take notes on whatever she could find. She scribbled down names and dates, making four separate lists – police, family, witnesses and suspects – drew arrows from some to others, circled key points and questioned possible connections. It felt good and it felt right. She felt useful.

Martin's mother Jean was still alive. The woman would still just be in her seventies, no age at all considering how long ago it felt since her son disappeared. The father had been gone for twenty years now, dying from a heart attack at the age of fifty-five. A heart attack brought on by heavy drinking, going by the hints in the press.

There was Martin's sister, Alice, now a mother of three herself, and an uncle, Benny Welsh, who was often mouthing off to the media about how his nephew should never be forgotten. He seemed to have become the family spokesperson, given how many times his name appeared in recent years.

Witness were relatively thin on the ground. The boys from school – Tierney, Brown, Wallace and others – were still around, as were Michael Hill and Harris McKenzie, two of the three drivers who'd seen him walking to or at the bus stop. That was pretty much it. Everyone else she found quoted was merely someone with opinions rather than information.

Suspects? Well, there were more of those. Reading between the lines of the press coverage, she decided the first was Martin's father, Alec. He was a drinker, even before his son went missing, and was said to have a temper on him. He'd been given a formal warning at work for thumping one of the other drivers, and a neighbour was quoted as saying that he wouldn't want to be in the killer's shoes if Alec Welsh got a hold of him.

The police had pulled all of the known and suspected abusers within thirty miles, finding reason enough to keep a couple of them in cells overnight. A guy named Eric McHattie had made some headlines, walked in with a blanket over his head and a bit of a mob waiting as he went through the door of the cop shop. He'd had some previous and no doubt some sly local bobby had let slip that he was on their list. McHattie had an alibi for the night Martin disappeared and, although it was only two alcoholic acquaintances, the police couldn't break it. Twelve years later, an angry father took a baseball bat to the man's head. If McHattie had been Martin's killer, he took the secret of it to his grave with him.

The name that came up again and again in connection with Martin's probable murder was a schoolteacher. A man named Alastair Haldane. He was Martin's history teacher and had taught him on the day of the disappearance. He was taken in for questioning, largely, it seemed, on the basis of local gossip and some of his colleagues saying he was particularly distracted in the days after it happened.

He was named in the press, albeit in a roundabout 'helping police with their enquiries' kind of way. He was named again and again. A press pack took up residence in his front garden for a while, asking for quotes and demanding to know 'the truth'. A mob mentality quickly and inevitably developed round Haldane. His windows were broken twice and his mother, whose house he lived in, claimed her life was made a misery by locals.

He was twenty-eight at the time and had been teaching at Calderrigg High for three years. Nice guy, said colleagues. Would never believe it of him, said others. Always pleasant, never any trouble, very helpful, dedicated to his pupils. The support wasn't unanimous, though. No smoke without fire, said one unnamed newspaper source. Too friendly with some pupils, said another. Always something odd about him, implied a few.

She counted three trips to the police station, two by invitation, one by demand. The third lasted as long as the law allowed but then he was back on the streets. No evidence. No body. Just a whole heap of suspicion.

There were photographs of him, too. Reasonably tall, spectacles, fair hair in a side parting. Awkward-looking but, then, who wouldn't be, walking into a police station with newspaper cameras pointed at you? In some pictures he was walking proud, aiming for unconcerned. In others he looked terrified, shying away from the prying eyes of the lens.

Harris McKenzie, the driver of the bus that Martin should have been on, also came under strong suspicion. The woman who got off with her child at Martin's stop on the edge of town couldn't say whether there had been anyone waiting there. She'd been too busy manoeuvring buggy and baby to notice anyone standing there or whether they got on after she'd left.

'Did Martin really not get on bus?' one tabloid queried. It was tantamount to calling the driver a liar, but not quite.

McKenzie had a record. Not much more than a couple of old convictions for breach of the peace and one for assault, but it was enough to interest the police. He too had been invited to the station for a chat, doubtless having his story questioned over and over. If there was no one else on the bus and no one to see them for a stop or two, then that left McKenzie with the dangerously double-edged sword of no witnesses and no alibi.

A quick calculation showed McKenzie to be seventy-six but she couldn't find any mention of him after the fifteenth anniversary in 1988, so whether he was alive or dead was anyone's guess. Either way he, like Alec Welsh and Alastair Haldane, was never charged. No one was.

Martin Welsh had disappeared not just from that bus stop but from public record. She could find only a handful of references in the past ten years, and they were largely insignificant. There were a couple of anniversary features from 2013, although far fewer than for the thirtieth: a local newspaper item about vandalism in Calderrigg cemetery that damaged four headstones, including the one the Welsh family had erected for Martin; an unsuccessful petition to name a street in the village after him; and a story about his sister Alice being robbed in a street attack.

Apart from those fleeting mentions, it was as if he'd slipped away into the mist of time. She lay in bed, forty years on, and made a vow to find him.

She knew whom she was going to call for help but she had no idea if he would answer or even if he'd know who she was.

CHAPTER 24

Nathan liked to follow people sometimes.

Tracking, trailing, tailing, all without their having the first clue that it was happening. Most people are stupid but even the smarter ones have no idea. They go around thinking they're safe. Thinking no one is watching them. Nothing could be further from the truth.

There are eyes everywhere. We're constantly being watched. Street cameras. Shop cameras. Traffic cameras. Cameras on houses. Cameras on car dashboards. Government cameras. Cameras in your computer. More than they tell you about. Much more.

And people are watching you too. Don't think they're not.

The man a few steps behind you, the unseen eyes in the window above, the couple standing on the other side of the street nudging each other and nodding towards you. Every step. Every movement. Everyone is watching you. Sometimes they look just because they're there; sometimes they watch because it's their job to.

You need to protect yourself against the eyes. Walk in

the shadows and in the crowd, hide when you can. Nathan knew. They were all looking for him, probably always had been but definitely now. But Nathan was ready for them. Prepared.

Being aware was being protected. He was constantly thinking of CCTV and cops and people and threats. And he listened. That's what people forgot to do most. Listen. People were dumb. Nathan listened to everything and everyone around him, and so he knew when they were coming for him. He was always ready.

The pills helped, too, not the ones they wanted him to take but the others. They kept him alert. Like jungle soldiers or desert warriors. He could hear everything, see everything, dodge everything.

People didn't see Nathan. He saw them. He made sure of that.

Following people was an art. There were rules to follow and tricks to use.

Don't get too close. Don't make it at all obvious. Don't ever get in their eye line. If they don't see you then they don't know you're there. Watch out for shop windows or mirrors. Treat reflections as your enemy. Change your clothes. Change your hair. Change the way you walk. Change the way you think.

If you need to, you drop them. You can always pick them up again, but better that than they see you. So just walk on by without a sideways glance if you feel a threat of discovery.

If they go in somewhere, a shop or an office, maybe, then you find somewhere suitable to wait it out. It can be visible as long as there's a reason for your being there, a bus stop, maybe, or a café. Don't hang around in public view without reason. If you do, then you're as stupid as they are and just asking to be noticed.

As a rule, the bigger the crowd the bigger the safety margin, but also the more difficult the tail. Keep closer to the shorter ones, let the taller ones go a bit. Use colours, hairstyles, clothing, whatever you can fasten on to. Keep them in sight. Keep out of theirs.

Despite its being Saturday afternoon, there weren't too many people on Anderston Quay but enough of a crowd to hide in. The Clyde was to his left, so he didn't need to worry about anyone coming from that side. The office buildings all along the other side of the road were full of eyes, though. Hundreds of them. All hiding behind darkened windows and slanted blinds. Those he had to be careful of.

The person he was tailing was maybe twenty yards ahead and still unaware of Nathan's existence. Six foot or so and wearing a bright-blue puffer jacket. Easily seen, easily followed.

Nathan had been behind him since the man had left Bacchus on Glassford Street in the Merchant City and then strolled down to the Broomielaw. All too simple. No sense of self-protection and no awareness of any possible threat. He was disgustingly stupid.

He'd been loud in the pub. Letting everyone know he had a phone and friends. Loud, drunk and obnoxious. No one liked him. Nathan didn't like him. Nathan had sat in the corner, unseen, and listened.

The guy was on his phone again now, texting as he went and making people swerve as he walked without looking where he was going. Not looking up was rude. Not looking around him was potentially fatal.

You could tell a lot about people just by looking. Nathan was good at that. He could see when they were proud or sad. He could tell the worried ones and the dangerous ones. He knew when they were selfish, arrogant or just useless. The stupid ones, most of them, he could spot a mile off.

The blue puffer jacket walked lazily, no hurry to get anywhere, and had just spent two hours drinking in a pub on his own. He was a waster. On top of that, he turned his head very obviously to look at people who passed to see if he'd been noticed. That bothered Nathan because it was wrong and because he didn't like the guy looking round.

He was in his early twenties and wore skinny blue denims that barely reached his boots and a flannel shirt under the jacket. His hand was constantly working through his hair or his stupid beard.

They were nearing the traffic lights at the corner and the guy had a choice to make. Straight on to Finnieston Quay, left across the Squinty Bridge or right on to Finnieston Street. Nathan stopped to tie his shoelace, giving the target time to decide and making sure he didn't close in on him. If he had to stop at the lights to cross then Nathan had to avoid being next to him. That might ruin everything.

He chose left, over the bridge to the south side of the river. It was the road less travelled and there were fewer people around him now, so Nathan backed off further. That bright-blue puffer jacket, so good at keeping the howling April wind out and yet so noticeable. The idiot would have been better off getting cold.

CHAPTER 25

Alzheimer's was as strange a disease as it was terrible. Often, five minutes ago didn't exist while fifty years ago seemed like yesterday. She knew far more about it than she'd like but far less than was of any use.

She'd seen it in her dad long before either of them would admit it was a reality. Little things like losing his keys or getting stuck in the middle of a sentence because he couldn't find the right word. He'd forget people's names or just lose track of what he was saying. Little things that began to add up to a bigger thing.

It was the first time he forgot *her* name that signalled to both that it was serious. His daughter, his only child. He couldn't remember her name. They both laughed it off but she was sure it had scared him as much as it did her.

Of course, it started happening more often. Forgotten meetings, repeated conversations, bumps with the car, getting lost. Still they denied it, still it got worse.

He drove through a red light at Anniesland Cross and smashed into a car turning right. No one was badly hurt but it was the day they couldn't ignore it any longer. He agreed to go to the doctor and the diagnosis was the one they'd both expected and dreaded.

They learned about Alzheimer's and they learned to deal with it. Sort of. They knew the short-term memory was usually the first thing to go, damage to the hippocampus, but that live events would be unaffected, for a time at least. So they enjoyed the benefit of that, talking long into the night about how he'd met her mother, his early days in the force, her childhood, any golden memory that they'd cherish while they could.

Even after he went into Clober Nursing Home, those long-term memories held firm. Some days they'd be so fresh he thought he was living them and they'd taken over from what had happened since. It could be a tangled mess, but on the good days the pathways joined up and he could walk down Memory Lane with a spring in his step.

They'd had some success a year earlier by bringing in an old Rangers player whom his dad had watched in his younger days and the pair of them chatted away as if the mud had only just been wiped away from the man's boots. It had done him so much good and maybe, just maybe, she could try something similar now.

He hadn't been on the original Martin Welsh case but his force had got called in a year down the line when the local cops had got nowhere. It was standard practice on an unsolved like that to bring in fresh eyes to look at everything from scratch.

She remembered him talking about the case, worrying over where he might have gone wrong, grieving about failing the family, the way that all good cops do on the ones they don't get to the bottom of.

What she didn't remember was the details. She'd been young and then she'd been busy. Too late now to wish she'd paid more attention except that maybe she could have a second chance.

It would be so much easier face to face, but that wasn't going to happen. Tony would freak if she left the house, and, anyway, she wouldn't take the risk. It was going to be by phone or nothing. She crossed her fingers and prayed it was a good day.

'Hello, Alan's room.'

'Hi, Jess, it's Rachel. Is he there?'

'Hi, Rachel. Yes, he's lying on his bed. Do you want a word?'

'Yes, please. How is he?'

'He's doing okay. He had his breakfast and we had a chat about the weather. He was worried the rain would be bad for his tomato plants. I told him they'd be fine and that seemed to keep him happy. Hang on, I'll get him.'

The moments between the phone getting passed over and her dad picking it up always seemed to take an eternity. It left so much time for doubts and fears to plunge into the void and leave her struggling. Would he know her, would he talk, would he be happy?

'Hello?'

He sounded stronger today. It wasn't necessarily a sign that he'd remember better than on the days he sounded weak and old but it still made her feel better. She liked him to sound like himself.

'Hi, Dad. It's Rachel.'

'I'm sorry. Who?'

'It's Rachel. Your daughter. How are you today, Dad?'

'I don't . . . I'm sorry, I don't know who . . .'

It hurt her every time no matter how much she readied herself for it. She'd learned not to push it too much, though: challenging him would most likely just distress him and that was the last thing she wanted.

'It's okay. Don't worry about it.'

'Okay.'

'I hear your tomato plants are doing well. That's good news, isn't it?'

'Yes, they are. Lots of rain but they're fine.'

'That's good, Dad. Listen . . .'

'I'm Alan.'

'Yes, of course. Alan, I wanted to talk to you about something. Do you remember the Martin Welsh case? The boy who—'

'The boy who went to school and never came home.'

'Yes!'

'Terrible, it was. His poor mother. She was still crying her eyes out a year later. The father was no use. He was a bad lot.'

Her heart soared. He was lucid and articulate. And he remembered.

'The local police said when it happened everyone in the village wanted to help. Do anything they could. A year later and they didn't want to know. They've turned on the father and the teacher. I think they're embarrassed about it all. They say it's given the village a bad name.'

Past tense had become present. He wasn't remembering now. He was living it.

'No one is talking. Say they've said all they've got to say. Makes it hard work. I'm worried we're never going to find out who did this.'

'Who do you think might have done it, Alan?'

'Eh? Oh there's a few possibles. I've got my suspicions about the lorry driver. Michael Hill. His story doesn't stack up. I want to talk to him again. And the bus driver, too. The father, though, a nasty bit of work, and he's got a right temper on him.'

'Anyone else, Alan?'

'Could be anyone. That's what scares me. Someone that drove past, saw the chance and picked the boy up and killed him. Some maniac that might be from nowhere near the village and nothing to do with what we know. So many back roads round here. He'd never be found.'

She had a question that bugged her.

'Alan, are you sure that Martin Welsh is dead? Are you sure he was murdered?'

'No.'

'*No?*'

'He probably was but we can't be sure. No body, see?'

'Can you think of anything else, Alan?'

'It's raining again. My tomato plants will be ruined.'

She told him she loved him and she'd call again soon. He'd already hung up the phone.

She went back onto KillingTime and went to her messages, pulling up the offer from RD, the person who was so desperate to buy the newspaper front page from her that he'd offered double what she'd paid.

> I've changed my mind and if you still want to buy the Martin Welsh front page then I'll consider selling it. Not for £250 though. I might take £300.

CHAPTER 26

The Clyde is the artery that lets life flow through Glasgow. It's the heartbeat of the place. It's where Glasgow was born and where it dies.

Nathan knew all great cities were built on rivers. They grew from need and opportunity, sprang up out of greed and necessity. The river brought trade, transport and protection, and took away some of the shit. Glasgow had made the Clyde and the Clyde had made Glasgow. It was an old line but it was true.

The Clyde came from hills and streams and was made into ships and an empire. It brought tobacco and cotton and sent out men to fight wars and build roads on foreign dirt. It put the blood in the city's veins and flesh on its bones. It was a cold, black sheet of life.

Nathan was above the river now, standing on South Portland Street Suspension Bridge. He stared with the rest of the crowd, the throng growing thicker round them with every scream. People came running to join them, fighting for room, straining to see, camera phones working overtime. Facebook had another treat coming.

The noise had moved downriver, cascading from bridge to bridge with the current, gaining in volume at each crossing. There was a huddle of bridges on this part of the river, fifteen of them squeezed into the two-mile stretch between the exhibition centre and Glasgow Green, and the sound had already passed over five of them. He imagined it had begun as just a shout of curiosity, a wonder if it could really be what it looked like. Maybe some kid ran to the middle of St Andrews Suspension Bridge and stood open-mouthed when seeing that was exactly what it was. The second person shrieked and, from that point, neither the screaming nor the shouting stopped at all.

He could see they'd come running. From walkways and pavements on either side of the river, anxious to see for themselves. He knew they'd all be denying their nature, making some excuse to themselves as to why they wanted to see it. Nathan wasn't denying his.

They still stared from the granite grey of the Victoria Bridge, stretching their necks from Gorbals Street on the south of the river to Clyde Street on the north. Scores of others hungered for their turn on the Glasgow Bridge up ahead while, in between, those on South Portland Street held their breaths.

The cause of the commotion was a mattress. A simple, white mattress. It had served some unknown person as a double bed before being dumped illegally at a fly-tipping site. It was now travelling where the river took it, its pace set by the tide and wind.

As it sailed under the suspension bridge, the riot of phone clicks reached a crescendo, drowned out only by a scuffling of feet and raised voices as the crowd wheeled round to follow it. Nathan turned more slowly than the others, letting them spin by him, seeing them for what they were. He heard the screams rise again as the mattress re-emerged on the other side, as if it had come as a fresh surprise that the body was still there. Still bloodied, still dead.

Police sirens could be heard in the distance now, called by people on one of the earlier bridges. The noise was edging closer but was no incentive to the leeches on the bridge to move or do anything other than stare and scream and photograph.

Boats were on their way, too, a police launch thundering against the current, a blue light signalling haste. They couldn't get there in time to save the poor bastard on the mattress though, that much was clear to them all.

His long, tousled hair was matted by a much darker shade, making an even greater contrast with his ice-pale skin and showing where his skull had been bashed in. His body was spread-eagled across the mattress, the long legs clad in skinny black jeans, the bright-blue puffer jacket shining in the gloom as he slept the longest sleep.

A helicopter roared overhead, slowly following the procession. It must be either TV news or the police. Either way, Nathan didn't like it much.

He watched the mattress float away from him with an odd mix of sadness and satisfaction. It was now everyone's, not just his, something he created but was having to share with the herd. They were devouring its spectacle as if they owned it. Some on the Glasgow Bridge were calling it to them, screaming at it to go faster so as to beat the cop launch before they missed out on their turn for a close-up view. A few of those around Nathan caught the mood and they shouted for it to hurry, too.

The boat got there first, collaring the mattress and hauling it in. The yobs booed, of course. Their fun had been spoiled and they acted like noisy drunks demanding more booze at a funeral.

You've got to love the river, Nathan thought as he began to slip away through the crowd. The Clyde was truly Glasgow's heartbeat. It giveth life and it taketh away.

CHAPTER 27

The orders from KillingTime were out for delivery. Online tracking told her some were due today and, although she didn't know which, she had a good idea of when they'd be delivered. She was ready, waiting and strangely anxious.

When she heard the doorbell, her feet slipped out from under the covers and she was over the side of the bed before the ringing had stopped. She wouldn't run, she'd promised herself that much, but she couldn't take the chance of missing the delivery.

She was halfway across the bedroom floor and the bell had stopped. She swore softly and hurried a little more, not knowing if there was someone standing outside waiting patiently or if he'd got back in his van, taking the package away with him. Or, worse still and potentially disastrous, was even now knocking on her neighbour's door to leave it there.

Her tummy ached in protest at the haste but she ignored it, padding across the hall and unlocking and opening the door in one movement. She was assaulted by a blast of cold air, reminding her she was standing there in bare feet and a short nightshirt. That didn't bother her as much as finding there was no one standing there. She cursed again and ventured out, seeing a man walking up next door's steps, a white package under his arms.

'Hey!' she called to him. 'Is that for me?'

He stopped midstride and looked across, seeing her state of undress and a smirk creasing his face. 'Rachel Narey?'

'Yes. Glad I caught you.'

'Me too,' he sleazed.

She bit her tongue and retreated to the door, standing half in and out, ready to close it as soon as she got the package from him. He was up the stairs in a flash, standing closer to her than he needed. She backed off slightly and caught hold of the door, ready to slam it in his face if necessary.

'Sign here, darling. Bit chilly to be out dressed like that, isn't it?'

She took the plastic stylus from him and made some incomprehensible signature on the screen of his handheld gizmo. Nodding at the package, she made to swap it for the document-signing machine but the delivery man held on to it.

'I could carry it inside for you if you want.'

She quickly reached out and pulled the parcel from his hands, at the same time raising the signing equipment till it was an inch from the man's nose. She leaned closer, seeing him start to smile. She whispered.

'If you don't fuck off right now, I'll take this box and stick it somewhere that will be very difficult for anyone to sign. Understand?'

He did. He backed off quickly enough that he nearly slipped down the steps. She shut the door and left him there. She leaned her back against the door and weighed the package, trying to work out which of her purchases it was. It was quite light, so maybe the Martin Welsh front page or the Watson letter. It could be one of the slaughter-graphs, definitely not the Susan Atkins frame but possibly the fireplace stone.

Whatever it was, it felt hot in her hand. Like stolen goods. Like guilt. Inside, restrained only by bubble wrap, evil was bursting to get out.

She made her way back upstairs, closing the door behind her and sat the package on the bed. Sitting down a foot away, she edged it from her with the tips of her fingers, then pulled it closer again. She looked at the postmark – Bermuda – and the neat handwritten address, trying to read what she could into it. Of course, the easy thing was just to open it, but she was stuck, held back by a mix of unease and anticipation.

Whichever of the items were inside, she knew she'd seen worse and touched worse, whether skin to skin or through latex gloves that never made you feel any more distant from whatever it was. She wanted it and didn't. Wanted to wait and couldn't.

Her head spun, drawn by a noise from downstairs. She knew it was the front door. Had the delivery creep come back? No, the door had opened and closed again. Shit! It was Tony.

She heard his footsteps on the stairs and knew she had to hide the package. She threw it under the bed and got herself under the covers as his tread got heavier and closer. The quilt was barely over her when the door opened.

She saw the immediate confusion on his face, his brows narrowing as he was obviously aware of her recent movement.

'You okay?'

'Of course. Why wouldn't I be?' She heard the annoyance in her voice, cross at him for coming home, irritated at herself for thinking it.

'No reason apart from the fact you're ill. Were you up?'

She glared at him. 'Am I not allowed to go to the toilet now? Maybe you want to get me a bag and a tube so I don't get up at all?'

He stopped and looked at her, staying calm and accepting her frustration.

'Do you need me to get you anything. Tea? Food?'

'No!' Damn it, she softened her voice. 'No, thanks. I'm okay. You not working?'

He wandered over and sat down beside her, kissing her lightly on the lips, his hand resting on her stomach. She enjoyed the touch but couldn't escape the thought of the package lying somewhere under the bed. Was it completely under the bed or was a bit of it sticking out? Would he see it?

'Yes, I'm working. I'm just back from Clyde Street. Thought I'd pop in, make sure everything was okay. Listen, I'm sorry that I worry, but I do. I can't help it.'

She managed to keep the sigh inside her. 'It's okay. I know you do and I know why. But I'm okay, just bored. Don't let me get in the way of you working.'

She could see him trying to work out if she was being sarcastic or understanding. How could he know if she wasn't sure herself?

'I take you haven't seen the news or else you'd know about Clyde Street.' He looked at her curiously, wondering why she was so uninterested. 'Do you want to hear about it?'

'Sure. Why not?'

She knew why not. Because she wanted him to leave so she could open the KillingTime parcel. It was wrong and it was unfair but she wanted to rip open that envelope and devour what was inside. It was under the bed, calling to her.

'I'm overwhelmed by your enthusiasm. Okay ... so today I photographed a body floating down the Clyde on a mattress.'

It was probably the Watson letter – that was the most likely going by the weight. Charles Denton Watson, known as Tex. He murdered seven people. She wanted to know what the letter said about him, what insights it gave into his personality. Was he ill or evil or both?

'A mattress. I didn't get close but, still, I'd never seen anything like it. They were queuing up on the bridges to get a look at it but by the time I got there ...'

Would she be able to tell that about Watson from the letter in the way she'd like to think she could if she met someone like him? She had a sense of a killer from having met more than her share of them. It was an indefinable thing, a very imprecise science, something born part of experience and part intuition.

'The victim had had his head beaten in, then stuck on the bloody mattress to float down the river in full public view.'

And, beyond whatever was in the letter, would she get a sense of *him*? His hand on the letter, his DNA all over it. His smell, his being. *Seven people murdered.*

'I managed to get some decent shots but the best of them would have been taken from the news helicopter. No way I can take anything to compete with that.'

It was just lying there, gathering dust by the second. She itched to get inside it.

'Well it sounds like you better get back to the office.'

'*What?*'

'You've got a lot to do and I'm tired and I'd rather get some sleep. Just go and give me some peace.'

'Peace?'

'Yes, peace. I'm supposed to be resting and you're fussing over me and telling me about work stuff that I shouldn't be hearing.'

'You're unbelievable.'

'Well you better start believing it. And do it while you're closing the door on the way out.'

He hadn't done or said anything wrong, they both knew it. Only she knew why. He looked at her, hoping she'd back down or apologise. She wouldn't. Sure, she hated herself for it but she wouldn't.

She could see he wanted to explode, shout at her, tell her what a cow she was being, but he was biting hard on his lip and holding it in. And he was doing that for her. She *was* being a cow.

'Okay. I'll see you later. Phone or text if you need anything.'

He said it on the turn and wasn't waiting for a reply. She watched his back and the closing door, struggling to resist the urge to hop out of bed as soon as it was shut behind him and rescue the package that was hidden beneath it. She had to force herself to wait until she heard his footsteps on the stairs and the angry closure of the front door. As soon as she heard it bang, she jumped out of bed and was on the floor in a second, scrambling over the carpet to grab the white envelope and yank it towards her.

She wasn't waiting any longer this time and tore into it with sharp fingers, scratching it open and pulling it wide. She gouged her way through the bubble wrap and eased the paperwork out, laying aside the accompanying invoice and finding to her disappointment that it wasn't the Watson letter or any of the other Tate-related pieces. Instead, she was holding a yellowing newspaper cover.

Friday, 4 May 1973. The photograph of the boy smiling out from the past. *Disappears.* That's what they'd had to limit themselves to. Not murdered, not kidnapped, just vanished. It was easy to read between the lines with the benefit of hindsight, though. Missing, presumed murdered, was the tone.

The village of Calderrigg, Lanarkshire, in turmoil, his parents desolate, the police searching. Neighbours were quoted about the friendly wee boy, never any trouble, devastated for his mother. The school was in shock, doing all it could to help and praying for his safe return.

She could feel the fear in the paper, the untold knowledge in every line. Martin was gone and he wouldn't be coming back. One minute he'd been at the bus stop in full public view, the next he'd disappeared.

Public view. The words made her remember what Tony had said, something that had passed right over her in her distraction over the package.

The victim had had his head beaten in, then stuck on the bloody mattress to float down the river in full public view.

She hadn't been listening, too caught up in the anticipation of the delivery to pay attention to what he'd said. In too much of a hurry to get rid of him, so she could indulge this new . . . whatever the hell it was.

Public view. Someone had put on a hell of a show. *Again.*

CHAPTER 28

'Hundreds of horrified city centre shoppers came face to face with a murder victim today right in the heart of Glasgow.'

The STV news reporter was suitably grave but you could tell she was loving it. She could barely keep the gleeful excitement out of her voice. Narey could see the woman was all but wetting herself she was so happy.

'People were forced to look on as a body floated down the Clyde between various busy bridges on a mattress. The victim, said to be in his early twenties, had been severely assaulted and witnesses spoke of seeing bloody head wounds that seemed the most likely cause of death.

'Large crowds gathered to see this bizarre and gruesome sight and screams could be heard for some distance. It was something that even people in this city, which is used to seeing violence and aggression, were shocked by.

'These extraordinary shots you are seeing now were taken from the Scottish Television helicopter as the mattress was taken up the Clyde by the current. You can clearly see the man's body in the centre of it. The images that will follow are close-ups of the mattress and some viewers may find them disturbing. If so, please look away now.'

Look away? She was daring them to stay. Look away if you're scared, if you're not strong enough, that's what she was saying.

The camera closed in on the mattress, focused on the body. Christ, there was no way this should be shown on TV. You could see the blood, you could see the damage to the skull. This was someone's son they were showing.

'Police Scotland say they are treating the man's death as murder. An inquiry team has been set up and an incident room assembled on the Clydeside near to where the body was seen in an attempt to question as many witnesses as possible. Police Scotland have not confirmed the victim's identity.'

Apart from some cringe-making interviews with witnesses, that was it. A few randoms told how they'd never seen anything like it, were pure shocked man, everybody was screaming and that, blood everywhere, like.

Narey's mind was racing, joining dots faster than she could find them. Come on, she was urging the news. Surely they've joined them too. Tell us. But no, nothing.

Instead, they went back to the studio and the presenter moved on to a related item.

'In a separate development, Police Scotland have revealed the whereabouts of murdered MSP's son Aiden McAlpine on the night he was killed. Caroline Denton reports . . .'

They switched to a studiously serious woman standing outside what Narey recognised as Kelvingrove Park. Caz Denton had probably just stubbed out a fag and quit giggling in time for the cameras to roll, doubtless counting down the clock to her first voddie and Coke. Kelvingrove? Narey jumped to conclusions right away.

'Thanks, Bill. I am standing at the entrance to Kelvingrove Park in Glasgow's West End and it is here that detectives have traced the last known movements of Aiden McAlpine. Officers have spent many hours trawling CCTV footage around the city in an effort to get a glimpse of Aiden and establish where he was the night before his body was found near the entrance to Queen Street Station.

'Today, those officers got a breakthrough. They spotted Aiden walking along Gibson Street and then turning into Kelvin Way just after midnight. He walks past where I am standing now, into the park and is then never seen again.

'DCI Denny Kelbie is the man leading the investigation into Aiden's death and joins me now.'

Narey's teeth clenched as the little shite appeared on her screen.

'DCI Kelbie, do you see this as a breakthrough in the McAlpine case?'

'Caroline, this is a significant development, something that we have worked hard to achieve, and I think it sheds much light on what may have happened to Aiden that night. There is much work still to be done, but your viewers can rest assured we will not rest until it is completed.'

Smug little shite.

'Please talk us through what you think happened the night Aiden was murdered, Chief Inspector.'

'Of course. As you say, we picked him up on camera as he walked along Gibson Street and watched him turn into

Kelvin Way. He entered the park alone, wearing the clothes that were found with him the following morning. We have studied footage from the camera covering this entrance for several hours after the time Aiden entered. He did not leave from here. We have similarly looked at other cameras and there is no sign of him leaving the park alive.'

'Do you believe he was murdered within the park?'

Kelbie looked grave. 'I don't want to jump to any conclusions, Caroline, but it's safe to say we are exploring the possibility of that being the case.'

Caz Denton furrowed her brow in a way that Narey had seen her do many times. She was going to ask the question.

'Chief Inspector, the park has a somewhat lurid reputation in the evenings, particularly after dark, particularly after midnight.'

Kelbie squirmed a bit but nodded. 'It does, yes.'

'In fact, it is known for being a refuge for drug addicts and sexual activity between gay men. Do you believe it was either of those pursuits that led Aiden to enter the park after midnight?'

Kelbie blanched and stumbled. 'There is no suggestion that Aiden McAlpine was a recreational drug user. A comprehensive analysis was done on his blood and there was no evidence whatsoever of illegal substances.'

Caz started at him and waited for him to continue. When he just swallowed awkwardly instead, she moved in.

'So you are saying he might have been here to meet men for sex?'

He frowned as if disapproving of the question but Narey wasn't buying it. 'That would be unhelpful speculation,

Caroline. We have no knowledge of that being the case and certainly wouldn't present it to the media before knowing it to be true.'

Caz had the merest hint of a smile on her face as the camera swung back to her. 'Thank you, Chief Inspector. So, Bill, these are the latest dramatic developments on the murder of the son of MSP Mark McAlpine. A tragic story which clearly has much yet to give us. Now, back to you in the studio. This is Caroline Denton for Scottish Television, outside Kelvingrove Park.'

So there it was. Kelbie had laid out the McAlpine murder as a gay slaying. And yet he hadn't, of course, said so.

'Bollocks!' Narey shouted at the TV. 'Bollocks! Complete bollocks.'

Or was it? McAlpine being killed for going after rent boys or whatever Kelbie was alluding to didn't match up with her own ideas, but that didn't make it wrong. Kelvingrove – of course you'd think along those lines. And if you were Kelbie you'd think it to the exclusion of everything else. She needed another viewpoint from inside the investigation.

'Hello?'

'Hey, Rico. How's it going?'

'Hey, Mum. Sorry, but I'm working just now.' He paused as if listening. 'Okay, okay. Give me a minute.'

She heard him walking, probably just far enough away that he couldn't be overheard.

'Are you trying to get me sacked, boss?'

'*Mum?*'

'First thing that came to mind.'

'I don't want to know why. So what's happening. Was the McAlpine kid gay?'

'Yes. Not that anyone gives a toss about that one way or another. We've asked around his friends and it seems he was but kept it quiet because of his father. Who didn't know, before you ask.'

'And of course Kelbie thinks that's why he was murdered.'

'He likes the line. He doesn't like that he's had to sell that to the father, who's gone apeshit. But Kelbie thinks paying for it in the park at night is why the son was killed, yes.'

'And what do you think?'

She heard him sigh heavily. Rico didn't like guessing.

'I think you shouldn't be asking me. You're off limits. And I don't know. Crawling into the park at that time and not crawling out again? Hard to ignore it.'

'But then hanging him out to dry for the world to see? Doesn't make sense. Not without some message saying that's why he'd done it. Some kind of sick warning to others.'

'Why are you even phoning me, boss? What happened to bed rest and quiet recuperation?'

'I'm bored off my tits, Rico. I'm not bothering anyone. Except you. Come on, what's happening?'

'That's it. We're trying to interview some park regulars in case any of them saw Aiden, but they're not quite so keen to talk to us. Kelbie is rattling cages. He doesn't seem to be a fan of the softly-softly approach.'

'He's such a twat.'

'Yes ma'am.'

'What about this body on the mattress?'

'No idea, we're not on it. I heard Addison's got it. Strange one, though. All I know is what's on the news. Kelbie wanted it, I know that much, but the brass said no.'

'Addison. Great.'

'Why?'

'Well there's no way he'll tell me anything, will he?'

'Shouldn't think so. He's not a soft touch like me. I better go. Kelbie's on the prowl. Take it easy, Mum.'

Rico either hadn't thought it or he wasn't willing to share it with her. No one was thinking there was a link? Surely someone must be. Or maybe she'd been in this room too long and was going stir crazy.

Killed for murderabilia or rent boys? Yes, maybe she was the crazy one. But she had an idea how she might find out.

CHAPTER 29

The Station Bar on Port Dundas Road had been Winter and Addison's local for six years. It was a proper pub and that suited them much better than any of the wine bars, craft breweries, prosecco palaces or gin joints that had sprung up in recent years. When all the hipster dives had shaved off their beards and been turned into nail bars, the likes of the Station would still be standing, as they always had.

It was rarely a two-pint destination for them. It was a four or six-pint venue, always an even number of course. It was a place to put the world to rights – and their worlds had enough wrongs to demand multiple drinks.

They'd be guaranteed to be left alone, and that helped. Plenty of the regulars knew what they did for a living but would give them space, either because of or despite that. The pub was named the Station because it served the thirst of the nearby cop shop, fire station and ambulance HQ. Working for the emergency services was very thirsty work.

It was half past ten before they could meet and that would doubtless mean a competition to see how much they could drink before last orders. And then a sprint to see how much they could get after it.

Winter turned up to find Addison already posted in the mezzanine with two Guinnesses, one that was already a casualty of war, and two halves of whisky.

Addison liked a drink. He liked it a lot. Winter often wondered if his friend was borderline alcoholic but usually decided against it. Maybe he was a functioning drunk in the way that much of the city was. He and they were just sociable. Sociable to a point that their livers would grumble with but their working lives could handle. Just.

'Whisky? That kind of day?'

Addison shrugged brightly. 'It's always that kind of day when you serve at the coalface of justice.'

'Oh Jeezus! It's one of those nights, is it? What's happened?'

'Nothing in particular. Just up to my arse in alligators as per usual, and now a new case on top of all the shit I already had to shovel. So how is Rachel? Really. And how are you, wee man?'

'Ach I'm fine. Forget about me. She's ... she's a bit stressed.'

'Let me guess. She's being a difficult patient.'

'Aye, you could say that. I'm glad to chew on a beer for a while, put it that way.'

Addison raised his glass in salute. 'So were you two ever going to tell us she's expecting? Although, given the time it took you to tell us you were a couple, maybe you were going to tell us just before the kid went to university.'

Winter shook his head. 'You know what she's like. She

didn't want anyone to know until they had to. She wanted to work on as long as she could and, while she was working, she didn't want anyone to judge her because she was pregnant or make excuses for her because she was.'

'Make excuses for her? She'd more likely have brought some gangster down in between contractions.'

Winter didn't laugh and Addison's face crumpled. 'Sorry. Just tell me to shut the fuck up.'

'It's okay. And it's all going to be okay. It's down to the doctors. And to her doing what she's told.'

'Good luck with *that*. She's never been good at doing what she's told. I've never managed to get her to do it.'

He knew Addy was right. She was as stubborn as a blood stain. He still couldn't get his head round her not being interested in the guy on the mattress. *He* was, though, and it was why he was meeting Addison now.

'So what's the new case?'

Addison took a sup at his pint, pausing mid-gulp to look suspiciously at Winter, wondering why he was asking.

'Mattress Man. I take it you've heard about him.'

Winter admitted that he had.

'Just what I needed. Mattress Man. The floating fatality, the corpse on the Clyde, the cadaver in the current. The body in the Broomielaw? You newspaper types like a good bit of alliteration, don't you?'

Winter drew deep on his Guinness. 'This is my fault somehow, is it?'

'Fuck's sake, wee man. Of course it's your fault. You're the media. The news manipulators. My job has just gone from overloaded to batshit crazy all because some poor sod goes for a nap and floats down the water as if Ryanair did cruises. How big are you going to use the picture of the hole in his head?'

'Addy, we didn't kill him or stick him on the mattress for the whole city to see.'

'No, you'll just stick it under everyone's nose till they either puke or demand to see it again. Or both. You'll make sure it's on every front page, every news bulletin every hour, every carton of milk and sack of potatoes. You'll not be happy until there's mobs on the streets demanding all mattresses be destroyed.'

Winter sank his Guinness as if it were the *Titanic*. 'You want another?'

'How did you guess?'

Winter glanced at the table as he stood up and knew Addison's whisky would be gone before he returned. He nudged his own glass across the table towards him. 'I'll get two more of these as well.'

'Very good. Get me a couple of packets of crisps, too. I may as well have a bar supper while I'm at it.'

'So who's the guy on the mattress?'

He got the look of suspicion again but he still got an answer.

'Name of Calvin. *Calvin*. I mean, seriously. Did his mammy just remember the name from the dad's boxer shorts and think that was what he was called?'

The room froze. Or Winter did.

'Calvin?'

'Yeah, as in Klein. This guy was called Calvin Brownlie.'

Winter didn't hear much of what was said next. He didn't know if it was on his face but wasn't sure how it could not be. *Calvin Brownlie.* The most public of killings.

'What do you think happened?' He managed to sound just professionally interested.

Addison peered at him over the rim of his pint. 'None of this appears in your rag with any possible suggestion that it came from me, right?'

'Right.'

'Okay. Then I don't really know how I figure it. The eejit disappears from the street and next thing he's floating on the Silentnight. It's Glasgow, shit happens. Chances are he's pissed off the wrong person, maybe shagged some gangtwat's girlfriend, and he goes for the long cruise on the nearest thing that's handy.'

Winter gave that wisdom due consideration and drank.

'Were all his clothes on him as far as you could see?' Nice, he thought to himself. Subtle.

Addison actually put down his glass. 'What?'

'Was there anything missing? Shoes or socks or something?'

'Wee man, what do you actually want to know?'

'I was just wondering . . .'

'Course you were.'

'. . . whether there was anything that maybe should have been there that wasn't.' He took a breath. 'The way that the clothes in the McAlpine killing went missing.'

Addison's whisky followed the Guinness as night follows day.

'Are you pumping me for a story or do you already have one?'

Winter considered the question. 'Bit of both. I've got a line but it needs firmed up.'

Addison laughed. 'Wee man, that means you *don't* have a story. You have a theory. What is it? You think someone is nicking evidence or selling it?'

Winter tried to keep the surprise from his face but couldn't. 'Maybe.'

'Yeah, maybe. Any idea who?'

'None.'

'Okay, let me think about that one. There might be something in it. And, if it leads to you getting a story and me finding a link that allows me to have the McAlpine case off Kelbie, then that would be something to drink to.'

'I'd say so.'

'Another pair of Guinness it is, then. But, before I go buy them, I'm going to test your loyalty, wee man.'

'Oh, good.'

Addison leaned in close to whisper.

'Calvin the Clydeside Corpse? He always wore a watch that had an inscription on it from his mum and dad that they gave him on his eighteenth birthday. Never left home without it. When he was picked up? No watch. Now, if that bit of info ends up in the *Standard* I'm going to boot your balls from here to Hampden. Got it?'

'Got it.'

CHAPTER 30

She wanted to be on the other side of the murderabilia sites, somewhere she could see what was actually going on. In the real world, her normal world, she would know where to go and who to talk to. She'd know who had the skinny and who was full of it.

That was what she needed now. To talk to those who knew how it worked. Or at least to know who they were.

None of it made much sense, and she wasn't confident that she was thinking clearly at all. This room, this bloody room, was strangling her, cutting off the oxygen to her brain. She needed out, one way or another.

Tony's computer was in the third bedroom, the one that he used as an office when there was no one staying over, which was most of the time. He used his laptop for day-to-day use but he kept the PC for storage and backup, and it was where all his photographs were. Sick as he was, he'd kept a copy of every photo on every job since he'd begun with the old Strathclyde force.

Before they'd moved in together, he even had a wall of them in the office of his flat. A neat square of twenty black-framed prints, four rows of five, of 'special' jobs. She could never quite decide whether the wall was a reason to dump him or love him. They were stunning in their own way, beautifully shot and grotesquely unnerving.

They were now all logged in his PC, out of sight but probably not out of his mind. If he could be relied on for anything, it was his dedication to the organised collecting of his work. Everything would be in there and everything would be in order. That was what she was counting on now.

She was also banking on the fact that she could read him like a book. The computer was password-protected, not from her as such, but just by habit. Anyone could try to log on.

She booted it up and waited for the sign-in screen to appear. Password, please. If she knew him at all then she'd be fine.

She typed 'Metinides'. The name of his muse, his hero, his inspiration, the Mexican tabloid photographer who chased fire engines and ambulances for over fifty years. Nothing. Hm. She tried again: 'Metinides1'. She was in. She'd need to remember to have a word with him about security.

She quickly found files of photographs, tens of thousands of them, but all thankfully searchable by both date and name. She went straight to A and found the person she was looking for. Archibald Atto.

Atto. Serial killer. Serial liar. A dark and extremely dangerous man. Convicted of four murders and undoubtedly responsible for many more. He'd been in prison for seventeen years but his reputation hadn't dimmed. This was partly because Atto had worked hard to keep his name in lights over that time, drip-feeding newsworthy hints to police about the extent of his killing. Also, three years ago, she and Winter had managed to con him into divulging the location of two shallow graves where he'd buried young female victims. That had made plenty of headlines.

Atto had kept a nasty trophy collection, items he'd taken from his prey as souvenirs. He'd kept rings and watches, necklaces and pendants, many of them from girls who had never even been identified. Winter had photographed some, in particular a piece that had once belonged to Atto's first victim. It was a distinctive, and now quite famous, silver fish brooch.

Sure enough, there it was in Tony's files. Photographs of an innocuous little piece of jewellery that Atto had ripped from a twenty-one-year-old named Christine Cormack, after he'd beaten, raped and strangled her. He'd kept it as a piece of ghoulish vanity and that was what finally convicted him of her murder. The brooch's notoriety was well known but, crucially, it had never been shown publicly.

The original piece was, she was sure, safely locked away, but that didn't matter. She had a photograph of it from three different angles and, as far as anyone else was concerned, she had the real thing in her possession. As far as the world of murderabilia was concerned, she was going to go online and sell it to the highest bidder.

CHAPTER 31

KillingTime seemed to offer the best chance of finding a way into the UK market as it seemed to specialise in British collectibles more than the others did. She'd previously registered herself as Huntress and now she was going to post her first – and probably only – item for sale.

The wording was tricky but she followed the language used by other sellers and tried to hype it the best she could.

> Silver fish brooch.
>
> Once owned by Archibald Atto. Once owned by Christine Cormack.
>
> Extremely rare and sought after item.
>
> 100% genuine. Authenticity guaranteed.
> Starting bid £500.

She uploaded the three photographs, stated that postage would be paid by the buyer, crossed her fingers and pressed enter. Within minutes, her item – fake as it was – was up for sale.

She was still playing Manson's music while she searched online. Her good intentions to get rid of it had fallen through a dark hole. She played it now while she waited.

Charlie Manson. Sixties singer-songwriter.

After she bought the album, she'd told herself she was playing it because she was wondering what he had to say, whether his lyrics reflected his evil. Whether there had been clues there all the time to show what he was capable of. Truth was, she just couldn't stop herself.

Dirges and protests, strumming guitar and striving to be the angry, insightful voice of the times. He was a bad man's Bob Dylan, full of rebellious hippy ideals and his own importance. Some of the titles jumped out of the catalogue. 'People Say I'm No Good'. 'Cease to Exist'. 'Devil Man'. 'Who to Blame'.

She thought she could hear the malice in his voice but was fully aware her judgement was laced with hindsight. Was she hearing murder? Or hatred? She should be able to recognise psychopathy; it was her job after all. There was definitely rage and resentment, but that was all part and parcel of being a sixties folk singer. Was there more than that, though? She kept playing and kept listening.

Manson's voice filled her room now, echoing to and from the blue walls. As she searched and watched and waited, Charlie crooned about how he didn't care what they said and how they could just sit there and burn. He sang about scratching symbols on a tombstone. It was the soundtrack to her day.

He was singing to her as she dipped into a feature of the site she'd either never noticed or had ignored. 'Wanted'. A section where users could put up their own murderabilia wish list. It was, of course, a haven for crazies.

Someone wanted underwear. Anyone's, basically, but a murderer's if possible. Another sought anything connected to a prolific Russian serial killer she'd never heard of until she came to this place. One eejit wanted murder porn.

> Wanted: Porn movies featuring female killers. Looking for VHS/DVD of sex tapes involving convicted female serials. Have nice semi-professional tape can sell/swap that has double murderer in various sex acts. Girl in movie is my ex-girlfriend.

She didn't know where to start with that one, other than wondering why the killer was his ex, but made a mental note to pass it on to the spooks, who could check out the guy's Internet history. He was a murder or a rape waiting to happen.

There was nothing specific in there that was of any use to her, but she did think she could use it. All she had to do was work out what it was she wanted.

While she did that, Charlie sang to her: 'Look at your game, girl. Look at your game, girl.'

She'd done some research on KillingTime and knew it averaged around two thousand hits a day. Murder was big business and meant it should be no more than a few minutes before someone clicked on the brooch.

There was a counter on the item description and she sat, her stomach a knot of excitement, and watched it climb. Within half an hour, the brooch had been viewed forty-two times. Something must have kicked in after that, maybe word spreading virally, because after an hour the view counter had hit two hundred and fifty three. She felt the entire murderabilia community was looking on.

She waited and watched. No bids came in despite the watch counter clicking over. Then came the messages.

Along with her newly created username of Huntress came an inbox where buyers or sellers could contact her to ask questions or seek further details. Sure enough, it soon started to fill up, message after message with the same basic theme. Her heart sank as she read them, quickly realising this wasn't going to be as easy as she'd hoped.

Atto's silver fish? Yeah, right.

You're trying to sell an item like that on here? You're either a cop, a reporter or an idiot. Maybe two out of the three.

Who are you kidding?

If you've got that, prove it.

If this is real I want it but I'd need to know much more before I parted with money to a newbie.

First item for sale is an Atto trophy? Sure. Sell me Jack the Ripper's hat while you're at it.

If you're for real then you're in the wrong place. Email me here if you actually have the brooch.

£500 for the silver fish brooch??? I'll take two.

Smells fishy to me. Or maybe smells like pig.

They weren't buying it. Neither literally nor metaphorically. The watch counter slowed to a stop. Interest in her Atto brooch was over.

She slumped back onto her pillow, her eyes staring at the ceiling as she closed the laptop over without looking at it. Whom had she been trying to kid? They'd confined her to bed because she wasn't of any use to anyone. And they'd been right. She couldn't even con a bunch of freaky collectors that she had something to sell.

Damn it! All she'd succeeded in doing was letting collectors know that someone was noseying into their community. She'd made it harder for herself. Made it worse.

Useless. Amateur. Dreamer. Couldn't even have a baby properly. Pathetic.

The first grab of pain was somewhere deep in her belly and came with a dizziness that took her breath away. If she hadn't already been lying down, then she'd likely have keeled over. It spasmed and tightened, doubling her at the waist and scaring her. She didn't know or care if the tears were from the pain or the fear.

It lasted for only a few moments but that was long enough. She reached for the phone to call him but stopped herself as she felt the pain roll back. Whatever it was it had passed and wasn't worth worrying him over. But it was sufficient to convince her she had to calm down – and quickly.

She went through the breathing exercises she'd been taught, clearing her mind of murder sites and messages and thoughts of failure, counting to twenty, then thirty, then fifty, steadying herself the best she could. Her pulse settled, her breathing with it until she released a long gasp of relief. It was okay, scary but okay. No harm done.

She sat up, pillows propped behind her, and rubbed a hand idly across her stomach, patting and reassuring. One voice inside her was telling her she had to do less. Another was telling her she had to do better.

The words from the messages came back to her whether she liked it or not.

You're trying to sell an item like that on here?

If you're for real then you're in the wrong place.

On *here*. The *wrong* place.

That meant there was a *right* place. That meant there was somewhere else. Somewhere the likes of the silver fish brooch might be expected to be sold.

Maybe she wasn't so useless after all.

CHAPTER 32

It was two days later when she heard Tony's footsteps on the stairs and immediately knew he was angry. His tread was heavy and quick, determined. He was coming straight for her and she didn't know why. Her mind flew to the things she'd ordered online and she was sure he'd found them. This was going to be messy.

The look on his face when he came through the door didn't encourage her any. He was in control, not ready to rant or rave, but he wasn't happy. She knew the look.

'How are you?'

'I'm fine.'

'Not stressed?'

'No.'

'Just doing as the doctor instructed?'

Shit. 'Yes.'

'And you're definitely not getting stressed?'

'No.'

'Quite relaxed?'

'Like a baby.'

'Well that's good to know. So maybe, without getting

agitated in any way, you could help explain something to me.'

'Okay . . .' She didn't know where this was going but she was pretty sure she didn't like it.

He reached into the bag that was slung over his shoulder and brought out a newspaper. He was already turning to an inside page but she caught a glimpse of the front page and saw it was the *Sun*, not his usual reading choice.

'Page nine,' he announced, finding what he was looking for and folding it over so that the page was visible. 'Family's fury at Atto Internet sale.'

Shit!

The subheading didn't make any better reading. 'Unknown seller cashes in on murder victim.'

Shit!

He looked at her, gauging her reaction, before starting to read the article to her.

'"The family of slain 21-year-old Christine Cormack were distraught last night to learn someone was selling her personal items to the highest bidder.

'"A brooch worn by the Glasgow girl and taken by her murderer, notorious serial killer Archibald Atto, was offered in a ghoulish online auction."'

He stopped and looked up at her again. 'Shall I go on?'

'Sure, why not?' She could hear how unconvincing she sounded.

'Okay. "Christine's sister, Pamela Kinross, said she was devastated to learn about the sale and condemned the person trying to profit from her sister's death as heartless and cruel. She said she had to break the news to her elderly mother before she learned of it from someone else."'

He pushed the paper closer to her. 'Do you want to read it?'

'Tony . . .'

He ignored her. 'You have to wonder who would do a thing like that. And *how* they could do it. How they could possibly get their hands on that brooch. But the thing that puzzles me most of all? The photograph that the seller used of the brooch. That was my photograph. Mine. No question about it. Strange, isn't it?'

She said nothing.

'Of course, you might think that maybe someone inside Police Scotland has taken the brooch and accessed my photograph from the files to advertise it.'

'That seems the most likely explanation.'

He smiled. 'Does it? Why would someone take the risk of stealing it and making it so public? That would be risky and stupid. And also, do you see this mark here on the photograph, just under the brooch? That's my mark. And it's only on the copy I kept for myself. Only on the copy that's in my personal files.'

Shit!

'Listen—'

'What the hell do you think you're playing at, Rachel? Tell me how you could possibly think this was a good idea.'

He was keeping his voice as calm as he could but she could see his hands were tight and his knuckles white.

'Look, Tony, I know I've been taken off this investigation but—'

'No. No, no, no. Don't even begin that sentence. Don't even think of doing this. You've been consigned to bed for a reason. You're ill. You're at risk. Our baby's at risk. You cannot do this.'

'I'm not doing anything. I was told to stay in bed, I'm staying in bed. I'm not going anywhere, not doing anything. But—'

'No buts. I don't want to hear it. You are supposed to be relaxing. No stress whatsoever. You agreed you would back away from this murderabilia shit and leave it to me.'

She sighed heavily. 'I *am* relaxed. Or I was until you started interrogating me. And I'm relaxed because I'm doing something. Tony, seriously. Doing nothing? It was driving me crazy. It was stressing me. I'm more relaxed now. Honestly.'

His hands went to his head and he turned slowly on the spot. 'Driving you crazy? What the hell are you trying to do? Jesus, Rachel, that girl's family ...'

She had to look away, that was something she ought to have accounted for but had chosen to ignore.

'Okay, I didn't mean that and didn't want that. I didn't think it all the way through. But, Tony, there is something going on here. I'm on the right track. I know it.'

He was open-mouthed, starting to speak and stopping again. He blew out his cheeks, threw the newspaper onto the bed and walked away, waving a hand at her dismissively as he left the room.

Shit!

Her head fell back onto the pillow and she stared at the ceiling above her. Shit, shit, shit!

She felt absolutely fine. She wasn't ill, not in any real sense. She'd felt like a fraud lying there. It was no surprise she wanted to work, surely. Surely. How could he not understand that?

The newspaper was staring up at her accusingly from the bed. Family's fury. Unknown seller cashes in. Sister devastated. Elderly mother.

She picked it up and forced herself to read on.

The brooch, in the shape of a silver fish, has been listed on a site called KillingTime which specialises in the sale of true crime collectibles, or murderabilia as it is known.

A spokesman for KillingTime last night refused to identify the seller, saying that it would breach their user protocol.

Pamela Kinross said that her family had never fully recovered from Christine's death and that incidents like this only served to reinforce their heartbreak.

'I don't understand what kind of person could do this. It seems vindictive to me. People might think this doesn't hurt anyone but I can assure them that simply isn't true. My mother is 87 years old and she cried herself to sleep last night.'

Shit!

It was ten minutes before he returned. Ten minutes before he'd calmed down enough to talk to her again.

'You know why you've got to rest, right? You know why I'm not happy with this?'

'Yes, I know. You're worried.'

'*Worried?* Rachel, I'm terrified. The thought of losing you or the baby ... I couldn't cope with either of those things happening.'

'They won't happen. Either of them. The doctors are on top of this. It's all going to be fine.'

'It's much more likely to be fine if you do what you're told. Seriously, what do you think you're up to? What was this all about?'

She exhaled hard. 'Sit down. You're making me anxious pacing around like that. Pull up a chair.'

'Have you heard of a short story called "The Yellow Wallpaper"?' she began.

'No. Should I have?'

'Probably not. I read it when I was in university. It's by an American writer called Charlotte Perkins Gilman. Written in the early 1890s. It's regarded as an important piece of feminist literature. Which probably explains why you've never heard of it.'

'Yeah me being such a sexist dinosaur and all that.'

'Exactly. Anyway, the story is about a woman whose husband is a doctor and takes her away for the summer to an old mansion he's rented. He's convinced her she had depression after giving birth and his treatment involves keeping her in one room of this old house and forbidding her from working. She keeps a journal but hides it from the husband and his sister, who's the housekeeper.'

He frowned. 'Am I the husband in this story because if I am—'

'Shush. So, she can't get out of the room apart from

going to the bathroom. She's not allowed to do anything. She gets no mental stimulation at all and so she becomes obsessed with the yellow wallpaper in the room.'

'Okay . . .'

'Pretty soon, all she can think about is yellow and yellow things. Not good yellow things like buttercups but "old, foul, bad yellow things". She fixates over the shapes in the wallpaper, sees the swirls change and move. She sees women hiding round the edges of the pattern and she begins to think she's one of them. She sees someone hiding on all fours behind the wallpaper.'

'So she goes crazy.'

She shook her head at his bluntness. 'Yes, she goes crazy. The husband eventually finds her creeping round the room on all fours, touching the wallpaper. Then she refuses to leave the room and starts to strip the wallpaper to free the woman that's imprisoned behind it.'

'And you're telling me this because . . .?'

'Because if I don't have something to keep my brain in gear then I'm going to be circling these walls and scraping that fucking blue paint off with my nails. And you wouldn't want that, would you? And I might not know where to stop and end up scratching out your pretty blue eyes as well.'

'Okay, I get that but this . . .' He waved his hand at the newspaper.

'I'm not sure you do get it. I've been stuck in here and my mind's had nowhere to go but in on itself and it's not helping. I've been going through these sites . . .'

'You shouldn't have been anywhere near it!'

'Probably not. But I couldn't help myself. Tony, I can't

just lie here and look at those bloody blue walls. They're my yellow wallpaper and I'm not going to let them beat me. Let me do something. Help me, watch me, monitor me, whatever you need. But don't let me start scratching that paint off.'

'You do realise you sound a bit crazy right now?'

'*Don't say that!*'

She'd shrieked it. Surprised herself as much as him. She saw the wary look on his face and tried to backtrack.

'Please don't say that. I'm worried I *am* going crazy. I keep having these dreams. About Sharon Tate – you know, the actress? I keep seeing her and she's pregnant and covered in blood and then I'm bleeding and it's—'

'Whoa. Shh.'

She'd scared him. He had his arms round her, doing the only thing he could think of. It was his holding her like that that made her cry rather than the dream or the fear for her sanity. Or she thought it was – she didn't know anything any more. The tears came thick and fast.

He held her till they stopped. Only then did he let her go enough that he could look her in the eye.

'You're not crazy. Let's get that straight first of all.'

'I've been coming close.'

'Yeah, well that's close enough. If doing something stops you from stressing more and losing it more, then fine. You can do something. But you're not doing it on your own. I'm with you. And I'm *watching* you.'

'Okay. But this guy that was killed and left on the mattress . . .'

He ignored her. 'I don't like it and I don't think it's a

good idea, but, as long as you only go online and make sure you tell me what you're doing, then okay. God help me, okay.'

'I love you. And maybe I need you to save me from this.'

'Yeah, maybe you do. But the guy on the mattress? Calvin Brownlie? We're going to have to talk about him.'

She heard something in his voice and it made her skin tighten.

'Why? What do you know?'

He told her everything about Calvin and she told him everything about Martin.

'Jesus Christ ...'

CHAPTER 33

Nathan didn't have a way, a method. There was no signature style, no identifiable pattern.

Any cop or profiler or psychologist looking for some *modus operandi* would be wasting their time. Nathan didn't work that way. He went with the wind.

Maybe that was why he'd never been caught. They didn't know there was a him, they didn't know there were links. They didn't even know some of them had happened.

Sometimes it was just opportunity and means; there wasn't necessarily a need for motive. Like the time he'd travelled up north, to the Aberdeenshire coast. He'd an idea what he might do but no idea who might be there to do it to. He was happy to go and see, wait his chance.

It was a place near Stonehaven. A beauty spot but cold and windy, even in May. The wind howled off the sea and swirled round your back, especially three hundred feet up on the cliffs. There was a path along the top that people walked, sometimes with their dogs. There was a great view over the sea, so he understood that. Dangerous, though, you'd think.

This woman was walking along the path and Nathan was coming from the other direction. She was attractive, or so he supposed, in her forties, brown hair streaming behind her in the wind. Nathan went to go to his left, towards the sea, at the same time as she went to her right. They both laughed and both changed to go to the other side and they laughed again. Nathan stepped back towards the hillside like a gentleman to let her pass.

She nodded her thanks and began to walk past him. Nathan simply leaned into her with his shoulder and she was gone. The look of astonishment on her face was quite funny. It was open-mouthed confusion more than fear. The fear came soon enough, though, a scream that curdled in the swirl and disappeared with her.

Nathan didn't bother looking over the edge. No point unless the woman had discovered the power of flight halfway down. He knew where she'd be and how she'd be. On the rocks below. Broken.

The newspapers said her name was Rosaleen Burke. Or was it Rosalind? Anyway, she was a mum of two girls, left them and her husband grieving when she jumped from the cliff top without even a suicide note. She was always so friendly and helpful, her neighbours told the press, but she'd been having a difficult time at work. It was agreed her death was a tragedy.

Nathan killed people. It was what he did.

He did his first when he was just seventeen years old. This kid named Brian Horsburgh had been at him for months, hassling him, making fun, pushing his buttons in a way he really shouldn't have. He'd call Nathan weird. Weirdo.

Mongo. Ripping him in front of the crowd. Nathan hated him. Hated him big time.

One day Brian Horsburgh fell in front of a train. People say he was pushed or knocked out and left there, but no one knew. Train destroyed him. Nothing much left for anyone to check. Some of the kids thought Nathan might have done it, but after what happened to Horsburgh they were too scared to come out and say so. That felt good. Felt better than Nathan had ever done before.

Once he started, he couldn't and didn't want to stop.

He'd strangled and he'd stabbed. He'd bludgeoned. On a number of occasions, he'd burned people alive. He had poisoned, he'd drowned and he'd cut throats. He'd gone through the book and he'd started again.

He'd killed through anger. He'd killed in cold blood. He'd done it for revenge, for money and for sexual thrills, out of curiosity, and sometimes just because. People had annoyed him, mocked him, got in his way. Maybe more than anything, he'd found a taste for it. Nothing, but nothing, had given him the thrill that did. Nothing else came close.

Once you'd done it, you wanted to do it again. You could try to fight it but it was your nature and you could never fight that for too long. It itched and itched until you ached to scratch it. And, once you did, it felt so damn good.

There was a taste. A physical taste. Your mouth watered for it. Once you knew, and once you accepted it, you found yourself hungering to taste it again. It was like blood in your mouth, like that taste of iron, or something else metallic and raw and alive. But it was more than just a taste. It was a sensation. Something your entire body felt.

Nathan had done this for a long time. And no one knew. No one even suspected. Few people even seemed to notice him. He'd worked out how to get away with things. When to do it and when to stop, when to move away, when to stay at home and hide.

He'd learned to change his car regularly, rarely keeping one for more than a year. No point in taking the risk of a particular make or model turning up at otherwise unrelated scenes. He had hobbies, bullshit ones, that explained absences to the few people who cared where he was. And he could lie like a politician, a banker and a teenager rolled into one.

What made it easier for him was that people didn't care and that people were stupid. People were reckless, brainless, continually putting themselves in danger, thinking it could never happen to them. You know what? It did. All the time.

The world is full of missing people who aren't missing at all. They're dead. Dead because they took risks, stupid risks. Putting themselves in the wrong place at the wrong time – and it's always the wrong time – just because they wanted sex or money or drugs or a thrill. You get the biggest, most short-lived thrill of them all that way.

Their families, who are at least equally stupid, just keep appealing for them to come home. As if a zombie were going to walk through the door one day, wanting dinner. They are long gone, most probably pushing up daisies in one of Nathan's favourite places. One of those woods that are so dense and unvisited that they are ripe for his needs.

Even Nathan doesn't know how many are in there. Dozens probably.

The central belt of Scotland pulls the whole country in, tight, in the middle. Like a belt. Like a noose. It squeezes it so tight that there's only seventy miles from west to east. Nearly three million people live in that little space yet there's also still room for a whole load of nothing in between.

Take a look at a map and see all the dark-green space that's east of Glasgow and west of Edinburgh. There's a whole load of forested mazes, country lanes and blink-and-you-miss-them villages. There are places where bodies will never be found, where it goes back so far and so dark that only deer or badgers or stray dogs ever bother to go.

There's a big barren triangle, stretching between the two cities and going north as far as Falkirk, the sides of it formed by the M80, M9 and M8. There are places in there that most people have never heard of or couldn't find on a map. Have you ever been to the Black Loch or to Nine Mile Burn? Do you know the woods near Caldercruix or the fields round Slamannan? Course you don't. Just like you don't know the woods near Polbeth, the ones above Avonbridge or the deep stuff north of Blackridge near Drumtassie Burn.

That was Nathan's country. His killing fields. His burial fields. There are places deep in there that he'd used like a potato patch. Come the harvest, the bodies would be coming up like prizewinners.

All these years he'd been hoping that day didn't come. Suited him just fine to have them buried deep, buried shallow, unfound and unloved, sometimes even unmissed. Made it so much simpler to keep doing it, to serve his nature.

Things had changed, though. It didn't matter now if the world knew. Instead, it would soon suit him for it to know. He'd done his thing without recognition for so long when so many others had their headlines. Now it was to be his time. And he'd make sure they remembered him for ever.

CHAPTER 34

It hadn't taken long for the person desperate to buy the Martin Welsh newspaper page to respond to her email.

> Yes, I still want to buy it. I am prepared to pay £300 as you asked. I see you have good feedback for paying so trust you will be the same at sending. Please send the newspaper, in good condition and with the necessary protection.

She'd smiled and spoken to the blue walls, liking them for the first time in an age. 'Will you walk into my parlour, said the spider to the fly.'

The walls had not replied and for that she was grateful. Nor did she reply to the desperado. She made him wait.

She still had two packages from her KillingTime spree to open. She'd done her best to ignore them and had tried to just write them off as a bad idea born out of temporary insanity, but they kept calling to her.

From inside the hall cupboard and behind a box, they cried out. Open us, open us. In the middle of the night they whispered and during the day when Tony wasn't there, they roared. Open us!

She gave in as she knew she would. Once you accept that the damage had been done by buying them, then the step to opening them and feasting on them is an easy one. Her will was weak, her craving strong.

Both packages sat on the bed and she weighed each in turn, like a fifteen-year-old trying to guess what was inside a Christmas present. In the end, like most teenagers, she gave up guessing and ripped the first one open.

Inside the brown envelope was a clear, plastic bag and inside that was a postcard, a written note, two photographs and an extra prized sealed in a plastic sheath. All from State Prison Corcoran in California, USA.

The words scribbled on the postcard said a lot about the sender. She didn't know what any of it meant but it said a lot.

> Tisket Tasket. The head man's basket. The head man said, man you don't need a head man, just accept the sum as a hole in your head as what you thought was your head man.

Scratched on a postcard in his own hand. And from his own crazy head. The head and hands of Charles Manson.

And that wasn't all. It was his head, his hands and his hair.

Long, dark strands of Manson's once-flowing locks were sealed in the plastic casing along with a handwritten note to confirm they'd been cut from his ponytail. She'd had to think hard about whether she really wanted to own that but, in the end, she decided to go for it. She wanted, needed, to know what it felt like. To get some sense of what these collectors were feeling and why they did it. She had to get inside *their* heads.

Tisket. Tasket. The head man's basket.

Charles Manson. Serving nine life sentences, two for murder and seven for conspiracy to murder. The boogie man. Blood all over the hands that wrote the card she was holding. Something inside her flinched and, although her fingers itched to drop it, she forced herself to cling on.

What did she feel? Revulsion. That more than anything. Interest, sure. Interest both professional and salacious. She forgave herself that as being shameful but human. Manson she was disgusted by. Whether evil or insane or just bad to the bone, he orchestrated the murders of nine people. Now he was selling his hair, his signature, his art, the music that was droning in the background at that very minute. He was selling hatred by the dollar.

The problem for her was that she had met, interviewed, comforted, and failed, far too many bereaved relatives to see this as anything other than sickening. Manson killed real people. Other real people had their lives ripped apart as a result. Many of those were still out there, nursing themselves through broken hearts while this kind of shit was bought and sold as memorabilia.

She was glad she'd bought it, though. For all that it turned her stomach, it helped her know what she was after. She'd touched it and she'd know its smell from now on.

The second package was torn open with less relish

because she now knew what was inside. She slowly ripped the top and tipped the contents onto the bed. A sealed plastic bag with a cardboard sleeve, branded 'Hellhouse of Hollywood'. Inside was a simple, broken piece of reddish stone that had once formed part of the fireplace in Cielo Drive. The Tate–Polanski residence. The Murder House.

The idea of collectibles is that they are worth what they are as long as they come in their original packaging. So toys are worth small fortunes as long as they haven't been opened, haven't been played with, haven't been touched or enjoyed. Open them, just once, and their value shrinks with the air.

She tore into the sealed packaging and let the contents fall into the palm of her hand.

It was cool and rough at the edges. She turned it between her fingers, getting a sense of it, feeling every cut and broken border. She smelled it. A nostril full of brick and mortar, maybe smoke. Maybe blood.

She knew she was feeling more than there was. It was just a piece of old brick. Something that had once been something whole and now was broken. The fireplace had been a silent witness to a terrible event, but it had shed no tears, felt no pain. It was brick, not blood.

She told herself that and repeated it when the stone wouldn't leave her hand. She felt more than the dust and the clay and the shale. She felt history and hurt and horror. The brick suddenly felt as hot as if the fireplace still burned, and she dropped it onto the bed, bundling it back into its envelope once it had cooled to the touch.

She put the lock of Manson's hair back in its packaging

too and she hid both again in the hall cupboard behind the box. Then she washed her hands.

Back on KillingTime, she returned to the message from RD. She'd made him wait long enough. She was the spider and she had a web waiting for him.

> Okay, I'll take your £300. I'll sell you the page.
> All I need is to know where to send it.

And to tell Tony where he has to go to find you.

CHAPTER 35

Robert Dalrymple opened the door warily, like someone expecting bad news.

Or maybe he'd received that already when Winter telephoned to say he'd be calling at his door to discuss the newspaper front page he'd bought to add to his Martin Welsh collection. He'd had to call back twice to make sure the man knew he was not going to give up and go away.

Winter got the distinct impression that the man was considering changing his mind now, though, and was about to close the door in his face. He held his front door ajar, one hand grasping it firmly so that he could quickly push it back towards Winter if needed.

He sized up both Winter and the situation, a nervous swallow confirming his uncertainty. He sighed deep and hard, then opened the door wide. 'Come in.'

The house was a cottage, standing in isolation at one end of the village of Balerno, just eight miles southwest of Edinburgh city centre. It was a picturesque little place, its main street all cobbled slopes, handsome houses and independent shops.

The cottage's whitewashed walls were woven with climbing plants while a neat window box sat on each sill, populated with happy yellow and purple flowers. The rear of the cottage seemed to lose itself in the woods, making for a back garden that went on for ever. Parked in front, tight up against the sandstone walls, was an ageing Volvo.

The house's owner was a tall, overweight man in his mid-sixties. His grey hair was confined to either side of his head, and he wore a fussy goatee. Silver spectacles added to the impression of a university professor, or maybe a historical novelist.

Whatever his role, Robert Dalrymple was not happy that he had company.

'I don't need to have this conversation, you do know that? I have done nothing illegal. This is just a hobby.'

'It's a rather strange hobby, don't you think?'

'That's a matter of opinion. I don't find anything strange about it, but I suppose I can appreciate why some people would. People who don't understand it.'

Dalrymple was very defensive but trying not to be. It was there in his voice, though, unmistakeably so.

'Perhaps you could tell me how you came to start collecting murderabilia. Or is that even what you call it?'

He shrugged, uneasy at letting Winter into his world.

'It's as good a name as any. A bit tacky, perhaps, but I didn't invent it. I guess it covers what it is. As to how I got started ... it just sort of grew. Look, Mr Winter, I really don't want any sensational tabloid exposé here. I think that would be really unfair. It's why I agreed to talk to you. To let you understand that it's not like that.'

'So what is it like? I'm keen to learn, Mr Dalrymple. To give your side of the story.'

The words sounded hollow to Winter, so God knows how unconvincing they were to Dalrymple. Lying for a living still didn't come naturally, even after a year in the job.

'It's no different to any other hobby. No different to stamp collecting or butterflies or beer mats. It's like anyone who collects movie memorabilia or old toys or antiques. People have interests, whatever sparks it, and they collect things they enjoy. Sometimes that can become a business, and then it's a win–win situation.'

Apart from those who've been murdered, Winter thought, but didn't say. He needed to ask some easier questions before he got to the more difficult ones. Archie Cameron had taught him that if there was one question that was likely to get him thrown out of an interview, then ask it last.

'What was the first thing you collected?'

Dalrymple was wrestling with himself over how much he could trust Winter. On a scale of one to ten, lack of trust probably registered at eleven. But the alternative was to leave Winter to write it as he pleased.

'A letter written from prison by Peter Manuel. It didn't say much except how he was innocent and the legal system was conspiring against him. It was written in his own hand from his cell in Barlinnie.'

'The same hands that had killed nine people?' Winter bit his tongue, too late, but Dalrymple didn't seem to notice or care.

'I suppose that was part of it. But it's a piece of history first and foremost. Manuel is the most notorious murderer in twentieth-century Scotland. He went on a killing spree that will never be replicated. I've no doubt that a relic belonging to him is as valid as that from a politician, a king or an artist.'

Winter nodded, seeing some of the merit of the argument, whether he liked to or not.

'And how did you get hold of it?'

'I bought it. Simple as that. I read that it was up for sale and I was willing to pay the asking price.'

'From whom?'

Dalrymple shook his head firmly. 'No. That's always sacrosanct. Identities are protected. No deals would be done if people didn't respect each other's right to privacy. Which leads me to *my* question. How did you know to come to my door?'

It was a query Winter was ready for. He intended to tell some but not all of the truth.

'The newspaper front page you bought concerning the disappearance of Martin Welsh? You bought it from me.'

'That was *you*? How . . .' The man was angry at being deceived. 'How did you get the piece in the first place?'

Winter gave the merest shrug of his shoulders. 'Identities must be protected. Privacy must be respected. You understand.'

'You bought it on KillingTime, but how did you get it before me?'

If you're not fast, you're last, Winter thought but didn't say. 'I got lucky, I guess.'

Winter could see the wheels turning in Dalrymple's head. Dubious of coincidences and not liking it. Dots being joined and guesses being made. It wouldn't matter much if he made the right guess or the wrong one. They now operated under some dubious code of honour among thieves.

'You're a journalist and yet you own this? Do you have other Martin Welsh items?' Dalrymple's enquiry was coy.

'Not as many as you, I'm sure. But, yes, I have more,' he lied.

'I would be interested if you have. What more can I tell you about my collection?'

'What else do you have? Am I right in saying I can see some of it hanging on your walls?'

Dalrymple looked over his shoulder as if surprised to see it hanging there. 'Yes. Some of it is framed. Letters, artwork, that kind of thing. I like to have it on display.'

'May I look?'

'Okay.' Winter got the distinct impression that Dalrymple was operating somewhere between being guarded and showing off.

'Before I show you anything, I must remind you that I will not be photographed, either alongside my collection or on my own. Okay?'

'I understand.'

'Fine. This . . .' – Dalrymple stopped in front of a black frame with a white inset – 'is a letter from Charles Ng. He raped and murdered somewhere between eleven and twenty-five people. There's a significant market in his memorabilia.'

'The more you kill the more you're worth?'

Dalrymple turned to look at him. 'Yes. Pretty much. Or the more rare it is. Ng took up painting in San Quentin. They're not particularly good but the value's not in the quality of the art. I have this piece . . .'

A simple white frame held an odd watercolour showing a mermaid reaching up to stroke the underside of a swimming shark. Winter couldn't separate the artwork, if it could even be called that, from its creator. This 'description' came from the disturbed mind, the same violent hands that had orchestrated the killing of so many. Was this piece worth more or less because it had been crafted by a mass murderer? And what did it say about the society that deemed it more?

The next frame incongruously held a painting of a clown. Winter stopped and stared at it, Dalrymple sensing, and delighting in, his confusion. 'It's a self-portrait by a children's entertainer by the name of Pogo the Clown. He was a big hit at children's parties until he got arrested under his real name. John Wayne Gacy.'

Winter moved from frame to frame, killer to killer, seeing an arrest warrant for Clyde Barrow and an original wanted poster for the 1920s American gangster Pretty Boy Floyd.

There were frames with just white sheets of paper containing nothing but signatures. Prison-cell sell-offs by men who'd never see daylight again. Dennis Nilsen. Peter Tobin. Ian Brady. Rodney Alcala. The creepiest of celebrities.

A deeper frame, more like a glass box, held a single piece of red half-brick.

'It's from Cromwell Street,' Dalrymple explained from behind him. 'Something like that couldn't be demolished without at least one person helping themselves to a souvenir.'

Cromwell Street. Home to Fred and Rose West. The house of horrors.

'And you had to have it?'

'Not just me. There are almost as many pieces of that house floating around as there of the Berlin Wall. It's popular.'

Winter choked back an answer and toyed with the man's ego instead. 'Do you have anything from the Wests that no one else might have?'

There was a hesitancy that had to mean yes but instead only a half-smile played on his fat lips. 'I'd never buy anything that was illegal. Everything I have is legitimate and above board.'

It was a yes disguised as a no passing itself off as *I'm not telling you*. Winter moved it on.

'Would I be right in saying your main collecting focus is the Martin Welsh case?'

Dalrymple was troubled, seemingly not sure how best to answer.

'I have a number of items connected to that case, yes. I'm not sure if it's my main focus.'

I am, thought Winter. 'Can you show me some of the things you have?'

'I'm really not sure that's appropriate. The case is still strictly active as no body has ever been found. Most of his family are very much alive, too, and I'd hate to cause them any more heartache.'

'Perhaps if you could just show me a couple of things that you have.'

He hesitated but gave in, conditionally. 'Okay, I will, but I'd rather you didn't include this in any article. Out of respect for his family. I wouldn't want them to think anyone was profiting from Martin's demise.'

Winter weighed it up and decided it gave him a bargaining chip. 'Okay, I won't.'

'I appreciate that. And I'm sure Martin's mother and sister would, too.'

Dalrymple went to a white door and pulled it back to reveal a walk-in cupboard. He closed the door behind him and emerged moments later with a large flat jewellery case that might have once held an expensive necklace. He flipped the catch and opened the case to reveal a letter in a protective plastic folder.

'This is a letter written to Martin by his mother after he disappeared. She wrote it for publication in a newspaper in the hope he might read it. It's an original and a one-off.'

'That must be worth quite a bit.'

The man looked offended at the very suggestion. 'That's as maybe, but it's not why I have it. I'm afraid you don't understand. It's not about the value. Let me show you something.'

He went back into the white-doored cupboard and Winter could see him reaching up towards a shelf. When he came back out, he had a small brown box held carefully in his hands.

He placed it on a hexagonal wooden table and eased off the lid. Winter had no option but to lean forward, consumed by curiosity, to see what was inside. There was a clear plastic bag, sealed at the top and preserving a square, yellowing object within.

He turned to look at Dalrymple, ready to ask what the bag held, and saw that the man had slipped on a pair of white cotton gloves. Like a very twisted magician, Winter thought.

He reached into the box, withdrawing the bag and opening it. He brought out a small book, its cover having no words on it but just a mottled design.

'Hold out your hand. And try not to sweat.'

The two instructions were suddenly contrary to each other. Winter placed his right hand out, palm up, and waited. Dalrymple placed the book gently onto his hand and left it there.

'The value of this is incredibly difficult to ascertain. Maybe it has none. Maybe it's priceless. You know of the Edinburgh grave robbers Burke and Hare?' Winter nodded. 'William Burke was convicted in 1828 for the crime of murder. He had delivered corpses to the eminent university surgeon Robert Knox. The irony is that, after his trial and execution, his body was sold to the same department for medical research that he'd previously sold to. His corpse was skinned and his skeleton remains in the university to this day. As for his skin, it too was sold. Some of it was made into objects, curios, you might say. Like the one you're holding in your hand.'

Sgriob. It was a word Winter hadn't thought of it in a while. It was a Gaelic word, an expression, referring to the buzz of anticipation on the lips before tasting a good whisky. He had his own version of that. His *sgriob* was buzzing now while he was holding the flayed peel of the serial killer on his own flesh.

Outwardly, and for Dalrymple's benefit, he flinched.

Dalrymple saw the reaction he was supposed to and smiled, lifting the book from Winter's hand. 'Let's not have you sweating on this now.'

He assiduously placed the book back in the plastic bag and the bag in the box. He stepped inside the walk-in cupboard, the door half-closing behind him, and re-emerged empty-handed. The show was over.

'So, I asked you earlier how you came to knock at my door. You didn't tell me the truth – or at least not all of it. Did you?'

He took Winter's stumbling, surprised silence as an admission of that truth. 'Because, although I did purchase that newspaper front page, I didn't have it delivered here.'

It had taken longer to get to this point than Winter had expected, but it was nonetheless inevitable for that. He explained the subterfuge to the man.

'No, you had it sent to what they call an accommodation service. An address off George Street in Edinburgh. I sent it guaranteed and trackable next-day delivery as requested and rightly assumed you would want it as soon as it arrived. I didn't have long to wait until you came for it and saw you leave with it tucked under your arm.'

Dalrymple's faced flushed, one part embarrassment to three parts anger.

'You had no right—'

'Well that's debatable. I'm going to go for "public

interest" on this one. But it does make me wonder: if all this is just a hobby like any other, if it's nothing to be ashamed of, why do you go to all the trouble of hiding it?'

The interview was ended immediately and he found himself standing outside the cottage door with it closed firmly in his face.

CHAPTER 36

She'd had the Sharon Tate nightmare again. The sight of her turning away, the blonde hair and then the bloodied nightdress as the figure disappeared into the blue wall. She'd woken up crying. Crying for herself or for Sharon, she wasn't quite sure. Tears of fear or of compassion, she didn't know. She burst out of sleep gasping for air and with soft sobs streaming down her cheeks. It scared her.

She was still following auction sales on KillingTime, monitoring bargains or just watching prices soar. It was research.

There were people out there ready to spend serious money to get what they wanted. Thousands of pounds or dollars on some piece of shit that happened to have been drawn or worn or sung by a murderer.

Sometimes she could see when they were paying over the odds and wondered whether it was just a buyer who didn't know the market or had so much money they didn't care. She'd find herself shouting at the laptop. *Idiots. Too much.*

She still found herself toying with the idea of buying things but managed to resist. Still, if there was something quirky or dark, she'd be interested in it. She'd look up killers she'd never heard of just because a collectible caught her eye. She'd become hooked as surely as if the murderabilia had been liquidised and shot into her veins through a hypodermic.

When she saw Sharon Tate's engagement ring was up for auction, she sat up in bed and brought the laptop closer to her. She felt a thrill go through her that she barely recognised but knew she didn't like.

She stared at the photograph. A large, oval, four-carat opal, surrounded by twenty-four garnet gems. Next to the image of the ring was another, showing Sharon wearing it. Her blonde hair tumbled either side of her face, eyes wide, eyebrows raised, lashes heavy, mouth open in a perfect bow. Her hand was by her mouth, one manicured nail tugging playfully at her lower lip, the opal ring clearly visible.

The clincher was that the site claimed Sharon was wearing the ring when she was butchered by the Manson Family. The starting price was eleven thousand dollars.

She didn't have eleven thousand dollars to blow on a ring. A new bathroom or kitchen, maybe, but not a ring. Not a ring someone was wearing when she was murdered. Yet she bookmarked the item and kept coming back, watching the bids climb and wondering if she could justify it as an investment. She'd rebuke herself, knowing it was only an excuse, and yet she'd check back and then check again.

She did some research on it, despite her sensible head urging her to close the laptop, and learned Polanski bought it for Sharon in 1967, the year before they got married in London and two years before she was murdered. Her morbid curiosity grew and grew. All the while, she could see the blonde fringe and the open mouth as the head turned away from her, disappearing out of view in a waking dream.

Then she read that Sharon hadn't been wearing the ring when she was killed after all. Not according to her sister Debra, who said the ring wasn't her style and she gave it to a friend long before she was killed. Debra said she'd never actually worn it, even though the photograph seemed to suggest otherwise. But then there was the deal breaker. Sharon couldn't wear any rings at the time of the killing because her fingers were too swollen from the pregnancy. Narey looked at her own thickening fingers and knew it was true.

Her interest in the ring fell off a cliff. It was because Sharon hadn't worn it, she told herself.

CHAPTER 37

Narey had learned long ago that Danny Neilson knew pretty much everything. If he didn't, he'd know someone who would.

Tony always said his uncle was the smartest man he'd ever known and she wasn't going to argue. Danny came loaded with both kinds of smart: wisdom born out of a life lived on the streets, and also knowledge, loads of it. And he'd been a cop, which meant he also understood her and what she might need.

Given how much she needed to keep this to herself, Danny seemed her best bet. The hi-tech nature of the subject wasn't ideal, but he'd know someone – he always did. The problem would be convincing him that she should be doing anything at all, but she thought she had the answer to that.

'Hey, Danny, it's Rachel.'

'Rach! Everything okay?'

'Oh, I'm fine. Everyone's worrying over nothing. I'm just bored silly.'

'You think? Well, I'm going to worry, if it's all right with you. It's my job.'

'Seeing as it's you, I'll let you get away with it. Listen, Dan, I wanted to pick your brains about something.'

He made a grunting noise that suggested scepticism. 'I'm already not liking the sound of this, but on you go.'

He was going to be hard work, but it would, hopefully, be worth it.

'Okay. There's things I want to find online. I'm sure what I want is there but I can't find it. I need to know if there's some . . . other place, somewhere under the radar that they might be. So I need someone to tell me where I can look. That make sense?'

He made the same sceptical sound. 'Wait a minute. Complete bed rest and relaxation, that's the way I heard it. Doesn't sound to me like that's what you're doing. I'm not sure I should be helping you at all.'

'I'm in bed – and no intention of getting out of it. As for relaxation, I can't relax with nothing to do. You know what that's like. You retired and hated it. Couldn't sit around doing nothing, right? Well that's the way I am right now. I'm much more likely to be relaxed and stress-free if I can at least give my brain a workout.'

The silence on the other end of the line was Danny weighing it up.

'It makes some sense. But it hardly answered my question. Tell me you're not doing anything that puts you or my new nephew or niece at risk.'

'*Great*-nephew or -niece. And, no, I'm not.'

'Nephew or niece. Great-Uncle Daniel makes it sound like I should be in the Wombles or a retirement home. I'm not ready for either of those yet. Okay, what do you want to find? And, more to the point, why do you want to find it?'

She didn't want to give up any more of this than she had to. Not yet, anyway.

'If someone wanted to sell something – or buy something, come to that – and the normal sites that dealt in it wouldn't touch it, is there somewhere else they'd go? I'm not expecting you to know but thought you might know someone who does.'

'You didn't expect me to know because I'm old and this is all young person's stuff? Give me some credit, Rachel. I may be a dinosaur but I've moved on a bit from learning about digital watches. I make a point of keeping up with whatever I need to know.'

'Sorry, Dan.'

'Don't be. Looking like a dinosaur is one of my best disguises. They never see me coming. As for where you'd go to buy or sell something dodgy online, have you heard of the dark net? Sometimes called the dark web or deep web?'

'I think so. Yes.'

'That's where you need to go.'

'As simple as that?'

'Ha. No. Nowhere near it. And that's where you should go. Nowhere near it. What's this all about, Rach? And I'm not buying it's just to stop you from being bored. That's what *The Jeremy Kyle Show* is for.'

'I've been nosing around and there's something that interests me. Think it will interest you, too.'

'Try me.'

'Martin Welsh.'

'The bus-stop boy?'

'Did you work the case?'

'No, but I know guys who did, and I follow it as close as any of my own. Like every cop, every parent, did. If you're a certain age, it's a huge case.'

'What if I said I might have a lead?'

Danny whistled. 'I'd say I'll be at yours in half an hour. Don't bother putting the kettle on, I'll do it when I get there.'

'I remember it like it was yesterday. Nineteen seventy-three. That spring and summer, it was all about Martin. The boy was everywhere. Plenty of us were hoping to get the call to join the investigation but it didn't come for me. I still read everything I could, watched every news bulletin, talked to everyone I knew who was working the case. You couldn't help but think it might as easily have been one of your own.'

'Who did you like for it at the time?'

He shrugged his big-bear shoulders. 'It was all second-hand guessing. Not my favourite way of policing. But ... I never liked the father. Alex Welsh just came across as a quick-tempered, violent, cowardly little sod. I didn't believe he was grieving the way he should. The way I know I would have. The mother was a wreck, a strong, strong wreck, but she was bleeding. The dad wasn't.'

'That's Scottish men and women for you.'

'Ha. Maybe, aye. Also, I know I'd have liked to have spoken more to the lorry driver, Michael Hill. It seemed awfully convenient to me that he was there at just that time and no one could know if the boy had got in or not. Nothing more to go on than that.'

'What about Alastair Haldane?'

'He was the popular choice, certainly. Quite a few of the cops on the case thought it was him but they had nothing much to go on. It was mainly local gossip and circumstantial. There was more than a whiff of mob rule about it. They did everything short of standing at the school gates with pitchforks. He didn't do it for me, though.'

'You don't think he killed Martin?'

'Like I say, I don't like guessing, but no. I don't think he did. He was just a bit weird and people had him convicted because of that. What do you make of this guy Dalrymple?'

She shrugged. 'I don't know. But I don't like the way he's so desperate to get things connected to Martin. My instincts tell me there's something there.'

'Mine too. So talk me through it some more, this thing you shouldn't be doing. I'm getting that it's all about crime collectibles, this Dalrymple plus Tony trying to buy the McAlpine kid's clothes from the guy at Hampden, but what do you actually think is going on here?'

'I'm not sure, Danny. I've had my head stuck in this thing so deep that I can't see out again. Maybe I'm just stir crazy. Or plain old-fashioned crazy. I've not been sleeping and, when I have, the dreams are weird. Really weird.'

'One thing I'm sure of: you're not crazy. Now, tell your old Uncle Danny all about it.'

'So how do I get into the dark web?'

'Well, first of all you shouldn't. You really shouldn't. But, if you do, you need special software for a start. Everything is encrypted to the *n*th degree. There's no way to hack it without the software.'

'Where do I get it?'

She heard him breathe out hard. 'You don't. I know a man who can get it. Leave it with me. I must be off my head but I'll sort it. Even then, though, you're still going to have to find a way into the places you want. You'll need passwords and an invitation.'

'Okay, let's worry about them later. What am I going to find when I get in there?'

'It's a vipers' nest. You can buy anything you want on there. It doesn't matter how illegal, how dangerous, how immoral, you can get it. Guns, drugs, sex, kids, those bastards trade in the worst of human depravity. It's unpoliced but guarded like Fort Knox. When the cyber cops do catch up, which isn't often enough, then they start again like cockroaches after a nuclear holocaust. My advice, which I know you'll ignore, is not to go near it. You don't know what you're doing.'

'Which is why I'm asking you.'

'I don't know either. I know *about* it but not how to operate in there. It's a different world. If you do go in, go slow. And watch your back.'

'You make it sound like I'm going into another country.'

'Worse. It's another world. Listen, you can be anyone you want on the dark net. Do anything you want. All you have to do is pay for it; all you need is to know where to look. But the problem with being anyone you want is that people make bad choices.

'You think people act bad on the Internet because they're

unknown? It's nothing compared to the dark side. It's depressing, Rachel. The way people act when they can be assured of being and remaining anonymous. They don't act well. They act very, very badly.

'Listen, we try to kid ourselves on that people are basically good, but the way they behave in the dark web tells us it's not true. The only thing that encourages them to behave decently is the fear of being caught. When that risk is removed, they revert to the animals they are.'

'Danny, I'm bringing a child into this world. I can't let myself believe it's that bad.'

He shrugged apologetically. 'Sorry, love. But there's only one reason the deep web is dark. And that's because human nature is dark. We've both seen enough of it to know that's true.'

She stared at him, hiding herself from the truth. 'So you can get me the software. But what about passwords and an invitation?'

He looked grim. 'Well, there might be a way.'

CHAPTER 38

It had been three years since Danny stood in the rain-lashed tarmac car park in front of HMP Blackridge along with Tony and wondered what awaited them inside its tall, grey walls. The weather was the same that day as this, although you'd have got very short odds from a bookie on its being any different. His sense of foreboding was the same, too.

He hadn't been convinced Atto would agree to see him, nor was he sure he wanted him to. The man was a monster, convicted of the murder of four young women but undoubtedly guilty of killing many others. Danny couldn't look at him without wanting to rip his head off.

He and Tony had gone to see Atto when a string of murders took place in the city that mimicked the Red Silk killings of the early seventies. These were crimes that Danny had investigated back then and that Atto was thought to be responsible for.

He turned his collar to the rain and let his mind wander inside, thinking what kind of reception he might get. Quite possibly, Atto was going to spit in his face and send him back on his way. Danny checked the time and knew there was nothing else to be done. He had to go in and he had to do it now.

The guard who led him to the visiting room had remembered him from a previous visit. A stocky guy with a bald bullet head and a scowl stitched to his face. He instructed him to sit at one side of the table and to keep his hands in sight at all times. When the forty-five-minute session was over, the prisoner would exit the room but Danny would remain seated. Did he understand? He did.

When the door to the room slid back, there was a sense of the man even before he was seen. There was a pause, quite probably for dramatic effect, before Atto stole into view. He was the same unremarkable everyman he'd always been but he looked distinctly older. More lines in his face and more grey in his hair, heavier too. He sat down and slowly made himself comfortable before he deigned to look at his visitor. He was making the point that he had the power.

When he finally lifted his head, his dark, dead eyes drifted over Danny as if measuring him for a coffin.

'Well, well, Mr Neilson. You never write, you never call . . . It's almost as if you don't care.'

Mister Neilson. Atto liked to remind Danny that he wasn't a cop any more. Any little edge he could find to put himself in charge. Danny's instinct was to tell him to get stuffed but today he needed Atto's help, so he reined it in.

'We can cut the shit if you want and just get straight to it.'

'Fine by me. What made you think I'd even see you? You're a piece of shit, Mr Neilson.'

'So why did you agree to let me visit?'

'I was curious. Wondering what it would have taken for you to show your face here again. Is it to do with the body found hanging at Queen Street?'

Danny's mouth betrayed him, opening just enough to let Atto know he'd been right. A smile spread slow and wide over the man's face. It had been a guess, a bloody guess. Danny cursed himself for showing it.

'Interesting. I saw your nephew's photograph that hit all the front pages. Nice picture. I was a bit disappointed that he switched professions, though. Journalists are such utter arseholes, don't you think, Mr Neilson? He'll never be as happy doing that as he was photographing dead bodies. He's got a dark heart. And I should know what that's like.'

'He's not like you, Atto. Nothing like it. His heart might be a bit dark but it's good. Not sure we can say that about you, can we?'

'So . . .' Atto ignored him and was thinking out loud. 'This poor bastard is found swinging from a rope, the MSP's son, and somehow that's brought you to visit me. Very interesting. Your nephew's police friend, Miss Narey, was investigating the case and then she wasn't. She got promoted, didn't she? I was so happy for the bitch.'

Danny didn't rise to it for all that his fist was curling into a ball.

'So you're here because of her. But why?'

'I want some information. And you can give it to me.'

Atto laughed. 'You're in a bad way if you're relying

on me for help, old man. In fact, you must be desperate because you know what the chances are of me wanting to help you after what you did.'

Three years earlier, Danny had taken away much of the thing Atto treasured most. His notoriety. And Atto hated him for it. Danny's only hope was to offer to give some of it back.

'The kid's clothing that Tony photographed? Some of it was missing. And I think it was taken so it could be sold. And I think you can help me with that.'

Atto grinned slyly. '*You* think that? Or she does? No matter, tell me what makes you think I know anything about that?'

Danny knew he was being played, could hear it in Atto's voice, but went along with it anyway. 'There is a market in such things. They call it murderabilia.'

'Is that so? *Fascinating.*'

He heard the tone. Teasing. Mocking. But it confirmed what he'd suspected and it gave him hope. He continued.

'People are selling things, things like the clothing that belonged to Aiden McAlpine. Things that have a value because they're connected to a murder. A high-profile murder. There are a couple of sites specialising in these sales. And among the things being sold on one of those sites were items of yours.'

All he got was a shrug. 'I'd be disappointed if there wasn't. I'm famous, you know.'

There it was, Atto's ego. His weak link.

'Aye, you used to be famous. But, you see, the interesting thing about that stuff was that two of them were put up for sale just two months ago. And the only person I can think could have sourced them to sell is you.'

Atto spread his arms. 'Maybe. But I'm in prison. In case you'd forgotten.'

'I thought we were going to cut the shit. You sold these or had them sold. I want you to tell me how it all works.'

'Why should I?'

'You want your face in the papers again. You want your name back in the headlines. Tony can give you that. Notorious murderer sells trophies while behind bars, that kind of thing. Just the way you like it.'

'Maybe.'

'Up to you. No one's talked about you for a long time and I can't see that changing unless you take this chance. You're yesterday's news.'

It stung, and the hate flared in Atto's eyes.

'If I'm yesterday's man, why are people so keen to buy anything they can that's connected to me? They snap it up because of who I am. Because of what I did. My name's worth money. My things are wanted because I *did* something.'

Keep talking, big man, keep talking.

'I could put my toenail clippings up for sale and some idiot would buy them. Because I'm *somebody*. I'm famous.'

'Only amongst the freaks that want this stuff. Not with the public. They've forgotten you.'

'Fuck you! I know you're winding me up but you're wrong. The ones you call freaks want me because the public knows me. If I make one of my trinkets available then they're snapped up right away. The little trophies I earned from some of the young ladies I'd met along the way.'

Young ladies. He meant the girls he'd murdered. Melanie Holt. Louise Shillington. Beverley Collins. Emma Rutherford. And the unknown rest.

A drawer had been found in Atto's house. A horror find of jewellery, twenty-six items in all. Brooches, ladies' watches, bracelets, pendants, rings and necklaces. Pieces that had been stripped from their owners, stripped from the dead.

'They were all found by the police.'

'All?' Atto sneered gleefully. 'Not all.'

'So you sell it. How? How do you do it from prison when you aren't even allowed Internet access.'

Danny knew the answer to his own question but he wanted to give Atto the chance to gloat and show off.

The smile was suitably smug. 'Getting hold of a mobile phone with Internet access is no problem. Expensive but not a problem. You think an iPhone is expensive on the high street? It sells for three times the price in here. Do you know what the record is for one person smuggling in phones hidden up their arse?'

Danny shook his head.

'Three. Plus a charger. Impressive or just stupid, what do you think?

'Probably both. I need to know who does the buying. Who are the collectors?'

'The collectors on these sites aren't the people you're looking for. It's kid's stuff. You'll only see a fraction of my sales on there and very rarely any of the good stuff.'

'So where?'

'The real sales, the heavy-duty items? They're done elsewhere, and most go to a particular group of collectors. It's all off the grid. Have you heard of the dark web?'

Bingo. 'Vaguely. Who are this group of collectors?'

'Never mind. You wouldn't even know where to look. I sell on a dark-net market. A cryptomarket called *Abbadon*. It's a place you can buy and sell the kind of things you're looking for.'

'Abbadon?'

'It's a Hebrew term. Means bottomless pit, the place of destruction. It's also the name of the angel of the abyss, a demon known as the destroyer.'

'Christ!'

Atto laughed. 'Oh, I doubt you'll find Christ in there, Mr Neilson. Just the Devil. And there will be no one that can save your soul because, if you're in there, you've already lost yours. Or sold it.'

'So how do I get in?'

'You don't. That's the whole point. It's by invitation only.

'And who can invite me?'

Atto's smile broadened into a malicious grin. 'Just me. I very much doubt anyone else you know can get you in. It's an interesting place.'

'Then do it and your name will be back up in lights again, just the way you like it.'

'Make sure you spell my name right.'

As Danny made his way out of Blackridge and across the car park in teeming rain, he did so armed with an invitation into hell. What he couldn't see was a man sitting alone in his prison cell with a large, satisfied grin on his face.

If he'd been able to see it, he would have assumed it was because the man's ego had been satisfied and he was purring at the prospect of publicity. He would have been wrong.

CHAPTER 39

She'd chosen Myra as her username on Abbadon. It seemed appropriate enough for being on a dark-net market. Sure, she didn't feel entirely comfortable naming herself after one of the UK's most infamous killers but she'd long since given up on the morals of the thing. It was about doing what she needed to.

Myra had the key to get inside. Myra had the software, the right words, and she had the bitcoins. She wanted to know what was out there and she was a serious player. Or at least she hoped she could convince them she was.

Myra was going to buy and she was going to chat and she was going to learn whatever she could.

As it turned out, being in was one thing, but getting anyone to deal with you was another. Not only was the site encrypted so as to keep out anyone without a key, but areas within Abbadon were also padlocked. Access to those were not granted without the say-so of those already inside the walls.

As soon as she entered, she was seen and challenged by a gatekeeper.

Who are you?

Newbie. Not to the field but to this market.

How did you find us?

A mutual friend.

Name?

No chance.

Name!?

No way. If it takes giving up someone's name to get in this place, then it's maybe not for me.

Nothing. She waited. It was probably only thirty seconds but seemed longer. Then the screen moved.

A member pointed the way?

Yes.

Tell me one thing.

Polar bears aren't all left-handed. It's a myth.

Okay. Fair enough. So what areas are you interested in Myra?

Scotland. Peter Tobin and Archibald Atto. And the Martin Welsh case.

Another wait.

> *Okay. Tobin we can do. Atto too. Martin Welsh will be more difficult but you're welcome to try and if you've got the funds then maybe it can happen.*

Well good.

> *Have you got the funds?*

I'm here to spend.

> *Not yet. You need to bring something to the table. This place isn't just for buying and we need to know you can be a provider. Can you do that?*

I think so.

> *Then do it. Then come back and talk.*

Okay.

> *Good luck, Myra . . .*

The last line sounded as much like a warning as good wishes. *You'll need it*. That was the subtext. Or else she was getting paranoid.

She'd been deep in it, this world of murderabilia. And she was getting deeper.

There was a guy her dad had arrested in the early eighties, an amateur boxer named Harry 'Hurricane' Donnelly.

Harry was very useful by all accounts, just twenty-two but lined up for a shot at the Scottish heavyweight title. Until it all went wrong.

He came home from a long training run to his house in Denny to find his manager in bed with his wife. Arthur Grant had been the one who suggested he should go for the run after work and sweet little Maureen had said it was a good idea. It might have been okay for everyone, except that Harry ran faster than they thought.

Harry beat them both to death. He said later he might have been able to walk away from what he'd seen but Maureen had laughed at him and then Arthur joined in. He lost it and pummelled them until the walls were sprayed with blood.

Harry went on the run for nearly two weeks and that was what really hit the headlines. He'd headed north, thinking he could hide out in the hills SAS-style. First he picked up supplies in the village shop in Plockton but a six-foot-four stranger built like a heavyweight gets recognised quite easily in a place like that. He moved on before the cops got there but then he was spotted in Applecross and again in Torridon. THE HURRICANE'S HIGHLAND HIDEWAY, the papers screamed. Sightings of the double murderer became a national pastime. The *Sun* put up a ten-thousand-pounds reward for information leading to his capture.

After ten days on the run, a farmer named Jack Jamieson saw the Hurricane on the road near Kinlochewe and decided to claim the money for himself. Jamieson was a big guy and armed with a pitchfork but, after a tussle witnessed by a neighbouring farmer, Harry Donnelly took the pitchfork and drove it through the man's heart.

His running didn't last long after that. The cops, led by her dad, arrived *en masse* and chased him to ground. He was photographed being dragged off the hills, stripped to the waist with a rucksack over his shoulders and looking like a bare-knuckle pin-up. He got twenty years and three proposals of marriage.

The drive to Glasgow took three hours, her dad and handcuffed Harry in the back seat. They talked because there was nothing else to do and Harry told him everything. A big, soft lump was how her dad described him. Nice lad who went a bit crazy. They talked boxing and football and her dad made the driver stop at Fort William to get Harry some food.

A few weeks later, Harry's lawyer turned up at the station asking to see her dad. He said how the Hurricane had liked him and said he was fair and that was all he could have asked for. Then he gave him a plastic carrier bag with Harry's boxing gloves in it. Well-used red leather, initialled 'HD' and made to fit the hands that beat two people to death. He'd signed them, too, as they were going to go into a charity auction, but now they were a present to say thanks for being the good cop.

Her dad always kept the gloves, a story to tell people when they came round. Now she had them. And now she had a use for them.

She scoured the surface murderabilia sites for anything relating to Harry Donnelly. There wasn't a lot and the few things available weren't cheap. However, after less than half an hour, she'd made three purchases and they'd already been dispatched.

She bought a fight poster: Harry the Hurricane against Bobby Dow for the western district heavyweight title, signed by Harry himself. It set her back a hundred pounds but she thought it was worth it. For just seventy-five quid, she also got hold of a handwritten letter he sent from HM Prison Peterhead to one of the women who wanted to marry him. And, finally, she splashed out two hundred pounds for a cassette recording of Harry singing 'Flower of Scotland' down the phone to another of the wannabe fiancées, the one he finally married in the prison chapel.

Now she had a bundle. A proper portfolio of murderabilia with the boxing gloves being the highlight. She had something she could take to Abbadon and hopefully be her ticket in. It wasn't maybe the level of gore that they'd expect but, short of digging up Harry's victims, it was all she had.

And it's genuine? All of it?

Yes.

Where did you get the gloves?

I'm not saying. But they're Donnelly's. I've got a photograph of him wearing them and you can also check the signature.

We will. Post a photograph of them.

Okay.

Why are you selling them on here and not on a surface site? If they're what you say they are then they're good items but nothing that couldn't be sold in a regular marketplace.

I'm proving that I can lay my hands on things. That I have contacts. I can be a provider.

We'll be the judge of that.

They were sceptical and challenging. They had her photographic proof for an age before they came back and accepted it was what she said. They asked again about its provenance, but she stonewalled them. She was sure it was part of the test. Say where you got it, say who sent you here, and we'll slam the door in your face.

She said nothing, said she would continue to say nothing. Okay, finally, they said yes. She was in.

Welcome to Abbadon.

CHAPTER 40

The Landscape Gardener

He collected his first piece of murderabilia when he was just eight years old.

Not that he knew that was what it was called or would have been able to spell it if he had. But, looking back, there was no doubting that was when it all began. And maybe there had been no stopping it.

There was a house just a few hundred yards from his parents', a white-painted cottage with a low wooden door that stood on its own at a crossroads on the outside of the village. The old woman who lived there was said to be a witch. Maybe it was because of the cottage or maybe because she had long grey hair and a pointed nose. Or maybe it was because she *was* a witch. She was in her seventies, the kids guessed, but that could easily have been ten years out either way.

Her name was Miss Astill and she lived on her own – apart, of course, from her three cats. They were hairy, wary beasts who denied any and all attempts to play with them, feed or stroke them. They'd be seen slipping in and out of the cottage or looking cautiously from behind clumps of grass. Go near them and they'd disappear.

The old lady wouldn't be in the village much, just the occasional sighting in the shop or maybe in church a couple of times a year, Christmas and Easter, and even then she didn't seem to talk to anyone. There was talk of a man who'd died in the war and of a son who either died in childbirth or had been kidnapped. All probably nonsense. No one really knew anything about her.

Then she was murdered.

It turned out she wasn't a witch at all, or at least not one with any powers or spells that could have saved her. She was just a lonely old lady with some money hidden under her bed.

The first anyone knew was when the door to the cottage was seen lying open to the wind. A friend of his dad had driven past about seven and seen it that way but didn't think it was any of his business to do anything about it. A bus half full of passengers had done the same less than an hour later. It was only when the postman came with two letters around 8.30 that someone actually went to the open door.

He called out for Miss Astill but, when he got no reply, he just slipped the letters into the hallway and turned back down the path. Something made him stop – he told the newspapers he didn't know what – and he went back to the cottage and called again. When there was still no reply, he went inside and found the old lady sprawled out on the living room floor with her head bashed in.

It was before the days of mobile phones and he had to run to the phone box in the village to call the police and an ambulance. The nearest police station was five miles away and, by the time they dragged the only copper from his breakfast, word of the woman's death had spread and half the village were camped outside the house.

His dad had taken up guard of sorts on the door, stopping anyone from going in. He was ex-army and knew enough to know there would be fingerprints and the like that the police wouldn't want messed with. He'd also seen dead bodies and didn't think anyone else needed to do the same.

He'd gone up to his dad and asked what was going on, even though he'd already been told, just trying for an excuse to see inside. He was told it wasn't anything he needed to be bothered about. Better that he just go on to school as he was supposed to. He'd nodded, said yes dad. Gary Elford's father had come up at that point, asking if it was true and was told it was. It's bad, his dad had said, blood everywhere. *Everywhere*. He'd always remembered that.

When the policeman eventually got there, his dad was relieved of his duty and told detectives were on their way. Everyone was cleared off, pushed back as far from the house as the copper could get them. Few of the kids had actually gone in to school and teachers had to come round to the cottage and drag them away.

They could talk of nothing but Miss Astill and her murder for weeks. It was her son, some reckoned, back from the dead or the kidnapping, who'd killed for his inheritance. It was the postman, others said – he'd just pretended to find the body. It was their teacher or Gary Elford's dad or gypsies or a crazed killer escaped from the nearest prison. The talk of blood grew until the floor was covered and the walls.

About a month later, two men from a town twelve miles away were arrested. One of them cracked and ratted out the other, said how they'd gone there to rob the old woman and his accomplice had brained her with a hammer when she started to shout. They both got put away. Two years for the one who talked and ten years for the one who didn't.

Their arrest came as a big relief for the postman, who really had been interesting the police. They were suspicious of his arriving first at the scene and wanted proof that he really had business being there. He'd insisted that he'd delivered two letters for Miss Astill, left them in the hallway next to the umbrella stand, as the door had been open. Trouble was, there was no sign of the letters anywhere. The cops were sure he was lying and were pressing him hard before the other pair started spending money they shouldn't have had and talking too loud when they were drunk.

Those letters had been just too tempting. At the time, if anyone had asked, he couldn't maybe have told why he took them, reaching behind his dad's legs while he talked to Mr Elford, hiding them inside his school jacket while no one was looking. He just knew he wanted them.

It didn't hurt anybody: the postman was cleared and Miss Astill had no use for them any more.

He read them hundreds of times. Always careful to make

sure no one was around, no one to see. He would read them under the covers of his bed and then hide them again. He'd fold them back carefully in their envelopes and make sure not to tear or mark them. They were special.

One was from a cousin, another woman, named Elizabeth. She didn't say much, just told Miss Astill not to worry and thanked her for her birthday gift. She told her everything would be okay.

The other letter was from the son. He'd really existed all along and was writing to his mother from London just to tell her he was doing fine and that he had a job. He hoped she was well and that she was thinking of him. He said he'd met a girl and was hoping to marry her. He said if they had kids he'd never let them go.

He never told anyone about those letters. Not even when his dad seemed suspicious and asked him directly about them. He was sure his dad had searched the house for them at the time but he'd never have found them where they were.

They were now safely locked away in a drawer in his own house, away from his own children, away from his wife. Those letters were his. His start. His beginning. From them, a collection grew as he did. He became the Landscape Gardener, he became one of the Four.

He still took those letters out regularly and read them, sensing Miss Astill on the paper even though she'd never held it. He sensed the innocent postman and the things that happened in that cottage.

Murderabilia. He knew what it was now. And it was his.

CHAPTER 41

Jean Welsh was a small, slight woman but she gave the impression that a hurricane couldn't blow her over. She was the sort of woman the west of Scotland specialised in. Tougher than any coalminer or gangster or heavy-handed husband. The world had thrown everything it had in her face and she'd wiped her mouth and started again.

She sat on one side of her kitchen table, a cigarette working nervously between fingers and lips, and Winter sat on the other. She'd made them both cups of tea and placed hers in front of her as a makeshift defensive barrier.

The dresser behind her had a framed photograph of her son, smiling out at them, for ever in the 1970s, for ever in his early teens. Winter did his best not to stare at it but she caught him looking.

'It's different to any of the ones they used in the papers or on TV. I kept it just for us. I like to see his face. I know I'm just kidding myself on, but it's like he's still here.'

She said it as much to herself as to him, but he got the impression she'd explained the photograph many times.

The kitchen was small but tidy, plenty big enough for

one but it must have been a squeeze when four of them lived here and sat around this table. He couldn't help but picture Martin sitting there, eating breakfast before leaving for his last day at school. Jean Welsh was right: it was as if he were still there.

They'd made small talk for a few minutes, polite and nervous diversions about the traffic and the weather that kept them away from Martin for a bit longer. When they did start talking about him, he noticed she kept switching between tenses. Martin is. Martin was. Even after all these years, part of her didn't accept it.

'This is for the *Scottish Standard*, you say? I don't read newspapers any more. And they don't bother coming to talk to me much these days, either.'

There was a question inherent in it. *Why now?*

Winter hadn't wanted to jump straight into the issue of Martin and murderabilia, but it was the only real answer he had. She saved him from having to say it, though.

'You know what always bothered me? The anniversaries. It was like everyone remembered him then. It was, "Oh poor wee Martin Welsh, let's all cry and hold a march or another television appeal." They all remembered him on the anniversaries but the anniversaries weren't any different to me to any other day of the year. I cried my eyes out every single bloody day. But on the anniversaries they all came out the woodwork and I had to share him. I hated that.

'And when he disappeared? Oh, the whole country was bloody heartbroken. "Poor Martin. His poor mother." It was all so *public*. Martin dying ripped my heart out, but being made to share that with everybody else wasn't fair.

It was like everyone wanted a bit of it. And it wasn't theirs. *He* wasn't theirs. He was mine. He came out of me. *Me.*'

Her eyes were reddening but her mouth was angry.

'A year after he was taken, a year after he died' – the word tasted like poison in her mouth – 'the whole village walked from his school to here. Three miles. *Three miles.* Big bloody deal. This village and the next one and most of the next. People came from Glasgow to walk. It was like they were so upset they had to show it. But it wasn't their place to be upset because they didn't know him. They didn't love him. Maybe they were scared for their own weans and that's why they did it, but it wasn't right. Did they think I really wanted to see hundreds of folk carrying banners with my boy's face on them? It was nothing to do with them. It was private.'

A single tear ran unbidden down her cheek and he could see her twitching at it, trying to will it back into her eye. She was hating herself for showing that in front of him, but, if she thought she was showing weakness, then she couldn't be more wrong.

'Didn't it help knowing that talking, keeping it all public like that, increased the chance of finding who'd taken Martin?'

She laughed in his face. 'It might have if it had actually helped. It didn't, though, did it? Nothing helped. Nothing brought him back or found who killed him. Our lives were all over the papers and the telly. For nothing.'

She stubbed her cigarette out in the ashtray to her side and another was lit within seconds. She jabbed it at him accusingly.

'The papers more or less came out and said my husband had done it. My Alec. Of course, everyone round here believed it. I could see the way they looked and knew what they were saying. The same bloody hypocrites who walked from the high school to the village were whispering away saying Alec had done for his own son. It was a disgrace saying that. Evil tongues on them, that's what they had. Evil tongues.'

Winter wanted to ask more but hesitated. He didn't want his own evil tongue to ask the next question. Jean Welsh had heard it before, though, and could see it sitting silently on his lips.

'You're wondering about my Alec, too, aren't you? I can see it in your face. Well, ask me. Ask me if he lifted his hand to me. Ask me if he would get so full of whisky that he couldn't keep his temper.'

She was daring him and he could picture her standing up defiantly to her husband's reddening face and bunched fists.

'Was your husband violent, Mrs Welsh?'

She laughed bitterly. 'He had a temper on him. Couldn't stand things not being the way he wanted. And when he'd a drink in him, which was most of the time, he'd lash out. I caught a few slaps. He always regretted it and sometimes he even told me. But he didn't kill our boy.'

'How can you be sure?'

'I knew the man.'

Winter persisted. 'Lots of people knew their partners but their partners still did terrible things.'

'Aye, I'm sure that's true. But those wives knew and ignored it. If I thought Alec had done it, I'd have killed him myself. He was a drunk and a coward but he wasn't a murderer. And certainly not his own. He loved Martin. And that's a fact.'

It was time to change tack.

'Mrs Welsh, do you know about the items relating to Martin's disappearance that are being sold?'

Her brow furrowed. 'Sold? What do you mean sold? Why would people be selling things?'

'That's partly why I'm here. There are people who collect things relating to . . .' – he nearly choked on the word – 'murders. They buy and sell and collect things. They've been doing that with items connected to Martin.'

'That's . . . that's *disgusting*.' She sounded as if she'd been slapped again. 'What kind of things?'

'Posters from when Martin went missing. Some items from school. The letter you sent to the newspapers. They have some of his clothes.'

'His *clothes*? How . . .?'

Mrs Welsh suddenly looked very small indeed. She shrank before his eyes as she contemplated her son's things being passed around like collectible stamps or football stickers. It took a lot for someone who'd suffered the life she had to find fresh disappointment with the world, but she just had.

'How would people even get them? His clothes?'

Winter shrugged. 'I'd be guessing but they could have been taken from the bin or if you'd given them to charity.'

'I threw them all out. I didn't want them and I didn't want anyone else to have them.' Disappointment had given way to fresh anger and he saw her brittle fingers go white at the knuckles as she folded her hands into tight, small fists.

'Who's selling these things? And who the hell is buying them?'

'That's what I'm trying to find out.'

'And you can stop them?'

He shook his head. 'Only if they're breaking the law, and that might be hard to prove. But I can name them and shame them.'

She thought about it for a moment before nodding. 'That's something. Do it if you can. Because it *is* shameful. It *is*.'

'I'm certainly going to try.'

'Thank you. But if you excuse me I'll no get my hopes up. Everyone else that's come to my door and said they'd try their best hasn't managed to do what they said. They said they'd do their best to find my son and they didn't. Then it was they'd find the person that took him and they didn't. Then it was they'd find my boy's body and they didn't. So I'm all out of hope that folk will do what they say. But I thank you for trying.'

Winter left the house feeling that he'd let the woman down before he'd even begun.

CHAPTER 42

The Jeweller

He had a technique that had never let him down. He knew it wasn't exclusively his but he'd refined it and made it work for him particularly sweetly. It was his own little niche in the murderabilia world. Or her niche, depending on how you looked at it.

He was straight. That's the first thing you need to know. This was a strictly business-only practice.

It was just like acting, he imagined. Not that he'd ever done any, not on the stage at least. Maybe everyone was an actor to some extent. He'd assume a role, a part, and he'd play it through. He was Alison. Alison Dale. Ali, to special friends.

Ali was single. Her job didn't give her time to get involved. She was attractive but not so attractive as to be unattainable. Kind. A good listener. She didn't mind faintly suggestive remarks. In fact, she quietly implied she might like it without quite saying so. Above all, she cared. She cared a lot. Ali was a good friend to those who needed it. And they certainly needed it.

Ali was blonde and blue-eyed. She didn't like to talk about her figure but she might admit she was in good shape. The horse riding and the running saw to that. And, yes, people said she was pretty. Men said that.

If you wanted a pen friend, someone happy to write – and receive – lots of letters, then you couldn't do better than Alison Dale. Ali to you. You could tell Ali anything. Anything at all.

And they did.

It first worked with a lifer in HMP Durham named Francie Rowlands. Alison wrote to him, claiming an interest in his case. Rowlands didn't stop to wonder why Alison would be interested in the case of a man who'd strangled his wife and daughter and buried both in the garden. He was just happy to have someone to talk to.

It helped that Alison was sympathetic. She understood that sometimes things just happened. That wasn't Francie's fault. We all have a breaking point and a person shouldn't pay for the rest of their life for one mistake. Francie loved that. Pretty quickly, it wasn't all he loved.

Soon he loved Ali so much that he told her how his wife drove him to kill her, practically begged him to do it with the way she'd behaved. She didn't understand him the way Ali did. She didn't understand that men had needs and moods that didn't make them bad, just human, just normal. Ali got that.

So he told Ali how he'd planned it. How he'd wanted to do it for weeks, maybe months. He laid bare the details of the murders in a way he never had in court or to the police. It was gold dust.

The Jeweller wasn't always Alison. Sometimes he was Nicole Ellis. Nicole was a campaigner for prison reform. She really cared about the inhuman way prisoners were treated. She was their friend. Nicole was popular in the UK but, man, was she ever a big hit in the US!

Nicole got particularly passionate about capital punishment and solitary confinement. She had empathy and the Death Row guys loved that. There was over two thousand miles between Aaron 'Whitey' Hooper in Eyman, the state prison in Arizona, and Wayne Barrett in Central Prison in Raleigh, North Carolina. That suited Nicole just fine, as there wasn't much chance of either finding out about the other. Both might have been upset to find she wasn't their one true love.

Whitey and Wayne were both waiting their turn to die and, while they did so, they poured their hearts out to Nicole. Whitey spilled his guts about the family of four whom he'd butchered and how it was all his daddy's fault for what he did when Whitey was a kid. Wayne wrote all about his seven-year spell as the Pine Woods Killer, telling her the stuff that didn't make it into the papers or onto TV. He let her know that there had been twelve victims, not nine, and that the voices were still there, still talking away to him in the middle of the night.

Nicole even had correspondence going with Charlie Manson for a while. They swapped a dozen letters but Charlie was too busy being in love with himself to fall for Nicole. All she was getting back was some crazy shit poems and songs that made no sense and, worse, weren't worth much. She ditched Charlie and wished him well.

Alison and Nicole were his favourites but sometimes he'd also been a social worker named Emma Hart, a kind and wealthy crusading grandmother called Olivia Wright, and a naïve but pretty student by the name of Jennifer Jackson. Hell, he'd even been a corruptible young nun named Sister Catherine.

The Jeweller didn't see anything wrong in it. Far from it. It worked a treat.

He got regular letters from some of the most infamous killers on the planet. Sometimes extremely intimate and revealing letters. He'd been told things the press and the police had no idea about. More than that, he'd been a good friend to those who needed one. He'd been loved and had brought happiness in return. How many of us can truly say that?

Best of all though, he knew, quite literally, where bodies were buried. That, my friend, was priceless.

CHAPTER 43

Within a minute of being in Abbadon, she knew she was in the right and the wrong place. It was like tripping through a waking nightmare.

On the face of it, it looked like any normal website. Well laid out, functional rather than flashy, it was like a dozen buy/sell and forum sites she'd used over the years. The difference was behind the forum subsections, inside the topics. The difference was in what you could buy.

Drugs or guns? No problem. Someone to supply them, someone to fire them? Easy. Someone taken care of? That could be arranged. Anything you wanted. Dreams and nightmares catered for.

Abbadon's speciality, though, was the one she'd come looking for. Collectibles.

She tentatively entered one of the American sections, seeing names both familiar and unknown leap out at her. Some of them, those who had killed most often, she knew. Others she had to look up, single killings that never made headlines even across the US, never mind across the Atlantic. And there were so, so many of them.

She couldn't quite believe what she was seeing. Anything and everything was for sale as long as you had the stomach for it.

Some guy named John Terence Bosko had murdered his brother. You could buy the brother's bloodied shirt. Arturo Aguilar had stabbed a man to death in a bar brawl and, somehow, the knife was for sale. Hollis Allan Newton had poisoned a family of three and, seemingly, not all of the poison had been taken into evidence.

The prices tended to match the fame: the more victims the more money, just as on surface sites such as KillingTime. Yet these items from little-known murders were higher because of the nature of it, because they were so hard to get.

Then she saw a figure that made her sit up. Twenty thousand dollars for a knife. Her eyes flashed back for the murderer's name but there wasn't one, just the victim. Hayley Elizabeth Poulsen. She didn't know the name at all and the sky-high price puzzled her. And no named killer.

It took her a while to grasp the concept. The figure for this knife wasn't so high *despite* the murder's lack of notoriety but *because* of it. She opened a new window and went to her search engine to confirm it. Hayley Poulsen was missing, presumed dead, not seen since she left her home in Akron, Ohio, in August 2013.

This was someone who hadn't been caught. This was an unsolved, where the victim hadn't even been found. The knife was, almost certainly, being sold by the killer.

She didn't know where to start processing that. Shock. Outrage for sure. Disgust. She wanted to phone the cops in Akron but stopped herself. That could, and would have to, wait. So, too, would a phone call to Hayley Poulsen's family. She forced herself to go on.

Some of the files didn't include things for sale but macabre wish lists. People seeking to buy things related to specific killers or crimes. Neither money nor morals seemed to be any hindrance. *Want Ed Gein furniture. Money no object for Albert Fish victim items. Bundy victim clothing wanted.* Anyone? It went on and on.

Some of the things that were or had been available must have been in circulation for many years without the rest of the world having a clue. She saw items from the twenties and thirties, gangland slayings and brutal murders, things that could only have got out there by someone being paid to turn a blind eye or to smuggle objects out.

The scale of it was overwhelming, and she had to stop and collect herself. Her stomach was tightening and she could feel the stabs of pain increasing as her stress levels grew with every new discovery. She wanted to stop just as much as she wanted to go on.

Just as the urge to get the hell out of it began to engulf her, she found a United Kingdom subsection and couldn't ignore it. She felt a trail grow warmer and was loath to leave it, no matter how twisted.

There were many fewer names but many more of them were familiar. Hindley and Brady. The Wests. Christie. Nilsen. Atto. Norris. Sutcliffe. You could buy belts, furniture, stolen underwear from victims, hammers ... Christ! Her stomach somersaulted. *Flesh.* You could buy human flesh.

Some sick bastard was offering the boiled flesh taken from the drains of Dennis Nilsen's flat in Cranley Gardens in Muswell Hill. The remains of his rent-boy victims.

She shouldn't be surprised, she told herself. But she still was. Nilsen killed them, cooked their body parts on his kitchen stove, then poured them down the sink. Liquefied, then solidified, the flesh clogged the drains and had to be removed. It was how Nilsen was finally caught.

'As seen in the police crime museum in London' was how the seller described it. Some of the congealed gunk had found its way into the Met's black museum and some of it had also found its way into Abbadon.

She leaned back on her pillow for a bit, nauseous at the thought. Her little lodger turned as her stomach did, resenting being disturbed. She patted her tummy, said an apology out loud, and carried on her trawl through hell.

Inside the UK piece of Abbadon, she saw another subdivision. 'Whitechapel'. She had no choice but to enter.

She'd wondered before why there were virtually no Jack the Ripper collectibles on the surface sites apart from a copy of the fake 'Dear Boss' letter and some collector cards worth a couple of pounds. Even though it was over a hundred years since the killings, they were still incredibly high-profile and she had no doubts that items would have survived.

Even before getting into all this, she'd read about the shawl that had supposedly been found on the body of Catherine Eddowes, the Ripper's fourth victim. The story being pushed was that a policeman, Sergeant Amos Simpson, took the surprisingly expensive silk shawl from the crime scene and asked if he could take it home to his wife. It turned up nearly a century later and was said to have both the victim's and the killer's DNA on it. Sure, that didn't seem far-fetched at all.

The shawl, said to be coated with Kate Eddowes's blood and the Ripper's semen but actually covered more in doubt than either of those, went on sale at auction for a touch under three million dollars. Not surprisingly, no one wanted it.

She'd wondered where such artefacts might be, and now she knew. They were all circulating underground, now, right in front of her eyes. Maybe they always had been in some shady, pre-Internet way, bought and sold by word of mouth, secret locations, used notes.

She ran through them, barely able to stop herself. Little things. Old things. Odd things. Incredibly expensive and much wanted things. Many of them came with disclaimers, some came with guarantees of provenance. Or as much guarantee as a hundred-plus years of separation can offer.

At least one of those things made her jaw drop. It came with the Abbadon stamp of certification in as much as everyone on the community seemed to have no doubt it was genuine.

Liz Stride's coat.

Elizabeth Stride, Ripper victim number three. Found in Berner Street, Whitechapel.

There was a photograph on the screen. A grainy crime-scene image of a wraith. More like a sketch than a photograph. The poor woman lying on her back, eyes closed, mouth bloated. Her lips were curled into a smile, as if she'd just been told a secret, a secret no one should ever know.

Lizzie Stride was wearing what looked like a black cloth coat. It sat high on the neck, with a raised crisscross pattern as part of the material. Now, that coat, 128 years on, was for sale.

Half of her wanted to know what was wrong with these people. The other half wanted to know how much. And she wanted to see it. A large and dirty part of her wanted to touch it, connect with it. A bit of that was professional but another, greater, portion was just rubbernecking. It was Jack the Ripper. And she wanted to know what it was like.

It took less than an hour to find what else Stride had on her person when she was murdered. A black skirt and black crêpe bonnet. A checked neck scarf, a dark-brown velveteen bodice, two petticoats, a white chemise, white stockings and spring-sided boots. In the pocket of her underskirt were a key, a piece of lead pencil, six large buttons, one small button, a comb, a spoon, a hook, a piece of muslin and two small pieces of paper.

She went to the site's search function and put in each item in turn. The white stockings were there. Available to buy. So too, were the collection of buttons. A poor woman's bits and bobs, a pocketful of mix-and-mend, now worth money because she had her head nearly cut from her body. *Blood money.*

She jotted down what she found, then searched Abbadon again.

A white pocket handkerchief said to belong to Mary Ann Nichols. An empty tin matchbox and a mustard tin containing two pawn tickets, both in the possession of Kate Eddowes when she was killed. A comb in a paper case, belonging to Annie Chapman. *Murder money.*

There was Ripper suspect murderabilia, too. A handwritten letter from Dr Neil Cream, almost certainly not Jack but the killer of at least four women and one man. A pair of kid gloves found on the drowned body of Montague John Druitt. A tie that had belonged to George Chapman, who poisoned three women during the Ripper era.

Hell, there were case files, too. Police case files. She couldn't believe that and had to go back online, and wasn't sure whether to be glad or not when she found out it was true. Several case files had gone missing over the years. She couldn't be sure what was truth and what was conspiracy theory, but the suggestion was that cops on the investigation had taken them as souvenirs, something to show their grandchildren that they'd worked the most famous murder case on the books.

There were few or no case files left. Those that hadn't been sneaked away were destroyed during the Blitz in World War Two along with most of the City of London files. Of course, there were bunker nuts online who believed this was just a convenient cover-up and that the files were removed to stop the truth being revealed.

She was sure that was probably bollocks but, God, she wanted to see those files. If only she had the million pounds that would be needed for a starting bid.

None of these Ripper items would have been illegal to own, although probably illegal to obtain originally. But they were hidden away on here, furtively removed from the righteous wrath of public opinion. Here they could be bought and sold without judgement. Except maybe the judgement that approved of it.

Each succeeding item sickened her more than the one before. Both the murders and murderers they were associated with and the trade in them. It was a cesspit.

She put in 'Scotland' and searched. And wished she hadn't.

Manuel. Atto. Tobin. Child killer Robert Black. Archibald Hall, the monster butler. Angus Sinclair, the World's End killer. Personal items, victims' clothing, even bloodied murder weapons. Things she never knew existed, even though she'd been involved in cases involving two of them.

She knew her pulse was throbbing and her stress levels were going through the roof. The pains at her middle were biting hard and often.

There was a listing that was selling items relating to an 'Unknown White Male in West Lothian, aged mid-30s, living rough and probably alcoholic'. The price was low because no one even knew the man had gone missing.

Some of this stuff couldn't be in circulation without the complicity or incompetence of cops, lawyers or court staff. Much of the rest could only be coming from people with direct – very direct – links to the killings. She couldn't take much more. She had to log out.

Her finger was above the exit door, her head swimming and her emotions choking, when she saw it. *Queen Street Station.*

Her finger was quicker than any misgivings she might have had. One click and she was in. Immediately, the words surged at her from the screen, nearly drowning her: 'Aiden McAlpine. Clothes. Photograph. Murder. Hanged. Best offer.'

The missing clothing. Aiden McAlpine's socks and underwear. It was here and it was for sale. And it was made very obvious that this time it was genuine.

CHAPTER 44

The Accountant

The interest had always been there as far as he could remember. He hadn't thought of it as anything unusual, far from it. He couldn't understand why anyone *wouldn't* be fascinated with it.

If it started with anything, it was with watching the movie *10 Rillington Place*. Maybe it wasn't the movie a fifteen-year-old boy should have been watching, but the address wasn't too far from where he lived in East Acton, and that had grabbed his attention. Once he started watching, he couldn't stop.

Richard Attenborough as John Christie and John Hurt as poor, stupid Timothy Evans. Murders, sex, lies. And it was all real. That was what captivated him. It was real.

Christie murdered eight people, all in that house, just two miles away. It made him feel close to it. It made him *feel* it. The Accountant had such a young and impressionable mind and the impression was made.

He sought out everything he could find. Books by the

dozen, other movies when he could. Reading, watching, immersing. British killers were his thing and, pretty soon, he knew them all and he knew all about them. By the time he was eighteen he could reel off dates, birthplaces, nicknames, names and ages of victims, sentences, judges, arresting officers. He became a walking encyclopedia of murder.

John Reginald Halliday Christie, born in Northowram in the West Riding of Yorkshire on the 8th of April 1899. Executed by hanging in Pentonville Prison, London, on the 15th of July 1953 by Albert Pierrepoint. Victims: Ruth Fuerst, Mùriel Eady, Beryl Evans, Geraldine Evans, Ethel Christie, Rita Nelson, Kathleen Maloney, Hectorina MacLennan.

Thomas Neill Cream. The Lambeth Poisoner. Born in Glasgow on the 27th of May 1850. Executed by hanging in Newgate Prison on November 15 1892. Victims: Nathan Stott, Ellen 'Nellie' Donworth, Matilda Clover, Alice Marsh, and Emma Shrivell. Probably more.

John George Haigh. The Acid Bath Murderer. Born in Stamford, Lincolnshire, on the 24th of July 1909. Executed by hanging in Wandsworth Prison on the 10th of August 1949 by Albert Pierrepoint. Victims: William McSwan, Donald McSwan, Amy McSwan, Dr Archibald Henderson, Rose Henderson, Olive Durand-Deacon. Three others, full names unknown.

Those were his favourites but he could do the same for Mary Ann Cotton, Peter Manuel, John Straffen, George Joseph Smith and many more. It was history the way it was never taught to him in school. History, real history, wasn't about battlefields or kings: it was about real people and how they lived. And how they died.

He first went to Rillington Place the day after watching the film at the cinema. It had been renamed Ruston Close by then but no one thought of it as anything other than what it *had* been. He stood and stared. Such an ordinary, ugly little house with its white door, grey walls and crooked downstairs window, right up against the wall that cut the street off from the world. It had all happened in there.

The people in the three other flats in the building had refused to move out for the filming of the movie but were all soon to be evicted, anyway, as the motorway was coming through. It was just so convenient that it was also going to turn Rillington Place into rubble.

He stood in the cold with his collar up and his eyes fixed on the ground-floor flat, his mind working overtime as it processed images of Christie and Evans, their wives and the other victims. His heart was thumping with the truth of it all and his head swam with excitement. Suddenly, he was across the road and through the white door before he knew it. There was an awakening as he realised he was inside and staring at the grubby door that had been Christie's. He ran his hand over its wooden surface and squeezed the handle. At his feet was a small, thin square of old red-and-blue-patterned carpet that served as a doormat. Moments later, he was back on the street and hurrying away, the carpet rolled up and under his jacket.

He didn't go back until the days of the demolition. There were plenty of gawkers then and plenty, too, who were taking advantage of it. One local, a builder, was selling bricks for a pound a time, mainly to American tourists. The same guy used to sell front doors that he found in skips just by getting the numbers one and zero from the local Woolworth's and screwing them on. Fifty quid a time he got for those.

The Accountant just laughed at them. He'd already got his own keepsake and it was the real thing. Sure, there had been nearly twenty years between Christie living there and his taking it, but that didn't matter. It was where it came from.

Now, he still sometimes drove round and parked on the new Bartle Road, maybe just looking from his car or, on drier days, getting out and strolling to the spot where the old house stood. Every now and again there were tourists there, except most didn't really know where the house had been. If he felt like it, which wasn't often, he'd point out the spot. There, he'd say, yes, there, that patch of St Andrew's Square. Can't you feel it? Can't you smell it?

Sometimes they got it and sometimes they didn't. He always did.

CHAPTER 45

Aiden McAlpine's missing clothing was marked at a starting bid of seven thousand pounds. Low morals came with a high price.

There was a photograph to accompany the sale. The one Tony had taken at the crime scene, the shadow of the body swaying over the abandoned clothes.

'This item has extra value owing to having gained worldwide publicity.'

Tony. His bloody picture had made this thing worth money by going viral. Although she'd no doubt that was the killer's intention all along.

The provenance was guaranteed. Not least it seemed because the seller's reputation assured it. His name, given simply as Big Sleep, was enough for anyone on Abbadon to know they could trust it was what it said it was.

Clearly, Big Sleep had sold before. He'd delivered and they knew he'd deliver again. The authenticity was not in dispute.

Something spoke to the back of her mind and her fingers moved back to the listing for the presumably murdered homeless man in West Lothian. Had she seen it or was she imagining it? She wasn't sure which answer she wanted to be right.

> Unknown White Male. West Lothian. For sale: Boots, jeans, jacket, bloodstained shirt, penknife, torn photograph of a woman, signed medical prescription. Offered as a lot but separate sales considered. Seller Big Sleep. Provenance guaranteed.

The clothes he was murdered in and the little he had on him. Who could have them other than the person who killed him? Big Sleep.

She tried to slow down and think, not rush past the obvious in the pursuit of other conclusions. The same person selling Aiden McAlpine's clothes was selling this murdered homeless guy's few possessions. And what else?

She searched. It took a while and her heart sank every time she found something. Some of it was present, still for sale; other items were archived. There was more, far more, than she'd expected or wanted.

It was like peeling layers off a rancid onion and finding more and more poison beneath.

An unnamed, probably unknown, young woman whose last location was given as Avonbridge, south of Falkirk. A female hitchhiker plucked from the M9 near Linlithgow, her name given as being 'probably' Annie Townsend. A Dutch student named Piet Dreese, who'd been walking the path of the Forth and Clyde canal. A woman, said to be in her sixties, who was described as vulnerable and who went unnamed.

The items for sale included clothing, possessions, murder weapons and even body parts. Two of the lots offered the victims' hair, as they'd been scalped.

Annie Townsend and the Dutch student she'd heard of; the others she ached to search for information on. There would be something, online or in police files. She'd go there, officially or not, but she wouldn't leave these people without a name. She couldn't let this go.

It wasn't all being sold by Big Sleep, though. Some things were being sold by others but still attributed, still linked to whom she took to be the killer. She could only guess that they were being resold, most probably for a profit.

The results spread across the central belt of Scotland like a cancer, each return making her more fearful of the scale of what she was seeing. And, worse still, she was sure she was only scraping the surface.

She made notes and pulled a map up on her laptop, sticking torn slices of Post-its on the screen until the pattern emerged. Every item she found relating to Big Sleep was inside the boundaries of the three main roads that cut through the centre of the country.

The M8 ran west to east, from Glasgow to Edinburgh, and from each end the M80 and the M9 ran diagonally northwest and northeast to form a raggedy triangle right in the heart of Scotland. If what she was seeing made any sense at all, if she had the brains left to decipher it, that triangle was where it had all happened.

She knew the area well enough to know there would

be countless places there where you could hide a body and be confident that it would never be found this side of Doomsday. There were lochs and reservoirs, thick woods and deep forests, rivers, bogs and quarries, all served by back roads far from the prying eyes of CCTV.

Shit! What the hell was out there?

A killer and God knew how many victims. Or was she seeing things that weren't there? Was she seeing bogymen in the blue walls and not able to tell reality from the crazy crap she was forcing herself to wade through online?

She wanted to trust herself, back her judgement and her gut and her experience, but she couldn't. She was the crazy woman who played Charles Manson music and searched for dead people's things. She was the cow who put her own baby at risk by doing what she knew she shouldn't.

An unknown serial killer who ploughed a furrow through the green belt between the cities? Fields and forests and lochs that had become graveyards for the missing? She was seeing too much and seeing nothing because of it. She couldn't process this, couldn't make sense of it.

She sensed the pains coming before the first one bit. They came in waves, each one faster and deeper and more painful than the one before. They made her gasp and bend double, made her baby curl and hide. They made her scream and cry.

No one could hear her and no one could help. She'd brought it on herself and all she could do was lie there, thinking, hurting, wondering, and waiting for it to pass.

CHAPTER 46

The Librarian

He'd never set out to be a collector and sometimes he still didn't think he was one. He was an accidental gatherer. A hoarder more than a buyer and seller. That was what he told himself.

He had issues with it and always had done. He accepted that the morality of it was indeed questionable and never tried to defend that to the few people who knew of his pieces. Their view was what it was and it was neither his place nor his inclination to change that.

If he defended it to himself it would be to say that the things he accumulated existed whether he acquired them or not. Any hurt, any associated stress or bad taste, would have been there anyway. If not him then someone. You might think that a convenient position, and he wouldn't argue.

He wouldn't be the first person to do something he knew was wrong and he would be far from the last. The smoker with lung disease who takes one more cigarette.

The problem drinker who has one more vodka. The addict who takes just one more hit. Just one more won't make any difference; just one more, then I'll stop. Just one more.

So he bought one more item. Then another. Every time he'd die inside a little, immediate regret and self-loathing that lasted as long as it took for him to want something else. And he always did.

But it was more about completion than want. If there was a gap, then it had to be filled. If there was an omission it had to be rectified. It was obsessional and compulsive. It couldn't have been ignored even if he'd chosen to ignore it.

The thought of someone else having something filled him with genuine dread. He knew that was irrational, but knowledge changed nothing. If someone had something of his it felt like theft. He hated the idea of someone owning or touching any item that ought to be his. On the very few occasions he lost out to someone else in an auction, or if someone got to a piece before he did, it would drive him crazy and he'd then do or pay whatever it took to get it for himself.

They didn't deserve to own these items because they didn't understand. Not as he did.

These things were special. They had such history to them and should not, must not, be in the hands of people who didn't fully get that. They'd be better off burned or buried than with someone who wanted them only for the thrill or to make a quick buck.

Crazy? Sure, why not? He'd accept that. But weren't all great passions based on a degree of madness? Whether it was love or compulsion, obsession or desire, they were all founded on a part of our brain that involved loss of control. They all swam in some form of lunacy, however mild. He'd happily admit to being as crazy as the next nut. At least he knew it.

CHAPTER 47

She was talking to people on Abbadon. People she didn't know and couldn't see.

Some of them were sellers, some collectors, some as crazy as she was. Maybe all of them were all of those things. She knew she shouldn't just as much as she knew she couldn't stop. It was her job, whether she was signed off or not. It wasn't the kind of thing you could walk away from, it was who you were.

But, more than that, she was in quicksand. The more she tried to climb out, the faster it sucked her back in. Abbadon was a nightmare that she couldn't wake from.

Some of them were questioning her. Suspicious of a new face, yet boldly unworried by any threat. They were anonymous, safe in their shadows, masks pulled down tight. They were the worst kinds of coward. The brave kind.

> 'Who told you about this place? Make sure you keep it to yourself. If you're not kosher, you'll be out.'

> 'I won't be dealing with you till I know you can be trusted. If you don't like that, then too bad. You're welcome to leave.'

Others just wanted to boast.

> 'I've got stuff you wouldn't believe. It would put me in prison but I don't give a fuck. It's not hurting anyone but why would I care anyway.'

> 'Don't listen to what the rest say. If you have good items, bring them to me. I pay top dollar, guaranteed. I have the cash and I'll take the best of what's out there.'

> 'The cops will never break this place. You can buy whatever you want. Christ, if people only knew.'

She asked questions. Slowly, drip-feeding them, then accelerating when she hit the straight.

> 'I've got some stuff but I want more. I want something from Big Sleep, whatever there is. How do I make sure I can get it before anyone else does?'

> 'Have you bought from Big Sleep? Can I trust he will deliver?'

'How does he get away with it?'

'Does anyone know who he is?'

The answers were varied but rarely helpful. Some were short and to the point. Immediately suspicious, immediately guarded, they just told her to get lost. Others gossiped but knew little. What little there was, she grabbed with both hands.

Big Sleep was prolific. He was death. He could be relied on to provide what he said he would and it was highly advisable to pay on time. No one was known to ever have met him, no one had as much as seen him. He worked predominantly in the central belt but had been known to venture north and occasionally across the border into northern England.

Buying from him was not easy, though. It seemed you had to be quick, loaded or connected. Particularly the last.

'He sells mainly to *them*. No one else gets a look-in.'

'Good luck trying to buy some. I've tried for years but *they* snap everything up.'

'Those bastards are a cartel. A bunch of us should get together and see how *they* like it.'

'It's the Four. They're all over Big Sleep's stuff.'

The name came up again and again. The Four.

No one said much. Mostly it was in fearful whispers. Even the brave cowards seemed reluctant to mouth off. Then came conversations that worried her.

> 'You ask too many questions. Your lease here might have to be terminated.'

> 'This place is fresh snow. You leave footprints with every step you take. You should remember that.'

When she asked about joining the Four, the reply was instant.

> 'We are the Four. Not the Five or the Six. This is a closed club and now a closed conversation. Now fuck off.'

The last discussion she had on Abbadon quickly became long and one-sided:

> Does it not worry you that you've no idea who you're talking to? That you can't see the face behind the name behind the seller? Aren't you afraid to ask questions about someone you know has killed a number of people? Seems to me to be a bit stupid to be so reckless. You ask about Big Sleep but he could be anyone you're talking to and you wouldn't know. For all you know, it could be me.

CHAPTER 48

The Four

It was what they called themselves and, soon enough, how they were known by those who knew little at all. Nothing dramatic, nothing ad-man snappy or chilling. Just practical, descriptive and anonymous. It also made it clear that the membership number was fixed. No one would be leaving and no one would be invited to join.

The Four. They were the best at what they did. The most serious in their field, head and shoulders above the amateurs, the enthusiasts, the weekend collectors. They would go farther, risk more, want more, get more. What others would dream of, *they* would accumulate. While the rest would scramble around buying and selling to make a scrap of cash, they would collect. They would keep.

They understood what the others didn't. They saw the real value in their collections, something way beyond money or acclaim. Something the amateurs wouldn't and couldn't understand. *They got it.*

Each of them had their own area of interest and

expertise, a particular killer or victim they centred on and collected whenever they could. They knew about and helped to feed each others' habits. If one became aware of something available that would appeal to another, then they'd tip them off or simply buy it if time was pressing.

They were a collective of collectors. A cartel if you listened to some, to those not allowed inside the circle. Jealous minds were small minds.

The Four first got together in the Crowne Plaza Hotel in Ventura, California. Meeting each other was completely unscheduled but, they decided with hindsight, utterly inevitable. They had all gone there, individually, to attend the World Murderabilia Convention, or MurderCon, as it was known to its devotees.

The Landscape Gardener and the Accountant had been to a MurderCon before, in Raleigh, North Carolina, and Detroit, Michigan, respectively. For the Jeweller and the Librarian it had been a step into the unknown, one they'd ached to do for years.

They weren't the only Brits in attendance, there were maybe a dozen in all among the hundreds of convention attendees. But they were most committed. They didn't know it but all they had to do was find each other.

The con took over the top floor of the hotel, the Bay View, as it was called, with its two large meeting rooms, adjoining corridors and views over the Pacific towards the Channel Islands. Down below, people walked on the wide, sandy beach and others walked dogs or threw Frisbees in the ninety-degree October heat. On the Bay View, they had no interest in such things. They had eyes only for what was on display.

There were stalls all over the top floor, conveniently out of sight of the tourists and the honeymooners. Everyone who turned a coin by selling murderabilia was selling it there. It wasn't all on display, some objects being too sensitive to be laid out for everyone to see.

The entire floor buzzed with collectors, mostly men, some more serious and knowledgeable than others. Some strange types among them for sure, some you wouldn't trust to watch your dog for fear they'd eat it, but plenty of ordinary, decent individuals too.

The Jeweller and the Landscape Gardener were the first of them to make contact, a wary conversation at the bar on hearing each other's accent. They teased it out of each other at first, hesitant admissions of things collected and how they did it. With each drink and each disclosure, they became a little bolder, a little more boastful, hinting at things of interest. After an hour, they knew they were cut from the same cloth, a darkness that recognised a mate. They maybe weren't yet ready to voice that mutual recognition but both sensed it.

The next morning, nursing agreeable hangovers, they were admiring a stand that had three human skulls, each on offer for a reasonable $1,500. The stallholder said the bleached, grinning skulls were imported from India and they'd be smart to buy before laws were tightened and prices went up. The Jeweller and the Landscape Gardener stood in captivated silence, comfortable enough now in each other's presence to unashamedly stare, their obvious rapture unconcealed.

'You have to wonder how they died,' said a voice from behind them. The accent made them flinch as much as the rudeness of the interruption. It was English, London probably. Close enough to be immediately uncomfortable.

'Murder or natural causes? What do you think?' The newcomer stared at the skulls as fiercely as they did. 'Something grisly, I'd reckon.'

The Jeweller and the Landscape Gardener had swapped quick glances. Accept or retreat? They decided to give him a chance.

'You *think* or you *hope* that it was grisly?' the Landscape Gardener tested him.

The man shrugged nonchalantly. 'Both. Chances are it was and it would definitely be more interesting, don't you think?'

They did. And they said so. The Accountant joined their company, another like mind welcomed.

It was later that afternoon that the Jeweller got talking to the Librarian. They found themselves after the same item: a shirt that had belonged to Richard Ramirez, the Night Stalker. The Librarian was trying not to let the stall-holder see how keen he was, feigning uninterest only to be called on it by the seller, who informed him that 'another Brit' was going to come back with an offer. The Jeweller duly appeared, having seen the Librarian hovering around Ramirez's black shirt.

The seller was delighted of course, and managed to jack up the price, eventually selling it to the Librarian for way more than either of them had intended to pay. The Jeweller had conceded defeat with a handshake and an offer to join him and some friends for a drink. The Librarian, already drunk on victory, happily agreed.

They took a table outside, far from the crowd, the four of them sitting on a pair of brown wicker couches, drinking ice-cold beers and being careful not to be overheard. It was bland at first, cautiously so, much to the frustration of each of them. The Accountant tried to push it a little but the trust wasn't there yet, and the others were still wary.

It was only when the Jeweller casually dropped Dennis Nilsen into conversation, to see what reaction he got, that they began to talk properly. It was a potential bomb, but he'd preferred to think of it as sending a hare running across a minefield. He saw heads lift and eyes dart right and left. He saw interest. A fevered discussion erupted over how idiotic Nilsen was to block the drains with the body parts of his victims, how surely he should have seen that coming. There was no debate about the morality of what he'd done before that. Killing and dismembering were fine; stupidity was criminal.

The Landscape Gardener picked up on that and tried his own luck with a mention of Fred and Rose West, joking – and yet not – that they were his favourites. That got knowing nods and encouraging laughs. That drew them all closer to the table. Did any of them have a brick from the demolition of Cromwell Street, the Jeweller asked quietly. One by one, they all gleefully confirmed that they did. Maybe they should put them together and build a monument, the Librarian suggested. That got a big laugh and some murmurs of, 'No we really should.'

Little by little, they opened up. Just a window cracked here, a door ajar there. The Accountant brought up Jack the Ripper and they all groaned. Cliché, they chorused, old-hat and overrated, thrills for tourists. They then all displayed detailed knowledge of each victim, each potential Jack. There was a full hour's discussion of Kosminski, Ostrog, Gull, Maybrick and the rest, every opinion fiercely held and contested. Jack might have been overhyped but he still represented the Holy Grail of murderabilia. They all craved a piece of Jack.

They wanted more than Jack, though. They wanted Manson and Bundy, Dahmer and Tobin and Gacy. They trotted out names and nicknames as if they were on TV commercials, citing Andrei Chikatilo, Gary Ridgway, David Berkowitz a.k.a. the Butcher of Rostov, the Green River Killer, Son of Sam. The four of them wanted more, much more, but were still shy of saying so, still wary of showing their all.

They were close though and getting closer. It wasn't just that they shared nationality. It was much more than that. There were those other eight Britons in and around the hotel for a start. At one point, they had to stop talking because a thirty-something car salesman from Wolverhampton named Lewis joined them uninvited, telling them how he could make just as much money from murderabilia as he could from second-hand cars. His grubby greed wasn't their mindset at all.

Others, like a shy shadow from North Wales, seemed overwhelmed by the whole convention and had clearly overreached himself. He was the type who had an interest in Jack the Ripper or the Zodiac Killer but it began and ended with wanting an answer to the mysteries. He just didn't get it.

There were Americans who came to it from the same viewpoint they did. It was obvious in their eyes and in the hunger of their voices, but they were still different. Too loud or too creepy, too brash or too dangerous or just too American. They all agreed they didn't like how the Americans dressed, lurid shirts and comically bad T-shirts with murderous puns. It was as if they were publicly revelling in it, showing off. Not British at all and not what they wanted.

It was partly what drew them closer, not just being the same as each other but being different from the locals and despising them. They were a group, they were separate from the herd. Maybe, just maybe, they could soon let it all go in front of each other.

By the Sunday evening it had happened. They'd all talked enough, trusted each other just enough, that they agreed to get together and see how much they truly had in common. They hired a private function room, ordered two bottles of bourbon, a bucket of ice and four glasses from reception. They locked the door and drank and talked. By three a.m., they'd told each other everything, all relishing the freedom of speaking without shame. By the time the first rays of morning light warmed the sands of Tortilla Flats another two hours later, they'd made a plan and a pact. They were the Four.

CHAPTER 49

Her mind was tumbling with everything she'd learned, or at least thought she had. She struggled to make sense of what was real, what was in her own bruised imagination and what had come from someone else's.

She searched for anything on Big Sleep or the Four but still she read anything and everything she could find on Martin Welsh. The Internet was so layered that there was information inside information. It had to be dug out like bones from the earth.

Martin was officially declared dead fifteen years after he disappeared. His mother accepted it with great reluctance, never wanting to give up on her son or accept the truth, if that was what it was. Reading between the lines, it was obvious that she'd been persuaded to do it so that insurance and compensation could be paid out. Everything about Jean Welsh screamed proud, and it must have cut her deep to have done what was necessary.

It was after that that the family carried out a 'burial' in Calderrigg Cemetery and put up a headstone so there was somewhere to visit and pay respects. One interview suggested Jean never visited because she knew her son wasn't there.

Narey found an article on Michael Hill, the lorry driver from Jedburgh who'd been interviewed after seeing Martin at the bus stop. It was ten years after the boy went missing and he was still angry at having being named and far from pleased at being interviewed.

He had a family and a job and he was very keen to keep both. He made it clear that being in the newspapers again wasn't helping that.

Above all, he made clear that he was innocent. She'd heard that before, but this guy was adamant. He resented even being asked about it.

He'd seen Martin, he wasn't denying that for a second. He'd gone to the police after seeing the newspaper photographs. He'd wanted to help any way he could. He had two daughters of his own and couldn't imagine what the parents were going through. Ten years on, he still couldn't.

He'd gone through hell back then at being suspected. The cops had treated him right, apart from a couple of them, and he knew why they'd done it, but it was rough. People pointed at him in the street and he knew they were whispering behind his back and making up all sorts of nonsense.

Michael just wanted to put it all behind him. If he could do anything, say anything, remember anything to help Martin's parents then he would. But he'd told the police everything at the time and they either listened or they didn't.

He went thought it again, however reluctantly. How he'd

seen Martin standing at the bus stop. He'd had to pull to a stop because there was a car turning right in front of him and he had to wait while it got room to turn.

If there was a particular reason he remembered the boy it was that he was staring into space. He remembered laughing at how dozy he seemed, not a care in the world, not noticing the lorry or the car or anything at all.

The car in front got a space and it turned and Michael drove on his way. He'd gone a bit, taken a look back in his mirror at the boy still daydreaming. And the only thing he could remember that might be any use at all to the police was the sight of a white van approaching the bus stop.

The van went past and was behind his lorry for a bit, then it was gone. He looked and he thought, but wasn't sure, that it had turned round. It may have turned right or left but there was a white van going back the other way.

He wasn't saying it was the same van. He was saying it may have been.

The bedroom door opened and Tony was walking towards the bed before she knew it. She had been so deep in the article she hadn't heard the front door open or close. Now he was feet away and getting closer.

She couldn't close the laptop without looking ridiculously suspicious, so could only hope he wouldn't look at what she was viewing. Fat chance.

He leaned over the laptop to kiss her and saw the article writ large on the screen, the lorry driver staring back at him. His face dropped.

'What did we say about leaving this alone? I thought we'd been through it.'

'We had. And . . . remember the yellow wallpaper? That still holds good. You wouldn't like me if I was crazy.'

'Not funny. You really think you can find something new in that case after all these years? I feel pretty shit for talking to Jean Welsh as if I can do something when there's barely a chance in hell that we can.'

She got annoyed at him for saying it. He may have been right, but this was her thing. Why couldn't he just leave her to it? She snapped at him. Again.

'There's no chance of doing anything if you believe that. This is my job, not yours, and I feel there is something more in this.'

'You *feel* it?'

'Yes! This Martin Welsh stuff didn't just come up again after all these years for no reason. It's come up because there is a connection to this other shit. I just don't know what it is yet.'

He didn't answer and she looked up to see him staring at the screen, brow furrowed.

'What is it?'

'Can you enlarge that picture?'

'This guy? The lorry driver?'

'No. The other one.'

She hit the key combination and made the other photo bigger if grainier. He studied it.

'What the hell is it?' she demanded.

He looked confused but sounded certain.

'That photo. It's him. It's the collector, Robert Dalrymple.'

'*What?* You sure?'

He frowned and looked again, closer this time. 'Yes, I'm

sure. He's much older but I'm sure it's him. Add the glasses, more weight, thinner hair. It's him.'

'Christ.'

'Why? Who is it?'

She swallowed and lifted her head to look at him.

'*That* is the teacher who was prime suspect for murdering Martin Welsh. That's Alastair Haldane.'

CHAPTER 50

The Sharon Tate dream was the sort where you were aware on one level that you were asleep and that it wasn't real. It's called lucid dreaming but at the time it seems no less real for knowing it for what it is.

So, when Rachel saw the blonde-haired woman standing with her back to her on the other side of the room, she now knew from experience who it was and what it was. Long before she walked away, before she turned half round and then disappeared into the blue wall. She knew. It was Sharon.

It was coming to her almost nightly, infecting and disturbing her sleep. Sometimes, she wouldn't know if she was dreaming or dreaming that she was dreaming. There was a spiral of confusion and fear that would end only when she woke gasping and distressed.

She saw her now, standing there and facing the other way. If she could see Sharon it meant she was dreaming, it meant she was asleep and safe, but that knowledge didn't help. She dreaded what was coming, the dress turning red and the dripping blood and her own bleeding, her baby bleeding out of her.

Turn round, she urged her. Turn round, Sharon. Please. If you turn round just this once then I'll see your face and it will all be okay. You won't die and I won't bleed and my baby won't die. Turn around. Just once.

And she did.

This *couldn't* be a dream because Sharon never turns around in the dream.

She turned and Rachel could see her face. So beautiful. Perfect. A movie star. She turned slightly more and she could see the swell of her belly and the obvious proof of her near-full-term pregnancy. It was going to be okay. Sharon was alive and looking at her, and that meant her baby was going to be born.

Then it came. The red. The white dress turning red before her eyes and the river of blood dripping from it. She wanted to cry but looked up again to see that it wasn't Sharon Tate standing there but herself. The so-pregnant woman with the blood-soaked dress was *her*.

She could do nothing but watch. It was a dream, she told herself that, but still wanted to scream. Suddenly, something fell from the bloodied vision of herself and hit the floor with a sickening bump. It was a baby, a baby boy. Tears flowed from both her and the woman that was her.

She looked and the boy, the lifeless baby boy, was Martin Welsh. The face from the poster but with the eyes cold and lifeless.

She wanted to scream for help but her mouth wouldn't

work and her head wouldn't move. All she could do was stare and when she looked she saw the man standing behind the woman. He'd killed them, killed them both. He was death and he terrified her.

CHAPTER 51

Winter parked at the far end of Balerno, a few hundred yards from Dalrymple's house, and walked the rest of the way on foot. He wanted to see before he was seen, gain any little advantage he could.

He stood in the shade of a tree where he had a vantage point facing the white-walled cottage, and waited. It took only a few minutes before he saw Dalrymple walk across in front of the bay window framed by climbing plants. He was at home.

Winter stood there for ten minutes, seeing Dalrymple on the move a further twice. After a few minutes more, reasonably sure now that the man was alone, he emerged from under the tree and approached the cottage door.

He knocked and waited, but no one came. He knocked louder and quickly repeated it. If Dalrymple was hoping an unwanted visitor would go away thinking there was no one in, he was going to be disappointed.

He had to knock once more before the door was hesitantly opened. The look of surprise and unhappiness on Dalrymple's face had already made the trip worthwhile.

'What do you want? I thought we'd finished with your interview.'

'There are a few more questions I'd like to ask you.'

This didn't seem to please him at all. 'No, I don't have time for this. I think I've said all I want to say about it. I'd really rather not go through this again.'

'I think it's important, Mr Dalrymple. Or should I call you Alastair?'

The man's face froze. Winter might as well have slapped him.

'You *are* Alastair Haldane, aren't you?'

Dalrymple stared over Winter's head, anxiously looking left and right, presumably in case anyone was in earshot. Seeing no one, he turned back to glare at the visitor on his doorstep.

'You'd better come in.'

Neither Dalrymple nor Haldane offered Winter a seat but he took one, anyway, positioning himself in the armchair, which gave him a full view of the living room. It let him watch his reluctant host pacc the floor.

'You do understand how this changes my article, I'm sure.'

'How did you find out?'

'I saw a photograph from a newspaper around the time of Martin Welsh's disappearance. You've changed but not so much I didn't recognise you.'

Dalrymple chewed at his lip till Winter worried he might bite a chunk of it off.

'All I did was change my name. There's nothing illegal about that.'

'You've got to realise how suspicious it looks, surely?'

'I can't do anything about how it looks. People have always thought what they wanted, anyway.'

'So why did you change it if you've nothing to hide?'

Dalrymple stopped pacing long enough to open and close his mouth. He composed himself and started again. Whatever he was going to say was swallowed down. 'I don't have to explain myself to you. Changing your name is a common and perfectly legal process. It's my right and I think you should leave.'

Winter was going nowhere.

'I'm giving you a chance to explain yourself. If I run a story about Martin Welsh's teacher, who collects murderabilia, including several items relating to Martin, *and* that he's hiding under a false identity, well it's going to look a lot better for you if you can explain why. I'm giving you the chance to put your side of the story. I'd recommend you take it.'

Dalrymple stopped marching and stared at him, seemingly trying to make his mind up.

'Have you got any idea what it was like? Being all but named as the person who murdered Martin Welsh? I was only twenty-five and I just didn't know how to cope with it. I was in every newspaper, every television news bulletin. My picture was everywhere. And I could do nothing to prove I was innocent. Nothing. I didn't have an alibi because I was home alone. I had no one to prove it.

'My windows were broken. People called me murderer, paedophile. And that works just great for your career when you're a teacher. Parents went to the school and said they didn't want their kids in my class. Enough of them said it until I was asked to leave. My lawyer said I could fight it but I'd still never work again. So I took a payoff and left.

'That broke my mother's heart. She'd been a teacher and all she wanted was for me to do the same. She believed me, probably the only one who did, but it still hurt her when I left the job. She was never quite the same after all that and she died ten years later. She just lost the will to go on.'

Dalrymple stopped and Winter thought the man was close to tears.

'I was engaged when Martin disappeared. Well, pretty soon my fiancée disappeared too. She couldn't handle it and, worse than that, although she never said so, she wondered if I did it. How could I blame her? The world was saying that I did it. And, once she'd gone, no one else wanted to know. Her leaving just convinced them they were right and I had to be guilty.

'So I left the area. I had to. But, in the new place, people still knew who I was; they still whispered when I went past in the street; they still talked behind my back or swore in my face. So I had to move again, this time to England, to Leicestershire, but this time I changed my name as well. I wasn't Alastair Haldane, teacher, any more, so I may as well not be Alastair Haldane at all. I became Robert Dalrymple. It made life . . . simpler. After a few years, with my hair cut and different glasses, a bit older and a new name, I moved back up to Balerno.'

'And did you start collecting before you became Robert Dalrymple or after?'

He swore low under his breath. Telling any of this was not his first choice.

'Martin's disappearance, his murder, it shocked me. It shocked everybody. But I was right at the centre of it. It was like being thrown into the middle of a whirlpool with no way out. I knew I was innocent but no one else seemed to believe it. I became fixated with it, with the police investigation, with what happened to him. I cut out every newspaper article I could find and I kept them, filed them. I couldn't really have told you why, but I did. And I couldn't stop.

'I started collecting other things, too. Magazine articles, videoing documentaries and the *Crimewatch* re-enactment. It got me into reading about other killings, other disappearances. And I began buying things related to those other cases, too. I guess I became a bit of an expert, a bit of a fanatic. And, when I got the chance, I bought things connected to Martin's murder. It didn't seem odd, not to me. I knew I hadn't done it. It just made me feel . . . I don't know, like I was doing something.'

'Something for *Martin*?'

'I don't care if you don't understand or don't believe me. It gives me a connection to it. Something I need. It's like the more I have the more I know. And maybe one day I'll know enough that I can prove to the world I'm innocent. And maybe I can help him.'

'It's not just that you're obsessed with it?'

Dalrymple's face glowed in anger.

'You don't know anything about it. Nothing. It's not obsession: it's . . . It's just something I need to do.'

'That pretty much sounds like the definition of obsession.'

Dalrymple lashed out an arm, deliberately knocking over a lamp and sending it spinning to the floor.

'My life has been ruined by this! Martin Welsh wasn't the only one who suffered that day. I'd have been married. I'd have kids. I'd have been a head teacher. My mother would have died old and happy. Don't come in here and lecture me. Just don't.'

The man's face was contorted into a twist of rage and the words were being spat out like nails. The rage had been sudden and fierce.

'Leave my house, please. Now!'

'Do you see why people might find your collection odd? Or distasteful given how close to the case you were?'

'No.'

'How it might look very suspicious to the police?'

'Are you threatening me? You've come into my house to threaten me? With what? With spurious allegations that have already been investigated and reinvestigated by the police and found to be nonsense? If you print one word suggesting I killed Martin Welsh then you and your newspaper will be sued.'

'I'm giving you the chance to—'

'No, you're not. You're after a story and that's all. So, yes, I changed my name. And, yes, I collect things. Neither of those changes the fact that I didn't kill Martin Welsh, that I had nothing to do with his disappearance and that the police cleared me on both counts. You can stick that in your paper.'

'Okay, I will. I'm not out to crucify you. But you can see why this would be of public interest.'

'No. I can see why the public would be interested in it. That's not the same thing at all. I can't stop you from writing about my collection or that I've changed my name. I'd rather you didn't and I'm asking you not to. I'm begging you not to. But, if you suggest that I killed Martin, I *will* sue.'

'I will make sure my boss knows that. But let me ask you one more thing: how do you fund your collection? You said you couldn't work as a teacher again and I assume this stuff doesn't come cheap.'

He frowned. A mind-your-own-business sort of grimace.

'My mother left me some money. Plus, although I'm retired now, I did get another job, just not as a teacher.'

'What did you do?'

'I became a librarian.'

CHAPTER 52

'So what did you tell him, this journalist? Didn't you just tell him to fuck off?'

Alastair Haldane glowered at the receiver and through it at the person on the other end.

'No. It wasn't as simple as that.'

'Sure it was. You should have slammed the door in his face and told him to do one. He had no right to question you.'

'He was *there*, though. He knew some of it already. Enough to bring him to my doorstep. He knew about my . . . more legitimate collecting. I admit I panicked a bit but I thought I had to talk to him about that and not make him more suspicious by shutting the door in his face as if I had something to hide.'

'But you do have something to hide. We all do. That's why you shouldn't have spoken to him. *Christ!* It's bad enough that we have this woman digging around the dark web looking for us, but you have to bring this as well.'

'I told him what he wanted to know, but it was stuff he already knew or could find out whether I talked or not. It's public more or less. All there, bought and sold on surface websites. Nothing that actually matters.'

'It *all* matters right now. Christ, you think it's a coincidence he's nosing around at the same time she's digging online? Don't be so naïve. And I'm not buying for a second that you just told him enough to get him out the door. I know you, remember? I know you'd have got all puffed up about your collection and couldn't help yourself. You were boasting about it to him, weren't you? You showed him some of your Martin Welsh stuff. Didn't you?'

The silence was a tacit admission.

'I knew it! You arsehole.'

'I was just trying to make sure he had what he wanted and he'd go away.'

A bitter laugh. 'Well that worked well, didn't it? *He came back*, and now he knows more. He knows who you are and he won't stop digging until he knows it all. You've put *all* of us at risk, you fucking idiot.'

'Don't talk to me like that. It's easy for you sitting there and not having to deal with it. He was at my door. In my house.'

There was a pause that dripped with malice.

'No, that's where you're wrong. I *am* going to have to deal with it. Because you didn't. We're all going to have to deal with it. With both of them.'

Haldane didn't like being spoken to like that but he liked even less what it meant. He asked, anyway.

'Deal with it? How?'

'I'm going to speak to the others, but we can't have our arrangement plastered all over the newspapers. We've got too much to lose. If this were all to come out … It just can't. So we have to stop it.'

'How?'

'We have the perfect tool at our disposal.'

'No …'

'*Yes*. We need to contact Nathan.'

CHAPTER 53

'Don't run it? Don't run the story? Are you kidding me?'

'No, I'm not.'

She was calm, which should have pleased him, but he was irritated by the way she was just lying back in bed and coolly telling him to ditch the best story he'd had in his year-long career as a journalist. It was a stick-on front-page lead. A splash. A certainty to be picked up and run with by every other media outlet in the country.

Alastair Haldane, prime suspect, living under an assumed name and collecting murderabilia about his alleged victim. It was golden. And she was telling him not to run it.

'Rach, I've had Archie Cameron on my back all week demanding to know when I was going to give him something that would justify all my time away from my desk. To justify *my job*. Now I've got that, and more, and you're saying I should forget it. He's going to boot my arse out the door and back onto the street.'

'Not if you play him right, he won't. Anyway, I'm saying don't run it *yet*. Dalrymple, Haldane, isn't going anywhere.

The longer you take to run it the more spooked he's going to be. You *will* run it. Just wait.'

'Wait? Play him right? Archie's been playing this game for over twenty years and I've been doing it for five minutes. He's going to see right through anything I try.'

'Not if I tell you how to play him,' she said with a smile.

'Very funny. First, tell me why. And it better be good. Why shouldn't we run it?'

'Because we haven't finished. *You* haven't finished. You've got half a story.'

'I've got enough of a story to fill the front page. I know that much.'

She laughed bitterly. 'Maybe that's the difference between the police and journalists. I'm used to working on a whole different level of proof. And I need a whole different kind of outcome.'

'Which is?'

'Justice.'

'Sounds kind of smug, doesn't it? Holier than thou?'

'Well, holier than *thou*, that's for sure. You think there's something wrong with wanting justice, wanting all the ends tied up in truth and not just some half-arsed exposé that gets a big headline but doesn't answer the real questions?'

He groaned wearily, beaten down by her self-righteousness. 'If you say so . . .'

'I do. But more than that: if you run it now then you'll tip everyone else off and you'll most likely miss out on the bigger story that's still to come.'

'The bigger story?'

'Who killed Martin Welsh.'

'So what do you suggest I tell Archie? He's not going to be happy if I go back in empty-handed. And he's certainly not going to buy me telling him that I'm fighting for truth, justice and the West Highland Way. He'll tell me to stick that where the sun don't shine. And he'll be quite right.'

'So you don't tell him that. Have I taught you nothing? And you don't go in empty-handed. You give him a story. Give him something that keeps him happy and keeps you in a job.'

'Uh-huh. And what's that?'

'You give him the story about Aiden McAlpine and Calvin Brownlie. You link two high-profile killings. You have the MSP's son. You have the lover trying to sell the clothes. You have a guaranteed front-page exclusive.'

'No, no, *no*. I've already made my mind up on that. The Brownlie kid was just stupid. He only did it because he was hurting. And it got him killed. My running that story is just going to rubbish his name for no good reason.'

'You really aren't going to make it as a journalist thinking like that. And I mean that as a compliment. But you're wrong: it *is* for a good reason. For a start, you need to give Archie Cameron something, but also you can do Calvin a bigger favour than keeping his name out of the paper. This is about finding out who killed him.'

'Jesus.'

'Whoever killed Aiden killed Calvin. That much seems obvious. And, if I'm right, he's killed others. I want to flush him out. You run this story and it might just spook him.'

'It might spook him enough to hide.'

'I don't think so. I don't think that's who he is. He isn't the kind to run: he's the kind to come out fighting.'

Archie Cameron's office door was open but he was on the phone. He wasn't saying much and seemed more intent on rubbing away at the little hair that was left on top of his head. He was making occasional 'uh-huh' noises of agreement but they didn't sound very convincing to Winter. It had all the hallmarks of a conversation with someone who couldn't be disagreed with. Management.

He sensed Winter standing there and looked up with a scowl, annoyed at being seen to be tugging his forelock to the bosses. He waved an arm angrily, a movement that Winter couldn't be sure meant come in or piss off. He assumed the one that suited him and took a chair in front of Archie's desk. He soon saw it was the wrong interpretation.

'Yes, well, I'll look at it. Uh-huh. Uh-huh. Of course. Yes. Okay.'

He hung up and glared at Winter. 'What the hell do you want?'

'Nice to see you too, Archie.'

'No. You see, here's where you're going wrong. To have any chance of coming in here and being a smartarse and getting away with it then you need to be actually contributing something to the paper. Like, say, a story now and again. Or some photographs. Or maybe even, God forbid, the front-page story you promised me. But, if you sit on your arse all week doing sweet fuck all and then try to be funny, I'm more likely to take a baseball bat to your head.'

This was going well.

'Right, sorry. I know I said I'd have something for you and I thought it would be before now but—'

'I don't want to hear any more buts.'

'But I've got it now.'

Archie looked sceptical. 'Now. Like *now* now? Like front-page now? Because I need front-page now.'

'I think it's front-page now. Well, front-page-in-about-two-hours kind of now. I haven't actually written it yet.'

'Fuck's sake! Okay, what is it?'

Winter made his pitch.

'And you're sure about this. All of it?'

'Certain.'

'And this person that you've quoted, the source close to these kids, it's someone real, right? Not just some shit you've made up, as I believe happens occasionally.'

'The person is real and so's the quote. But I can't name them. That's a deal breaker.'

'Deal breaker? We're not making a deal: *I'm* making a decision. Okay, here's how it's going to go. You get quotes from Mark McAlpine. And you make sure he's shouting from the rooftops. He's not going to be happy about the cops not knowing about this connection, so get him to say so. Okay?'

'Yes.'

'And you'll need a quote from the cops, too. They will look stupid and they hate that, so make sure you phone them five minutes before we press the button on this. I don't want to give them the chance to kill the story or hand it elsewhere as a spoiler.'

'Got it.'

'You do that and we run it on the front page. If it turns out to be right you get a gold star and a pat on the head. If it's wrong you pack your bags and I'll boot your arse on the way out of the door.'

Mark McAlpine didn't let anyone down.

Winter managed to get a call through to his office at the Parliament and, after a few minutes' wrangling with the MSP's assistant, McAlpine himself came on the line. Winter was in no doubt that it was in order to give him an earful, but that didn't matter. All he needed was the chance.

'*Yes?*' The tone was immediately confrontational.

'Mr McAlpine, It's Tony Winter of the *Standard*. I wanted to—'

'You've got a nerve. How dare you phone me and presume I'll give you my time?'

'I think it's something you'll want to hear. And something you ought to know.'

'Unless it's an apology, I don't think I want to hear it. And, unless you're going to tell me who murdered my son, then I don't need to know it.'

'It's neither of those things but it might help us find out who did kill him.'

The was a lengthy pause on the other end of the line before Winter finally heard a sharp burst of breath.

'Okay, but this better be good.'

He was in. 'You'll have read about the body found floating on the mattress on the Clyde. The young man named Calvin Brownlie.'

'Yes, of course. What about him?'

'He and your son were friends. Very close friends.'

McAlpine's voice was smaller now. 'What do you mean?'

'Aiden and Calvin were a couple at one point. Boyfriends. I think they were killed by the same person.'

'My son wasn't . . . How do you know this? Who told you this?' There was an accusation inherent in the question, as if he had a very good idea who'd told him.

'Someone who knew both of them. I won't say who. But I talked to Calvin before he was killed and I know it's true.'

'You knew this and the police didn't?'

'Yes, sir.'

'If you're wrong about this, I'll have you fired.'

'And if I'm right?'

'I'll have someone else fired.'

McAlpine then duly went apeshit on the record and Police Scotland were called every name under the sun, in particular Detective Chief Inspector Denny Kelbie.

Winter had his story.

CHAPTER 54

Death is a strange thing. Very few people get an insight into it, not the way Nathan had. Others get to see it just once, and even then only very briefly before they slip into whatever hell they endure for eternity.

Nathan didn't really know if there *was* some kind of hell. He didn't believe in God but he could easily be convinced about the existence of the Devil. And it stood to reason that, if he was real, then he had a place to live. And one thing was for certain: if there was a hell, then Nathan would be going there.

He'd sent many people on the road to death, taken them by the hand and shoved them through the door of no return. For him, much of it was about the look on their faces as they realised it was over. They'd be surprised or terrified, confused or hateful. Sometimes they were pleading, sometimes defiant. Sometimes they knew nothing about it until it was too late.

He'd learned that you never knew how it was going to be. The ones you expected to react one way would just as easily do something different. The big guys who would whimper for their mammy. The little women who stared back at him, refusing to give him the satisfaction of seeing them beg. It didn't matter to him either way.

He was fascinated, too, by the switch-off. Life to death in the blink of an eye. Blood and colour draining from them, brain a goner, organs beginning to rot. From this to that in a split second. Sometimes, though, you'd be sure they were done but a rogue electrical impulse still flickered somewhere and they'd kick out or throw a hand. That was weird.

He didn't know what happened after that but he wanted to. Lately, he'd wanted to know more than ever. Even if there wasn't a hell, was there a soul inside each of us? Or something else, some *thing* that kept going after the physical stuff had ended? Could we see, hear, think, feel, suffer?

He supposed people had always wanted to know but he'd never given it much thought until recently. Now, he needed to know. He'd stare at those he'd killed, looking for signs. All he ever saw, though, was the light going out and the body starting to decay. Every single time.

He found himself hoping for more but never getting it. So he'd do it again. Like a scientist. Like a doctor. Like an explorer.

He'd taken the subway to Hillhead and got out onto Byre's Road. It was a Saturday afternoon and he emerged into a tidal wave of people, deliberately standing still so the wave had to break round him, pissing off as many people as possible.

Quite a few turned round to glare or to mouth off, but that didn't bother Nathan much. He didn't care what they thought or said. More than that, the bigmouths and the hard men often changed their minds when they looked into Nathan's eyes. Whatever they saw there, they didn't like it much. He was used to seeing them lose their convictions, and he enjoyed that.

Maybe it was his ability to think how these people would look if they were dead. They could sense he was thinking it and it scared the shit out of them.

This street was just annoying. Too many people. None of them doing anything worthwhile. Shopping and eating, buying clothes and growing beards, drinking and drinking. Too many students, too many middle-aged teenagers, too much money and not enough sense. Stupid middle-class wankers looking for stupidly expensive coffees and cakes and coke.

He started past the whitewashed walls of the Curler's Rest, then McColls, people streaming by him, past the banks and the chip shops, the jewellers and the phone shops, past the library and the pastry places. Past people and their things.

Nathan walked slowly because no one else did. They were all hustling and harrying, hurrying to their next mocha choca or noseful of adrenalin. He walked slowly so they'd either have to avoid him or bump into him and apologise. Maybe it would make him stand out, but he wasn't worried about that, not today. Today was just for looking.

Death concentrated the mind. He knew that much for sure.

He'd watched people say prayers, sometimes silent and sometimes screaming, making their peace and their too-late apologies for past wrongs. He'd seen them mumble and wonder, Why them? What had they done? Truth was, they'd most often done nothing except stumble into Nathan's path. Sometimes they'd have the fear of the abyss written all over their faces, the terror of knowing they'd be making the jump but having no idea what was down there.

He'd strolled as far as Oran Mor and waited for the lights to change so he could cross over and walk down Great Western Road, away from town. Waiting, he stared up at the spire of the church that had become a pub and wondered if there had once been answers in there.

He'd believed when he was a kid, or at least was told that he did, which was much the same thing. That didn't last long, though. As soon as he realised what life was like, what people were like, he gave that nonsense up. It had crossed his mind again of late, whether the God people really knew something. Time would tell.

From the very moment he crossed and made his way onto Great Western Road, the number of people dropped off as though someone had closed a door in their faces. And that was a good thing. There was still plenty of traffic chugging by, but that didn't bother him. Machines were okay. Humans weren't.

He walked parallel to Grosvenor Terrace, just a few feet the other side of the hedge, where the big beige Hilton was. He'd walk back that way but walking it only once was the better idea. Grosvenor became Kew Terrace, another expensive leafy strip with barely room for cars to negotiate, a line of trees separating them from the commuter drag.

After Kew was Bellhaven Terrace but that too would wait till the return trip.

He walked in the shadow of the bus lane, coughing at the endless exhaust fumes that smoked him as he walked. Not that he'd need to worry. He was dying anyway and a hail of carbon dioxide bullets couldn't make it any worse.

His illness did make him think differently about death. No less curious but definitely more fearful. It was the not knowing. He understood now that was what freaked people, not having a clue if there was a heaven or a hell, some endless drudge in between, or just immediate nothingness.

Cancer.

Cancer was a bastard. Something he couldn't fight, couldn't kill. Something he couldn't kneel down and beg to, even if he wanted. It was stronger than he was, more evil and more indiscriminate, too. It scared him and nothing had scared him in a long time.

When he reached the point of the road where Bellhaven Terrace was visible over the hedge and though the trees, he tried not to look but couldn't help himself. A grand line of houses, Victorian sandstone and a thousand windows onto the world. Stop looking, he told himself. Do it on the way back, shielded from the road by the greenery.

He turned left at the crossroads onto Horselethill Road, which climbed towards Dowanhill, walked past the entrance to Bellhaven Terrace without so much as a sideways glance, and walked another thirty yards or so to Bellhaven Terrace Lane, which ran behind the houses. It was one of those strange little thoroughfares that the West

End had so many of. It was a long, narrow cobbled lane that could as easily have been in the countryside.

Gated doors led to backyards, bushes bloomed and odd wee cottages sprouted up where you'd least expect them. This was the back way in and he needed to check it out. The houses on Bellhaven Terrace looked bigger and taller from this side, scruffier, too, as if all the tarting up had been kept for people driving past the front.

He'd stand out on the lane if he was seen, though, he knew that. It was a bit of a worry but not what it might have been before. He'd come to understand the beneficial aspect of dying. Death was so frightening that there was nothing else to be scared of. It freed him from other concerns.

He retraced his steps to Horselethill and then on to Bellhaven Terrace itself. Posh people's houses, even the bits that only half peeped up from below the street level. He imagined they were maybe servants' rooms back in the day. Now, they let anyone in there.

Main door off the street leading to other doors inside, blond stone, big bay windows some with Mackintosh friezes, flowers everywhere. Yeah, it was a nice place for sure. He could see why they'd moved in here.

He walked slowly. Not getting in people's way this time. Just looking. Just checking things out.

He was going to die but he wasn't the only one.

CHAPTER 55

Denny Kelbie maybe wasn't the smartest cop since Sherlock but he was a street fighter. He'd been dragged up in one of the rougher of the east end's rough areas and knew how to kick and gouge in the mud and the blood and the beer. If he was going down, he'd be going down swinging.

Narey sat up in bed, propped up on two pillows, and marvelled at the man's performance on the evening news. Caz Denton had her microphone thrust into Kelbie's face but, rather than duck away or admit that he'd messed up, he came out punching.

'DCI Kelbie, would it be fair to say Police Scotland are embarrassed about the revelations of the relationship between Aiden McAlpine and Calvin Brownlie?'

'No, Caroline, I wouldn't say that at all.'

'But surely the police should have known before it was revealed in a national newspaper that two such high-profile murder suspects were involved together. Is that not an embarrassment?'

Kelbie snarled and smiled at the same time. 'Caroline, let me make it clear that what Police Scotland let it be known that they know and what they actually know can often be two quite different things. The fact that this *newspaper* claimed to have revealed something certainly doesn't mean that we were unaware of it.'

'So you did know that Aiden and Calvin were once lovers?'

'Caroline' – he affected a small laugh that couldn't have been any more patronising if he'd patted her on the head with it – 'I am running a murder investigation here. That comes with responsibilities and with tactical decisions that go way above the needs or indeed the understanding of the media. There are things I will reveal when the time is right and will keep secret when it is in the interests of the case to do so.'

There was a pause and Narey knew it was Caz Denton trying to decide whether to shove her microphone somewhere her viewers wouldn't hear it. She wouldn't, but she sure as hell wanted to.

'With all respect, Chief Inspector, that isn't answering the question. Did you know of the relationship between the two victims before it was published in the *Scottish Standard*?'

Kelbie's face tightened and Narey was sure he was pushing himself up on his toes the way he did when he wanted to look taller and more intimidating. 'It answered your question, Caroline. I'm sure your viewers understood that, even if you didn't. There are operational reasons for not revealing case detail and this instance falls firmly under that. Moreover, there are sensitivities owed to the victims' families and we have respected that even if the newspaper in question hasn't. The sexual preferences of these two young men have been dragged through the press in an unseemly manner that was quite unnecessary.'

He was on a roll now, blustering his way into living rooms across the country.

'The murder of Calvin Brownlie reinforced our belief that the murder of Aiden McAlpine was one of homosexual prejudice. Our enquiries continue with that in mind while not ruling out other avenues of investigation. Caroline, when we identified the tragic young man floating on the mattress on the Clyde, it would have been the easy thing for me to immediately go on national television and boast about how we'd been right in our thinking about the murder of Aiden McAlpine. We did not do that because that is not the way we conduct our business. We leave such cheap and nasty theatricals to the press.'

Caz was probably standing open-mouthed at the man's brass neck but still managed to thank him for his time, sign off and send it back to the studio. There would have been a cigarette in her mouth and a two-fingered salute raised to Kelbie by the time the studio presenter appeared.

Narey almost admired it. Almost. He'd had to go on TV to defend his own incompetence but left boasting about how he'd been right all along and having a potshot at Tony for having the cheek to know something he didn't.

The wee shite had got away with another one but he wouldn't for much longer. He was wrong and she was sure of it. Kelbie couldn't sort this mess out. Only she could and that thought scared her as much as it excited her.

CHAPTER 56

Nathan hadn't always read the papers or watched TV to see what had been said about the things he'd done. The thrill had been in the doing, not in the retelling, not in glorying in cold leftovers. He was happier when nothing was written and no one knew.

It changed, slowly. He took to looking, more out of self-protection than excitement. If he knew what was being said, then he'd know if he needed to run or hide, whether he'd need to dig and rebury. Once he started reading and watching the news for mentions of himself, his other self, then he couldn't stop.

It amused him when they were wrong, like *way* wrong. He'd read cops being quoted or see them talking to cameras and laugh at out loud at how far off they could be. He supposed they had to give the media something, anything, to make it seem they knew what they were doing, so ordinary people could sleep at night.

It was like when he'd taken the girl who'd been walking the Telegraph Road into Longriggend. Sandra Gillespie, that was her name. That road is long and as straight as an arrow so you can see anyone on it from a distance away and nothing but empty fields on either side. By the time he'd got close to passing her, he'd already made his mind up. He stopped and got out of the car with a map in his hand, making like he needed to ask for directions. She was bundled into the back of the van and never seen again.

The police blamed her boyfriend, a guy called Steven or Simon or something. The cops said they'd had a row and he'd killed her and buried her somewhere. The boyfriend said she'd walked the Telegraph Road but they didn't believe him. No one other than Nathan had seen her on the road and Steven or Simon got twelve years in prison.

They were getting it wrong again now. He'd watched the news and saw the cop in charge, a wee guy named Kelbie, saying how it was because Aiden McAlpine and Calvin Brownlie were gay. He was slavering at the mouth about homophobia and how that was the key to breaking the case.

It was rubbish. Nathan didn't care one way or the other. Sex was never something he'd been bothered about. This Kelbie was like a dog with the wrong bone, clinging to it for all he was worth.

Sure, he'd taken the boy from the park, that much was right. But only because he'd followed him long enough to know that was the best place to make his move. It was dark and secretive and anyone who saw anything was going to be reluctant to talk to the cops.

That one had been about the boy's dad, the MSP. Mark McAlpine had been the Minister for Public Health when

Nathan was eventually diagnosed, the man who the Internet said had responsibility for things like doctors.

Nathan had written to him, angry for sure but polite all the same. Not ranting or anything, just wanting to know what would be done. To save it happening to anyone else. Maybe he'd used language he shouldn't have done but that didn't mean he should have been ignored. The very least he should have got was a reply.

When two weeks had gone and he'd heard nothing, he phoned. The man who answered sounded as if he were just out of school, said that McAlpine wasn't there, said he was in a meeting. Three times Nathan phoned and three times the man was in a meeting. One of those times, Nathan heard him speaking in the background, he was sure of it. That was when he'd made his mind up.

He'd already had a plan, an exit strategy if you like. The plan was not to go quietly. He was going to do more of the things he'd done and do them more publicly. He'd have found the tools to work with, through planning or chance, but then Mark McAlpine delivered his son into Nathan's path and he didn't need to look any further.

He knew it wasn't the son's fault, but that didn't matter. He had to suffer for the sins of the father, and Mark McAlpine had to know the pain that Nathan knew, had to learn what it felt like to look at death.

Then, when he found out that the other guy, the Brownlie kid, had been selling off clothes and saying they were the ones Aiden McAlpine had been wearing, he had to act. He couldn't let that go. That was taking the piss, and Nathan wouldn't stand for it.

It was like stealing money from his pocket and his name from the headlines. None of them knew who Nathan was but they soon would. There was a letter, left to be found as and when it was needed. If the cancer took him or something else did, then the letter would ensure his immortality. It laid claim to all that he'd done. All that he should be credited with.

It didn't tell everything. He owed some duty of silence to those he'd come to side with, the few who were like him and those whom they sold to. Nathan could keep a secret.

He hadn't always realised there was money to be made in what he did and in the things he'd kept. Maybe he should have known everything had a price, everything had a value, but he was too busy doing what he did to think about it or care. Then he learned about murderabilia. Such a strange word. A strange thing, too, he guessed. But there was money in it.

He saw what things were going for. Items that were much less than what he had. Much of the stuff that was going for big bucks was second-hand. All once removed from the event. His things were very much first-hand.

He made himself a profile, created in an Internet café so there was nothing tracing back to him, and offered to sell an item of clothing. Just a shirt. A bloody shirt. Things happened quickly after that.

The offers came thick and fast, each one higher than the one before, but he never got a chance to accept any of them. He got an email, clearly from the police, asking where he'd got such a thing and to identify himself. He didn't reply. An hour later he was glad to be kicked off the site he'd posted it on.

The collectors, the ones who called themselves the Four, they'd sought him out. At first they'd come looking just for what he was selling but when they sensed who he was, just how he'd obtained what he had, then they became very interested. They let him know they had money and were prepared to spend it.

It was explained to him how he'd been selling in the wrong place and that there was somewhere safer for all of them, somewhere the cops wouldn't go or even know about. Abbadon. They invited him in and made him king.

Nathan had never been fêted like that before. Respected. Worshipped even. It felt good and it made him rich. His hidden cabbage patches suddenly sprouted money. They wanted everything he had.

And everything he could get.

They'd had this conversation about Robert Knox, the anatomist who bought the bodies from Burke and Hare. A useful arrangement, they'd called it. The doctor was a respected man, they said, didn't know where the corpses came from, didn't have to know. But he paid Burke and Hare well. An arrangement that suited everyone. All except the dead.

It was on Abbadon that he'd got talking to Archibald Atto. Until then, Atto had simply been someone he'd read about, the guy on the television news who'd killed all those girls. The famous version of him. Famous because he'd been caught.

The first time Atto had messaged and revealed himself, Nathan wasn't sure what to make of it. There was a thrill, almost as if he'd been contacted by a celebrity, but also worry and a sense of contest. They swapped stories, giving a little more each time, trust growing, telling things only the other would understand.

Nathan never said who he was, though. That was a step he wouldn't take. He could only be Big Sleep, and Atto accepted it. There was a kind of comradeship, a bond for sure. Two people who knew.

Atto sold through Abbadon, too, and had done for a while, his own stash of keepsakes being snapped up by the Four. He made money out of it, but Nathan got the impression it was all a game to him, getting off on his own notoriety. Atto said he used the Four at least as much as *he* used them.

It was Atto whom the old ex-cop had gone to when he wanted information. He went looking for a way in and Atto had given him a map and a key and pointed him in the right direction. So simple.

Smart man, though, is Archibald Atto. Devious bastard too.

The old guy and the journalist had stitched him up before, something that a man like Atto was never going to forget. When they wandered back into his life, he saw an opportunity. He saw revenge. He didn't just point the way to Abbadon, thought Nathan: he sent them to me. An arrangement that would suit everyone.

All except the dead.

CHAPTER 57

It was already dark by the time Winter got to Balerno. He parked as he'd done the time before, well away from Haldane's cottage, and hoofed it from there.

The house was shrouded in gloom, swallowed up by the woods behind it so that only the sheen of the whitewashed walls and the shade of two lights hung out of the forest's mouth. One of the lights burned in the living room that Winter had been in twice, while the other was fainter and probably deeper inside the cottage.

He stole into the cover of the trees across the road, now a familiar hiding place, and he waited. He took a few shots of the house through his longest lens but made sure not to use a flash in case Haldane spotted it. He opened up the aperture instead and let in all the light he could. It was enough to do the job and keep him veiled.

A couple of minutes later, his phone vibrated silently in his pocket. He knew it would be her and deliberated over whether to ignore the text. He knew he couldn't take the risk of stressing her out by not replying, so reluctantly took the phone from his pocket.

So he's still at home? Just sit tight.

He swore silently. It was bad enough her pulling his strings when they were in the same room. Just as well he loved her.

His photographs were going straight to the cloud and popping up within seconds on the window she had open on her laptop. She was seeing what he was. And ready to comment on it whether he liked it or not.

Sit tight was what I was planning to do.
But thanks for the advice.

Sit tight was exactly what he did, for a little over an hour. He had friends who had done this kind of thing, either surveillance work for security firms or as paparazzi for the papers, and they'd told him about the arse-numbing monotony of sitting in one place for so long, but he'd never really understood it until now. His knees locked, his neck was stiff and his back ached. His fingers did too until he realised the complete needlessness of holding onto his camera.

What's going on!?

Nothing.

And it was a whole load of nothing until the rear cottage light went out and, seconds later, the front room light followed it. His mind just had time to wonder whether Haldane had gone to bed when . . . There! The front door opened and the man emerged, coat on and collar turned up. He didn't look around as he strode to the old black Volvo, got in and drove off away from the village.

Winter took two quick shots of the departing car and awaited the inevitable reaction on his phone.

Stay where you are for a bit in case he's forgotten something. He might turn around.

Yes, boss.

Shut up and do what you're told ;)

He waited five minutes then slipped out of the trees and across the road. There was a side gate that led to what he was sure was Haldane's garden, backing onto the woods. He groped at the door and swore to himself when it didn't open. Locked. The whitewashed walls were easily six feet high. Damn it. He took another look around then stepped back to give himself room to get a foot up onto the handle and from there levered himself to the top of the wall. He took one look to see where he would be landing and swung himself over the top, dropping almost soundlessly onto grass

He leaned his back against the door, breathing hard and listening for the unlikely sound of footsteps or a shout suggesting he'd been seen. There was nothing but the wind stealing through the trees and the unseen scurry of small animals.

There was even less light in the garden than outside, the overhang of trees from the forest blackening the night still further. As far as gardens not being overlooked were concerned, this was an estate agent's dream, with the wall to one side and the dense woods protecting the rest.

He – or, more to the point, she – was sure the garden would give him the easiest and safest way into the house. He wanted to work quickly, not knowing when Haldane would return, but the privacy of the garden would at least buy him time to find a way in.

He could make out two lines of slabbed path that ran at ninety degrees from each other and skirted mature flower beds, the colours neutered under the pale moonlight. He stole down one side towards the house until his eye was caught by something shining dully to his left. He stood still, trying to work out what it was. Tall and thin, it seemed out of place.

He turned and walked across a patch of lawn until he was next to it. It was a round, metal post that rose a good foot above his head. A pole for hanging a washing line? No. His phone's torchlight picked out a rusting, white, square metal flag at the top. BUS STOP.

Running a hand up and down its roughcast surface, he felt a chill on his spine that mimicked his own movement. Pulling at it, he found the pole was planted deep into the garden, very much a permanent fixture.

He took a burst of photographs and resolved not to answer the text that he'd soon get. He didn't have an answer for her. He could only see what she could.

Sure enough, as he worked his way back to the house, his phone shook in his hand as her message came through, then buzzed again in frustration a minute later when it had been ignored.

Tell me that's not what it looks like

It sure looks like it, he thought.

He inched along the path, walking more by feel than sight, his head full of the implications of the bus stop sign. He had begun to reach for his phone to text her when he was forced to stop in his tracks. There were footsteps on the road outside.

He shoved the phone in his pocket to douse what little light it offered, and stood still. The footsteps got closer, voices too. Shit. Don't text, he urged her. Even on mute, don't text.

There were two voices. Two people. He couldn't make out what they were saying but he realised they were now right outside Haldane's garden and just a few yards away. He held his breath and debated his options if the garden door opened. Fight or flight or bullshit his way out of it?

There was something said and then the snap and sizzle of a match being struck. That was quickly followed by a sharp bark. A dog reminding its owner it was there. He held his breath some more until the footsteps started up again, voices chattering till they faded.

He finally let his breath loose with a weary shake of his head. He didn't need this.

As he reached the other side of the garden, his phone's torch picked out a door that he could see led into a conservatory, the moonlight glinting on its sloping glass roof. It seemed the most promising way in and he headed towards it. There was a good chance the conservatory would have an open lock or if not, one that was easily negotiated.

He had taken just two steps when his shin cracked painfully into something solid.

He sank onto one knee, rubbing at his shin and doing his best not to swear. What the hell had he walked into? He shone his torch towards it and saw a slab of upright grey stone. No wonder it hurt: the thing was two-inch-thick granite with corners that would cut down a rhino.

He looked closer. *Jesus!*

Open-mouthed, he picked up his camera and adjusted the aperture. To hell with any risk, he needed flash. He shot from every angle, a few close-up shots and one further back to frame it in the lean of Haldane's house.

The photographs flew to the cloud like angels and he waited.

Is that what it looks like?

Yes

Can't be. In Haldane's garden?

Yes!

He slid onto his haunches and looked at it, camera by his side.

Martin Welsh's gravestone.

CHAPTER 58

The words on the stone were macabre in the mix of moonlight and torch.

Martin Alexander Welsh
January 16 1959 to May 7 1973
Beloved son of Alexander and Jean Welsh
Loving brother of Alice
He doesn't lie here but in our hearts.
Never forgotten.

The last line reflected the fact that Martin's body was never found but the ripping up and movement of the headstone gave it even greater poignancy. Winter's breath was caught in his throat. For all that the boy wasn't buried beneath him, he felt just as if he were stamping all over his grave. He felt as if he were intruding, even though the gravestone had no right being there. He wasn't the culprit: Haldane was.

The headstones that were damaged in Calderrigg Cemetery. The family had put a new one in its place.

This ... this had to be the original. Had it actually been vandalism or something calculated to get the stone out? Haldane was the collector. And he'd collected big time.

His phone had been jumping at his side as if it were alive. He finally relented, dragging his eyes away from the carved granite and inspected the messages that were desperate to be read.

I'm not sure I believe what I'm seeing

Any sign of how long it's been there?

What is the ground like around it?

Forget going inside. We have enough and DO NOT want to alert him

Get out of there NOW. Phone me from the car

Winter heaved an exasperated sigh and got to his feet. He retraced his steps through the garden, stopping at the door to listen for the sound of returning dog walkers. There was a bolt on the garden side that would have let him out easily but there was no way of locking it again from the other side, so he had to repeat his trick of climbing the wall, this time landing with a bit of a clatter on the road. Just a few minutes later, he'd got back to his car, driven to the opposite end of the village and parked again. She answered his call immediately.

'Did anyone see you leave?'

'Nope. There was no one around. I guess I might have been seen getting back into the car but no one would have thought anything of it, even in a place this size.'

'Okay, good. We need to think what to do next, and it helps a lot if no one knows and we've got time to work it out.'

'No one saw me leave. A couple of people walked past while I was inside but I'd been in for a good few minutes before they arrived.'

'How long do you think the headstone had been there? Was it covered up by anything? Shrubs or flowers or some manmade thing? And the bus stop sign, could it be seen from the road? They're usually pretty tall.'

'Which question do you want me to answer first?'

'Sorry, sorry. Any one you want.'

'I've really no idea how long it had been there. Maybe I'd have a bit of a clue if I'd seen it in daylight, but who knows? The earth didn't seem like it had been disturbed any time recently so my guess would be it's been there a while. When did the stone get taken from the cemetery?'

'March 2007.'

'Well probably then, don't you think? Or not long after it. There were some tall, dark-leaved things growing by it and the fronds – is that what you call them? – were hanging over the headstone. Hard to say if that was deliberate or not, but they did hide it a bit.'

'It sounds like he doesn't have any visitors to his garden if he wasn't worried about it being seen. Was it locked?'

'Yes, bolted from inside. The bolt was rusted pretty stiff, too, so I don't think it had been opened in long time.'

'You didn't open the bolt to get back out, did you?'

He let the silence hang until she apologised.

'Sorry, I'm used to working with halfwits.'

'Yes and they must love being micro-managed all the time.'

'I don't . . . Anyway, what about the bus stop sign. Could it be seen from the street?'

'No chance. It's taller than the wall but it's far enough into the garden that it can only be seen from inside. It's stuck in a corner, too. The only people that could see it would be by Haldane's invitation only.'

'And he never mentioned these parts of his collection when he was boasting to you about the other stuff?'

'I think I'd have remembered.'

'Oh, shut up and stop being so precious. I'm just thinking out loud. Just get yourself home. I need someone to make me a cup of tea.'

She ended the call and Winter picked up his camera, flicking through the images he'd just taken.

The house, Haldane leaving, the bus stop sign.

And the headstone.

The more distant shot with Haldane's house and conservatory behind it placed it firmly in the location. The close-up was the money shot, though. Beloved son. Loving brother. He doesn't lie here but in our hearts.

One day, this photograph would fill a front page. But not today.

CHAPTER 59

Nathan hated his doctor. Genuinely, absolutely, utterly hated him.

Doctor Death. Doctor Doom. The Quack who needed a Smack. Doctor George Jeffries GP. Gormless Prick. Greasy Prat. Gimpy Pisshead. Glorified Pill Pusher. Glib Ponce. Grubby Pig.

Doctor Jeffries. The bearer of bad news. The incompetent Doctor J.

He worked out of a practice in Mount Florida. Four of them on the nameplate and yet you still had next to no chance of getting seen. Phone for an appointment, or try to, find the lines jammed and then call back every two minutes, and it's still engaged. Even if you win the lottery and get through, the odds are still against your actually seeing a doctor.

You can't book for more than a week ahead and there's no chance of getting an appointment for the next few days. If it's an emergency, then maybe, if you're lucky, you could go in and wait and see. Is it an emergency, though? What, you've been feeling it for a few months? Well it's hardly an emergency, is it? Try again next week.

And then of course you finally get an appointment and the quack is fucking useless. What's the point if they first can't diagnose it, then can't cure it. The specialists? Not much better, but at least maybe they'd have had a chance if Doctor Dickhead had read the symptoms right in the first place.

It took three appointments – each one harder to get than the one before – and four months before it was finally diagnosed. By then it was too late: the bastard had its teeth in him and would never let go till it killed him.

Sometimes Nathan thought it was partly his own fault. Maybe he could have pushed it harder; maybe he should have complained more, not suffered it, then moaned afterwards. But that was letting them off the hook; it was letting *him* off.

Jeffries with his bad breath and smug smile. With his silly little specs and garish ties. With his patronising, nothing-to-worry-about attitude. You're run down. Just take it easy for a bit. Four or five years training for a medical degree and they tell you to take some vitamins and give yourself a shake. That worked well, didn't it?

Nathan hadn't made too much of a fuss. It wasn't his way. The whole medical practice, especially old useless Grubby Pig, probably thought he'd taken it really well and not blamed anyone else for it. Just a bit of bad luck, really, nothing they could have done.

It wasn't what he was really thinking. He was thinking about a spiked railing going through Jeffries's head. Or a car knocking him down, then reversing over him. Or maybe tying him to a chair and then letting him experience what pain really was so that just maybe he'd finally realise that a smug smile of sympathy wasn't going to make anything feel better.

He'd been thinking about George Jeffries for a while now. Every time made it worse. Every time he thought of him, he wanted to *do* something worse. He'd been imagining greater and more complicated punishments. Something that Glib Ponce really deserved.

He could see the doctor's face when he closed his own eyes. See him when he tried to sleep and when he couldn't, see him when he paced the floor and in the early hours and when he finally woke from his bloodied dreams. The big, pink, patronising face of Greasy Prat, smiling at him. Always smiling, the grin getting big and wider and cheesier every time he saw it.

Nathan wondered why the man did that, why any doctor would do it. Smile. Is it supposed to make bad news easier to swallow? To show you that they care? Maybe they teach it at their posh universities. Bedside manner, that was what they called it. How to get the plebs to accept you don't know what you're doing but at least you know more than they do, and you're a nice person. *Fuck that shit!*

There was an undertaker's just five doors down from the surgery on Cathcart Road where the quacks did their stuff. Handy, really. Dr Jeffries and his fellow snake-oil-guessing merchants could mess up but offer a discount with their neighbours on a shop-with-them, shop-with-us basis. From where Nathan sat in his car, he could see the front door of both operations and was studying them in turn.

At least one of them was honest. R. K. Harkins and Sons

did what it said on the tin. They filled you full of embalming fluid, slapped on some makeup so you looked more like yourself than you had done in a long time, dressed you in your Sunday best and sent you on your way to the next world with a quiet smile fixed on your face. A fake smile, a drawn smile.

The doctors? They'd have been as well sending him to the next-door chemist for an aspirin or to the butcher's two down to sell himself off as meat. For all the good they'd done him, he'd have been better off going to the curry house next door and taking his chances with them.

Nathan had no time for people trying to take the piss out of him, and that was what Jeffries and the rest of them had done. Like that kid Calvin who had tried to make out he was selling what was Nathan's. The trophies that Nathan had earned. He couldn't let that go any more than he could let Brian Horsburgh get away with making fun of him when he was seventeen. The Brownlie kid had to be made an example of.

There were double yellows on both sides of the street in front of the surgery but Nathan had found a rare space just before the lines began and sat there and waited. Nobody paid him any attention, sitting low in the driver's seat with a hat pulled down on his forehead. Instead, the world just shuffled on past towards the bookie's and the newsagent's, a pair of old ladies compared complaints on the pavement, and the occasional junkie staggered in for iced doughnuts and yum-yums at the bakery.

Nathan knew by now that he couldn't quite be sure when Jeffries would leave the practice. Sometimes he'd make a break for it before seven; others he'd still be there nearer to eight. It was all about getting to know his routine. Wednesdays, as this was, he'd more likely be later. Maybe he did paperwork that night or sent half-arsed apology letters to the patients he failed. Maybe he just practised his smile in the mirror before he went home. No matter, Nathan would wait and then he'd follow.

There he was. Last man out and locking the door behind him. His collar turned up to the rain and his silly specs already starting to need wiper blades. His fat, pink face glowed under the street light and he looked around as if expecting a burst of applause. He tugged his raincoat tighter to him and began to walk. Nathan already knew the first few turns he'd take, knew where he was going, so he sat tight and waited it out. Let him walk, let him lead the way to his car.

Jeffries's usual parking spot was on Bennan Square, just ten to fifteen minutes' walk away, crossing the invisible border into Govanhill. A football-pitch-sized rectangle of green formed an oasis in the middle of the surrounding ex-council housing. It didn't have much more than two squares of grass, trees and the odd park bench but it was a nice spot on a summer's day. On a night like this, it was dark, isolated and quiet, making the path through the middle a dangerous shortcut.

Nathan made his move, trusting Doctor Dickhead to be a creature of habit, and hoping he'd been able to get his spot that morning. He drove slowly, carefully, took his turn off Allison Street and looked for him. Yes, good, good. He was walking close to the tenements, hoping to avoid as much of the rain as he could. As if that were the only thing he had to worry about.

Nathan passed him without a sideways glance and made his way round to the far side of Bennan Square, his fingers crossed on the steering wheel. Just off the corner, he saw Jeffries's white Honda Civic and sailed past it, turning into Brereton Street, parked up and got out. Timing, it was all about timing, but he had the length of time it took to cross the park to play with. That was his window of opportunity.

As he entered the park, the first thing he did was to look around and make sure no one else was daft enough to be in there in the dark and the rain. He was pleased to see the rest of Govanhill had more sense than the doctor.

He walked slowly, giving him time, and there, sure enough, he saw the tall figure wrapped in the raincoat, hustling along the path. Nathan had his hands in his pockets, his head lowered, doing his best to be as unthreatening as possible. Jeffries had certainly seen him but there was no way he'd recognise him, not with wet spectacles and the gloom.

He edged towards the left of the path, letting Jeffries take the right, letting him feel secure. He walked half a stride beyond him before slipping his right hand out of his pocket and swinging it through the air, catching Jeffries square on the temple and watching him fold like a wet rag with barely a whimper.

Nathan slipped the cosh back into his pocket and bent to place an arm under each of the doctor's armpits. The man's deadweight stalled him for a moment but, once he got him moving, it was easy to haul him off the path and into the thick bushes that grew just a yard or two away.

He dumped him there, Jeffries's head on the wet grass and his mouth gaping like a fish. Alive but out cold. Not for long but long enough for Nathan to go through his pockets, taking his wallet and car keys, slipping off his spectacles and placing them safely in his own jacket pocket.

Nathan crouched, keeping his knees off the grass and avoiding their getting tell-tale wet, looking and listening to make sure no one was aware of what had happened. Satisfied, he waited, delivering small slaps to the side of the doc's face to bring him round. It took a few of them, stinging more each time to make the point, before Jeffries began to stir.

He enjoyed the look of recognition when it finally came. At first it was just a gasp of breath and a muddle of confusion as to where he was. After a bit the eyes focused and then remembered; only then did he know who Nathan was. *You? Why?*

Nathan didn't let him speak the words, only think them. He clasped a hand firmly over the man's mouth, both holding him down and silencing him.

'You killed me,' he whispered to him. 'You sentenced me to death and smiled at me. You shouldn't have done that.'

Jeffries wriggled under his hand, protesting with his eyes and doubtless making all kinds of bullshit excuses and apologies. It was all too little and too late. Nathan didn't want to hear it.

He swung the cosh again, cracking hard against the doctor's skull. Jeffries passed out immediately but Nathan swung it once more for good measure, harder this time, hearing bone break as he did so. He needed silence.

Sure, the easy thing would have been to tape the man's mouth closed, something he'd done on maybe a dozen occasions before. That wouldn't work this time, though, not given what Nathan planned to do.

He brought the Stanley knife from his pocket with one hand and squeezed Jeffries's mouth into a smile with the other. He looked down at him for a moment, hating him and hating his lips, hating the shape they made.

He was going to cut the smug smile clean off the doctor's face. And then he was going to kill him.

CHAPTER 60

'I'm telling ye. She's Danny Hamilton's big sister.'

'No way, man. Danny Hamilton's got a face like a bag of spanners.'

'Still his sister but. You've got it bad for her, eh?'

'Naw.'

'Aye ye huv, Hutchy. Cannae stop talking aboot her. You pure love her.'

'Bolt, ya nugget. I jist fancy her. A bit. Nuttin' special.'

'Aye, right. Tell ye what. If you dog school with me the day then I'll no tell Danny that you're pure wanking off over his sister.'

'Naw. Ah'm no skipping school, Briggo. My dad'll kill me if he finds out.'

'Aww, come on. How's he gonnae know, eh?'

'He's like a walking lie detector, him. Cannae get anything past him. Well, no unless you're my mam. She's the only one can con him. Does it all the time.'

'Telling you, he'll never know. Naeb'dy will. We go into school, register, maybe go to Maths first thing, then we leg it. Spend the day down the arcade. I'm no getting up at the arsecrack of dawn to deliver these papers and then no spending the money. We can go to Mickey D's as well.'

'Naw!'

'Aye. Ye know ye want tae. Let's get these bags back to the shop before old man Maan sends out a search party then I'll see ye after brekkie.'

'Naw.'

'Shitebag.'

'Fuck you.'

The boys took the path through the gardens on Bennan Square, the same route they took every morning after delivering the papers and meeting up to walk back together to the shop on Cathcart Road. The gardens were a bit close to Hutchy's house for comfort but the pair were still gallus enough to stop and have a smoke on the benches. It was their ritual, deserved after a hard morning shoving copies of the *Daily Record* through letterboxes.

It was barely daylight but, as they turned into the gardens, Hutchy saw the leg sticking out where a leg shouldn't be. He nearly crapped himself but managed to keep his calm just enough to turn it into bravado.

'Jeezo, man, look. A jaikie sleeping in the bushes.'

Briggo followed his gaze and grinned wide. 'Let's boot him then leg it.'

'Ya mentalist. Aye, awrite then. Bags first kick.'

'Naw, it was ma idea.'

They edged closer, making sure the man was asleep and seeing his arms spread wide, legs splayed on the grass and his head tumbled back into the flowerbed. Hutchy and Briggo stood over him, the truth slowly dawning.

They saw his eyes rolled back in his head and they saw the bloody mess in the middle of his face. They saw he was too well dressed to be a junkie or a jaikie. Neither boy found the ability to move his feet but each eventually managed to swivel his head towards the other.

'Fuck's sake, man.'

'Ah know.'

'Scared, Hutchy?'

'Naw. You?'

'Naw.'

It was quiet in the gardens. Quiet enough that Hutchy could hear his own heart beating. He'd never seen a dead body before. He didn't think he wanted to ever see one again.

From the corner of his eye, he saw Briggo reach into his back pocket and bring out his phone, swiping through the options on the screen.

'You calling the cops?'

'Ma fuck. I'm taking pictures.'

'Whit?'

'Naebody's gonnna believe this otherwise. This is going on ma Facebook.'

Hutchy fished out his own phone and followed suit, even though his stomach urged him not to. The pair of them clicked through their fear like whistling through a graveyard. Big baws that's what they had. Big baws.

The scream nearly made them crap themselves. It pierced the air and rang round the gardens, shattering the morning calm. The boys turned and saw a little red-haired girl, her eyes as wide as the Clyde and her lungs bursting. It was Hutchy's little sister, Megan.

'Aw, shite! Shite!'

Hutchy took a step and clamped his hand over the girl's mouth, at the same time spinning her away from the body to take it away from her view.

'Dinnae look, Megs. And stop that screaming. Dad'll kill me.'

The girl sank her teeth into his hand and bit down with all her strength. Hutchy yelped and let her go. Megan spun on her heels and looked at the body again, screaming louder and longer than before.

All round the square, doors and windows were opening. Heads sticking out, people emerging to see what the hell was going on. Hutchy and Briggo looked at each other, the pretence of hiding their fear gone. They stuffed their phones in their pockets out of sight and backed away from the corpse as the residents of Bennan Square began to filter through the gates and into to the gardens. They were in for it now.

This was old-school for Winter. Photographing bodies. It didn't get old, didn't get better or worse, neither more nor less exciting. It was what it was.

The difference from the days when this was what he was specifically paid to do was that he was now on the outside looking in, his lens effortlessly shortening the distance across the railings and into the garden where the man's body lay spread-eagled.

He'd got a call from one of the uniform guys, Sandy Murray. A tip-off that would be worth a beer or two and a favour owed in return. It was well worth it, particularly as he got the alert early enough to beat the crowds, including most of the crime-scene guys.

They were here now and had a hustle on, trying to rig up a tent to keep out prying eyes, but they couldn't beat his trigger finger. Click. The stricken body. Click. The bloodied face. Click. The hideous, sculpted hole. Click. The ragged flaps of skin and teeth and gums that looked funny where the lips used to be. Click. Click. Click.

Old-school. The man had been dead for hours, somewhere between five and ten was Winter's guess. Nothing particularly scientific, just plenty of practice. The ashen purple of his skin, the rigidity of his limbs and the cold brown of the blood that smeared his face like a kid who'd gorged on chocolate.

Those were the nuts and bolts of it, the physical engineering that the forensics would be all over. There was more, though, and he couldn't miss it. Every instinct, old and new, was screaming at him that this was more of the same.

Whoever had done this had made no attempt to hide the body, far from it. The corpse was left with the intention of its being found. It was all so obviously, deliberately public. Like Aiden McAlpine. Like Calvin Brownlie.

People stood around Bennan Square and stared. Half-dressed men and women, their morning rituals interrupted by screams and sirens. Winter's camera froze them as they pointed and gossiped, some with mouths open, others shaking heads in disbelief that it had come to their doorstep. Younger faces were pressed up against windows, banished indoors but wide-eyed and desperate for something to tell at school.

The only youngsters on the street, two boys in their mid-teens, stood alongside a pair of uniformed cops, looking small and scared in their shadow. One of the two just shook his head sullenly, unable or unwilling to come up with words, his eyes darting nervously round the square. The other boy jabbered away, anxious to be heard, or just to hear it himself.

Winter caught them in a single frame that he immediately knew was a front-page photograph if only he had the lack of heart to use it. The boys looking at each other, shared fear and excitement, a moment passing between them that no one else could hope to understand.

In an instant, they disappeared from view as two other figures emerged on the fringes of his lens, getting larger as they marched straight towards him. One had his hand up, ordering Winter to stop and trying to block his view.

He didn't know either of them, and that meant his chances of arguing his case were minimal. His time was up. No matter, he had his pictures and he knew what he had to do next.

There was a cop out there whom he *did* know – and it was time they talked.

It took till nearly six before he was able to call, copy written and filed, photographs selected and approved. Addison was still in the station, sounding tired and grouchy, neither of which was particularly unusual.

'Hey, wee man. No, I'm still at the coal face. Been in here for six hours and starting to go stir crazy.'

Winter thought of Rachel cooped up in the bedroom and threatening to scrape off the paint.

'That's bad for you. It's well documented that the mind works better with respite from work and that social interaction increases mental stimulation.'

'Yeah? Next you'll be telling me that pubs are better than health spas and I can get Guinness on prescription from inhuman resources.'

'They say it's the perfect cure.'

'The TSB in half an hour?'

'I'll be there in twenty minutes.'

Winter got there first, two pints poured and guarded at the bar while watching and waiting for a suitable spot to become vacant. He was a third of the way down his pint of black when he saw a couple in the mezzanine start to fiddle with their coats. He was by the table before they'd stood.

'Jump in our graves so quick?' the man demanded, albeit with what passed for a smile.

'You know what it's like in here when it's busy. Got to be fast.'

The guy just grunted and the woman shook her head at him by way of apology. There hadn't been any need, though. Winter knew what it was: the age-old local ritual of booze-fed adrenalin that leads to confusing aggression for humour. They'd all been there and worn the war medals.

Addison was through the door two minutes later and had scooped a mouthful of Guinness in the time it took his coat to fall from his shoulders to the chair. It was the parched supping of someone with more questions than answers.

'So what do you want?'

Winter mocked indignation, hands wide. 'Seriously? I can't ask my best pal out for a beer without him thinking I want something?'

'What do you want?' Addison repeated. 'You're not my best pal any more. You're a scumbag journalist now, so of course you want something.'

'Arsehole.'

'Cheers.' He took another healthy mouthful of the black stuff. 'Don't make me ask again. What do you want?'

'I want to know about the murder this morning in Govanhill. In Bennan Square.'

'Uh-huh. And why should I do that? I told you how Calvin Brownlie's watch had gone missing but I get the feeling you've been holding out on me. Is that going to change?'

Winter hesitated but knew he had to give to get. He nodded.

'Ask me, then.'

'What do you make of it? And what about Kelbie? Does he think it's related to the other two killings? And was there anything missing?'

'You want to know a lot, wee man. But before I answer, I've got a question for you.'

'Of course it's off the record and of course I won't quote you.'

'I might not have been going to ask that.'

'Were you?'

'Yes, but I might not have been. Don't be such a smartarse. Look, I don't know if the guy in Bennan Square is related to the others but it was the first thing I thought. From what I hear, Kelbie is still convinced Aiden McAlpine was some kind of homophobic killing and is busy trying to keep the MSP happy. Which isn't proving very easy after you lit a fire under him with those missing clothes. Was there anything missing this morning? Well, maybe. And maybe I shouldn't tell you.'

Winter looked back at him. 'Maybe you shouldn't. But maybe I do know a few things you don't. And that Kelbie doesn't. This could be a two-way thing.'

'I was hoping you'd say that. Now that you're a scumbag reporter, this could be the start of a beautiful friendship.'

'I thought it always was.'

'Yeah but now it could actually be useful for me as well as for you. Okay, the guy this morning usually wore spectacles but they weren't on or anywhere near his body. No one seems to be reading too much into it, just thinking they got knocked off in the struggle prior to him being killed or someone nicked them. You and I know better. Now tell me what you've got.'

Winter told him. Some but not all. That he couldn't do. Not yet.

CHAPTER 61

It felt odd that the only real and regular contact she had with the outside world – the real world, not the strange world she'd recently stumbled into – was someone who didn't always know who she was.

She hated the anticipation of the first few moments of a call with her dad. It was the not knowing. Would he recognise her voice? Would he know her name? Would he speak at all?

Of course, it was the hope that really killed her. Despite all logic and experience telling her otherwise, she knew she made every call with a wish that *he'd* answer, her old dad, her real dad, the way he was before that evil fucking disease took him. She hoped, but it never was.

Sometimes, it was nearly him. Enough of him that they could talk and she would smile and be happy for both of them. Those rare golden days.

It was killing her not to be able to see him, though. Good days or bad days or worse days, it wouldn't matter so much as long as she could see him and know he was safe and well. As well as he could be. But being able only to hear a voice, a voice that rarely sounded like him, was a damn poor substitute.

The phone was ringing and she hated the sound of it. The sound of not knowing.

It clicked and the line was open. There was just silence but that was usual. She had this horrible image of him staring at the receiver not knowing what to do or say. That, sadly, was the norm, but she still had to try.

'Hello. Alan's room.'

It was Jess. She'd probably been there and let him try to answer it himself first. She was so good with him. Good enough that Rachel was a bit jealous of it in a way that shamed her.

'Hey, Jess. How is he?'

'Hi, Rachel. He's okay today. I think it might be good. Hang on.'

She heard the carer talking to him. It's Rachel. Your daughter. *Rachel.*

'Hello?'

He sounded weak and distant. Fragile. But he'd answered.

'Hi, Dad. It's Rachel.'

A long pause.

'Rachel?'

'Yes, Dad. How are you today?'

'I . . . I don't know. How are you?'

'I'm okay, Dad. I'm sorry I can't come to see you today. But I will as soon as I can. Promise.'

'Okay.'

He didn't get that. She could tell that he didn't. He probably wasn't going to get what she was going to tell him, either. But she had to. It was a golden day. He knew who she was, or seemed to. It could be weeks before she'd get that chance again.

'You're going to be a granddad.'

'What?'

'A grandfather. You're going to be a grandfather.'

Silence. She thought she knew his confusion. Most frequently, when he knew who she was, he thought she was somewhere between twelve and sixteen, still at school. Maybe she shouldn't have mentioned it.

'A baby?'

'Yes, Dad. I'm having a baby.'

'Oh.'

More silence. He may have been thinking or could as easily have lost the train of thought altogether.

'A baby?'

'Yes, Dad.'

'Okay. Well, don't worry. It will all be all right. Me and your mum will help with everything.'

Tears began to roll down her face. Damn hormones, she told herself.

'Thanks, Dad. I knew you'd understand. I love you. Thank you.'

Silence. Then, 'For what?'

She nearly laughed. Their golden moment had shone so fleeting and bright. She didn't want to ruin it. Not today.

'Bye, Dad, I love you.'

She waited and hoped, as she always did. She told herself it didn't matter if he got it and if he replied the way she wanted. She knew he loved her and that wasn't changed by his illness or how he was on any given day or at any given hour. She particularly told herself that on the days when he didn't answer or when he asked who she was. Those days when a little bit of her heart was broken off.

It didn't really matter if he said it back. Not really.

'Bye, Rachel. I love you too.'

Oh, it mattered. It mattered all kinds of everything.

CHAPTER 62

Nathan wasn't a – what was the word? – pyromaniac, that was it. He wasn't one of those. He didn't get a hard-on from starting fires like some nutcase. But he knew what he was doing.

He'd even been paid for it in the past and there was good money in it. You'd maybe think any idiot could start a fire and that was probably true. But doing it and getting away with it, that was a different thing altogether. He'd done it often enough and clean enough that those who needed things done knew that he was a man they could trust to do it right.

It was just the same as calling a hit on someone or getting a new bathroom put in. You got a pro, not some amateur who'd only set you back a pocketful of change. He was as good as any pro.

The thing with fire, though, is you've got to respect it. Don't do that and you get your fingers burned. Fire is a wild fucking beast and, like any animal, you've got to be the boss. Take control but respect what it can do. Fear what it can do. Most people think they know how powerful fire can be but they don't, not until they have to confront it. It's the most powerful weapon in the world if you use it right; almost impossible to stop once it gets going. It can take out hundreds, even thousands, of miles of forest and you can't kill it. It can make a building disappear.

The real beauty with fire is that accidents do happen. People get careless, they get drunk, they knock things over. Any number of ways a fire can start. If you're bothered about cops or anyone else not knowing it was murder, then fire is a good way to go.

The cops might suspect it's murder but knowing it and proving it are other things and they can't do that if it's done right. Any idiot can start a fire but a pro can make it look like an accident.

Nathan never felt bad for any of the places he torched any more than he did for any of the people he killed. They were just bricks and mortar, concrete coffins. It didn't matter to him what they looked like or how old they were. Usually, they were just figures on an insurance form, pounds and pence waiting to be counted. Some places actually deserved to be burned, though. Like this one. A horrible low bungalow, its dreary walls pebble-dashed in rainy grey, all the windows the same and with the same curtains drawn closed on every one. It was like a dead whale with its eyes shut.

A single small sign was all that declared its purpose. Clober Nursing Home. One of God's waiting rooms.

Nathan didn't know how many coffin dodgers were inside and he didn't particularly care. All that mattered was that people didn't leave the place. Once they were in, they were in to stay. So he could be confident that the person he wanted to be in there would be.

He'd watched the place long enough to be sure they had all settled down for the night. The odd lamp still burned but most were in sleeps that they'd likely never rise from. It would be a blessing, for whatever that was worth.

For old codgers like them, fires must be a regular risk. Very forgetful, very careless. Just close their eyes for a minute and they drop off. Not that it mattered if anyone knew it was deliberate. As long as one person was fairly sure that it was.

There was just one fire exit in the building. That and the front door and windows were the only way out. The front door was also his most likely way in. A place like this – why would anyone want to break in and why would anyone bother with heavy security?

It was easy prey. A steal down the darkened path, a bit of specialist plastic in the jamb, a wiggle or two and he was inside. Nice and quiet, just in case.

You need three things to start and sustain a fire. It's what they call the fire triangle. Oxygen, a fuel source and heat. One, two, three, go. That's your basic fire.

To really get a blaze you up the stakes. You make sure two of the factors are on your side as much as possible. Up the fuel load, increase the oxygen content. The first you do by adding flammable material or adding an accelerant. The second by opening windows to get an air flow.

As he padded round the care home in the near dark, he knew how simple this was going to be. Plenty of combustible material. Curtains, furniture, bedding. Plenty of accelerants too. Nail polish remover, hair lacquers, cleaning products, maybe some alcohol. He was going to keep this simple.

He moved to the heart of the building, hearing the low hum of sleeping humans around him. Smoke alarms dotted the ceiling but he doubted they would beat the speed of his fire. There were two fire extinguishers, but they wouldn't come close to matching the fire's power.

He opened the door to a large open-plan space that he assumed worked as a day room. Sofas and chairs, a television set, a side table with tall, white candles on it. This was the place.

Taking the bottle from the inside pocket of his jacket, he unscrewed the top and splashed the contents freely over one of the sofas and the carpet around it, trailing it towards the door. Once the path was set, he opened two of the windows. The better the air flow the better he liked it. Going back to the centre of the room, he struck a match and lit the candles on the table, which was no more than a foot away from the couch. He watched them burn for a few moments, enjoying the anticipation. They were a convenient starting point, enough to put doubt in the mind of the fire investigators, but he'd have found another way if he'd needed to.

With a gloved hand, he nudged one candle into the other causing it to topple onto the sofa and the flame to bite into the doused fabric. Sparkle time.

He stepped to the side, ready to flee, ready to help the fire on its way if it was needed. There was no need. It began with a low rumble and quickly grew to a cough and a bark. Flames jumped and the fire was on.

He made his way quickly to the door, making sure he would outpace the heat that was racing at his heels. He pushed the door wide and paused in the corridor just long enough to open another window and lay the contents of another bottle of liquid along the carpet before leaving through the front door.

He stood in the shadows of the trees in the road opposite the nursing home and watched. There. There it was. The first curl of yellow flame rising above the height of the windowsill. And there. The first pane of glass blown out by the heat.

Nothing would stop it now. It would eat the building alive.

CHAPTER 63

The first scream came well after the first window had blown out. A high-pitched female shriek from the member of the night staff who heard the smoke alarm first. Not the alarm in the day room, because it had been switched off, but one towards the rear of the home. By that time, the fire was thriving. By that time, it was virtually unstoppable.

Jess Docherty threw back her bedroom door and was greeted by searing heat and flames licking at the walls. The scream burst out of her and she began to retreat back into her room for her own safety before she realised what she had to do. She banged on the bedroom door of the other person working nights, Maggie Dornan, just a few feet down the corridor.

The woman emerged, dazed but wide-eyed and quickly let loose a scream of her own.

'Get them out!' Jess roared at her. 'We've got to get them out!'

Maggie looked terrified and lost, tears streaming down her face. She screamed again and Jess slapped her.

'Open the doors, wake them up and get them out.'

Maggie nodded, but it took a shove from Jess before she moved, thumping on the nearest door and opening it. All along the corridor they went, heads low trying to avoid the smoke that curled its way into their lungs.

Jess charged into George Young's room. Old Mr Young they called him, poor old soul who coughed from morning till night and could barely walk a few feet unaided. He was sitting upright in his bed, his mouth and eyes wide open.

'Come on, George. Get up and come with me. Now!'

Unblinking, he threw his legs over the side of the bed and got unsteadily to his feet. Jess strode across and put herself under his arm, taking the weight of him on her shoulder. She was a good foot shorter than he was but he was bent near double. Together they shuffled towards the door.

'What's happening?'

'It's a fire, George. We've got to hurry. Come on, best you can.'

The old man half walked, half let himself be carried. His breathing was laboured and broke into a bark as they got into the corridor. She looked back to see a wall of flame and knew they wouldn't, couldn't, get them all out.

Maggie Dornan was nowhere to be seen. Jess swore out loud and marched the old man on towards the front door. 'Come on, George. Nearly there.'

The door was open when they reached it and she manoeuvred George into the space, taking a quick breather as she leaned him against the frame. Outside, a few feet away, Maggie was on her knees, coughing violently.

'Maggie! Jeezus, we've got to get them out of there. They'll all die!'

'I can't go back in there. It's too late!'

'We've got to.'

Maggie just shook her head and buried her face in her arms. Jess pulled old George along another few feet and kicked the other woman in the shins. 'Take him. Get him away from the building. I'm going back in. Make sure the fire brigade's on its way.'

The corridor was ablaze when she turned, a tunnel of fire. Through the heat haze and the flames, she could see frail bodies on the move. With just a moment's hesitation, she ducked her head and plunged into it.

The first person she reached was a woman, screaming and scrambling on her knees. Without stopping to see who she was, Jess dragged her along towards the door, scraping her across the carpet. She dumped her on the other side of the doorway and went back inside.

She shouldn't have favourites, she knew that and had been told it often enough, but if she could save only one then she knew who it would be. His room was at the far end of the corridor and she was going there.

A thin, bald man was slumped against the wall unconscious, the smoke taking him or maybe a heart attack. She said a prayer to a God she didn't believe in and pushed on past him, her own lungs searing and filling up.

The building roared all around her, crackling and shouting. Her eyes were streaming and her throat was closing over, her nightdress was on fire and she had to beat at it violently to stamp out the flame. Someone bumped against her and she felt a body fall through the smoke. Turning to see who it was, she stumbled, one leg giving way beneath her, and she fell to the floor. Down the corridor, she thought she saw a door open and legs emerge beneath the worst of the smoke.

She pushed on her arms and began to rise again but there was someone else stumbling in the swirl and he or she crashed over her and landed on her back. She screamed in frustration and the effort burned her throat.

It was getting darker and yet brighter as the fire raged. No one was moving that she could see. Her eyes were so painful, she felt the need to just close them for a moment. She fought it but they ached and bled. She let them slide over and they immediately felt so much better that she let them stay shut a little longer.

Somewhere beyond herself, she heard the wail of a siren calling to her. Was it there to rescue her or drag her onto the rocks? It was close by and yet so far away. She slipped one more time as the darkness closed in on her and swallowed her whole.

CHAPTER 64

Rachel sat upright in bed the moment the phone rang at five in the morning. She was immediately wide awake and one look at the time on the bedside clock was enough to scare her.

She began to reach for the phone but he stretched his arm across her and stopped her from picking it up.

'I'll get it.'

She heard the same worry in his voice that she felt inside. Her stomach tightened and she didn't know if it was the pre-eclampsia or fear. Probably both.

Her mind raced. It took a few moments to remember she wasn't working, that she was off all cases. That really just left one thing. One person.

'Hello?'

A pause.

'She's not here just now. I'm her partner. I can take a message.'

He was protecting her and she didn't like it. Didn't like that he had to.

'*What?*'

His eyes were wide. His mouth open.

'But is he . . .?'

His eyes closed. His face crumpled.

Her heart dropped to her stomach like a plane dropping out of thc sky.

When his eyes opened again he was nodding, saying okay, right, okay, I will.

He hung up the phone and turned to look at her. She didn't want him to speak.

She already knew what he was going to say.

'Rach, it's your dad.'

She knew.

'He's dead.'

She knew.

It was what she didn't yet know that was going to rip her in two.

CHAPTER 65

He didn't let her go to the nursing home or the hospital. There was nothing to be gained from either, only risk.

Stopping her wasn't exactly easy. She'd screamed at him, threatened to rip his head off if he didn't get out of her way. All he could do was hold her and try to quieten her, try to reason beyond everything that was utterly unreasonable.

She had to stay and she had to calm down. It was all he had.

In the end it was the pain that stopped her. She was still in his arms when she bent double and her knees gave way. The pain ripped through her middle and she had to give in, letting him guide her back into bed.

He phoned the doctor, then held her till the pain subsided and only the tears remained.

She'd known for a long time that her dad would go. That he didn't have long left. But this! Oh, my God, this!

She could have taken it if he'd passed away in his sleep as she'd expected him to. It would still have been heartbreaking but it would have been expected and almost a blessing. It had been so hard for him, such a proud man and so strong that to have all that stripped away was so unfair. She'd even have forgiven herself for being a bit relieved that he didn't have to suffer that any more. But this . . .

The sheer horror of it. It made her want to throw up. Made her want to scream. She couldn't let it into her head, couldn't picture it for an instant.

And worse, much worse than even that, it was her fault. It was all because of her.

The doctor had arrived within half an hour and had sedated her. She was swimming in that now, a horrible soup of half-thought and half-dream and all nightmare. She kept seeing her dad's face, his young face, when she was a girl. Smiling, patient, understanding, always there. On the edge of her thought, though, there was a fire burning. Flames that kept trying to get into her picture. She had to fight to keep them away, fight not to think of him like that. She could only think of him alive. Alive and kind and strong and smart and loving.

Tony had waited for the doctor, then phoned his Uncle Danny to come over and sit with her. He was there now, her guard, somewhere above and beside her in the mist. Keeping her safe and keeping her from leaving.

The irony was Danny was like a second dad to her. As if there could be another. Just one dad. Fuck off, Danny. Leave me alone.

It was her fault. All her fault.

She was clinging to his last words and they were all that was keeping her from drowning. 'Bye, Rachel. I love you.'

I love you too, Daddy. I love you too.

The flames were licking closer, setting a slow torch to her memories. She couldn't keep it away much longer. Then everything would burn and she'd deserve it.

CHAPTER 66

Winter stood, stunned, outside the cordon that kept onlookers away from the burned-out shell of Clober Nursing Home. Fire investigators busied themselves and uniformed cops were going door to door looking for anyone who may have been up in the middle of the night.

Addison was there, chatting to the lead fire officer, both looking grim. He saw Winter and waved, holding up a hand to suggest two minutes. Winter nodded back, not sure what else to do.

The building's walls were charred black. Ravaged. Windows were blown out and the doors were buckled. He guessed the fire had been out for a couple of hours, but he could still feel its heat even from thirty yards away.

He'd visited the care home maybe twenty, thirty times. He'd never liked the place. The staff were good enough but he hated her dad being caged in there. Now he'd give anything to have it back like that.

He hated what this had done to her and what it *would* do to her. It terrified him what it might do to her health, to the baby.

'How are you doing, wee man? Stupid question, I know.'

Addison had ducked under the cordon and put a hand on his shoulder, dragging his gaze away from what was left of Clober. It struck Winter how unusual it felt, the contact. They weren't the type that would touch or hug, nothing much beyond a handshake at New Year. Why was that? Why didn't they? They should.

'I just can't believe it. Rachel was talking to him on the phone just last night. He was in good form, too. I'm scared for her, Addy.'

'Christ, it's not like she hasn't got enough to cope with. He was a good man, her dad. Didn't deserve this. None of them did.'

'How many?'

'Eight residents and one member of staff. Three got out but one of those, an old lady, is suffering badly from smoke inhalation and she's touch-and-go to make it.'

'Shit.'

'It's horrendous. Newspapers have all been and gone. You've missed it.'

'Not why I'm here.'

'I know. Sorry. I can't help being a twat.'

'Who was the member of staff?'

'What?'

'The member of staff that died. Who was it?'

'Name of Jess Docherty.'

'Jess? Christ.'

'You know her?'

'She was close with Rachel's dad. Really good with him. She did some shifts with us at the house to cover when we were working.'

'That was her? Jesus, I'm sorry, man.'

Winter was shaking his head angrily, staring at the nursing home. Addison studied him.

'When are you going to tell me, Tony?'

'What do you mean?'

'Cut the shite. I don't button up the back. Jim Bradley, the fire lead, says it looks accidental at first glance, but he's definitely suspicious. The fire was too good, too strong, too many things fallen just into place. And a cop's father is inside? Suspicious as fuck, I'd say.'

Winter didn't have words. Where would he start?

The lack of an answer was all Addison needed, though.

'We've already had the conversation about you holding out on me. Was this deliberate? If you know anything about this, you've got to spill. Don't give me any crap. This is serious.'

'I can see it's serious. It was Rachel's dad. I'm up to here with serious. I know it's fucking serious.'

Addison stared at him and Winter glared back. They inched closer without either moving. Addison broke it off before they butted heads.

'You've got some slack for Rachel and her dad but it's running out fast. Tell her I'm thinking about her. And about what happened.'

'I will.'

'And you know where I am when you want to talk.'

Winter nodded, a concession in the movement. 'Yeah. I do.'

'So make it soon.'

CHAPTER 67

'That fire was no accident. We both know that.'

He wanted to argue the point with her, for her sake, but he couldn't. They'd rattled cages and there had been a consequence. Believing anything else would be dangerously naïve.

So, instead of trying to make her feel better with paper-thin reassurances, Winter could only accept it at face value. The question wasn't whether the fire was deliberate or whether it was a way of getting at Rachel: the question was what they did about it.

'Tony, my dad died because of me. And don't tell me otherwise, because you know it's true. That was a warning. To me, to us. A warning to stay away. Someone killed him and those other old people just to make a statement.'

He wanted to argue with that too but couldn't. She wouldn't thank him for patronising her with what would basically be lies. Her emotions, her entire mental health, were on a knife-edge and he couldn't take risks with that. He had to walk as carefully as she did.

It wasn't just the pre-eclampsia, not just the fears for their unborn child. He was scared for her.

She was still talking, babbling really, steaming off a fraction of the tension she was boiling in but still leaving an ocean of it on simmer.

'So it leaves us with a decision to make.'

She let that hang there, a huge question mark that begged an answer. The time of his getting away with just nodding an agreeing was disappearing. He knew that, within moments, he'd need to be in or out and he had to make absolutely sure he got it right. For both their sakes.

They were sitting curled up together in an alcove under the stairs where the previous owners had built in a cushioned drawer-space that doubled as a reading nook. It also made a good place to hide away from the world.

'We either get scared off as they want or else we don't,' she pressed on. 'We stay away from whatever it is or we don't. We let them get away with killing my dad or we don't.'

The tipping point had been reached and his silence was no longer an option.

'No one is letting anyone get away with killing your dad. Don't lay that on me, because it's not fair.' He felt her begin to unwind in readiness to protest, but he subdued her by pulling her in tighter. 'I understand, I really do. But it's not the only consideration. This isn't just about you and me. It's him or her as well.' He patted her belly to make his point. 'I'm not saying no. I'm just making sure we know exactly what's at stake.'

'You think I've forgotten I'm pregnant?'

'No. But you might have forgotten you're ill. And you definitely seem to have forgotten you're off the case. *And* that we have someone who can help us with this. But ... as long as we know all that, ask me the question.'

She squirmed and spiralled under his arms until she turned her body enough that she was looking him in the eyes.

'Do we let them get away with it? Do we back off? Or do we finish this?'

He had to be in or out. And he had to be right. He had to weigh the risk of doing this against the risk of not. Which was likely to do her more harm?

'You do not leave this house. You get back into bed and you take as much care of you and our baby as you can. You do nothing without talking to me and you get the hell off those murderabilia sites. I don't want to regret anything from this moment on.'

'Do we finish this?'

'Yes. We finish it.'

CHAPTER 68

Something had been niggling her way at the back of her mind for a while. It had bothered her in the way that a fly might when you know it's round your ear but you can't see or hear it. You just know it's there and you can't ignore it.

It wasn't a fly, though: it was a thought, a guess, more than a guess, a knowledge that she'd ignored. It was an idea whistling on the fringes of her thinking but banished somewhere deeper so her subconscious could work it out without being disturbed by real-time things. She'd always worked that way, almost from day one on the job. Maybe everyone's mind worked like that, but she knew hers did. If she had a problem, then often it was better not to try to wrestle it into submission but to let her brain get at it on its own.

She'd lost count of the number of times she'd sat up in bed, wakened from sleep with the solution right at the front of her mind. Or even just doing something completely different, such as driving or showering, and suddenly the answer popped up when she least expected it.

This time, she found it somewhere in the deep-blue

depths of the bedroom wall. She'd been staring at it, hating it, examining it, wondering whether it was peacock blue or cerulean when it came to her. Something Tony had said. Maybe he'd meant it as a throwaway remark or maybe he too had the thought she now had.

It was suddenly simple. And obvious. If it was correct at all. Shit, was it? She thought it through from all angles now, her conscious challenging the workings of her subconscious. She'd known it all along, she just didn't know that she did. But was she right?

Once she was sure in her own mind, she still had a decision to make. Follow her own agenda or do the right thing? Go all lone wolf or get the right help? She could barely think for the excitement of what she'd worked out, but she *had* to. She had to cut through the adrenalin and think.

In the end, that was easy. This wasn't about her and couldn't be. She was off the case but she'd never be off the job. Doing anything other than the right thing wasn't an option to her, not nay more.

She stretched across the bed, her body complaining at the movement. She paused, sensing the onset of the pain but determined to suffer it. This had to be done.

She called Tony and told him her thinking, leaving him speechless for a while. When he found his voice he tried to point her in the right direction but she stopped him, saying she already knew the way.

She flipped through the contacts folder on her phone again and pressed call. It rang and rang and she was about to hang up when Addison answered.

'Yeah?'

'It's Rachel.'

'You okay? You don't sound too good.'

'I'm fine. Listen to me. I need you to get a search warrant. You have to do whatever it takes to get it.'

There was a quiet laugh at the other end of the line.

'I've been waiting for this call for a while but now it's here, you've got me worried. What the hell do you want?'

When she told him, she got nothing but silence from the other end of the phone for a long time. Addison was not a man often stuck for words and she could imagine his face screwed up in disbelief.

'You're kidding me, right?'

'Nope.'

'Fucking hell. And you're not even sure of this?'

'No. But I think I'm right. I'm as sure as I can be without knowing it.'

He laughed but she heard the strain in his voice.

'You need to give me something I can take to the Fiscal. I'm not going in there to tell them you've got a feeling.'

It was her turn to go silent. She didn't have much more than that to offer.

'You need to get it done, Addy. If I'm right . . .'

'You better be, Rachel. Christ, you better be.'

CHAPTER 69

The narrow streets of Balerno buzzed with early-morning rumour and the rumble of machinery trundling through the village. Curtains were pulled back and tousled heads pressed against glass to see what the hell was going on.

They saw the yellow and blue of police cars as they glided before and after a van loaded with forensic equipment and two others towing heavily laden trailers covered in tarpaulin. It was barely daylight and Police Scotland were going to work.

The cavalcade made its way slowly through the village and didn't stop until it got to the white-walled cottage at the end. The lead cop car parked a few feet away and two uniformed officers got out and made for the front entrance.

The first of them banged loudly on the door, three crashing knocks that might have wakened the dead. The sergeant paused only briefly before he repeated it. He was pulling back his fist to thump the door for a final time when it opened before him. A tall figure was pulling on a pair of silver spectacles and looking bewildered.

'What's going on?'

'Mr Robert Dalrymple?'

'Yes. What's happened?'

The sergeant held up paperwork for the man to see. 'We have a warrant to search your house and garden. I'm asking you to step aside and allow us to do so.'

The man's face blanched and he could only stammer. 'What? Why? No, no. I'm calling my lawyer. You have no right.'

The cop pushed the warrant into Dalrymple's hand. 'We do have the right and this will confirm that. You of course have the right to have legal representation present but I suggest you hurry up. We *are* going to search.'

'No, you can't. I won't allow it.' Dalrymple started to shut the door but a size-eleven boot was quickly wedged into the space.

'It really is in your best interest to cooperate, sir. Anything else might be deemed obstructing a police officer in the execution of his duty.'

'And you wouldn't want that, would you, sir?' The voice came from behind the cops and Dalrymple looked up to see Addison approach.

'Are you in charge here? I demand to know what's going on.'

'Am I in charge? It's an interesting question. Some would say never fully. Almost always on the verge of losing control, really. What's going on is that we have, as the sergeant explained, a warrant to search these premises and we intend to do so. If you want a lawyer present then you have roughly the time it takes to get that lot set up.'

Addison jerked a thumb behind him and Dalrymple

followed his gaze to see the men begin to unload the van and the trailer. His eyes locked on the sight of shovels, stakes and planks of wood.

'I . . . I'm phoning my lawyer. I refuse permission for any of you to enter until she gets here.'

'Yeah, sure. Sergeant . . .'

The uniform nodded and followed Dalrymple inside, standing over him as the man grabbed the phone and dialled, still protesting in vain. His call was answered and he began jabbering into the phone.

'It's Robert Dalrymple . . . Yes . . . Yes . . . I have police at my door with a search warrant. Yes, they're inside now. No, they haven't told me. Can you get here? Please, hurry. Okay, okay, I will.'

He slammed down the phone and whirled, eyes blazing.

'My solicitor is on her way. She wants to validate the warrant and asks that you wait until she gets here before proceeding.'

Addison looked at his watch and shrugged. 'Sure. I've got all day and we're not going anywhere, Mr Haldane.'

The man flushed. 'My name is Dalrymple.'

'Whatever. This search is going to happen whether your lawyer likes it or not. Why don't you and I have a chat until she gets here? You can save everyone some time and effort. You'd like to do that, wouldn't you?'

'What is this all about?'

Addison faked disappointment. 'Now that doesn't sound very helpful at all. You *know* what this is about. It's about Martin Welsh.'

The name couldn't have come as a surprise to Dalrymple

but he still jumped as if he'd been slapped. His mouth opened and closed, finally twisting into an attempt at defiance.

'We've been through all this. I was cleared. Completely. How dare you bring this up after all this time?'

It was a good question, Addison thought. He dared because he trusted Narey. He had faith in her judgement, even though he knew she wasn't thinking as clearly as she might. He was putting all his trust and hope in her being right.

The lawyer was there in less than half an hour, looking harassed and angry at having been dragged out of her bed without warning. She demanded to see the warrant and to speak to her client. The sergeant calmly made sure that she could do both. Five minutes after arriving, she was back on the doorstep of the whitewashed cottage and making unhappy noises while admitting she had no power to stop the search.

'This is completely unnecessary, though, Inspector. This could have been handled quite differently and without this circus at such a time of the morning. My client would have cooperated with any request. You didn't need to make a dawn raid.'

Addison smiled. 'I've always liked dawn raids, much more exciting. Come on, you can have breakfast in front of the telly any morning. Surely this is more fun. No? Okay, please yourself. I want to have another chat with your client before we get going. Give him a chance to help himself. That okay with you?'

The solicitor looked as though she wanted to argue

but didn't have either the energy or the right. Instead, she smiled sourly and held an arm out towards the cottage interior. 'Be my guest, Inspector.'

Addison took a few steps inside and found Dalrymple waiting, nervously cleaning his spectacles and scratching at his grey goatee.

'Do you want to tell me what we'll find in your garden, Mr Haldane?'

He blustered. 'I told you. My name is Dalrymple.'

'Right. Do you want to tell us what we'll find?'

'Nothing. You'll find nothing.'

'Really?'

The man was furiously debating with himself. Maybe thinking whether to confess, or maybe whether to run or to swing a punch. Addison recognised the fight-or-flight signals and welcomed the possibility of his doing either. Nothing says guilt like trying to hook a cop or jump out of a window.

Dalrymple let him down on that score, though. He flipped his gaze back and forth between Addison and his lawyer, before finally answering.

'There's a gravestone. You'll find a gravestone in the garden.'

'Whose?'

'Mart—' He swallowed hard. 'Martin Welsh's. It's just a headstone. Nothing illegal. I bought it.'

Addison nodded slowly, as if learning this for the first time, and making a show of looking at the lawyer. 'I'm not so sure it isn't illegal, Mr Haldane. Ms Cousins here might confirm that for us. Who did you buy it from? Martin's family?'

He had the decency to look ashamed. 'No.'

'Then from whom?'

'I . . . I don't know.'

Addison laughed loudly. 'If I had a pound for every time I'd heard that one I'd own my own brewery, but I've never heard it said of a gravestone before. It's a new one, I'll give you that. Did it fall off the back of a lorry?'

The man said nothing.

'What else are we going to find, Mr Haldane?'

'Nothing.'

'You sure?'

'Yes.'

Addison smiled but inside he was worried: the man sounded convincing this time. They were going to dig a hole for themselves, one way or another.

He went to the front door and waved his arm, beckoning the troops towards him. A succession of uniformed officers and forensics climbed out of their vehicles and a number of them began to climb into white protective suits. Slightly further back, an unmarked car opened and out climbed the only member of the press who'd been given permission to capture the scenes.

Winter had had the law laid down to him. Nothing that would identify officers or forensics personnel, no photographs inside the house or garden. Otherwise, the exclusive is yours. He'd grabbed it gratefully.

He had his camera in his hands and was firing off shots of the cops and crime-scene guys busying themselves around the property, being careful not to show faces. And he'd already captured Dalrymple/Haldane standing, mouth open, on his doorstep with a uniformed cop in his face. As he passed the front door, he moved close to Addison.

'Is he talking?'

'Nope. It's all going to be down to finding something.'

'And you think we will?'

'Well we're soon going to find out.'

CHAPTER 70

The search warrant gave access to Dalrymple's property by any and all reasonable entry points. It also gave the police the right to bulldoze their way through such entrances if admission was denied. The choice was simple: unlock the gate to the garden or we knock it down.

Dalrymple grudgingly found a heavy iron key and the door edged open slowly and noisily, as reluctant as its owner. For the first time in many years, it shook off its rust and rolled back to let the world inside.

Winter watched with mounting frustration. He'd readily agreed to his exclusion from the garden as it had been non-negotiable, but now he was regretting it. He had front-page pictures in the bag, but the real money shot was inside the wall and out of view. And it was more than just the photograph: it was what it would mean. He wanted to know that as soon as it was revealed, and he needed it to be right. Being stuck outside was going to strain what was left of his nerve.

His phone had already vibrated a few times in his back pocket but he'd largely ignored it. He knew it was her, demanding updates, anxious to know if she'd been right. He'd sent one reply to say the cops were inside but that was it. There was nothing more he could tell her and nothing he could do. It was out of their hands.

'Where did you get this from?'

Addison was kneeling in front of Martin Welsh's headstone, brushing aside the foliage to trace the lettering with his right hand.

Beloved son ...
Loving brother ...
Never forgotten.

Dalrymple shared glances with his solicitor and Addison knew she'd briefed him on what to say.

'I bought it.'

'Have you remembered who you brought it from?'

'I never knew his name.'

'And you never asked.'

'No.'

'But you knew it was stolen? That it had been taken unlawfully from Calderrigg cemetery?'

He looked at his lawyer again and she gave the slightest of nods.

'Yes. I knew that there was a chance it had been stolen.'

'A chance?' Addison laughed in his face. 'Yeah, a very good chance. Robert Dalrymple, also known as Alastair Haldane, I am charging you with the crime of reset in that you did receive and keep property knowing that it has been appropriated by theft. You do not have to say anything but anything you do say may be noted in evidence. Do you want to say anything else?'

Dalrymple shook his head.

'I thought not. Okay, Ms Cousins I'd like you and your client to move inside the house, please. This may take some time and you can view proceedings from the window. But I need you to move. Now.'

Addison waved an arm and a stream of officers filed through the garden door. They carried shovels, stakes, hard hats and harnesses; others carried plastic buckets and blue tarpaulin sheets. Finally, two pairs of cops squeezed through, the first carrying a jackhammer and the second pushing a contraption that look like a modified, hi-tech shopping trolley. Fresh alarm spread across Dalrymple's face.

'You're digging up the headstone? *Why?* Why take it away? It won't serve any purpose.'

'We're not digging up the headstone – not yet, anyway. We're digging up your garden.'

'You'll ruin it. It's taken years to get it like this. You can't!'

'Watch me. But do it from inside the house.'

The lawyer broke in. 'This is beyond the scope of any reasonable warrant, Inspector. This is harassment. We will sue.'

'If we don't find anything, then be my guest.' Addison sounded more confident than he felt but they had no option but to go on. They'd be hung for the lamb, they may as well be hung for the sheep.

The machine that was shaped like a low-slung shopping

trolley was, in fact, ground-penetrating radar equipment. A yellow and black monitor was fixed to the handles that steered it and wires attached that to what looked like two large, yellow batteries, and from there to two pieces of metal that were flat to the ground.

An engineer got behind it and walked the machine across the lawn near the headstone. His eyes never left the monitor and no one's eyes left him. He repeated the manoeuvre, his expression never changing, no matter how much Addison tried to read it.

When he'd finally finished, he approached Addison, his shoulders already forming a discouraging shrug.

'I can't be sure. There's a lot of clay in the soil and that's not ideal for making a reading.'

'*Christ!* Has the ground been disturbed?'

'Probably. But not necessarily in the way you're hoping.'

'Is there anything down there?'

'Nothing in the first few feet. After that I can't be sure. I'm reading something but my guess is that it's rocks. It's got to be your call.'

Addison lifted his head to sigh and locked eyes with the lawyer, who was staring at him through the cottage windows. Safe to say she didn't look very happy. His call.

'Fuck it! Sergeant Lyons, get your men started. We've got a hole to dig.'

The job was laborious. They took the radar at its word and used the jackhammer to burst through the first few feet of soil, but, after that, men dropped into the resulting hole with shovels and proceeded at a much slower and more careful pace.

Planks of wood were laid across the hole and sheets of tarpaulin laid down to collect the shifted dirt. Every shovelful of earth was sifted, analysed and metal-detected. For an hour, every one of them came up blank.

Addison kept them going, switching the men doing the digging every half-hour and encouraging them to work as quickly as they could. They were down five feet and his own belief was dwindling.

He'd turned away from the dig and from the penetrating stare of Dalrymple's lawyer, and was now looking out over the back wall into the woods. Maybe if he just climbed that wall and ran, they'd never find him. It was beginning to sound like an inviting alternative to getting his balls chewed off by everyone from Kelbie to the DCS and the lawyer.

That was when he heard it.

A clang of metal against something hard and resistant. The noise swept the garden and everyone inside the walls froze instantly.

'It's brick or rock,' the cop in the hole announced. He jabbed his shovel a couple of feet away from where he'd just struck and got the same result. 'There's a whole layer of it.'

Addison waved the radar engineer back over and the man eased his way

The engineer was lowered down into the hole and knelt on the bottom layer so he could brush away soil with his hand. He stood up again almost immediately.

'Rocks. That's what I was reading. But these aren't here naturally. I think you want to dig them out.'

'Too right I do. Keep going, lads. But take your time.'

Shovels were replaced by trowels and the two cops in the hole scraped space round each small rock – their work lit by torches on the hard hats – passing them up by hand then tackling the next. They concentrated on a foot-square area, desperate to see how far the rocks went.

'That's it,' one of the cops shouted up. 'The layer is about three rocks deep but I'm through it. There's soil again. I'm going to scrape that away, too.'

It was just moments later when the same officer stood up and faced Addison, who was peering into the hole from its edge.

'There's something just below this layer of soil. We'll need to take all of those rocks out to get at it properly but . . .'

'But?'

'But, from what I can feel and see, it's a cotton blanket and there's something wrapped in it. I got a handful of it and I'd swear it's bones. There's a body buried under there.'

Addison turned to the window and saw Dalrymple standing beside his lawyer. His eyes were firmly closed.

CHAPTER 71

The work to remove the remaining rocks took over an hour. The two cops in the hole worked as fast as their fingers and the space allowed, trying to keep their bodyweight on the edges and not press down any further on what was below. Two further officers stood either side of Robert Dalrymple to ensure he didn't feel the need to leave.

As the bottom layers of rock were exposed, one of the two cops climbed out, leaving his colleague to finish the job. He lifted the rocks one by one, revealing a surface of soil that was broken sporadically by dirty spears of cotton pushing through from below.

The shape was clear to see from above. It was long and narrow, maybe five feet from tip to toe and no more than a foot across. It was a body. A boy's body.

The last cop was pulled out of the hole, clearing the area so it could be photographed as it was and then leaving the final touches to the forensics.

Two white-suited figures kneeled on the edge of the hole that led to Martin Welsh's gravestone and flooded the cavity with light as they took shot after shot of the risen shape six feet below them.

Some forty yards away, across the wall and across the road, Winter photographed, too. From his precarious perch, hidden high in the branches of an ancient oak tree, his camera trigger fired and fired. He photographed them photographing it.

He twisted slightly and let the camera hang round his neck so that he could reach into his back pocket and rescue his phone. Just one text, just one line: 'You were right.'

It took the crime-scene guys just forty-five minutes to brush away the thin layer of soil that covered the blanket, each grain placed in a bucket and passed back up to the surface. When that was removed, they carefully peeled back the blanket to reveal the white bones and grinning skull that rested beneath.

Addison stared down into the hole, relieved they'd been right and angry they'd been right. He turned to the nearest cop and ordered him to bring Dalrymple and his lawyer to the graveside.

The ultimate piece of murderabilia is how Narey had described it. A grave. Not just a stolen headstone but the actual grave of one of the country's most famous murder victims. Dalrymple had a collector's dream and a family's nightmare.

The man had tears streaming down his face when two cops frogmarched him to the graveside. His lawyer, standing just a couple of feet away, looked horrified.

Addison stood opposite, the gaping grave between them. Dalrymple stared down into the depth.

'Is that the body of Martin Welsh?'

A huge, choking sob escaped from his mouth but he said nothing.

'*Is that the body of Martin Welsh*?'

Dalrymple nodded pathetically.

'Answer me!'

'Yes!'

'Inspector, I must—'

Addison cut the lawyer off. 'That arrest for reset that I read to you earlier? Well I've got another one for you. Robert Dalrymple, also known as Alastair Haldane, I am arresting you on suspicion of unlawful interference of human remains. And I am arresting you on suspicion of the murder of Martin—'

Dalrymple's head snapped up, the tears disappearing.

'No! I didn't kill him. I swear to you I didn't.'

'No, of course not. He just tripped and fell into a hole in your garden.'

'I didn't kill him!'

Dalrymple lost it. He shook off the grip of one of the constables and made to leap into the grave. His feet had cleared the ground and his body arched back when his jump was partially arrested by the other cop.

He was left half in and half out of the hole, the burly officer struggling to hold back his weight till two colleagues rushed to help him.

Addison kneeled beside Dalrymple's head and whispered low enough that the lawyer couldn't hear.

'I'm so tempted to let you fall into that grave and cover you with enough soil that you never get out. The only thing that's stopping me is that poor kid in there doesn't deserve to spend eternity with a piece of shit like you for company.'

He stood, his boot just a couple of centimetres from Dalrymple's face. 'Drag him up. And don't be too gentle. As I was saying, Robert Dalrymple, I am arresting you on suspicion of the murder of Martin Welsh. You do not have to say anything but anything you do say may be noted in evidence.'

'I didn't kill him. I didn't kill him!' He was screaming.

'Yeah. Sure.'

CHAPTER 72

Dalrymple and his lawyer, Victoria Cousins, sat at one side of the table, both looking thoroughly depressed. She'd appeared hassled when she'd been called to his door just after daybreak but that was nothing to how she seemed now. She had a possible child killer for a client and didn't like it.

He was distraught, staring blindly at the table in front of him and wiping tears from his cheeks. Looking old and broken, he rubbed obsessively at his spectacles. Addison saw someone on the verge of a breakdown and knew it was a useful place for an interviewee to be.

The video was running. Rico Giannandrea sat alongside Addison, and one statement seemed to be on loop.

'I didn't kill him.'

'So why was he buried in your back garden?'

'I didn't kill him.'

'Mr Dalrymple, you need to give us some explanation of how he came to be there.'

'I didn't kill him.'

'You knew he was there. You're not denying that, are you?'

'No. But I didn't—'

'So you knew he was buried there. And you were complicit in his body being placed there?'

'I—'

'Inspector, my client will not recognise a question involving the word complicit. It assumes guilt.'

'Well, yes, I'd have thought so. Okay, let's try this. Did you put the body there? Did you arrange for the body to be put there? Do you know how the body got there?'

Dalrymple seemed absent. His brow furrowed and his eyes straying left and right.

'I didn't kill him.'

'But you had his body buried in your garden! You're seriously expecting me to believe you didn't kill him?'

'Yes!'

'Inspector!'

'So you have to help me. If you didn't kill him, how did he get there? At least tell me how that happened. Help yourself.'

'I bought—'

'Mr Dalrymple, don't . . . Inspector . . .'

Addison ignored her. 'You bought what? You bought the body?'

'Yes.'

The word fell out of him like something that tasted bad in his mouth, and he wanted rid of it.

'Okay, tell me how that happened. Who did you buy it from?'

'I can't.'

'Right. Then how can I believe you? You know it looks

much more likely that you killed Martin. You were his teacher and you have his fucking body buried in your back garden. What do you think anyone is going to believe?'

'I did. I bought it. *I did.*'

'Okay. Tell me. How did you buy it? Who did you buy it from?'

Dalrymple's eyes widened and there was something Addison couldn't quite catch.

'A man.'

'A man? The man who killed Martin?'

Dalrymple was in his sixties but shrugged like a twelve-year-old. His lawyer stepped in to help him.

'My client cannot conjecture about who killed Martin Welsh. He has already told you he didn't do it. If he did interact with someone, he cannot know what he'd done.'

'Uh-huh. Okay. Mr Dalrymple, did you believe that the person who sold you Martin's body had killed him?'

'Mr Dalrymple, don't answer—'

'Yes.'

'Okay, good. So you believed you were purchasing the corpse of a murder victim from the person who murdered him. Is that right?'

'Yes.'

'Inspector! I need to speak to my client alone.'

'Mr Dalrymple, the person that sold you the body, was that *you*? Did you kill Martin and then sell the corpse to yourself? Is that what you're telling me?'

'No!'

'You killed Martin Welsh, didn't you?'

'I bought the body. I didn't kill him.'

'Inspector! I cannot allow my client to incriminate himself. I want to speak to him and I'm asking you to suspend this interview.'

Addison was on his feet before she'd finished. A break was going to suit him, too. He had a call to make.

'The weird thing is, I think I might believe him.'

Narey sat up in bed, phone glued to her ear, trying to take in what Addison was saying. 'Me too. It fits. I'm not going as far as to say it makes sense because it doesn't, but it *fits* that he'd do that. He's a collector. A serious collector. If anyone would acquire something as grotesque as a body, it's him.'

'So if he didn't kill Martin then the person that sold him his body did.'

'Yes. And he's sold plenty more.'

'You still know more about this than you're telling me, Rachel.'

'I haven't known it long and some it is guesswork, but I think there's someone out there who's been killing for years. A serial killer we didn't even know was operating. I spoke to my dad and he said his fear was it was just some random who drove past, saw the chance and picked Martin Welsh up and killed him. Some maniac who had nothing to do with what we know. I think he was right. Except I think the same person has done it again and again.'

'Jesus Christ! How many . . .? I mean, what are we dealing with here?'

'I hate to think. But if I'm even remotely right then lots of it. The person who can best tell us, apart from the man who's done it, is sitting in your interview room.'

There was a long pause as Addison mentally released his murder suspect and tried to figure out how to make him a useful witness instead.

'I think he's scared. When I asked him about who he bought the body from, he changed. His eyes widened and he was shitting himself. He'd rather have gone away for this than tell me the truth.'

'Then you need to work out what he's more afraid of and use it. Offer to protect him from the killer and let him know only you can do that. We need whatever it is that he knows. I think you should ask him about the Four.'

'The *what*?'

She explained and he listened.

CHAPTER 73

'Okay, Mr Dalrymple. Let's start again.'

The man formerly known as Alastair Haldane looked much older than he'd done just a few hours before. His eyes were held up by dark circles and his brow was furrowed deep.

'Are you ready to talk to me?'

Dalrymple looked drained but summoned up enough energy to nod.

'Good. Now here's how I think it should work. I will start by believing what you say, that you didn't kill Martin Welsh. That okay with you? And, in return, you tell me the truth. All of it. It's the only way I think it can work.'

Dalrymple and his lawyer exchanged looks that weren't well served by a lack of words. He wanted help and she struggled to offer it. Her only true advice would be to recommend silence, and Addison was stealing that option away by offering him a possible way out.

'Why should I believe you?'

'Because you've no choice. Because I already know some of the things you need to tell me. I know you've spent years trying to keep everything secret but it hasn't worked. Not as well as you think it has. You've got to realise that. It's all over, Alastair. Now it's about how you deal with it.'

The man's head came up at the sound of his real first name. Probably the first time anyone had called him that in many years.

'What do you think you know?'

'No. You tell me. The truth, the whole truth and nothing but the truth. If you want me to believe you, then it's the only way to go.'

'No, I don't think you—'

'Why don't you start by telling me about the Four?'

Dalrymple's lower jaw dropped by just a quarter of an inch but it was enough for Addison to know he'd get what he wanted. Now, all he had to do was steel himself to hear it.

'Firstly, I did not kill Martin Welsh. I was as shocked as anyone else when he disappeared. He was a nice boy, nothing remarkable about him, not particularly smart, but I liked him. So when I was accused of . . . all that . . . it hurt. You can't know what it was like. Everyone thought I'd murdered him. The police, the school, his village, his parents, other parents. Everyone. I was *hated*. It got to the stage I hated myself. I'd have been as well killing him for all it cost me.'

That silenced the room. Even his lawyer sat open-mouthed, unable to intercede to defend him.

'I don't mean . . . You don't understand. It ruined my life. I had *no* life left. Everything was affected by Martin.

Everything was *about* Martin. I read everything I could, cut it all out of the newspapers, then got worried if I missed anything. I became a collector and it just . . . grew. I think it probably got out of hand.'

As much as Addison wanted to stuff that understatement down Dalrymple's throat, he resisted. 'So you bought everything you could about Martin?'

'Yes. After a while, I *had* to. The thought of anyone else having anything—'

'And what about the Four?'

Dalrymple hesitated, eyes blinking as he couldn't decide which way to go.

'That's all over, Alastair. You've got to know that. It might have been fun while it lasted but it's over now. You have to give me something and that means choosing between them and him.'

Victoria Cousins offered her client a small shrug, then a nod of encouragement. Do it. Tell him.

'We met in the USA. Ventura, California. It was a murderabilia convention and we got on well with each other. We realised we had . . . mutual interests. We formed a pact, a bond.'

'And what was the pact?'

'That we'd work together, to get the best collectibles that were available, helping each other to the exclusion of all others. We'd corner the market by pricing everyone else out of it. We all had our areas of interest and we'd respect that. If someone else saw a Martin Welsh piece before I did, then he'd acquire it so that it could be given over to me. And I would do the same for them.'

'Who did the rest want to collect?'

He looked distressed, the pains of treachery written across his face. But he gave it up just the same.

'For one of them it's Dennis Nilsen. For another it's Fred and Rose West. The third collects anything he can about John Christie, Rillington Place and all that. We collect other things, too, but those are the exempt areas where the others agree not to go.'

'And where did you do your collecting?'

'At first it was on surface sites like KillingTime and Murder Mart but, as we bought more and had more clout in the trade, we started to go elsewhere.'

'Like Abbadon and Whitechapel?'

Addison enjoyed the surprise on the man's face and the look of defeat that quickly followed it. He didn't have much resistance left. 'Yes.'

'Tell me about it.'

'We all wanted to buy things that the mainstream sites couldn't give us. Things that couldn't be bought openly but that we knew were out there. So we went dark and found Abbadon, then helped form Whitechapel inside it. We could . . . we could buy whatever we wanted. And, because we were together, we could control the place.'

'Can't beat a sense of power, right?'

It didn't get a reply, just a glare that proved Addison had been right.

'And how did you come into contact with the person calling himself Big Sleep?'

The fear flashed in Dalrymple's eyes again. Unmissable, unmistakable. Addison could see he was terrified of him.

'We saw him selling items that interested us. Items that wouldn't normally be on an open market. We contacted him and invited him to operate somewhere that would work better for all of us. He got to know about my interest in Martin and said he might have some things I'd like. For the right price.'

He paused to grab at the glass of water in front of him, swallowing heavily. Addison enjoyed his discomfort,

'I wasn't sure whether to believe him. Whether he could really get the things he said. But when he sent me a photograph of Martin's clothes . . . I knew. I knew right away they were his. He wanted a lot of money but it was worth it to me.'

'And did you ask him how he got them?'

'No.'

'How did you think he got them?'

'I didn't want to know.'

'But you *did* know!'

'I suppose I guessed. But I didn't ask and he didn't offer to tell.'

'Very convenient for both of you. What happened next?'

'I paid the price he asked and he arranged for me to pick the clothes up at a drop-off point near Nine Mile Burn in Midlothian. I was scared, not knowing what to expect, but Martin's shoes and shirt were in a box, exactly where he said they'd be.'

'And you bought more?'

'Yes. In time, I bought everything he had. The rest of Martin's clothing, his schoolbag, his homework jotters and books.'

'And then you bought Martin?'

'No. Not like that. Not then. It was years later. First, I'd introduced Big Sleep to the others. He said he had other things we might be interested in. And he had. Items we didn't even know existed. That *no one* knew about. He offered us a lot.'

'Oh, the rest of your little gang must have been pleased with you, bringing them such a good source of material. Did you ever meet him, any of you?'

'No, never. That was the deal. All we ever got to know was his name, or at least what he told us his name was. Nathan.'

'And did none of you stop to think this was wrong?'

'No. We are just collectors. The objects were there already, we just paid to have them. We didn't kill anyone.'

'No but *he* did! And you all knew it.'

'He never once said he'd killed any of these people. He just left us to assume he had.'

'And did any of you doubt that?'

The reply was quiet and shamed. 'No. Not for a second.'

Dalrymple catalogued the things they'd all bought from Nathan. It was a long and squalid list. Body parts, blankets that had held corpses, weapons, wallets and jewellery, clothing, teeth, hair. There was no end to what he could offer and what they were prepared to buy.

'Why did you keep doing it? Why did you keep buying this shit from him?'

'We became addicted. I think that's the only word for it. We didn't stop because we couldn't stop. And also we didn't want to say no to Nathan.'

'Because you were afraid of him?'

'Yes.'

'You could have gone to the police.'

The laugh was twisted. 'No, that option was long gone even if we'd wanted to. We were in too deep. And we were obsessed with it. All of us.'

'So when he came to you with Martin's body ...'

Tears began rolling down Dalrymple's face. Self-pity or shame, Addison didn't much care which, but he wanted to slap them away.

'He contacted me and asked if I wanted something special. Something to complete my collection. When he told me what it was ...'

He downed another glass of water, refilling it from the jug in the middle of the table and drinking more. He was falling apart.

'I was horrified. Genuinely. Martin's books and clothing was one thing but this ... I said no but he kept pressing, telling me he'd dig them up and throw them away, encouraging me to buy them. It was a game for him, to make me as bad as him. I know that's what he wanted. In the end, I gave in. I couldn't say no. I didn't want to ...'

'How did you get the body?'

'Bones. It was just his bones. That was all that was left of him. I went to a different spot near Nile Mile Burn and they were waiting for me. Four separate boxes. I took them home and dug the grave. When it was ready, I laid him out the way he should be, then covered him up. Respectfully.'

'Jesus Christ! What about the headstone? Did you already have that?'

'No. He got it for me later. From the one Martin's family had put up for him. To complete me, he said.'

'Did this Nathan ever tell you how Martin was killed?'

'Yes. In a roundabout sort of way. He didn't tell me directly, not that he did it, but said what had happened. He made me pay for it.'

'*And?*'

'He said that Martin was standing at the bus stop and a white van pulled up – *his* white van of course – and the driver offered Martin a lift. He was reluctant at first but got in. It took him a while to notice the van had taken the wrong road but, when he started to protest, he was smashed over the head with a hammer. He was then driven to a place the driver knew and was murdered.'

A white van. Michael Hill, the lorry driver, had been right all along. So too had Rachel's father. Lone wolf, a random driver in a white van had seen a chance and taken the boy to kill him. Forty-three years it had taken but now they knew. The knowledge gave Addison no satisfaction at all.

'What is Nathan's surname?'

'I don't know.'

'Where does he live? What does he do?'

'I don't know.'

'How do I contact him on Abbadon?'

'You don't. You can't. He'd see you coming a mile away. Believe me, there's no way he's going to communicate with you.'

'Believe you? I suppose I'm going to have to. But you

must know that my believing you means that you will go to prison, quite possibly for what's left of your life.'

'I only collected things!'

Addison laughed in his face. 'Right. Among that collection is a book made from the skin of Burke the grave robber, isn't there?'

Dalrymple didn't ask how Addison knew but nodded curtly.

'Well I'm no historian but I know a bit about Burke and Hare. And the surgeon, the anatomist, Robert Knox, right? He bought the corpses the bodysnatchers stole from the graves but, when that dried up, Burke and Hare got inventive. They cut out the middle man and killed people so they could sell the bodies to Knox. Am I right?'

'Yes but—'

'And Knox's great crime, even if it couldn't be proven, was that he knew. He *knew* they were killing to order and he paid them what they wanted. Now Knox just about got away with that because he was an eminent surgeon, but that's not going to work for you. We're talking conspiracy to murder.'

'What? No! We didn't—'

'Oh, but you did.'

'Inspector! There's no—'

Dalrymple's lawyer reminded them of her presence but not for long. Her defence died in her throat. She was collecting herself for a second attempt but was so far out of her depth she was struggling to get her head above water.

'No point in arguing with me, Ms Cousins. That will be

for the Procurator Fiscal to decide. All your client can do is help himself. By helping me.'

Dalrymple was broken. 'What do you want?'

'I want to know who they are. And where I can find them.'

CHAPTER 74

They had done everything they could to keep the discovery of Martin Welsh's remains out of the press and away from anyone who didn't absolutely need to know. That wouldn't hold for long and they knew they had to work quickly and quietly.

They had taken a risk informing Martin's mother, but Winter had been adamant she had to be told and Addison had backed him all the way to the top. So the news Jean Welsh had waited on and dreaded for over forty years was finally delivered to her door. She reacted by dissolving into tears but the breakdown lasted all of two minutes before she pulled herself together and announced she would start arranging a proper funeral for her boy.

What happened next needed the help of three police forces and Addison had to go to his Chief Constable to make the necessary contacts, ones high enough in each chain of command that they could keep the operation under wraps.

Much as he wanted to be in three places at once, Addison couldn't. Instead he and Winter were in the most northerly of the three locations, Richmond in North Yorkshire. Winter was along at his dispensation, negotiated with the Chief Constable, much to the disgust of a certain DCI Denny Kelbie.

Kelbie was going to have more than that to worry about, though.

The information that Addison extracted from Dalrymple went beyond the Four's historical connections to the man they knew as Big Sleep. The collectors had bought or agreed to buy items from the murders of Aiden McAlpine, Calvin Brownlie and Dr George Jeffries. One killer, as yet unknown but closer than ever before.

It had shown Kelbie's investigation up as a shambles. His head would soon be served up on a plate to appease a very angry MSP and several gay-rights groups. For Winter and Addison that was an added bonus, some welcome light among all the dark.

It was nearly two in the morning and they shivered inside an unmarked van with blacked-out windows just north of the banks of the River Swale. The van was about to drive into Frenchgate in the town centre and get inside the Landscape Gardener's house before he knew they were there. And certainly before he could reach for a phone or laptop.

Similar scenarios were going to be played out in Lewisham in south London and Clifton in Bristol, home to the Accountant and the Jeweller respectively. At precisely two, the signal would be given and all three residences would be raided. All teams had warrants that gave them the right to search everywhere and examine everything.

The van was on the move now, gliding slowly into the end of Frenchgate to park some forty yards from the target's house. The three cops who were squeezed into the van alongside Addison and Winter didn't seem pleased to have two Jocks for company, and they were particularly suspicious of the fact that one of them was a journalist. A large shaven-headed guy who Addison had decided was ex-army had already twice turned quickly so that the helmet strapped to his shoulder zipped past Winter's nose. When he did it a third time, Addison let him have it, quietly but firmly.

'Sergeant! If you do that once more then I'm going to have to educate you in the way we do things in Glasgow when someone takes the piss.'

'I don't know what you mean, sir.'

'Do it again and you'll find out.'

'Yes, sir.'

The local inspector, Brian Huddlestone, sitting in the front seat, turned round to protect his man, ready to fire some verbal volley at Addison, when an alarm sounded quietly. Ten seconds to go.

'Right. In ten,' Huddlestone announced. 'On my count. Ten, nine ...'

When he got to one, then 'go', Winter was the first to move. He turned sharply towards the door, causing the heavy photographic bag on his back to smash into the face of the cop who had hassled him. There was no time for apologies, just enough for grins between Winter and Addison as they jumped out of the van.

The lead cop smashed open the front door in the blink

of an eye and the rest poured inside. Two of them hared up the stairs, making for the bedroom so they could isolate the Landscape Gardener before he could do anything they didn't want.

Brendan Fallon was found bleary-eyed, sitting up naked in bed with his wife as the two cops charged in to arrest him and read him his rights. He was still shouting and protesting his innocence when Addison and Winter joined the show along with Huddlestone.

The inspector looked questioningly at his two officers, one of whom nodded sharply in return. Huddlestone reached for the radio piece at his shoulder.

'Richmond locked down.'

He listened for one reply, then the other. All three collectors had been detained and read their rights. None of them had been able to get to any communication device or get rid of evidence. Now they could search the three properties at their leisure.

Word soon drifted back from London and Bristol of caches of collectibles of John Reginald Christie and Dennis Nilsen. Murder-scene pieces from Rillington Place, Cranley Gardens and Melrose Avenue. The disturbing but relatively unsurprising was quickly followed by bulletin reports of congealed flesh, murder implements and atrophied body parts. They found photographs and clothing as well as letters that officers said were goldmines of information.

In Richmond, they found a host of collectibles related to Fred and Rose West on display. Framed pieces of the demolished Cromwell Street house, a couple of official documents signed by Fred, and newspaper front pages about the House of Horrors.

The first real surprise was when they slid open the drawers of a tall chest in Fallon's second bedroom. The oak dresser seemed innocuous enough but, inside, the four drawers were all lined with purple velvet and each held a single piece of clothing in protective cellophane wrapping. The clothes, two blouses, a dress and a pair of flared jeans, were all made for young women and seemed dated in terms of fashion.

Both blouses were bloodstained, the dress was torn and the jeans engrained in dirt. Everyone in the room thought the same thing. Teenage victims of Fred and Rose.

'You'll sue? Good luck with that, freak.'

Fallon's eyes widened on hearing Addison's accent.

'You're *Scottish*? The fucking Librarian. I knew that bastard would fold.' He slipped one arm out of his captor's grasp and had to be held a second time.

'You'll pay for this. You're too stupid to realise we knew you were coming. Is one of you with that bitch that went on Abbadon? She'll wish she never came after us. Nathan will sort her. Get your hands off me!'

Addison and Winter looked at each other. 'Rachel . . .'

CHAPTER 75

Narey had been asleep for maybe an hour when she heard something that stirred her awake. She opened her eyes with a dream of Sharon Tate just slipping from her view. Had she dreamed the noise too?

She strained her ears and eyes in the dark but couldn't make anything out. Then, there, again. A squeak of floorboard. It was an old house, she told herself. It squeaked and groaned like geriatric mice.

There was something else, though, something faint beyond the squeaks. Breathing. She could hear someone breathing.

She slapped an arm to the other side of the bed to see if Tony had come home, sliding in beside her while she slept. Her hand hit only duvet and pillow.

Every sense was on full alert, her own breath caught in her throat. She could sense it, feel it, there was someone else in the room.

She fumbled for the bedside light and switched it on. Standing a few feet from the end of the bed was a man dressed in black with a balaclava covering his face.

The window. Her ear to the street. The one she'd insisted Tony leave open just enough for her to hear the world go by on Great Western Road. That was how he'd got in. Stupid, so stupid.

The man was slight, although reasonably tall. Wiry. Dressed in black with wild eyes staring at her through the peepholes of the balaclava. He didn't say a word but the eyes betrayed his pleasure at her reaction.

Her stomach heaved in fear. The fact that the man felt no need to move, either to flee or attack, worried her hugely. He was calm, unflustered. He'd done this before.

'Who are you? What the hell are you doing in here?'

She asked it, although knowing the answer. Not a name or a person as such. But she knew who he was and what he'd done. He was the Big Sleep. He was death.

'My name is Nathan Phimister. I'm going to kill you.'

The simplicity of the statement terrified her. She edged back in the bed away from him but stopped once she realised what she was doing. Showing him fear wasn't going to help.

'Why?' It was a stupid question but it just burst out of her while she thought what to do.

'You've been looking for me, haven't you? Well now I'm here. Happy?'

'Just get out. Go. I won't say anything. Just go.'

He laughed at her. 'Yeah? Sure you won't. Anyway, you made such an effort to get me here, it would be rude if I just left.'

'*Please!*'

'No chance.'

His legs were spread, as if ready to spring, ready to attack.

'Get the fuck out of here. Now.'

He just laughed again. 'No. We both know that's not going to happen. You're my next. Maybe my last.'

She had a mental flash of Sharon Tate. Eight and a half months pregnant. Intruders in her house. The dreams of the long blonde hair swaying as she slipped from view. The horror that had woken her from sleep was now real and standing by the end of her bed.

Images of the Tate slaying flooded her mind. She should never have looked at those things. All she could see in her head were the blood and the bodies. All she could think of was the murder of that unborn child.

She put an arm over her stomach and cradled her refugee. This bastard wasn't getting at her baby.

She had to push him. Change this somehow. Reason with him. Beg him. Anything. Ask questions that she didn't want to hear answers to.

'My dad. Was that you?'

He nodded slowly.

The rage flooded through her. Her hands formed claws and she bared her teeth. She wanted to rip his head off. She began to lever herself against the bed to get up, but he took a step forward threateningly. She stopped, not caring for herself, but it wasn't just her own life she'd be risking.

'You killed all those people. All those pensioners.'

'Nah, I just killed your old man. The rest didn't matter. Just collateral. I've killed a lot more than that, darling.'

The easy breezy way he said it chilled her, scared her, enraged her. He couldn't care less. It all meant nothing to him.

'Martin Welsh?'

'One of my first. Hadn't planned it. I drove past in my van and saw him standing there, so I stopped to offer him a lift. He got in and I drove to a place I know. Buried him there where no one would find him. Deep in the woods.'

'And he's still there?' She knew the answer but wanted to hear it all.

'No. He rose. Someone made it worth my while to go back and dig him up. Someone wanted him.'

He reached up to his head and, after just a moment's hesitation, pulled the balaclava back from his face. He didn't care if she saw what he looked like. In no way could that be good.

The face was gaunt and pale with two distinct lines stretched from either side of his nose to his jaw. There was sparse fair hair on the sides of his skull but the top was shiny and freckled with cancerous looking blotches. With the mask removed, she could see thin lips pared back from uneven teeth. He could have been a young seventy or an old fifty.

She felt the beginning of a searing pain that rose from her groin and spread like burning needles across her body. It spasmed and stung, stabbed and grabbed. She clutched at her stomach with her left hand and the man's eyes followed her movement, seeing her bump and recognising it for what it was.

'Please. *Please*. Don't do this. My baby . . .'

'Look, bitch, I don't have any mercy for you. You're going to die.'

Did he say that? Had she heard him right, or was she hallucinating? That was what she kept hearing in her dreams, what Susan Atkins said to Sharon Tate.

The pain seized her again, her shoulders rising from the bed as it forced her to double at the waist. She had to breathe. Count and breathe and slow it all down. She remembered what the doctor had told her. Breathe for two. Breathe for two. She exhaled the panic air and took in one long slow breath for her and let it go, following it with one for her baby. The pain grabs were slowing, just pinching rather than wounding, and she hoped it would pass.

He was staring at her, curious at her discomfort and maybe enjoying it. He was rubbing at the side of his temple with his left hand, idly massaging the skin and the bone beneath. She watched his right hand slip inside the dark jacket and re-emerge glinting as the light caught the surface of something metal and sharp.

The sight of the knife, the blade turning slowly in his hand, caused the stomach seizures to pick up again. He took a stride forward, his eyes burning cold, the knife gripped hard and pulled back ready to strike. Sharon Tate, eight and half months pregnant and stabbed sixteen times.

One last try. Talking through the pain that bit her.

'You don't want to do this. Not to me.'

'Oh, but I do. Especially to you. You're worth money to me and you're worth headlines. A pregnant cop. Guaranteed headlines. The whole world will know. And I'll be well paid for things from this.'

'The Four won't be buying anything from you any more. They're being arrested. It's probably done by now.'

His surprise quickly morphed into a shrug. 'No matter. Someone else will pay. There's always someone else.'

'If you kill a cop, they'll never stop till they find you.'

'I don't care. Don't you get it? *I don't care*. I'm dying. Just like you're going to. And I *want* to be known. I want to be remembered for a hundred years.'

'Remembered for being a murderer?'

'It's what I am. People can't fight their nature. Even if they can't be lions like me, then they're vultures, circling overhead till they get their own piece of the carcass. That's what people are. Lions or vultures. Or carcass. Like you.'

'Don't be so sure.'

She forced herself to stretch despite the pain so she could keep her head high and her eyes on him. Her left arm protectively cradled her stomach and she said a silent apology to her unborn child for what was about to happen. She wasn't sure she had time to rip the bedcovers back so she waited, letting him get closer and closer before she pulled the trigger and shot through them.

The noise was tremendous. The man staggered back with a look of shock plastered across his face and a growing hole in his chest. She swept the covers back with her left hand, raising the gun she'd had hidden there and aimed again. The cramps stabbed at her, causing her jaw to clench, her teeth biting down hard. She squeezed the trigger and another bullet blasted into him, knocking him off his feet.

You can buy anything on the dark web, and she'd bought a gun.

She was thrown back, too, hitting the mattress hard as her breathing convulsed into rapid irregular bursts. The pain was crippling her and she was sure she was going to pass out. Breathe for two, she told herself. Breathe for two. Count and breathe.

The black continued to close in but she managed to twist her body so that she could crawl to the edge of the bed and peer over, the gun still shaking in her right hand. He was sprawled, one leg tangled beneath his body, his arms wide. By his side, the knife lay like a stain on the bedroom carpet.

He was dead. Eyes wide, mouth open. His blood leaked from him. There was what seemed to be a crooked smile on his face.

Inside her, something curled into a ball and hid. She let her eyes close and gave in to the dark that swamped her, falling deep and deeper till the gun slipped from her hand and hit the floor. It bounced once but no one heard it.

EPILOGUE

WINTER-NAREY. On 23 September to Rachel and Tony, a daughter, Alanna. Mother and child doing well, father extremely tired.

NAREY. Died on 2 May, Alan Morton Narey, retired Detective Inspector of Central Scotland Police. Beloved husband of Christine and father of Rachel. Memorial service 15 December at the University of Glasgow.

MR A. WINTER AND MS R. L. NAREY. The marriage took place on Friday, 2 December, between Anthony, son of the late David Winter and the late Maureen Winter, and Rachel Louise, daughter of the late Alan Narey and the late Helen Narey.

AVAILABLE. Starting bids £5,000. A white Ford Transit van once belonging to Nathan Phimister. Provenance guaranteed. Other items relating to same individual may be available on request.

Acknowledgements

I owe a huge vote of thanks to a number of people, including family and friends, for their support and encouragement during the writing of this book. In particular, to my wonderful editor Jo Dickinson and all at Simon & Schuster; to my indefatigable agent Mark "Stan" Stanton; and to my partner, the astonishing Alexandra Sokoloff. Many thanks too to Tim Sheppard for finding Rachel Narey's mother when she was lost.

The heart of this book was written far from Glasgow, in the mountains above Temecula in southern California. My thanks go to Dorland Mountain Arts Colony for the gift of such a beautiful and peaceful place to work.

Research for *Murderabilia* inevitably meant delving directly into its world. In that, I was helped by people I cannot name from whom I bought things I cannot mention. However, my debt is to the victims, such as Sharon Tate, rather than to those who stole their lives. This book is for them.

Craig Robertson

In Place of Death

A young man enters the culverted remains of an ancient Glasgow stream, looking for thrills. Deep below the city, it is decaying and claustrophobic and gets more so with every step. As the ceiling lowers to no more than a couple of feet above the ground, the man finds his path blocked by another person. Someone with his throat cut.

As DS Rachel Narey leads the official investigation, photographer Tony Winter follows a lead of his own, through the shadowy world of urbexers, people who pursue a dangerous and illegal hobby, a world that Winter knows more about than he lets on. And it soon becomes clear that the murderer has killed before, and has no qualms about doing so again.

'Doing for **Glasgow**, what Rankin did for **Edinburgh**'
Mirror

'**A tense torch-lit trek** through a hidden city you never knew existed' Christopher Brookmyre

Paperback ISBN 978-1-4711-2779-3
Ebook ISBN 978-1-4711-2780-9

Craig Robertson

The Last Refuge

You can run from your past
but you can never hide from yourself

When John Callum arrives on the Faroe Islands, determined to sever all ties with his previous life and make a new start, he is surprised by how quickly he is welcomed into the close-knit community. But no matter what he changes in his outward life, the debilitating nightmares that haunt him just won't stop.

Then the sleepy peace is shattered by an almost unheard of crime on the Island: murder. A specialist team of detectives arrives from Denmark to help the local police, who are completely ill-equipped for a manhunt of this scale. But when tensions arise, and the community closes rank to protect its own, outsider John will have to watch his back. But more terrifying than that, why can't he shake the suspicion that the crime could have had something to do with him?

Paperback ISBN 978-1-4711-2775-5
Ebook ISBN 978-1-4711-2776-2

Craig Robertson

Witness the Dead

Red Silk is back . . .

Scotland 1972. Glasgow is haunted by a murderer nicknamed Red Silk – a feared serial killer who selects his victims in the city's nightclubs. The case remains unsolved but Archibald Atto, later imprisoned for other murders, is thought to be Red Silk.

In modern-day Glasgow, DS Rachel Narey is called to a gruesome crime scene at the city's Necropolis. The body of a young woman lies stretched out over a tomb. Her body bears a three-letter message from her killer.

Now retired, former detective Danny Neilson spots a link between the new murder and those he investigated in 1972 – details that no copycat killer could have known about. But Atto is still behind bars. Must Danny face up to his fears that they never caught their man? Determined finally to crack the case, Danny, along with his nephew, police photographer Tony Winter, pays Atto a visit. But they soon discover that they are going to need the combined efforts of police forces past and present to bring a twisted killer to justice.

Move over MacBride! *Witness the Dead* is the compelling new thriller from Scotland's hottest new talent.

Paperback ISBN 978-0-85720-420-2
Ebook ISBN 978-0-85720-421-9